A GALAXY UNKNOWN

TRADER VYX

Book 4

BY

THOMAS DEPRIMA

Vinnia Publishing - U.S.A.

Trader Vyx

A Galaxy Unknown series – Book 4
Copyright ©2002, 2012 by Thomas J. DePrima

ISBN-10 : **1619310082**

ISBN-13 : **978-1-61931-008-7**

2nd Edition

Amazon Distribution

Cover art by: Martin J. Cannon

Appendices containing political and technical data highly pertinent to this series are included at the back of this book.

To contact the author, or see information about his other novels, visit:

http://www.deprima.com

Many thanks to Ted King for his technical expertise and encouragement, and to Michael A. Norcutt for his suggestions, proofreading, and for acting as my military protocol advisor. And kudos to my artist, Martin Cannon, for the fantastic cover artwork that features a Tsgardi warrior.

This series of novels includes:

A Galaxy Unknown...

A Galaxy Unknown
Valor at Vauzlee
The Clones of Mawcett
Trader Vyx
Milor!
Castle Vroman
Against All Odds
Return to Dakistee

Other series and novels by the author:

AGU: Border Patrol...

Citizen X

When The Spirit...

When The Spirit Moves You
When The Spirit Calls

A World Without Secrets

Table of Contents

Chapter One
~ October 4th, 2272 ~

He strained to hear the slightest of noises above his own laborious breathing. They were still out there somewhere in the darkness; he was sure of that now. Three times during the past hour he'd thought he'd lost the ones who hunted him, and three times they'd turned up again at his back. He needed to rest, but the relentless pursuit wouldn't allow it. To stop was to die, and he wasn't ready to surrender his life just yet.

He sensed, rather than consciously saw, the movement and immediately flung his agile, five-foot-eleven-inch body sideways into the blackness of an abandoned building. The rotted wood of the old doorframe where he'd attempted to conceal himself just seconds before exploded into hundreds of tiny pieces as three lattice projectiles struck it. Twisting as he flew through the air, Vyx tucked in his head and curled into a tight ball so he could execute a quick roll. A plume of dust and dirt erupted upwards as he landed hard on a sagging wooden floor covered with years of accumulated filth. His roll left him crouched in position to spring again, and a swift look around was all he needed to choose his direction of flight.

As he sprinted towards the rear of the building and the only other doorway illuminated by the soft rays of diffused moonlight outside, he strove to see the path in front of him. He couldn't afford the time needed to pick his way slowly through the building, so he desperately hoped there were no gaps in the flooring or accumulations of trash left by former building occupants that would trip him in the darkness.

Emerging at the rear of the deserted building, he flattened himself against the outside wall, gulping the hot, dry air of a peaceful summer night as quietly as possible. He didn't have the luxury of standing in the doorway while he slowly scanned the street; he'd have been clearly outlined in the moonlight for any who had followed him into the building. The wall offered a modicum of protection from visual scanning, but it offered little concealment from a thermal scanner. When nothing moved in response to his sudden appearance, he made a dash for the end of the street. The buildings on this block were all occupied by local citizens, so he couldn't seek shelter here. On the Gollasko Colony, bursting into an occupied house would earn him a quick trip to the Body Disposal Depot. For that matter, he might have had his ticket punched early by disturbing the wrong party in the abandoned building. Like the wild west of America's nineteenth century, people shot first and questioned later. On Gollasko, justice was dispensed from the fastest gun, and everyone had an irrevocable license to kill.

Making it to the end of the street without seeing anyone— and more importantly without drawing fire— gave him new hope. If he could just make it back to his hotel, he might be safe. Armed guards patrolled the lobby, and sensors linked to automatic weapons safeguarded all other possible entrances to the building after dark. If only he hadn't lost his pistol so early in the fight he might have been able to reduce the odds by now. He knew there were at least three of them and that they had to be using some kind of electronic tracking device. If he knew what they had, he might be able to give them the slip, but it could be thermal, infrared, auditory, or olfactory. It might even be a combination of all four. The newest devices used by the Space Marines employed all four sensory systems, and the arms merchant employing these hunters usually had the latest and best for his own people.

Instead of trying to hide, which would be a waste of time, he sprinted down several streets and then ducked into a doorway to catch his breath. Nothing moved behind, but his pursuers had appeared from nowhere before, so he didn't spend any more time there than necessary. No sense giving them a stationary target on which to lock their weapons. As soon as he was able to breathe easily, he ran on, his hotel still at least eight long blocks away.

It took less than ten minutes to cover the distance to the hotel, but he was again breathing with difficulty when it came into sight. Rather than making an immediate dash for the hotel's front entrance, he stayed in the shadows of a building across the street and observed the movements of pedestrians as he filled and refilled his lungs with air. He was just about to step out when he caught a glimpse of almost imperceptible movement several doorways down from the hotel entrance. Pulling back, he stared intently at the recessed entrance of the closed shop.

It was another fifteen minutes before he saw any additional movement. Because he had been staring into a darkened area for a prolonged period, his eyes and mind had begun to play tricks on him, but he was sure there was someone there— someone who didn't belong there, certainly not at this hour anyway.

Other than the front doors, all entranceways to the hotel were barred after dark, so he didn't have a chance of getting to his room and reaching his backup weapons. If he had a weapon, he'd make a run for the hotel entrance, relying on his skill with a pistol to get him there. Without a weapon he was about as dangerous as one of the painted targets on a weapons practice range.

He backtracked a block without exposing himself to the watcher in the doorway so he could think and plan without danger of being spotted. He hated being weaponless, but the arms merchant he had met with tonight would have been suspicious if he'd come wearing all of his hardware. They'd allowed him to enter with his laser pistol only because there had been seven heavily armed bodyguards in the room during the negotiations. He'd had several blades hidden about his body, but they were of little use in the current situation.

Shev Rivemwilth, an Alyysian trader and arms merchant well known in the illegal arms trade, rarely left the sanctuary of the Gollasko Colony and never ventured into Galactic Alliance regulated space where his arrest would ensure he never saw free sky overhead again. It was widely rumored that he was a front man— in the loosest sense of the word 'man'— for the giant Raider organization that had become the scourge of the galaxy. The ugly creature neither acknowledged nor denied an association with the Raiders.

As members of a race that had migrated in non-FTL ships from many thousands of light-years across the galaxy, Alyysia claimed no home world in Galactic Alliance space, although small colonies existed on several different worlds. Their unique physiology allowed them to be frozen solid and then thawed and revived when they reached their destination. Typically about four feet, six-inches tall when standing upright, they looked a bit like erect versions of Terran toads. They all wore the same dark gray cloaks that covered most of their yellow skin. Being neither male nor female, the Alyysia were true hermaphrodites that could reproduce without contact with another of their species.

The meeting had started well enough. Vyx had set his translation device for Alyysian and they had gotten the pleasantries out of the way quickly. Then Vyx had spelled out what he was looking to purchase. After a bit of haggling and examination of a merchandise sample, an agreement on price had been reached. Shev Rivemwilth had specified that payment would be required in two parts— half before and half upon delivery. Vyx had just agreed to the terms and was standing to leave when a convicted Tsgardi killer named Recozzi entered from the corridor.

A race more closely resembling tall Terran baboons than humans, Tsgardis often filed their normally sharp teeth to even sharper points to make their appearance more menacing. Their warriors were well known for their ruthless ferocity but not for their intelligence. They walked upright, but their gait was normally stooped. When in the company of humans, the more intelligent made an effort to stand and walk erect.

Immediately recognizing Vyx as a Space Command undercover operative, Recozzi had uttered a profanity and grabbed for his weapon. Vyx had managed to pull his weapon first and with a slight sweep had sliced off the top of Recozzi's head just below his eyes. Shev Rivemwilth had leapt for safety behind a sofa as Recozzi's body, now almost lifeless, continued firing his automatic weapon as he fell. An errant shot had hit Rivemwilth in one of his two hearts, and putrid, yellow-green blood had begun spurting over the floor and furniture. Recozzi's fire had also caught two of the bodyguards, who then let loose with their own weapons as they fell. By some miracle, Vyx had only received a burning graze from someone's laser weapon. Diving for the open door as weapons fire continued the light show inside the room, he had lost his pistol and decided it wouldn't be prudent to reenter the room in order to retrieve it.

Vyx had literally run for his life and made it safely to the street after descending the single flight of stairs in just three leaps. He'd been half a block away when the first shots had been fired in his direction. Over the next hour, he'd played a game of cat and mouse with Shev's bodyguards. It had been no fun being the mouse.

The first light of dawn found Vyx still alive and still on the run. Long shadows were his only companions as he loped down deserted streets. Although no fire had come his way since the earlier shot at the abandoned building hours ago, the hairs on the back of his neck continued to bristle. He felt sure the hunters weren't far behind. It was the first time since he'd come dirt-side that he'd appreciated the shorter diurnal cycle of this planet. A twenty-two-hour, forty-minute daily revolution meant the sun rose that much sooner, and with the coming of the new day, the odds that he might actually survive increased dramatically. He'd be able to purchase a new weapon as the stores opened in a couple of hours, while people moving about on previously abandoned streets would provide him with some welcome cover. Armed and less conspicuous, he might yet have a chance to reach his hotel room.

It cost Vyx three times what it usually fetched, but the old laser pistol was worth every penny under the circumstances. The shop owner 'generously' threw in two extra power packs, both fully charged. Vyx tucked the pistol into his belt and warily exited the dilapidated pawn shop. The owner could probably take the rest of the week off on what he had made from the sale of that pistol.

Walking cautiously towards the hotel, Vyx mingled with the early morning pedestrian traffic on the sidewalk. It would seem a surreal sight to anyone accustomed to life on most civilized planets, but every person on the street, except for the smallest of children, was carrying a pistol or rifle. Amazingly, there was very little violent crime in the colony. Occasionally a drunk would be rolled, but no vandals broke into homes here. The ones who had tried it had long ago been delivered to the Body Disposal Depot, and with the entire citizenry armed, the surviving lowlifes were too smart to attempt it.

Vyx got to within eighteen meters of the hotel before one of the hunters from the previous evening stepped out of the doorway where he had waited all night and opened fire. Prepared for any movement from that location, Vyx dove for cover behind a waiting taxi as the first shot came his way. The second went wide as well, and it was the last 'free' shot the killer got. Before he could fire a third time towards Vyx, the local citizenry opened fire on him. He must have only recently arrived in the colony because he was apparently unaware that one should never fire a weapon on a crowded street here. The populace wasn't specifically trying to protect Vyx; it was just an automatic reaction to an ignorant fool firing into a crowd.

For several seconds, lead, lattice, and laser fire poured into the doorway from every direction. When the Tsgardi warrior fell to the ground, he had more holes in him than a brand new box of data rings. His two shots had missed Vyx, but two colony citizens were down. One was dead from a three-round lattice weapon burst to the chest, while the other had received a grazing laser weapon injury to his leg. It was anybody's guess if the Tsgardi was responsible for the lattice weapon fatality, but the laser weapon injury had to have been caused by a local. People crowded around the hunter's body to see if they recognized him, but no one claimed any familiarity, which was further testimony that he was new here.

Vyx made it into the hotel while everyone's attention was diverted and before the sanitation truck arrived to pick up the two bodies. The guards in the lobby were on heightened alert as a result of the shootout in the street, but they didn't stop Vyx from proceeding to his room after he flashed his keycard for the door.

As soon as the reinforced Ferro-carbon alloy door of his room was closed and locked behind him, Vyx took a deep breath and released it slowly. He then retrieved the backup pistol from his spacechest's hidden compartment and slipped it into his empty holster. The pistol he had just purchased was placed on the dresser and he would carry it in his belt when he left the room again, but first he had to report in.

Another pocket in the spacechest yielded a miniature radio transmitter. He stuck the three-centimeter-wide satellite dish against the windowpane and aligned it using its audio locator capability. The RF signal from his radio would be transmitted to the tiny, fist-sized satellite he had placed in geosynchronous orbit around the planet upon his arrival. The satellite would then compress the encrypted message before retransmitting it on a designated IDS frequency. It would take almost seventy hours to travel the two hundred ten light-years to the Intelligence Section at Higgins Space Command Base, so it would be at least six days before he received a response.

From a subcutaneous pouch in his chest beneath his left arm, Vyx retrieved a tiny recording wafer. It contained a full account of his trip to the arms merchant from the time he had left his hotel room the night before until his return. A chip attached to the optic nerve of his left eye provided the image, and a chip embedded in each of the audio canals of his ears provided stereo audio tracks. Recorded information traveled through his lymphatic system for delivery to the wireless recording device mounted over the ribs beneath his left arm so no transmission signal could ever be picked up by detection scanners. He delicately slid the tiny silicon wafer, not much thicker than an ordinary piece of writing paper, into his audio transmitter and pressed the send button.

His report sent, Vyx could relax. He took a hot shower and climbed into bed to get some much-needed sleep. He should be safe as long as he stayed in the hotel, but his pistol went onto the nightstand next to the bed anyway.

Chapter Two
~ October 6th, 2272 ~

Commander Jenetta Carver set two huge water bowls on the floor so that Cayla and Tayna, her Taurentlus-Thur Jumakas, could drink when they were thirsty. They had already received the first of their two daily meals. The two enormous pets, with glossy coats of black fur and large, bright yellow eyes that seemed to glow, brushed lightly against her legs as a sign of affection. She stooped to pet them for several minutes before continuing with her morning chores.

Resembling Terran Jaguars, although smaller at only a hundred sixty pounds each, the Jumakas would remain sedately in Jenetta's quarters while she went to work. She would have preferred to take them to work as she had when she was the commanding officer of Dixon SCB, but that wasn't possible. They could use the shower stall in the bathroom to relieve their bodily needs during the day. The automated cleaning process in all suites was programmed to remove pet waste, then clean and disinfect the stall as soon as the animal vacated it.

Before leaving her rooms in the Bachelor Officer Quarters, the attractive blonde checked her reflection in the mirror to make sure her uniform appeared clean and crisp. Satisfied, she left her apartment, stopping to face the door to another apartment some ten meters down the corridor. The automatic visitor announcement system would identify her and alert the apartment's occupant that she was at the door.

After half a minute's wait, the door opened and another Space Command officer, virtually identical to Commander Carver, stepped out into the corridor and smiled. The only distinguishable difference between the two women was their rank and uniform ribbons. The second officer wore the rank insignia of a lieutenant(jg), represented as one wide and one narrow stripe on each epaulet.

From the elevator that delivered the two women to the lobby, it was only a short walk to the Officers' mess hall, so they didn't bother hailing a cab. A number of people glanced their way and smiled as they passed, with most of the males sighing silently as they enjoyed a brief fantasy or two. Seeing Commander Carver with one, or both, of her gorgeous sisters was not unusual. The wide discrepancy in rank was owed to the fact that her two sisters, both clones, hadn't yet reached their second birthday.

After breakfast, the two five-foot, eleven-inch women proceeded together to their new duty assignments in the Intelligence Section of the Space Command Headquarters division of Higgins Space Center.

Located in geosynchronous orbit above the planetary capital of Vinnia, Higgins ranked among the busiest of SC bases. It functioned both as a StratCom-One base and a major freight hub. Easily visible to the naked eye from the planet below, the massive space station resembled an oval-cut, blue opal gemstone surrounded by a sixty-kilometer silver neck-lace. The necklace, of course, was the docking ring where dozens of massive ships could dock with the station simultan-eously. Roadway tunnels, connecting the base to the docking ring, appeared like spokes in a wheel.

Upon arriving at the Intelligence Section, the two women paused in the admittance area to sign in and be identified. A wall of clear security polycarbonate, virtually impenetrable by any portable weapon, separated them from the duty officer.

"Commander Jenetta Carver and Lieutenant Christa Carver reporting as ordered," Jenetta said to the lieutenant on duty after pressing the face of her Space Command ring.

"Good morning, Commander. Good morning, Lieutenant," they heard in their CT's as the duty officer spoke. "Please step up to the retinal scanner."

Subcutaneously located against the skull behind the left ear of every Space Command officer was a cranial transducer. Normally referred to as a CT, the devices were no larger than the tip of the needle-like insertion tool used to implant the miniscule devices in every cadet upon entrance to a Space Command Academy. Used mainly for communications, they also permitted sensors aboard a ship or base to identify an individual. The identification permitted immediate access to low security areas and unlocked equipment for which the individual was authorized. Additional identification verification was required for high security areas.

As the senior officer, Jenetta stepped to the retinal scanner first. The machine immediately said, "Identity confirmed as being Commander Jenetta Alicia Carver."

After Christa was scanned, the machine said, "Retinal identity confirmed as being Commander Jenetta Alicia Carver. CT confirmed as being that of Lieutenant(jg) Christa Carver."

In response to the confused look on the face of the duty officer, Jenetta said, "Lieutenants Christa and Eliza Carver's retinal scans are identical to mine, as are their fingerprints."

"Yes, ma'am. I understand, but I'm not sure how to log the system's noted anomaly. Please allow me a few seconds to check the Pass-down Log." After scanning information on her monitor for a few seconds, the duty officer said, "Ah, here it is, ma'am." She touched several points on her monitor and said, "Please enter," as she pressed the button to open the security door.

Once Jenetta and Christa were inside the clear wall, the duty officer said, "Lieutenant, report to Encryption in room D248. Lieutenant Commander Mirshra is expecting you. Commander, please report to Captain Kanes' office. You know the way, I believe?"

"Yes, I do. Thank you, Lieutenant."

As they entered the main corridor, Jenetta gave Christa directions to the Encryption Center since it was knowledge she had gained after Christa was born and then walked to

Captain Kanes' office suite. She was only kept waiting for a few minutes before being passed through to the Captain's office.

"Good morning, sir," Jenetta said as she entered the spacious work area. The walls remained almost as barren as when Kanes had moved into the office. The only interruptions on the four off-white surfaces were two large portraits that hung behind Kanes' desk. One was of Admiral Moore, the Admiral of the Fleet, and the other was of the current Chairman of the Galactic Alliance Council.

"Good morning, Jen," Kanes said as he finished taking a drink from his coffee cup and set it down on his desk. Pointing to a carafe on a conference table, he said, "Help yourself to some coffee, then pull up a chair."

"Thank you, sir."

After pouring herself a mug of the steaming black liquid from the carafe, she took a seat in a chair across from Kanes. Taking a sip of the coffee she said, "Delicious, sir. Your own blend?"

"It's one of my few self-indulgences," he said. "I blend a carafe each morning to bring to the office, then tolerate the coffee from my beverage synthesizer for the rest of the day."

"Have you tried tweaking the program that makes your coffee here?"

"No. I didn't know that was possible."

"You can't alter the established recipes, but you can add your own as long as you assign unique names to the new variations."

"I've never heard that."

"Few people have, and I doubt it's published anywhere. I only discovered it while trying to alter the established recipes in my office synthesizer on Dixon. I hacked my way into the synthesizer recipe cube only to discover that the encoded recipes were 'burned' in. They couldn't be altered or overwritten. I suppose it's a protection mechanism to ensure that people can't be poisoned or made ill by a hacker. But I did discover that it was possible to add new recipes."

"How do I accomplish that?"

"If you'll write out the recipes you'd like to add, I'll encode them and prepare a data wafer. Then it'll take just a couple of seconds to upload the information into your synthesizer's memory cube. Once loaded, the new recipes are alterable until you tell the system to make them permanent, so you can tweak them until you get them set the way you want."

"Will this affect any other synthesizer on the base?"

"No, sir, just yours unless other units are manually updated with the same data. If your unit experiences a problem and the synthesizer recipe cube is swapped out by engineering, you'll have to upload the changes again."

"Wonderful, I'll write out my special recipe blends this afternoon."

"Okay, sir. And I'm sure you must have something else in mind for me to do while I'm here."

"Yes, I do. I realize this is only a temporary assignment until the *Prometheus* returns to port, but I hope your month here will be productive and rewarding. I've had Christa assigned to the encryption section because of your expertise with encoding algorithms." He paused to grin. "We had a devil of a job a few years ago getting past the encryption you set up on your personal log ring."

"I knew you'd crack it, sir. It was a fairly simple formula only intended to keep curious eyes from my diary entries."

"It took our entire lab four days to crack it."

"Four days? Really? The entire lab?"

Kanes grinned again. "I suspect you knew exactly how long it would take us to read the entries."

Jenetta returned the grin. "I estimated four or five days if your people were good. I calculated that the simplicity of the design would actually add to the confusion of anyone trying to read the data. Since the encryption key uses the last date and time the journal was accessed, or where access was even attempted, you can't just continually throw a stream of varying keys at it and hope to get lucky. It's unlikely anyone could ever happen across it by accident. If your people cracked it in four days, they're good."

"The best. I think Christa will enjoy her time working there. Perhaps she'll decide to request a transfer to stay with us instead of reporting to the *Chiron* when it arrives in a month."

"Yes, sir, but I wouldn't count on it. One day perhaps, but right now my sisters and I only want to be aboard a ship in space. Did you want me to work in Encryption also?"

"No, I have another project in mind for you. We have a problem on the Gollasko Colony. We sent one of our undercover people there to buy weapons from an arms merchant, and right now he's holed up in a hotel room, fearful of leaving the building because some very nasty types want his head. That's just part of the problem. The deal he was involved in went bad because a convicted Tsgardi killer named Recozzi showed up just in time to cause problems. There was a shootout and our man killed Recozzi. Being the arresting officer, he'd testified against Recozzi at his trial, so they knew each other well. Recozzi had been sentenced to life without parole."

"How did Recozzi escape?"

"He didn't. He's still at the penal colony on Saquer Major."

"He's still at the penal colony, *and* he was just killed in a gun battle on Gollasko? That's a rather unique accomplishment."

"Yes. As soon as we got the report we contacted the warden at the facility, and he confirmed that Recozzi is still there and apparently healthy."

"Has he been cloned?"

"We don't know yet, but God, I hope not. We just got the issue of cloning settled with your sisters and the seventy-seven others 'born' on Dakistee."

"How unique are Tsgardi elbow-prints?"

"All of our researchers agree that they're as unique as Terran fingerprints. And when combined with DNA and retinal images, identification should be one hundred percent positive. Our doctors and researchers are currently examining every elbow-print on file to see if we can learn anything new."

"Could the records at the prison have been altered?"

"We'll know shortly. We had the prisoner reprinted and requested copies so we can compare them to ours. Everything is being analyzed right now."

"Is our operative safe where he is?"

"Somewhat. He'll stay in the hotel, taking all his meals there. The hotel has its own security force, so it depends on how badly the hunters want him. We've learned that the main subject in our investigation, Shev Rivemwilth, was critically injured in the melee. One of his hearts was blasted by an errant shot and he lost a lot of blood. It isn't yet known if he'll survive. We're trying to arrange an extraction for our man."

"*One* of his hearts? Since 'Shev' is an honorific normally used when greeting an Alyysian, I assume Rivemwilth is an Alyysian."

"That toad doesn't know the meaning of honor. But yes, he's an Alyysian."

"Why are we trying to buy arms from an Alyysian, sir?"

"They're Space Command weapons, and we're trying to trace the source. We've heard for some time that SC weapons were being sold on the black market, but we've never been able to get our hands on any. We want to learn if the weapons are original manufacture from one of our authorized industrial complexes or if they've been copied by someone and are being produced elsewhere. If they come from us, we intend to stop the flow, recover everything that we can, and prosecute those responsible. And if they're being manufactured by others within Space Command regulated space, we intend to track them down and stop them. Whenever we hear any rumors about the weapons, Rivemwilth's name is associated. He's obviously behind the thefts or the illegal manufacture.

We want him as much as we want to recover the weapons and stop the flow, but he stays holed up in the Gollasko colony most of the time. We won't shed any tears if he doesn't recover, but it might mean the end of our investigation. His accomplices might never be found and punished for their crimes."

"Aren't we prohibited from operating in the Frontier Zone?"

"There's no *legal* prohibition that prevents us from operating there. Space Command simply doesn't have the ships and manpower to enforce GA regulations in the Zone, so SC ship captains are ordered to 'ignore' the lawlessness there lest we get dragged into law enforcement activities that escalate beyond our control and reflect badly on the service when we fail to correct the situation. It's better that everyone simply believe we're not permitted to operate there."

Jenetta nodded. "What can I do to help?"

"I want you to go through all the files from the investigation and give me your assessment."

Jenetta didn't respond for a few seconds, then said, "Sir, I'm not trained in criminal investigation procedures. My field of study at the Academy was astrophysics."

"I realize that, Jen, but we've been working on this case for two years and our best criminal experts haven't been able to make any inroads. I'm hoping you might bring a fresh perspective to the investigation. That, combined with some scrap of information you may have picked up from the contacts you made while functioning as Base Commander of the Dixon Space Command Base, might reorient our investigation."

"My contacts were mainly freighter captains and Space Command officers, not arms dealers or manufacturers."

"Yes, but I know you also met some of the seedier types who frequent space ports. You couldn't avoid it, being the base commander and chief administrator. You sent me a lot of intel during the year you were there, hoping it would help us find your sister Christa while she was a prisoner of the Tsgardi."

Jenetta sighed to herself. "Very well, sir. I'll do my best, but I think you've picked the wrong person for this job."

"Just do your usual thorough job and I'll be happy." Standing up, Kanes said, "Come on, I'll show you to the office you've been assigned for the next few weeks."

Kanes escorted Jenetta to a small office in a restricted corridor that required another retinal scan for entry. The computer, having already been informed of her job assignment, had established the appropriate access levels for information retrieval and movement within the section's corridors. The computer recognized her voice, and a complete index of everything pertaining to the investigation was available on her screen when it was activated. She had also been assigned an aide who would work in an outer office. Kanes wished her luck and returned to his own office.

Jenetta sat down at the desk, grimaced, and began reading through the thousands of documents that had accumulated since the investigation began. When her eyes started to ache, she had the computer read the reports to her as she stretched her legs and poured a cup of coffee from the decanter her aide had brought in earlier. Her office didn't have a beverage synthesizer.

At the end of the first week, Jenetta was still reading, or being read, case documents. She was feeling the frustration shared by all people put into jobs for which they are ill-prepared. It seemed that the professional investigators had covered every possible facet. As each document was completed, she fit it into the larger picture she was assembling in her mind and did her best to keep her interest up, but she knew she would surely have gone out of her head if this had been a permanent assignment. Fortunately, her temporary duty would be over in a few weeks and she'd be reporting back aboard the battleship *Prometheus*.

Christa was faring a little better than Jenetta. She was being used mainly to break the encryption codes of intercepted messages, but she also had a hand in developing new encryption techniques for Space Command. Of the three women, Eliza had it the best. Upon their return from Nordakia, she'd immediately been assigned as third watch helmsman aboard the battleship *Bellona*. It was still in port, so she had little to do while on duty. She was able to meet Jenetta and Christa in the Officers' mess every other evening for dinner.

"When are you leaving port, Eliza?" Jenetta asked as she cut into the second of two large pieces of chocolate cake she had selected for dessert. They were sitting outside the hearing range of other diners so they felt comfortable talking in lowered voices.

"I was just notified that we're leaving Monday. Apparently something's come up rather quickly because we weren't scheduled to leave for another two weeks."

"Any idea where you're going?" Christa asked.

"You tell me. I'm just a junior officer. You're both working in the Intelligence Section now."

"We don't have any knowledge of ship assignments," Jenetta said. "Everything is very compartmentalized. I don't have access to Christa's area and she doesn't have access to mine."

"Not true," Christa said. "I could simply change my rank insignia and walk into your office. Unless you had it pass-word encoded, I could also access your computer interface and pass myself off as you without any trouble. Our retinal scans, fingerprints, and DNA are identical, remember? Even our voice prints are identical. You could also pass for me, and either of us could pass for Eliza."

"You're forgetting the cranial transducer that was implanted after you joined Space Command," Jenetta said. "It's not just for communication, you know. You'd never get into my office, and I'd only get into yours because of my high security clearance. However, even without the CT I wouldn't be worried about us pretending to be one another because I know me, but it raises the issue of the other clones. There are seven copies each of the eleven scientists on Dakistee who discovered the cloning equipment. Right now they're all back on the planet working at the dig sites so no problem, but what about the future?"

"You mean what happens if one secures a position in a sensitive area?"

"Yes. Civilians don't have CT's or implanted ID chips. If they've been in prison, they have permanent criminal marker tags in their bodies but otherwise nothing. There would be seven other people who were indistinguishable from the rightful holder of the position. Any of them could swap positions and no one would be able to tell. We have a problem right now with a convict in the penal colony on Saquer Major. A duplicate was just slain while trying to kill one of our people at the Gollasko Colony."

"A duplicate?" Eliza said.

"The slain convict recognized the undercover Space Command operative who had arrested him a few years ago and drew his weapon. Our man had no choice but to draw and fire. The question remains though: How can an incarcerated killer be in two places at the same time?"

"Has to be a clone," Christa said.

"We accounted for all the clones made on Dakistee," Jenetta said confidently.

"Did we?" Christa asked.

"We know exactly who was made on the equipment that made *us*. Are you suggesting there might be another machine we don't know about?" Eliza asked.

"It's possible," Christa responded. "One machine wouldn't have been able to reproduce the entire population of the planet if the original inhabitants had succeeded in neutralizing the cause of their sterility."

"You're suggesting that a Tsgardi found another site on the planet, learned to operate the equipment, and cloned himself?" Jenetta said, half as a question and half as a statement.

"Why not? The cloning process where Eliza and I were created was initiated when a laborer innocently placed a lamp on what appeared to be a table."

"If your hypothesis is correct, there could be a couple of hundred copies of that criminal running around by now," Jenetta said.

"Not a happy thought if he's as dangerous as you say."

"I think I should give Captain Kanes a call and relate what we've discussed. Excuse me." Jenetta touched the SC ring on her right hand with her left forefinger and said, "Captain Kanes." Touching the ring signaled the base communications computer to establish a link to her cranial transducer. The vibrations produced by her vocal cords traveled through her skull and were picked up by the CT before being transmitted on the carrier wave emitted by the base's computer. After a few seconds, she heard a reply in the tiny CT. Sent out only on her assigned frequency, neither Eliza nor Christa could hear the response, but to Jenetta it sounded as if Kanes was speaking directly into her left ear.

"Yes, sir. Sorry to bother you, but are you available for a private meeting? Something has come up that I think you should hear. I can't speak about it on an open line." Jenetta paused for a reply, then, "Yes, sir. Fifteen minutes in your office. Carver, out." The sign-off instructed the computer to stop emitting the carrier.

Twelve minutes later, Jenetta arrived at the Intelligence Section and waited in Kanes' outer office until he got there. She stood up quickly as he entered and motioned her to follow. He unlocked his office doors with his handprint and she followed him in.

"What's so urgent, Jen?"

"My sisters and I were speaking earlier, and I mentioned the possibility that the Tsgardi criminal might have been cloned. Christa suggested that he might have been cloned using Dakistee equipment."

"No, that's impossible. We have all that equipment here at Higgins. I can assure you that no Tsgardi has been cloned at this base."

"Yes, sir. We discussed the possibility that there might be additional facilities on the planet and that somehow the Tsgardi found one and managed to activate it. One cloning location would not have been adequate to clone the entire population since it took almost seven days to make a clone and there were only twenty-five artificial wombs. One facility could only make thirteen hundred clones each year."

Kanes looked intently at her for a few moments, then walked around his office for a few minutes as he thought. Jenetta just stood in silence, waiting for him to speak.

"It's possible," he said finally. "Unlikely, but possible. Not unlikely that there could be more facilities but that a Tsgardi could locate one and manage to initiate the process. They're not exactly intellectuals. A light destroyer has been stationed in orbit around the planet since the cloning incident occurred, but a small shuttle *could* possibly sneak in and out if they knew the ship's orbital path and schedule, and that could be easily determined by someone on the surface with basic equipment. The facility where our cloning equipment was found has been continually occupied as an outpost, even though the equipment was transported here two and a half years ago, but as you suggest, there *could* be additional locations. By the way, the criminal at the penal colony has been conclusively identified as Recozzi by every test we have, so a clone appears to be more a possibility than ever."

"Then it seems that you have to decide if a complete search of Dakistee should be commenced."

"Yes, but we're talking about an entire planet. It could take an army of investigators years to cover the surface, and it still might not be found. There may *be* nothing to find."

"Normally I'd suggest just searching for emanations from power sources, but we know the material used in the construction of the facility that housed the cloning lab we dismantled totally shielded the entire installation, making it invisible to sensors."

"True. We could be looking at it with sensors from two meters away and never identify it. And— there's the issue of how Recozzi might have escaped from Saquer Major, produced a clone, and then returned with no one being aware of his absence."

"There's another related topic that my sisters and I discussed, sir."

"Yes?"

"We talked about the difficulty of identifying the clones on Dakistee since they're all identical, right down to their retinal images, fingerprints, and DNA. Unlike my sisters, they don't have CT's to identify them."

"That was taken care of long ago, Jen. When the clones were given their physicals here at Higgins, a laser was used to slightly alter their retinal images and fingerprints. The alterations took a fraction of an instant, didn't cause any discomfort, and didn't affect their eyesight or sensation of touch. Each clone has a unique identity now."

"I see. Why wasn't that done to Eliza?"

"It was. Twice. But the unique physiology she inherited from you immediately reversed the changes both times. The process that the Raiders subjected you to while you were their prisoner, the one that keeps you looking like a twenty-one-year-old and makes your body heal ten times faster than regular humans, defeated all our attempts to create unique identities for Eliza and Christa. You know that your recuperative abilities have erased any signs of changes such as broken bones, including the one that occurred when you were seven and fell out of a tree. Even the tiny scar on the outside of your left leg that you've carried for most of your life completely disappeared when your DNA was altered. The scar where you were shot by the Raider officer just before the Battle for Higgins disappeared in just a couple of weeks. Your body seems to have a programmed image and won't allow even the slightest deviation. It immediately begins to restore that programmed image as part of its healing process whenever any alterations are attempted."

"Yes, I've tried to have the SLAVE imprint that the Raiders put on my chest removed or covered up, but it's resisted all my attempts. Skin grafts flake off as dead skin in a few days."

"It's part of the programmed image in the DNA the Raiders created for you. By now it would be difficult to find any trace of your original DNA. We'd have to take a sample from deep inside a bone, and even that won't be possible in another five or six years. By then every cell in your body will contain the new DNA."

"So there's nothing that can be done to make us appear unique?"

"With changes disappearing in a few days as the body reverts to the original image, it doesn't make sense to continue making them. We'll have to rely on the identification signal from the CT's."

"Yes, sir. I understand. I assure you that you have nothing to fear from our sharing a single identity."

"We know that, Commander," he said smiling. "If we had even the slightest concern, none of you would ever have been allowed inside this highly secure area."

Chapter Three
~ October 10th, 2272 ~

Vyx awoke with a start. Someone was outside the door of his hotel room. He immediately reached for the pistol on the nightstand in an automatic reaction. He pointed his laser pistol towards the door and waited, hardly even breathing. A white envelope slid almost noiselessly into the room from under the door and he heard footsteps trailing off down the corridor. He waited for several minutes before getting out of bed in case it was merely a ploy to get him over near the door. The room's draperies were closed over the bulletproof glass, but anyone with a decent thermal imager could place his position in the room. A bomb placed against the outside of the door could be detonated by the watcher to kill him when he retrieved the envelope. For that matter, the envelope itself could be a weapon. It could explode and blow his hands off, leaving him to bleed to death, or it could have been dipped in a poison that would kill him on contact.

Opening his suitcase, he slipped on a pair of impermeable gloves before picking up the envelope. An innocuous-looking viewpad placed on the envelope tested the paper and contents for poisons and explosives. No traces were found. Vyx supposed that if they wanted him badly enough to resort to sophisticated means of assassination, they would probably have just put a rocket into his bedroom from across the street. The bulletproof glass wouldn't stop that, and he knew they had the necessary weapons.

Ripping open the envelope, he found the note to be from Shev Rivemwilth. In it, Rivemwilth apologized for any misunderstandings. He explained that his associates had believed Vyx responsible for the attack on his person. He said the hunters had been called off once Rivemwilth regained consciousness and could talk. It was only afterwards that they had pieced together what had happened. They'd found Vyx's pistol inside the room and discovered it was set for a narrow beam, accounting for the separated skull portion of the Tsgardi who had started the fight. Rivemwilth and his two bodyguards had been shot with a lattice pistol, the sort preferred by the Tsgardi.

Lattice weapons had long ago been outlawed by the Galactic Alliance, but they remained the favored personal weapon of Raiders and other criminals because they could be fired aboard ship with the certain knowledge that they wouldn't puncture the hull. Like laser pistols, they used energy in place of chemical propellants, but they fired an actual projectile rather than an energy beam. Each fifty-millimeter-long projectile was composed of four narrow pieces of flat spring-steel. Loaded under great pressure into hundred-round magazines, projectiles were stored in compressed form. When pulled into the chamber, the projectile instantly expanded into a latticework tubule with a twelve-millimeter diameter. Spun by an electronically rifled chamber, the fired projectile bored through whatever it struck, like a hollow drill bit with a leading edge as sharp as any straight-edge razor. Since it wasn't attempting to push its way through the material as a lead projectile would, it didn't require nearly the mass. Rather, it cut its way through like the narrow blade of a filleting knife. Where a laser pistol sealed the wound as it made it, the lattice pistol left large, gaping holes that allowed a person's life force to bleed out in minutes from wounds in what were normally considered non-vital areas.

Rivemwilth went on to say that he would rather have been shot by the laser. His second heart would simply have taken over immediately for the destroyed one, but the lattice weapon opened a large hole and Rivemwilth had almost expired from the loss of blood. He said he was still willing to proceed with the arms deal if Vyx was interested and invited him to return to the building where they had talked as soon as Rivemwilth was well enough.

Tossing the note on the dresser, Vyx thought about the offer. It might be a trap to lure him out of the hotel, but if it was genuine, he might be able to salvage his mission. His goal had only been to purchase the weapons, not attempt an arrest of anyone here in the colony. Since the colony was located deep in the Frontier Zone, he wasn't supposed to perform arrests here anyway except under specific orders.

* * *

Jenetta concluded her second week of work in the Intelligence Section without any greater sense of job satisfaction than that of the first week. Her only consolation in being stationed at the Higgins Space Station was Lieutenant Commander Zane Spence. They'd dated off and on since the handsome young attorney, posted to the Judge Advocate General's office at Higgins, had defended her during her court-martial.

On this night, she and Zane visited Gregory's, a favorite restaurant on the civilian concourse. The food was always delicious and the retro look of the restaurant appealed to Jenetta's sense of aesthetics. Real wood had been brought to the station for the construction of the interior and then stained a red walnut color, giving the restaurant the subdued but elegant look of expensive restaurants from the twentieth century. The earth tones of red, yellow, and brown were pervasive throughout, and the interior was warm and inviting with none of the glitzy chrome and bright neon used elsewhere throughout the concourse. Gregory, always the most gregarious and congenial of hosts, welcomed them warmly.

"Commander Carver, Commander Spence," he said effusively, when he spotted the tall couple entering the waiting area, "come in, come in. I have your table all ready for you."

Jenetta and Zane looked at one another, then walked past other patrons waiting to be seated as they followed Gregory to a table that bore a 'reserved' sign. Gregory held the chair for Jenetta, while Zane settled his six-foot, one-inch frame into the chair opposite. Being escorted to a reserved table might once have been confusing since they hadn't made reservations, but Jenetta and Zane knew that Gregory always kept one or two tables in reserved status even when the restaurant was fully booked so he would never have to turn away favored or important patrons. Having important persons dine in an establishment was a recommendation in itself and well worth the cost of leaving a table unused and ready at all times. Commander Jenetta Carver was both a favored and important patron. Neither Jenetta nor Zane said a word as Gregory nonchalantly picked up the sign and slipped it beneath his arm.

"I'm pleased to welcome you tonight. My chefs have prepared a wonderful selection of entrees. Would you like to start with a bottle of wine from the Sebastian colony? We just received a shipment of '58 Pink Channay. It's most excellent."

Zane nodded. "That sounds wonderful."

Gregory smiled. "Your waiter will be with you momentarily. I'll get the wine."

"You seem preoccupied, Jen," Zane said after Gregory had brought the wine and the waiter had taken their food order.

Jenetta looked into the blue-green eyes of the handsome JAG officer and smiled. "I'm sorry. I was thinking about work."

"Anything you can share?"

"No, I'm sorry."

"I understand. Forget I said anything. Say, I picked up a copy of the second book about Dakistee today. I only had time to read a few chapters, but what I read is wonderful."

"Eliza did a fantastic job with it," Jenetta said. "It could turn out to be another bestseller."

"I wouldn't be surprised. People are fascinated that such an advanced culture existed twenty thousand years ago, and they hunger for any information about it. Several other books have been published by the archeologists and their clones, but nobody has shown the insight and depth of knowledge about those former inhabitants that you and your sisters have exhibited."

"And yet," Jenetta said, "for all of their technology, they couldn't stop their race from going the way of the large dinosaurs on Earth."

"The answer appears to lie in diversification. The Dakistee people live on in their descendants who colonized Nordakia and Obotymot. As we expand our presence in the universe, there's little chance that a single cataclysmic event, or even multiple events, can totally wipe out our race."

"Universe? Zane, we have yet to even explore five percent of our *galaxy*. At a hundred thousand light-years across, it would take our fastest ships two hundred seventy-five years to reach the farthest solar systems, and that's if we don't stop to visit along the way, which sort of totally defeats the idea of exploration. Although we've found hundreds of sentient life forms living within Galactic Alliance space, only a few dozen have the intelligence to one day begin venturing into space, and only a third of those are currently capable of extra-world travel."

"I heard some scuttlebutt," Zane said in a lowered voice, "that the Galactic Alliance is planning to move the Frontier further out."

"Really? How much further out?"

"A hundred parsecs, extending across the entire length of the current Galactic Alliance border with open space."

"A hundred parsecs? Oh, no! A three hundred-twenty-six light-year swath of additional frontier along our entire border with open space? That will more than double the current Frontier Zone."

"No, it won't. The old Frontier Zone will convert to regulated Galactic Alliance space."

"My God," Jenetta said in a hushed yet appalled tone, "they can't be serious."

"My friend on Earth tells me they're *very* serious. The hope is that it will push the vermin farther back. Once the current Frontier Zone is re-designated, Space Command will immediately assume complete authority over all ships in that space and enforce interdiction laws. In the Frontier Zone, we normally only answer distress calls. We don't stop ships and search their cargo for slaves, illegal weapons, substances, and other illegal contraband. As soon as a criminal crosses over the Zone border, they're essentially safe from pursuit."

"That guideline was only established because we didn't have adequate ships or people to cover the hundred parsecs of Frontier Zone space along the entire Galactic Alliance border. An expansion like you're talking about would add tens of thousands of stars, planets, and moons in this quadrant of the galaxy. We're stretched far too thin as it is. We've only just begun to get a handle on the Raider problem in our present space."

"They're addressing that. The Space Command budget will be increased *dramatically* as part of the expansion because assessments to planets now permitted to join the Galactic Alliance will provide substantially increased funds for law enforcement efforts. The annual appropriation for the construction of new ships is being *doubled*, and a brand new GSC Space Academy is being planned for construction on Nordakia. The first ten Nordakians were commissioned as officers of Space Command after their graduation on Earth last year, and there are presently over two hundred Nordakian cadets in the two academies. Class size at the beginning of the new school term was increased from three hundred fifty to six hundred at each school. The GAC knows that the expansion means we're going to need new officers, and plenty of them."

"But it will take years to build the ships and staff them."

"There's an old Chinese proverb: 'A journey of a thousand miles begins with a single step.'"

"There's another," Jenetta remarked, grinning, "that says 'paper can't wrap fire.' A paper fleet certainly isn't going to control the current Frontier Zone when it's re-designated."

"I've also heard there's talk of the Nordakian Space Force being merged into Space Command."

Jenetta shook her head slightly. "It would swell our ranks quickly, but I doubt it will happen."

"Why not?" Zane asked.

"Their training is inadequate by our Academy standards. I know that from firsthand experience because I've toured the Space Force bases and schools. Academy-trained officers would resist following the orders of a former Nordakian officer who was placed in command if they mistrusted his training and experience. It could lead to some very difficult situations."

"Even if it was you? You hold the rank of captain in the Nordakian Space Force. As I remember, you're only on loan to Space Command."

"That's different, and I'm on permanent assignment to GSC. Like you, I'm a Terran who was educated at the Northern Hemisphere Space Academy on Earth, and I was already a Lieutenant Commander in GSC when I was honored by being made a citizen of Nordakia and commissioned in their Space Force. The GAC arranged that 'on loan' silliness to further cement relations with Nordakia."

"Still, if the services are combined, you'd probably be advanced to the rank of captain immediately and we wouldn't be able to see each other anymore. You know the unwritten law about minimal social association with officers more than one level of rank from your own."

"Zane," Jenetta said, sensitive to his feelings on the issue, "I know you're disappointed that I've been promoted ahead of you, but you'll be promoted soon. You're named on the Promotion Selection List for Commander that just came out."

"Yes, but I still have to wait for a position to become available. It might be good for me if the GSC is greatly expanded. There'll be a lot of new positions created."

"How close is this proposed expansion to actually becoming a reality?"

"So close that my source isn't talking about it as being proposed. He says it can happen as soon as two weeks from now. They're just debating over the actual language of the resolution before going public. Word has already started to leak out though, so you'll probably see it in the news in the next few days."

"What about the planets in the newly delineated territory that don't wish to be part of the Galactic Alliance?"

"They really have no choice in the matter if they're located within the new border. Since we don't involve ourselves in the internal matters of planetary governments, it won't affect control of their governments or anything, but other problems will arise. Considering that the Galactic Alliance doesn't permit trade or association with planets that haven't develop-ed rudimentary space travel capability, those planets that have already been trading with advanced cultures might suddenly find themselves isolated except for trade with smugglers who choose to ignore GA law.

"It seems unfair to drag them into the GA," Jenetta said, "and then restrict access to former trading partners."

"The GAC believes that restricting access by more advanc-ed cultures allows societies to evolve more naturally without outside influence. Once they develop their own space travel capability, they'll be welcomed into the Alliance and can become an active trading partner with the more advanced member planets."

"Except that the GA doesn't accept member planets that are located in the Frontier Zone."

"That's been a problem— one that's been discussed at great lengths by the Galactic Alliance Council. The fact is that we just haven't been able to exercise control over all of the territory claimed by the GA."

"Is that the only reason?" Jenetta asked.

"Basically. They'd love to accept everyone applying for membership, but we just haven't been able to provide protect-ion and law enforcement in the Frontier Zone, so the Council limited GA membership to those planets located within the inner border. Until Space Command is able to enforce all the laws of the Galactic Alliance within the Frontier Zone, I can't see the planets there being affected by a 'paper' expansion.

They'll continue to carry out trade with anyone, just as they have before. We're really only establishing a new outer boundary and announcing that no part of our Frontier Zone can be co-opted by life forms from outside the Galactic Alliance or integrated into anyone else's coalition, federation, empire, or dominion.

"Of course some solar systems within the Zone may still object to becoming part of GA space. I assume those cases will be treated in the same manner as such solar systems were treated in the initial creation and again after the first expansion of the Alliance. The objecting solar system will be totally isolated, and no vessel from any Alliance planet will be permitted to enter their system or even trade with them at space stations or freight hubs. Likewise, their vessels will not be permitted to visit or trade with any Alliance member planets or space stations. Eventually, most of the previously isolated systems petitioned to have their status changed because they learned what they were missing out on as their civilizations matured."

"If your rumor is accurate," Jenetta said, "Space Command is about to be handed a major headache."

Zane's scuttlebutt was not only accurate, it was extremely accurate. Upon reporting for duty on Monday, Jenetta found an important memo in her message queue. Copied to all senior officers in the Intelligence Section, the memo stated that the Galactic Alliance Council was working on a resolution that would officially shift the Frontier Zone a hundred parsecs further out, and the former area would become regulated Galactic Alliance space.

Jenetta was summoned to a briefing for senior officers in Kanes' office at 1000 hours. The meeting was primarily for officers with the rank of Lieutenant Commander or above, but the two Lieutenants assigned to his Strategic Planning Committee were there as well.

"Good morning," Kanes began after everyone had taken their seats at the large conference table or seats around the walls of the room after places at the table were filled. "I'm sure you've all read the memo about the frontier zone by now. The GAC has privately deliberated on this expansion for some time, and they feel that with the Raiders so weakened from previous engagements, the time has come to act. Since the new territory hasn't been claimed by anyone previously, there shouldn't be any challenge to our authority. A number of worlds within the old Frontier Zone have been petitioning for inclusion in the GA for years, and now they'll be welcomed as full voting members. The official announcement will be made in a couple of weeks, but as with most issues where politicians and their office staffs are involved, the word has already leaked out. The first task for this command is to figure out how to exercise control over the new sectors of space that will adjoin our current mission area.

"In order for us to adequately patrol the new space, our fleet size must be, at the very least, doubled. The GAC has promised that it will be, but realistically it will take many years to build enough new ships to cover it satisfactorily. A number of older warships taken out of service over the past decade are being refitted for patrol duties in rear areas where we have few problems so that the newer, faster ships can be freed up for patrol in the new space. Space Command is also *finally* changing the mandatory ship officers' retirement age from sixty-five to eighty-five, and mandatory retirement age for base personnel is being changed from eighty-five to one hundred. The former age limits were a holdover from when people rarely lived beyond ninety years. Now that people are averaging a hundred thirty-six years with nano-bot medicine and many make it to one hundred fifty, this change is long overdue. Time spent in stasis will now be completely discounted from the officer's age when computing mandatory retirement dates instead of being computed at twenty-five percent as was the case previously.

"I'll be speaking with each section chief over the next few days to discuss how this impacts your section. Any questions?"

"When will this expansion take effect, sir?" Commander Edgar asked.

"As soon as the resolution is officially presented, voted upon, and passed. I understand the wording is 'effective immediately,' but we still have the formalities of government to observe. Of course, the criminals living in the old Frontier Zone will have weeks to escape into the new zone since the word is already out, but we're positioning as many ships as possible so we can begin interdiction activities as soon as the okay is given by Space Command Supreme HQ."

"The Alliance currently shares borders with three other nations, sir," Commander Brantford said. "How is that situation to be handled? We obviously can't expand the Frontier Zone into their territory."

"Where we cannot expand our borders a full one hundred parsecs, our new border will abut our neighbor's border."

"Will home port assignments be changing, sir?" Commander Murray asked.

"I'm sure they will. Space Command will be stretched pretty thin for quite a while. A lot of ships will immediately be re-assigned to home ports closer to the old Frontier Zone. In this region of space, that means Dixon since it's the closest base to the old border. A number of new bases will have to be constructed since we don't currently have any in the old Frontier Zone, and they'll need to have ships assigned to them for protection. But that will probably take decades to happen."

"How does it affect our search for the remaining Raider bases, sir?" Jenetta asked.

"Very little, and that remains a top priority. We'll continue to gather data, and we'll move when we have a definite location. We believe that both Raider-Four and Raider-Five are in our expanded sector area, so we'll now be empowered to seek them out as well." When ten seconds had passed without any further questions, Captain Kanes said, "If there're no further questions, you're dismissed."

People would be thinking about how the news affected them and their job functions over the next several days. As the group rose to leave, Kanes said, "Commander Carver, remain behind, please."

When the office was clear of the others, Kanes asked, "Have you formulated any new ideas on our arms problem?"

"Nothing yet, sir. I'm still reviewing the material from the case."

"We've received a vid of Vyx's meeting with Rivemwilth, so we have the serial number from the sample weapon he was able to examine. It certainly appeared genuine. We're tracking it from manufacture to locate the point where it went missing. It should help point a finger at our problem."

"Is there anything I can do to help?"

"Just continue your review of the case file and make whatever suggestions come to mind."

"Yes, sir. Sir, the Gollasko Colony will fall within regulated space once the border shifts."

"Yes, that's correct."

"What about the Alyysian arms merchant that's been using the Colony as his base of operations? Rivemwilth's capture could provide all the information we need to close down the pipeline of stolen weapons and arrest everyone involved."

"Yes, but I doubt he's still there. He's probably already on his way to what will become the new Frontier Zone. If he's still at Gollasko when the resolution passes and we can get a ship there, we'll take him into custody immediately."

"Even though there's no formal planetary government on Gollasko?"

"Because of it. In the absence of a planetary government, we can treat it as we would a ship in space. If there was a formal planetary government, we'd have to apply for extradition or wait until he tried to leave the planet because we can't interfere in the planetary administration."

"Yes, sir. Sir, after we took down Raider-Three I expected Space Command to immediately seek out and capture Raider-Two. We thought we knew the general vicinity of that base."

"We did search, Jen, but we weren't able to find it. Apparently we were wrong when we speculated on its general position using the history of past attack locations by Raider ships. Space Command has had a dozen ships searching every asteroid, moon, and planet within ten light-years from our projection point since I returned from Dixon."

"And they haven't found anything in almost a year and a half?"

"Not a sign. The search has been called off now so those ships can be assigned patrol duty in the new area of space that will soon come under Space Command jurisdiction, but they were on their second pass through so it's unlikely they would have found anything."

"Yes, sir. I'm sure the Raiders will reveal themselves again. We'll find them."

"I'm not so sure. The Raiders have ceased all pirating activities in GA space. The word we get is that they've retrenched their operation, concentrating on their old rackets of drugs, weapons, slaves, and prostitution. Without the attacks on shipping, we can't plot their locations."

"Then we'll have to find their hideouts by other means."

Kanes nodded. "Dismissed, Commander."

Returning to her office, Jenetta poured a steaming cup of coffee from the decanter her aide brought in and listened as the computer resumed reading aloud where it had left off earlier.

* * *

The *Chiron* and *Prometheus* arrived in port within hours of one another on Friday, the *Prometheus* actually arriving days ahead of schedule after receiving new orders in connection with the Galactic Alliance's plan to expand the borders. At the end of the workday, Jenetta and Christa were excused from further duties at Intelligence so they could report aboard their ships. Both ships were scheduled to depart within forty-eight hours, so Jenetta quickly prepared a final report of her investigation and brought it to Captain Kanes.

"I'm sorry I couldn't recommend any new course of action, sir. Your investigators and operatives have done such a thorough job that I couldn't come up with any new ideas."

"It was worth a shot, Jen. We're still actively pursuing the case. We've discovered that the weapon shown to Vyx was part of a shipment sent to the munitions depot on Delos-Anon. The records show that a freighter delivered the sealed cargo container, but none of the weapons shipped in that container were ever logged into the armory. We're following up on that trail."

"It sounds like you've located your leak."

"Almost— at least one— but we still want all the people involved. Somebody stole those weapons from the depot, and someone purchased them and distributed them. We want those individuals also."

"Yes, sir. Will you be traveling with the *Prometheus* when she leaves port?"

"No, I can't get away right now. This border expansion has significantly altered my plans."

"I wish you luck with the investigation, sir."

"And you have a safe trip. Thanks for looking over the case. If anything comes to mind, drop me a note."

"I will, sir. Goodbye."

"Good-bye, Jen."

Jenetta and Christa had given Eliza a little send-off party the evening before the *Bellona* left port, and now it was their turn to say goodbye to each other. After dinner they had their final chat as they walked through the civilian concourse.

"It may be a while before we see each other again," Christa said.

"Very likely, but we'll keep in touch. There should be quite a bit of time aboard ship to compose messages to each other, the boys, Regina, Marisa, and mom and dad."

"I'll call at least once a week as long as communications aren't blocked."

"Com blackouts don't usually last very long," Jenetta said. "They're usually only employed before an upcoming action."

"If we're operating in the newly expanded space, the captains may not want to give away our position."

"Perhaps, but it'll take four months at the top speed of the *Prometheus* or *Chiron* just to reach the border of the current Frontier Zone and then ten more to reach the new Zone."

"Have you said goodbye to Zane?"

"Not yet. I'll call him after we get back to quarters."

"Just a phone call?" Christa asked teasingly.

"He's been busy working every night this past week. He's preparing the case for a general court martial that begins next week."

"Prosecution or defense?"

"Defense, of course. He prefers that side of the aisle."

"You probably won't see him for a year or more."

"I know, but I can't make him interrupt his work on a case. It's too important."

"Let's head back to the BOQ. I'm anxious to start getting packed."

"Okay, but don't rush too much. You might be aboard the ship for a very long time."

"Yes," Christa said, grinning, "isn't it wonderful?"

Chapter Four
~ October 24th, 2272 ~

Jenetta completed her packing in the morning and prepared to leave for the *Prometheus*. Zane hadn't been in his quarters when she'd called last night, so she'd left a message and then started her preparations for moving to the ship. After stacking her smaller cases atop her 'oh-gee' spacechest just inside the front door of the small apartment, she took a final walk around to make sure she had taken everything. Her last act was to check for a message from Zane. There wasn't one, so she punched in the forwarding code. Any new messages would be routed directly to the ship.

Satisfied that she wasn't leaving anything behind other than her packed cases, she called her cats to her side and left the apartment. As she entered the lift with her cats, a rider who had come down from an upper floor moved as far back into the car as possible, a worried expression on his face.

"Don't worry, Lieutenant," Jenetta said, "They won't bother you."

"Yes, ma'am, if you say so," the lieutenant said, never taking his eyes off the animals. "I was just thinking that I hope they've had their breakfast already." After the car reached the lobby, he waited until Jenetta and her cats were well clear before he stepped out.

Jenetta received the usual looks as she walked to the *Prometheus*. She and the cats had actually become a fairly common sight since she had begun taking them to the base gym every morning for her workout. The big cats would sit and watch as she exercised or practiced her kickboxing, and then lope alongside her as she ran or jogged on the exercise track.

The two Marine sentries and the duty officer at the entrance ramp smartened their stance and saluted Jenetta as she reached the ship.

"Permission to come aboard?" Jenetta said to the young lieutenant as she returned the salutes.

"Granted, Commander," the duty officer said. "Welcome back, ma'am."

"Thank you, Lieutenant Nivan. Congratulations on your promotion."

"Thank you, ma'am. Congratulations on your promotion also. I haven't seen you since you became base commander at Dixon."

"Seems like a very long time ago, but it's only been two years. It's good to be home. Carry on, Lieutenant."

"Yes, ma'am."

Jenetta headed for the bridge, but she ran into a number of friends along the way and stopped to chat for a few minutes with each, offering congratulations to a couple of them who had been promoted since they last met. The two Marine sentries, one at the entrance to the bridge corridor and the other next to the door of the captain's quarters, braced to attention as she approached and passed. Neither challenged her for being accompanied by the two large cats. Arriving on the bridge, she was greeted by a Lieutenant Commander whom she only knew by name. She hadn't looked over his personnel file yet, but she estimated that he was in his early forties. He was of average height and wore his wavy black hair as long as regulations permitted.

"Good morning, Commander Eaton," Jenetta said, smiling. "I'm Commander Carver."

"Yes, ma'am," he said, returning her smile. "I recognized you immediately. It's a pleasure to meet you at last."

"Likewise. How's your friend, Lieutenant Flores?"

"He's fine, ma'am," Eaton said, obviously surprised by the question. "I didn't think you'd remember him. He's still on the *San Francisco*. He's made it to the Selection List for

Lieutenant Commander and he's hoping something might open up this year."

"I remember him and our conversation in my dining room on Dixon very well. There's a very good chance that a lot of new positions will be created over the next few years. Wish him luck for me when you speak to him."

"I will, ma'am. Are you here to take your position as executive officer?"

"Yes, I am. Is the Captain about?"

"He's in his briefing room."

"Thank you, Commander, I'll see if he's free. You and I can talk again later."

"Yes, ma'am."

Walking to the captain's briefing room on the larboard side of the bridge, Jenetta waited while the computer announced her presence. When the door opened in response to the Captain's directive to 'come', she entered with her cats. Memories of her months as the first captain of this battleship flooded into her consciousness as she again saw the richly furnished interior.

Coming to attention in front of a real wood desk seemingly large enough to alternate as a landing pad for a space tug, she said, "Commander Carver reporting for duty, sir."

The SimWindow behind Captain Gavin was presently displaying a live exterior view of a docking ring section at Higgins. A long, comfortable-looking sofa covered with the same deliciously soft dark brown leather used for the room's three 'oh-gee' chairs sat patiently waiting for occupants against one wall. The walls of the four-meter-square room were paneled with real oak finished in a light honey color, not the synthetic products that only simulated wood, and the topaz carpeting gave the impression of being ten centimeters deep.

"At ease, Jen," Gavin said. Gesturing towards one of the over-stuffed chairs, he added, "Have a seat. We've missed you while you were away."

Gavin's hair was still a dark brown with a touch of grey at the temples. Just shy of six feet tall, he had a strong face with good features. He was approaching his mid-sixties, but a strong exercise regimen kept his body fit.

Jenetta relaxed and sat down. "And I've missed everyone here, sir. I'm very happy to be back aboard."

Looking down with a bemused look at the two enormous animals at her sides, Captain Gavin asked, "Are these the two *pussycats* Admiral Holt spoke to me about?"

Jenetta smiled at his expression. "I expect so, sir. He said the decision to exempt me from the regulation allowing only one pet per crewmember was entirely up to you."

"Yes, he said he had no objection in this instance, but I'm always concerned about setting precedents in such matters."

"Yes, sir, I understand. I don't want to break them up because they rely on each other for companionship when I'm out of my quarters. I'm afraid that one might get into mischief if left alone."

"What would you do with them if I didn't waive the rule?"

"I'd see if Captain Powers of the *Chiron* will permit them, and if so I'd ask Christa to take them with her."

"I read about the assassination attempt on your life while you were on Dixon. I understand that your pets made short work of the attacker. Have they ever attacked anyone else?"

"No, sir. They would only do that if I were assaulted or if they were attacked or tormented. They're normally as gentle and playful as pussycats."

"I can't imagine anyone being foolhardy enough to torment this pair."

Jenetta grinned. "It wouldn't be the smartest thing to do. They won't cause any trouble, sir. I give you my word."

Captain Gavin hesitated for a few seconds. "I don't want you to be deprived of your pets, Jen. You may keep both onboard as long as they remain in your quarters. I can't have such large animals roaming the ship freely."

"Yes, sir. They'd stay in my quarters if I told them to, even if I left the corridor doors wide open. But I need to take them to the gym each day when I exercise. They need exercise also."

"That's acceptable. Commander Tighe, the officer who was filling in for you while you were assigned to Dixon and then to Headquarters, has already left the ship. You can move into your quarters immediately."

"Thank you, sir. I was informed that the ship would be leaving port tomorrow?"

"Yes, our scheduled departure time is 2000 hours."

"Isn't that a bit unusual? The crew hasn't had a chance for liberty."

"We had two months of liberty while the ship was in spacedock."

"Spacedock? Was there a problem, sir?"

"Our keel was fitted with a special docking collar. It's for a prototype scout ship assigned to the *Prometheus*."

"Why couldn't the scout ship simply use one of the existing flight bays?"

"The ship is far too large. Only the top portion is enclosed when it's docked in the new collar."

"How large is it, sir?"

"The specs are in the computer, but it's roughly a third the length of a light destroyer."

Jenetta's eyes opened wider. "That would make it about a hundred fifteen meters in length. I've never heard of a scout ship being over thirty meters."

"It's a new design. The *Chiron* has also been fitted with a docking collar, but only one prototype ship is ready right now. Ours was delivered just hours before we left the space dock. The *Chiron* will receive theirs when it's completed."

"Each battleship in the fleet will be getting such a scout ship?"

"Eventually. If we'd had one at Dakistee, the Tsgardi would never have been able to terrorize the planet while we went to answer the distress call. We could have separated and left the scout ship in orbit over the planet. It would have been more than a match for the Tsgardi vessel that attacked you."

"It's armed?"

"It has almost as much armament as a light destroyer. In fact, if you look at the exterior, it looks like a smaller version of one. It has phased array lasers, torpedo tubes, and a flight bay large enough for three fighters and a shuttle. But that's where the similarity ends. Its revolutionary new engine design will let it dance circles around the fleet's destroyers. It'll even outdistance the *Prometheus* and *Chiron* in a race."

"It can beat the *Prometheus*? A ship that small is faster than Light-412?"

"I was told that the engines are rated at Light-450, and that they could possibly exceed Light-487 at full power, but that's top secret for now. The helmsman can only bring it to Light-225, the official speed, and that appears to be the top speed to anyone visiting the bridge, but the commanding officer can override the speed governor from the command chair on the bridge and have the ship perform at more than twice the rated speed."

"What protection does it have?"

"The inner hull plating is titanium, and there's a self-sealing membrane between the two hull layers. The outer plating is a new material developed during Space Command's attempts to reproduce the material we found on Dakistee."

"That's wonderful. The ship will be almost indestructible."

"Not quite. They haven't exactly been able to reproduce the Dakistee material yet, but this stuff is many times denser and more durable than titanium so they decided to go ahead with its use on the prototype. It can't be damaged by laser fire but could sustain damage from a torpedo strike. The amount of damage will depend on the size of the torpedo, casing strength, velocity at impact, the type of warhead, and the structural integrity of the location where the strike occurs. A nuclear warhead that explodes immediately next to the hull can damage it, but bomb-pumped laser or high-explosive warheads that don't penetrate should have negligible effect. They're calling the new material Dakinium."

"Does the ship have an official designation?"

"It's GSC-SD001 and has been named the *Colorado*."

"After the state?"

"The river."

Jenetta smiled and nodded. "I like that. Like the river, it can be slow and peaceful, or fast and dangerous."

"As soon as we're underway, you'll have an opportunity to become familiar with it. By the time we reach the current Frontier Zone, I want my senior officers to know that ship as well as they know the *Prometheus*. It's your job to see that they do."

"Yes, sir. I can see where the new ship adds an entirely new dimension of effectiveness."

"Why don't you get settled in, Jen. We can talk more about it later. Have you met Commander Eaton?"

"I stopped and spoke with him for a few minutes while I was on my way to see you, sir. I wanted to resolve the issue of my cats as soon as possible. I told him we'd speak again later."

"You'll find we have a number of new crewmen on board since you were my second officer."

"Yes, sir. I'll go through the personnel roster as soon as I have a chance. What's our mission for this trip, sir?"

"So far I've only been told that we're to enforce the laws of the Galactic Alliance, concentrating our efforts in the expanded territory. I believe they want as many ships as possible performing interdiction activities against ships trying to get out of the formerly lawless space. But by the time we get there, the criminal element will have had months to get into the new Frontier Zone, so things might be fairly peaceful. You'll have second watch and Commander Eaton will have the third."

"Yes, sir."

"If that's all, you're dismissed, Commander."

"Yes, sir."

"And—" Captain Gavin began, softening his tone from his normal laconic military demeanor, "welcome back, Jen. I'm really glad to have you back with us."

Jenetta smiled warmly. "Thank you, sir. I can't adequately express how happy I am to be back and still maintain proper military decorum."

Captain Gavin grinned.

Jenetta stood and turned to leave, the cats rising without being told and staying by her side as she left the briefing room and walked through the bridge. Her quarters were just down the corridor, and her door opened as she approached it.

As executive officer, Jenetta's quarters were second in size only to the captain's. Her sitting room, bedroom, and bath were as large as the ones she'd had as captain aboard the cruiser *Song*, but she didn't have the private dining room, galley, conference-room-sized office, and attached steward's quarters afforded to captains of large warships. The cats seemed to recognize immediately that this would be their new home, probably because they had watched as Jenetta packed her things in the BOQ, and they left her side now to explore the suite. Her large sitting room and office had a connecting door and doors onto the corridor, and the centrally-situated bathroom was accessible from either the sitting room or the bedroom. All four rooms had been thoroughly cleaned by housekeeping bots since Commander Tighe had vacated the quarters. While she was there, the laundry robot came in to see if any clean sheets or towels were needed and then checked to see if there was any dirty laundry to be picked up. The cats sniffed briefly at the bot and then ignored it, being quite used to laundry and housekeeping bots. The bot stopped briefly until they finished their inspection, then continued with its assigned tasks. Jenetta called the base housing office to make sure her bags would be brought to the ship as soon as possible and then checked her duty schedule on the computer in her office.

After telling the cats to remain in her quarters, Jenetta left to begin her workday. Unlike the first time she had functioned as first officer when the *Prometheus* was newly commissioned, the ship's personnel knew their jobs, and their daily tasks had become routine. Jenetta had time to look through the personnel files to see who had been promoted, who had left the ship, and who had joined the crew. She even had time to visit the new scout ship.

The *Colorado* was impressive. The bridge was cramped when compared to that of the *Prometheus* but positively enormous when compared to that of a normal scout ship. There were regular stations for helm, navigation, communications, tactical, and weapons fire control, in addition to the captain's and first officer's chairs. The stations were spacious, and the bridge reminded Jenetta of the bridge on the freighter *Vordoth*, her first command. The captain's briefing room was austere compared to that of the *Prometheus*, but most briefing rooms would have to be described as such. Naturally smaller, it had a standard-sized desk, several chairs, and a sofa, but lacked the rich, real wood paneling and deep pile rug.

After thoroughly examining the bridge, Jenetta began checking out the rest of the ship. It seemed as though she had only just begun when it was time to report to the bridge for her watch.

Although they were in port and there was little to do, regulations required that the *Prometheus'* bridge be fully staffed around the clock. It gave Jenetta a chance to talk with the watch personnel and begin to develop a relationship with the ones she didn't know from her previous time aboard ship. One whom she did know from her previous duty aboard the *Prometheus* was Lieutenant Kerrey, the helmsman. At five-feet, eight-inches, Kerrey was three inches shorter than Jenetta, but she had known him since he was four inches taller.

"Hello, Lieutenant. How have you been?" Jenetta asked as she looked into the smiling chestnut eyes of the curly-haired officer as he arrived on the bridge for his watch.

"Great, Commander. Welcome back. It hasn't been the same without you."

"Thank you. I'm happy to be back. How did you wind up on my watch? I seem to remember seeing your name listed as helmsman with the first watch crew."

"I traded with Lieutenant Osawa. The Captain approved our swapping duty watches."

Jenetta nodded. "I'm happy to have you on my watch, Don. Have you had a chance to look over the *Colorado* yet?"

"Not yet, Commander. Access has been restricted ever since it was brought aboard."

"Once we've left port and things have settled down, I'll see that you're granted access. I'll be setting up a training schedule for crewmen to man the ship. Would you be interested?"

"Yes, ma'am!" he said enthusiastically.

"Okay, I'll put your name on the training schedule."

"Thank you, Commander."

"You're welcome. You've earned the right to be a part of the first team."

"What's the purpose of the ship, Commander?"

"To increase our effectiveness as we perform the duties assigned to us. When we launch the *Colorado*, we become a multi-ship force."

"You're saying it's armed? I thought it was like an oversized shuttle."

"It's only similarity to a shuttle is that it's housed in a bay on the *Prometheus*, if you can call its docking collar a bay. Once it's launched, it becomes a lightweight destroyer, although significantly smaller than a normal light destroyer. The designation is GSC-SD001. It stands for Scout Destroyer 001."

"Now I'm *really* excited. I can't wait to see it."

"Be patient for a couple of days and you'll have an opportunity for a close inspection."

When Lieutenant Commander Eaton reported for third watch, Jenetta invited him to sit down and talk.

After briefing him on the status of the ship, Jenetta said, "You've been the second officer for some time, so I'm sure there's nothing beyond normal instructions that I need to relate in preparation for your watch. Do you have any questions for me?"

"No, ma'am. At least nothing pertaining to the ship's operation. As you say, I've been a watch officer for some time."

"What is it you'd like to know?"

"I was curious about your cats and how you came to have a pair of jaguars."

Jenetta smiled. "Actually, they're Taurentlus-Thur Jumakas, not Terran Jaguars, although they look very similar. Jumakas are about a hundred pounds lighter than jaguars. My pets are fully grown but only weigh in at about a hundred and sixty pounds each. You're probably aware that Jumakas were domesticated on Taurentlus-Thur hundreds of years ago and are frequently used as nighttime security animals for businesses, much as canines are used in Terran businesses. Their appearance and physiology is like that of Terran cats, but they're actually much more like Terran dogs in temperament. Mine came as part of the inventory from a precious stones store that had been liquidated after the owner passed away. An Alyysian that I had to arrest asked me to sell off his inventory. I sold everything for him and deposited the money into an account that will be turned over to him when he's freed from prison in about a year. I kept the cats as my commission. That occurred while I was the Base Commander at Dixon. They've been with me ever since."

"Have they ever given you any problems?"

"None. They stay in my quarters, except when I take them to exercise with me. With them protecting me, I know I couldn't be safer."

"The word is that you're pretty good at protecting yourself."

"It's nice to have the extra eyes and ears. I sleep very soundly with Cayla and Tayna next to my bed."

"I can understand that. With three hundred twenty pounds of muscle, claws, and teeth protecting me, I'd sleep pretty soundly myself."

As the chronometer on the bridge sounded eight times, Jenetta smiled and said, "I see it's time for the watch change, so you have the bridge, Commander. I'll see you tomorrow."

"Aye, ma'am. Goodnight."

Jenetta's cases had been delivered from the BOQ and she took the time to unpack and put everything away before climbing into bed. Checking her bedside com unit, she saw that Zane still hadn't answered her message.

In the morning, Jenetta headed for the ship's gym with her cats. She spent an hour working out and thirty minutes running around the track with the cats before returning to her quarters to shower and prepare for the day. She enjoyed a couple of healthy breakfasts in the Officers' mess, then returned to her office with an armful of fruit to begin work. Matters relating to victualing and preparing the ship for an extended voyage consumed several hours, and then individual meetings with all senior officers to coordinate final preparations for departure took up the rest of her office hours for the day. She would have loved to spend some more time aboard the *Colorado*, but that would have to wait until after they were under way.

Jenetta arrived on the bridge to begin her watch just before 1600 and spent a very busy four hours coordinating the final activities related to their departure. At 1950 she gave the order to seal the ship and prepare to leave port. The captain returned to the bridge just before 2000 but didn't intervene.

He just stood near the tactical station and observed. After each department had reported in that all was secure and ready for departure, and port control had issued clearance and departure instructions for the ship, Jenetta gave the order to depressurize the airlock tunnel and then release the docking clamps. As the clamps were released, the airlock tunnel retracted automatically into the dock. The ship was immediately floating free.

"Reverse thrusters, twenty ticks," Jenetta ordered at exactly 2000 hours.

"Reverse thrusters operating, twenty ticks," the helmsman reported.

The large display screen at the front of the bridge that normally showed the view from the bow shifted to show a view from the stern. A small inset image now showed the view from the bow as the large ship backed away from the docking pier.

As the *Prometheus* cleared the pier and other ships, Jenetta said, "Starboard bow thrusters, ten ticks."

"Starboard bow thrusters operating, ten ticks," the helmsman repeated.

The ship began turning in a slow, counter-clockwise motion as the thrusters engaged. As it reached a certain point in its arc, Jenetta said, "Larboard bow thrusters, five ticks."

"Larboard bow thrusters operating, five ticks," the helmsman reported.

The ship slowed its turn but was still moving back away from the spaceport pier when Jenetta said, "Helm, sub-light engines at minimum power until we clear all station traffic. Engage sub-light engines."

"Aye, Commander, engaging sub-light engines, power at minimum."

The view on the large display screen changed again to show the view from the bow, and the ship moved forward slowly until it cleared the docked ships and the ships in planetary orbit. Once clear of all traffic, the helmsman called, "Clear of all traffic and our course is laid in, Commander."

"Are we aligned with our course, and is our path clear?"

"Yes, ma'am."

"Tactical, what's the status of the Autotect grid?"

"The Autotect grid is green, Commander."

The sizeable tactical station aboard the *Prometheus* was designed to accommodate no fewer than seven officers. The lead tactician, usually a commander or at least a lieutenant commander, sat amid an almost complete circle of displays and electronic control consoles. Facing him or her on the outside of the circle were six stations for the rest of the tac team. A bevy of holo-screens hung suspended over the encircling hardware so the lead could see what each tac team member was seeing.

The ship's ACS, or anti-collision sensors, had the potential to 'see' another vessel from hours away, even when both ships were proceeding at top FTL speed towards one another, *if* both vessels were transmitting a proper Autotect code. The signals traveled on an Inter-Dimensional Band in hyperspace at a speed of point-zero-five-one-three light-years per minute. Green meant that no other ships were reporting a course that intersected with the *Prometheus'* projected course in such a way as to present a danger.

"Tactical, what's the status of the DeTect grid?"

"The DeTect grid is green, Commander."

The ship's DeTect equipment used a special frequency in hyperspace to 'see' everything within four billion kilometers of a ship. The quality of the image wasn't very good, but the computers could identify the movement of any ships, extra-terrestrial bodies, or miscellany that posed a threat to the ship's navigation.

"Helm, build our envelope and proceed on course at Light-375."

As a temporal envelope fully engulfed the ship, the helmsman keyed in the speed setting. Jenetta turned to Captain Gavin and said, "We're away, Captain."

"Carry on, Commander," the captain said, then turned and left the bridge.

Jenetta settled into the command chair and watched the front viewscreen as the ship rocketed forward on its designated course towards the Frontier Zone.

Following her morning workout and breakfast, Jenetta returned to her quarters and recorded a message to her brother Andy, congratulating him on his promotion to Lt. Commander. She'd been too tired to respond to his vidMail after she'd come off duty and viewed his message. Then she spent a couple of hours dealing with shipboard matters before placing a call to the chief engineer, Lieutenant Commander Cameron.

"Bill, it's Jen. I'm going to spend some time aboard the *Colorado* this morning. Are you free to join me?"

"Absolutely! I've been itching to take a good look inside her, but she's been off limits."

"The captain has instructed me to familiarize myself with it and to train crews in its operation, so I've lifted the blanket restriction and established access for certain senior officers. As the crews are established, they'll also receive access privileges, but this is your chance to scrutinize things without tripping over a couple of dozen enlisted crewmen."

"I can hardly wait."

"I'll meet you there. Your access privileges are already in effect. I'm headed down there now."

"I'll meet you in the bay."

Lieutenant Commander Cameron was standing in the new bay gazing up at the superstructure of the scout ship when Jenetta arrived. At forty-seven, Bill was still at the top of his game. Standing five-foot-ten, he kept himself reasonably fit.

He had rugged good looks, dark brown hair, and brown, hound-dog eyes.

The bay, or more accurately the airtight docking collar, was easily ten times the size of a normal flight bay.

"It's enormous," Bill said, looking up at the *Colorado*.

"It's no shuttle," Jenetta said. "It's a real ship."

"I was in a shuttle checking over the shipyard's work when it was delivered, but it was dwarfed by the *Prometheus*. Seeing it like this really hits home. And we're only seeing the uppermost two decks."

"Let's go inside and look around. I spent some time on the bridge the other day. It's impressive."

Over the next few hours, Jenetta and Bill looked through the engineering section while comparing the equipment to the computer's specs and diagrams.

"This is crazy, Jen," Bill finally said in an exasperated voice. "From what I've heard, half this stuff is still experimental."

"This *is* the prototype, after all. They must feel it's been proven well enough to release it for active service. They're already building more scout destroyers for the other battleships from this same design."

"According to the computer, this ship has only logged *two* days of space trials. New ship designs are supposed to log ninety days before being released for fleet duty. And ships containing radical new engine designs are supposed to be tested until they've logged six months or more without a serious problem. We don't even know how this new outer skin is going to hold up."

"It saved our bacon on Dakistee. I think it should do the job."

"That was on a planetary surface with a warm nitrogen-oxygen atmosphere. We're talking about using it in the frigid vacuum of outer space. Remember the Titanic!"

"The Titanic?"

"The steamship that went down in the North Atlantic in 1912."

"I don't follow you."

"After an investigation of the damage about a century later, it was discovered that the steel and rivets used for the hull had become extremely brittle in the frigid waters. When the ship slid along the iceberg, rivets popped and hull plates cracked or buckled far more than they should have."

"I'm sure the shipyard tested the Dakinium plating under all the conditions we'll face."

"Probably, but there's no test like the real thing. And what about this new engine design? I only read about it in our engineering research updates a few months ago. I had no idea it was actually being built. Now I find that it's a reality. They can't have had time to test it properly."

"Maybe that's *our* job. Things are moving pretty fast since the GAC decided to expand our borders."

"Things shouldn't move so fast that safety is compromised."

"Do you feel it's unsafe?" Jenetta asked.

"I don't know, Jen. And that's the point! I don't think it could have been properly tested."

"We have months before we reach the old border. Spend some time going over the engines and satisfy yourself that there's no imminent danger. In a month we'll start doing some space trials of our own, unless you've found something to convince me we shouldn't."

"We can't stop to perform proper space trials. We have to reach the old border and begin our interdiction operations."

"The *Colorado* can launch and travel alongside the *Prometheus*. We'll have a couple of months to test the new engine design."

"The captain can't slow us to Light-225 so we can do that."

"Captain Gavin will do whatever is necessary to help safeguard the lives of his crew. Besides," Jenetta said, smiling, "Light-225 is only the officially listed speed. The

Colorado can easily beat the *Prometheus* to the old frontier border."

Bill's lower jaw dropped. "It's faster than the *Prometheus*? Faster than Light-412?"

Jenetta nodded slowly.

"My God! What's its top speed?"

"Light-487, but that's classified. Only the ship's commanding officer can override the Light-225 governor by entering a special password through the console at the command chair."

"Light-487?" Bill repeated in awe. *"In a ship this small?* No wonder the drive system looks so radical. It has to be."

"If the claim is accurate, there isn't another ship in the galaxy that can touch it, at least not until the other scout ships are ready for delivery. I'd like to log as many trial hours in the *Colorado* as we can before we actually need it for operations."

"Okay, I'll spend as much time with it as I can. Who can I bring in?"

"Only your senior engineers for now. I'm going to be bringing in bridge crews to train on the ship's controls. Let me know if you need to take anything off line or deactivate any of the bridge consoles."

"Will do. When will the bridge crews be coming in?"

"Tomorrow. I've already established the preliminary duty schedules."

Chapter Five
~ October 27th, 2272 ~

Vyx approached the meeting place with considerable trepidation. Shev Rivemwilth had sent another note, this one saying that he was now healthy enough to conclude the arms deal. The meeting would be in the same ramshackle house Vyx had visited last time. He'd brought half the payment with him, along with a small arsenal of weapons. His backup laser pistol rested comfortably in its well-oiled holster, and the older laser pistol he'd bought at the pawnshop was stuck in his waistband. Concealed in various places on his body were half a dozen knives and two old lead projectile weapons like the ones common on Earth two centuries earlier. The ancient 9mm pistols were able to pass through most screening devices set to pick up the energy signatures given off by laser and lattice weapons.

Climbing the stairs to the second floor under the watchful eyes of two burly Terran bodyguards, Vyx stiffened noticeably when one pointed to the laser weapons and held out his hand. Vyx shook his head very slightly and tensed his body for action, but the bodyguard simply stepped out of the way so he could pass. They must have orders to let him pass with his weapons but attempted to have him surrender them anyway, Vyx thought. He wondered if they were two of the hunters who had given him such a rough night the last time he was here. He hesitated and then walked past the guards, the hairs on the back of his neck tingling.

Entering the apartment, Vyx saw Shev Rivemwilth reclining on a sofa.

"Come in, Trader, come in. Take a seat over here next to me. I'm sorry for not getting up, but I'm still convalescing. My strength is returning, but slowly. I've had a new artificial heart installed but it's been causing me some pain. I debated whether or not to get it since my one heart could really handle everything, but I finally decided I should have it as a backup in case something happened to my remaining original."

"I'm happy to see you survived the lattice wound, Shev. I never expected to see that Tsgardi here. Apparently he never expected to see me here either."

"Why do you suppose he pulled his pistol and started shooting?"

"We met a few years ago during a deal. He tried to sell me a load of laser pistols he had salvaged from somewhere. I examined them and found that the pulse modulation circuitry in every unit was fried. I told him to take the junk to the nearest reclamation center and turn it in for scrap. He got mad and told me that if he ever saw me again, he'd kill me."

"I suppose this was the first time you'd met again?"

Vyx nodded. "Yes, or one of us wouldn't have been around for our most recent meeting. I know the Tsgardi don't make idle threats. It was only my weapons that saved me during our previous encounter."

"It's unfortunate it occurred during *our* deal, but Tsgardi are known for letting their egos and tempers reign supreme. Good sense never seems to fit into their equations. Are you ready to conclude our arrangements?"

"I brought the first half of the payment," Vyx said, passing over the envelope.

Rivemwilth carefully examined the certified credit draft from the Gollasko Colony Bank before sliding it into a small, pouch-like device on the coffee table. After a few seconds, the pouch glowed green, then winked out. It was obviously some kind of wireless verification device. Satisfied, Rivemwilth said, "Very good. How soon would you like to take delivery?"

"You have the weapons here?"

"Not here in the building, but they're not far away."

"I'll have the remainder of the payment as soon as you can deliver the weapons to my ship at the spaceport."

"You can have them in two hours. Which landing pad?"

"36-Delta."

"Very well, two hours at 36-Delta. My associate, Mr. Gutz," Shev Rivemwilth said, pointing to one of his Terran guards, "will make the delivery and accept the final payment. I have something for you, by the way."

Rivemwilth opened a decorative wooden box on the coffee table and took out Vyx's original laser pistol. Vyx tensed in case it was a ploy to aim the pistol at him under the pretext of returning it, but Rivemwilth extended his arm with the pistol pointed to the side. Vyx took it, noticing that the power pack was fully discharged, and stuck it in his waistband.

"Thanks. I've grown very fond of this pistol. I've missed its comforting feel."

"You'll need it when the Tsgardi come looking for you. The one you killed comes from a very large family. Undoubtedly one or more will be looking for your scalp."

"A blood feud?"

"Tsgardi can be so foolish. There's no profit in vengeance. Especially when the one being avenged started the trouble to begin with."

"Perhaps the family won't even hear of his demise."

"No chance of that. I have several Tsgardis working for me and they've already sent word to his family. You don't have to worry about the group here, though. They aren't related to him."

"Won't the family offer a bounty?"

"Possibly, but you shouldn't worry about any of my people trying to collect. I don't allow them to take work on the side, and I doubt that the family would offer them enough to permanently leave my employ."

"That's reassuring."

"But you should still be wary."

"I'll keep my eyes open. Thanks for the warning."

Vyx stood up and walked from the room. He descended the stairs slowly, a much more dignified departure than the last time he was here. Walking the several blocks to the bank, he secured another draft for the remaining payment and then made arrangements to hire two security guards from a protection services company that was located next door to the bank. The guards were a doltish-looking pair, and he wondered if he could trust them any more than the arms delivery people, but he was desperate and needed backup to serve as a deterrent to possible trouble.

As he left the protection company offices with the two guards, Vyx hailed a cab to take them all out to the spaceport. If transportation had been available after the shootout, he'd have been long gone, but like most everything else on this colony, even the driverless taxis stopped working as soon as it was dark. As they settled into the seats, he stated the destination to the auditory interface and deposited the fare into the slot in the credits box.

His spacecraft, which he had named *Scorpion*, was parked in an unguarded section of the port. Security wasn't really necessary as all ships in this area were equipped with self-protect systems. It's doubtful that anyone tampering with one of these ships would be around to celebrate his next birthday. For that reason, few travelers stayed aboard any of the parked vessels. If anyone happened to be next to a ship with a faulty self-protect system, their ship could be damaged or destroyed as well, even though ships were separated by ten-meter-high, double-reinforced blast walls. The hotels in town were cheap, so it was wise to stay in one if other accommodations weren't available.

Vyx carefully disabled the security system that would detonate in the entrance airlock if anyone attempted to break in and opened the cargo bay door. He left the second system activated— the one that would destroy much of the bridge if anyone tampered with the controls there— and sat down to wait for the arms delivery. The two guards took up positions outside where they could watch the transaction. Their presence was obvious enough that the delivery people would see them but close to available cover if trouble started. And they'd still have a good field of fire.

Gutz and half a dozen others arrived right on time. The weapons were contained in three large 'oh-gee' vans, and Vyx examined each piece after it was unloaded from the truck and carried over to his ship. After the last piece was examined, Vyx handed the draft to Gutz, and the delivery people departed in a gust of opposed gravity waves. The security guards helped Vyx load the crates into the ship and then received payment for their services. He stayed aboard after they left and recorded the serial numbers from each weapon by holding it up to the light where his left eye could see it clearly.

Before leaving, he reset the security system that would detonate if anyone tried to break in to retrieve the weapons, then ordered a taxi that would take him to his hotel. Once back in his room, he inserted the recording wafer into his transmitter and sent the information to Space Command. He would have to stay here until a reply came back— a six day wait, at least.

* * *

Jenetta gave the engineering staff a full month to study the new temporal envelope generator and crawl through the spotlessly clean bowels of the *Colorado*. On SC warships, the envelope generator retracted into a heavily armored repository on top of the ship when not in use. The docking collar gave the engineers a pressurized space dock in which to work, allowing them to disassemble entire sections of the generator for examination. And there wasn't a wiring panel in the ship that wasn't pulled apart and studied in their search for flaws. At the end of the thirty days, Jenetta sat down with Lieutenant Commander Cameron to discuss his findings.

"What do you think, Bill?"

"I hate to admit it, but we couldn't find a single problem. At least nothing that disagreed with the specifications, even though I don't completely understand why they did some things the way they did them. But they're in agreement with the manuals in the computer."

"What didn't you understand?" Jenetta asked.

"A lot of small things. For example, I'm confused over the way they're regulating the antimatter flow with the vacuum restrictors. They have the anti-hydrogen stream being varied according to the rate of particle deceleration in the secondary containment chamber. It doesn't make sense to me that they would tie these two system functions together, and they don't give an explanation or reason in the manual. There are a number of things like that, functions that are inconsistent with my knowledge of FTL equipment design and operation."

"I'm sure the designers had good reason for the changes. Can you ask someone back at the design labs to explain the inconsistencies?"

"I've sent several queries, but I haven't received a single response yet."

"Other than your confusion over the design of the new engine, do you know of any reason why we shouldn't start space trials?"

"No," he mumbled, almost irritably. "As I said, everything is within spec." Brightening a little, he said, "I'd like to accompany the first trial so I can monitor things."

"Sure, Bill. You're the chief engineer so you'll make the assignments for the engineering teams. Don't bring all your top people though. We don't want to leave the *Prometheus* without any senior engineers if something were to happen."

Cameron stared at Jenetta with a strange expression on his face. "You're not making me feel any better about this, Jen."

Jenetta grinned widely. "You're just nervous because it's new technology that you're unfamiliar with."

"I'm nervous because the engine dynamics defy many of the principals of FTL engines as I understand them."

"Look at it this way, Bill. This ship is supposed to travel twice as fast as any other ship its size, right?"

"Uh, yeah," he said guardedly.

"Then it seems to me that things would have to work a *little* differently to accomplish that."

"Yes, ma'am," he said, grinning, "but I don't have to like it until I understand it."

Two days later, the *Prometheus* dropped out of FTL speed just long enough to launch the *Colorado*. A minimal crew of thirty-two had been selected for this first trip, with sixteen of them being engineering crewmen. Jenetta would act as the commanding officer, and the first test would last for ten days unless a major problem developed. The *Colorado* was to travel on a course parallel to that of the *Prometheus*, one kilometer off the larboard side. The scout ship would accelerate to Light-37 and hold that speed for one hour, increasing the speed by Light-37 each hour thereafter until it reached Light-407. It would then maintain that speed for the remainder of the trial. The *Colorado* would remain in constant telemetric communication with the *Prometheus*, relaying engine and ship sensor data as quickly as it was collected.

* * *

Since Vyx no longer had to hide from Rivemwilth's bodyguards, and it would take months or maybe years before any of the Tsgardi could arrive from their home planet if they were even coming to avenge Recozzi, Vyx began to hang out around the city instead of holing up in his hotel room while he waited for new orders. As the days passed he became accepted as a regular at several taverns. The taverns he patronized didn't close at dark, but the number of patrons dropped significantly in the later hours. Only a small group of taverns stayed open until midnight, and a couple actually stayed open all night as there were no laws prohibiting the sale and consumption of alcohol at any hour on any day of the week. The early closures were simply a matter of economics. There just wasn't enough business for more taverns to remain open throughout the night.

Vyx didn't receive a message with new orders for almost ten days, then scowled and muttered an epithet when he read them. He was ordered to remain at the Gollasko Colony and observe the movements of criminals, particularly Rivemwilth, until further orders were received. His jaw dropped as he continued reading the message and learned that the current Frontier Zone was about to become regulated Galactic Alliance space. He was told to keep this in strictest confidence and that the news would be broadcast when the GAC resolution was formally proposed and adopted.

*   *   *

Four days into the ten-day trial run, the crew of the *Colorado* was exhausted, most of them having spent long hours constantly monitoring every function of the ship. The engineering staff had been kept busy adjusting and recalibrating equipment and, in some cases, repairing it.

Jenetta went looking for Lieutenant Commander Cameron at the end of her watch on the fourth day and found him seated at a computer console in Engineering with his head resting on his chest as he tried to keep his eyes open and focused on the monitor.

"Bill, you look terrible. How much sleep did you get last night?"

"I managed to get a few hours in when I dozed off here at the console. I'm still trying to understand the process, although I can't fault the performance of the engines. I wish everything else was performing as well. We've maintained a steady speed of Light-407 since the first day. You know, Jen, this design will revolutionize travel in Space Command ships. The drive system requires substantially less energy, so smaller power plants won't be the hindrance to faster envelope generation that they've been in the past. From what I can see, our older ships can be retrofitted for minimal cost since the basic temporal generator design is the same on all military ships. Every ship in the fleet should be capable of our speed."

"That's great, but right now you need some more sleep. I want you to go to your quarters and stay there for at least eight hours. And no using your computer while you're there." Jenetta smiled. "That's an order, Commander."

Lieutenant Commander Cameron looked up at her and grinned. "Aye, Captain, I'm going."

Jenetta patted him on the shoulder and left, returning to her own quarters. She needed some sleep also, but first she needed to exercise her cats. They had been cooped up in her quarters since coming aboard. She changed into her sweats, then led the cats to the flight bay where they all ran for more than a half hour before returning to Jenetta's quarters. After a quick shower she climbed into bed and quickly fell into a deep sleep while the cats stretched out and slept beside her bed.

At the end of the ten-day test, the two ships dropped to sub-light speeds and Lt. Kerrey effortlessly maneuvered the *Colorado* into the special docking collar on the *Prometheus*. The engines had performed flawlessly, but there had been various equipment failures elsewhere throughout the ship. The malfunctions were the sort always found in new ships with all new equipment. Some were due to improper install-ation and others were just the result of component failure during an initial burn-in period. The *Prometheus'* storerooms were adequately stocked with everything they would need to repair the systems aboard the *Colorado*, and Jenetta had approved access by the entire engineering staff so the repairs could be handled more expeditiously. There would be another trial run in a month's time once all the collected data had been reviewed and the repairs completed.

As soon as the ship was secure, Jenetta took her cats to her quarters and then reported to the bridge. The captain was in his briefing room, and she walked to his doors and waited for them to open. As she came to an easy attention in front of the captain's desk, she said, "Commander Carver reporting back, sir."

"Hi, Jen. Sit down. How did it go? I've read your daily reports, of course."

"As I said in my reports, the test was very successful, sir. We had various problems, but they were to be expected and nothing to be alarmed over. I think Lieutenant Commander Cameron has actually begun to like the new drive system."

The captain smiled. "That's something, I guess. Chief engineers rarely like anything radically new. They have to tinker with it for a while and maybe take it apart and put it back together a couple of times before they can convince themselves that it really is better."

"Yes, sir, but he still has some reservations. It would have been better if the shipyard had given him some hands-on training time during your layover there."

"The design is so new that they haven't developed any training programs or materials. This thing with moving the borders is forcing everyone to cut corners. We just have to hope safety wasn't compromised. The shipyard wanted to keep the *Colorado* for ninety more days and really test it, but they had to start work on new ships and begin retrofitting the decommissioned ships for active duty. Once we received new orders dispatching us to the Frontier Zone, they either had to release it to us or see it sit around for a few years until we got back. So it fell to us to conduct the space trials after they certified that the new design had passed the initial tests. I've been forwarding all your reports and operational data to them."

"Lieutenant Cameron feels that older ships can be retrofit with the new design so all our ships will be able to achieve the *Colorado's* top speed."

"That would be great," Gavin said. "The battleships would no longer have to slow down to accommodate the less powerful ships in a task force."

"The engineering staff will be working on the *Colorado* during the next few weeks and we'll have another space trial when the work is done. I think I'll let Commander Eaton take it out next time if you approve, sir."

"That's fine. He's a good officer and the experience will be good for him. We'll be nearby if there's a problem with the ship."

"Yes, sir."

"Do you feel ready to resume your duties as Second Watch Commander, or do you need a day to get re-acclimated?"

"I'm ready now, sir."

"Fine, inform Lieutenant Commander Sharpe that he'll return to first watch tomorrow morning as my senior bridge officer."

"Yes, sir."

"I'll see you at 1600 hours. Dismissed."

"Yes, sir." Jenetta stood, turned, and left the briefing room. Walking to her office, she called up her computer messages to see what problems had accumulated in her absence. As the list appeared, she saw that Commander Eaton had done a good job as acting first officer and she wouldn't have to spend a week handling a myriad of small troubles, but she did spend the hours until her watch clearing up the few problems that remained unresolved.

* * *

The *Prometheus'* engineering staff performed another complete analysis of the *Colorado's* systems and equipment during the weeks after the first space trial while the *Prometheus'* crew slipped into the normal routines found on any long voyage. Long-range sensors occasionally picked up a distant ship, and under normal circumstances the *Prometheus* would have investigated, but this wasn't a normal patrol so they didn't even hail them.

Near the end of their second month in space, the *Prometheus* received numerous news broadcasts that announced the adoption of the resolution extending Alliance borders by a hundred parsecs and converting the former frontier into regulated Alliance space. Those criminals who hadn't already gotten the word would now be scurrying to reach the redefined Frontier Zone, and the *Prometheus* was still almost two months from the point where it would cross into the previous Frontier Zone.

Jenetta received messages on a regular basis from her parents, brothers, and sisters, and had plenty of time to respond. She could almost predict which day of the week she would hear from which sibling or parent. She usually sent a single message to both her parents, but they responded separately. Her mother usually gave her the local gossip while her father talked about how politics were affecting the Space Command bureaucracy. Jenetta was surprised when she received a message from her mom on a Wednesday because she normally heard from her on Saturday.

"Hi, honey. I just had to call and tell you the news. Your father is returning to active duty with Space Command. Isn't that wonderful? They put out a call for retired line officers who were still younger than seventy-five. Dad called immediately and was promised one of the older cruisers that will be re-commissioned after a retrofit. He's been running around like a schoolboy since then. I'm so happy for him. I think he was tired of playing golf every day but didn't know what else to do with himself. Now that he's seen what retirement's like, perhaps he'll stay in Space Command until he reaches the new mandatory retirement age. He might even get that star he once wanted. I always told him he was much too young to retire. I knew he wouldn't be happy playing golf every day for sixty years or more. He acted as if we were living hundreds of years ago when people only lived to seventy or eighty instead of a normal hundred thirty-five.

"I know you communicate regularly with your brothers and sisters, but just in case you haven't heard, everyone is healthy and happy. Billy, Richie, Andy, Christa, and Eliza are all headed to the new space territory, like you. Only Jimmy's ship is staying on its routine patrol of the deca-section around 8667-2351 and he's upset with missing all the excitement, but dad says patrol duty there is just as important as out where you are.

"Marisa finally moved out of that tiny apartment and into the house she and Richie picked out after they married last year. She had to wait until the former owners completed construction of their new house, and then there was a lot of remodeling and redecorating to be done. But it's finally completed, and it turned out simply gorgeous. She has such wonderful taste and a real flair for decorating. It's too bad you can't be here for the house-warming party, but even Richie can't make it. I know how busy you are so I'll pick up a gift that I can give to her in your name.

"Oops, there's the timer so I have to go. Take care of yourself, dear. I love you."

The image on the screen winked out, and Jenetta immediately recorded a message to her father, welcoming him back to the fleet and congratulating him on his appointment as a cruiser captain. After routing the message to the outgoing queue, Jenetta walked to the *Colorado's* docking bay where preparations were underway for the start of the second space trial. Bill Cameron was there, conversing with a couple of his people. After completing his conversation, he joined Jenetta where she was standing.

"Almost ready to depart, Commander," he said. "My chief assistant, Lieutenant Grassley, will head up the engineering team this trip. I think we solved most of the problems with our last trip."

"Okay, Bill. If anything happens we'll be right alongside like last time."

Jenetta boarded the smaller ship and walked to the bridge where Commander Eaton stood with his helmsman and navigator, discussing the equipment. Tim Eaton stopped talking and turned to Jenetta as she approached.

"Almost ready to get underway, Tim?"

"Yes, ma'am. We'll be ready to separate at 1100 hours as scheduled."

"Good. I'll inform the Captain that we should drop out of light at 1045. Have a good trip. I'll see you in thirty days."

"Yes, ma'am," Tim said, smiling. "We won't be far away if you need us."

"Enjoy your first command, Captain."

"Thank you, ma'am. I've been looking forward to it."

Jenetta smiled and left the ship. An officer's first command was always special and marked a point of passage, even if just a kilometer from their regular post. Jenetta thought nostalgically about her first time as a ship's captain when she'd been asked to assume control of the freighter *Vordoth* after it had been attacked by Raiders.

At 1045 hours the *Prometheus* dropped out of FTL speed. When the *Colorado* confirmed that the ship was sealed and the air in the docking collar had been evacuated to containment tanks, the collar seals retracted and the docking clamps were released, allowing the ship to float free of the *Prometheus*. In several minutes the smaller ship had moved to a kilometer off the larboard side and then both ships accelerated to Light-412. They would travel together as a pair for the next thirty days as the crew of the *Colorado* monitored every bit of equipment on the ship and transmitted the live information to the *Prometheus'* computer.

*   *   *

After three months on Gollasko, Vyx had been generally accepted into the criminal circles. It had become widely known that he'd done business with Shev Rivemwilth, and that fact alone opened doors that might otherwise have remained permanently sealed. A person in Vyx's line, by necessity, had few friends. His life literally depended on no one finding out that he was an undercover agent for Space Command. The only people who could usually be trusted to keep that secret were other people who work for Space Command Intelligence, and it so happened that there were two at the Gollasko Colony.

Gordon 'Nels' Nelligen had operated a small electronics repair business in the colony for several years and was well known. He had a good reputation for being able to fix anything electronic and a slightly more dubious reputation for being a better-than-average card player. He could be found in his shop during the day and at one of the card tables in the L'il

Nugget Tavern almost every evening. A lot of useful information could be picked up where friends and business associates gathered to play a few friendly hands of cards while quenching their thirst.

Another frequent face at the card tables was that of Albert Byers. During the day he served up mediocre food at a local hash house, but after work he headed to either the L'il Nugget or the SkyRider Tavern. While Nelligen was tall and thin, Byers was short and a little heavy around the middle. A resident of the Colony for over five years, he was well known in every tavern.

Vyx had been apprised of their presence at the Colony but hadn't yet needed to contact either of the other operatives. They also knew of his presence and were prepared to assist if he requested help, but they were information gatherers rather than line agents. Vyx didn't think either would be of much use in a dangerous situation.

News that the Alliance was moving the frontier border spread like wildfire in a hayfield. Merchants specializing in illegal products desperately began looking for ways to liquidate their inventories. Vyx was courted by every dealer on the planet, including Shev Rivemwilth, as they tried to sell off everything they couldn't take with them. Vyx learned where most arms merchants were headed as they talked almost openly about their plans to reach the new Frontier Zone and reestablish their operations. They believed they had six more months before Space Command arrived, but they all intended to be gone in a month's time since the new frontier was more than half a year away at Light-187. Vyx always replied that he was naturally leaving as well and announced his new base of operations as being the mining colony of Scruscotto. Most of the mining operations there were small independents so he wouldn't have to worry about a big company's security guards, and the planet was only five light-years inside the new Frontier Zone.

* * *

The second space trial of the *Colorado* went smoother than the first but still had its share of difficulties. The biggest problem occurred when the food synthesizers in the crew mess hall broke down and much of the crew was forced to live on field rations from the emergency supplies for three days. Normally, synthesizers were only used for off-hours dining, so the number of machines was limited. The few synthesizers in the NCOs' and Officers' dining rooms couldn't provide meals for the entire crew, as small as it was for this test, and they hadn't brought any fresh food along for this trial. The problem was finally located and the crew food synthesizers were brought back on-line. Other problems were minor and the engineers aboard were able to repair them or bypass them until the proper parts could be retrieved from the *Prometheus'* stores.

After docking with the *Prometheus*, the *Colorado* was again turned over to Commander Cameron's staff for analysis of the problems and proper repair of those systems where temporary repairs or bypasses had been performed. Commander Cameron started pulling things apart as soon as he was allowed aboard.

The *Colorado's* systems were disassembled, inspected, and reassembled in time for the third scheduled space trial that would commence at the start of the fourth month into the voyage. The captain called Jenetta to his briefing room on the morning the *Colorado* was scheduled to begin the test.

"Jen, this is the final trial for the *Colorado*, regardless of the outcome. We must complete the trials before we enter the former Frontier Zone."

"Yes, sir. We'll wrap things up by the thirtieth day as planned. That will give us a full day before entering the old zone."

"This thirty-day trial decides whether the *Colorado* can be used in interdiction activities or not. If the ship fails to perform properly, it will remain docked with the *Prometheus* until we return to a space dock facility where the problems can be addressed."

"Yes, sir. So far the problems haven't been out of the ordinary and shouldn't require that the ship be laid up for the rest of the voyage. This third trial will concentrate on tight maneuvering instead of the simple straight-line travel we've been engaged in— at least as tight as can be accomplished at more than a hundred thirty million kilometers per second."

As the ship was readied for its final space trial, it was fully stocked with almost everything the full crew complement of a hundred eighty-five would normally carry for an extended voyage, including fresh food and a platoon of Marines. Jenetta took her cats aboard early and left them in the captain's quarters while she saw to the final details of the month-long voyage.

At 1030 hours the ship was sealed and they began working their way through the departure checklist. The *Prometheus* dropped out of FTL at 1045 hours and the *Colorado's* docking clamps were released a couple of seconds before 1100 hours. Floating free, the small ship moved to a position a kilometer off the larboard side of the *Prometheus*, and on a signal from the mother-ship, both ships began accelerating to Light-412.

After a week of travel, Jenetta was extremely pleased with the performance of the *Colorado*. The work the engineers had done in adjusting, calibrating, and general tweaking made the ship perform as well as any ship that had been in service for an extended period. They seemed to have corrected every problem, and Commander Cameron slowly relaxed his constant vigil. He even began to take breaks for meals instead of eating as he worked.

During the second week they began to test the ship's maneuverability. The *Prometheus* remained in constant communication and at the end of each series of tests they would slow and allow the *Colorado* to catch up before resuming Light-412.

On the twenty-ninth day, all tests had been completed except one. The *Colorado* had performed flawlessly, and Jenetta looked forward to certifying the ship as ready for active duty. The final series of tests were the speed tests. Thus far they had only attempted Light-412, and the ship had maintained that speed without problem. Now they would test the engines at full power. Space Command had said that Light-487 was possible, although a full power test hadn't been made at the Mars facility during the initial tests. If that claim was true, then this would be the fastest flight of any ship in the known galaxy.

Jenetta had the communications officer notify the *Prometheus* that the *Colorado* was about to apply full power to the engines at 1100 hours. It was agreed that the *Colorado* would travel at top speed for six hours and then slow to Light-225 until the *Prometheus* caught up. The *Prometheus* would simply maintain its top speed of Light-412 until they met up again.

With Commander Cameron set to monitor the ship's performance from the Engineering deck, Jenetta gave the order to the helmsman to apply full power. Rather than keying in a specific speed value— the normal method— the helmsman toggled the selector switch from 'speed' to 'engine power,' then keyed in one hundred. As the command was entered, there was a sudden flash and everything on the bridge went dark.

Chapter Six
~ February 22nd, 2273 ~

A second later, the bridge's emergency lighting flicked on.

"What happened, helm?" Jenetta asked quickly.

"I don't know, Captain," Lieutenant Kerrey replied. "I keyed in the power change and the console readout flashed briefly."

"What's our current speed?"

"All console readouts are now blank, ma'am. Nothing's functioning."

"Com, ask Commander Cameron what's happening."

"The com station is dead, Captain. I don't have any power at all."

Jenetta lifted her right hand and pressed the front of her Space Command ring before saying, "Commander Cameron, respond please."

After waiting several seconds she pressed the ring again and said, "All Engineering personnel, this is the captain. Anyone respond, please."

When nothing was received after thirty seconds, Jenetta jumped out of her chair and headed for the door to the corridor. Over her shoulder she shouted, "Lieutenant Kerrey, you have the bridge," and then promptly ran into the door when it failed to open automatically. She bounced back a half meter but managed to keep her footing. Fortunately, she had been leading with her left shoulder because she had been issuing the order to Lieutenant Kerrey as she hurried.

"I guess the doors aren't working either," Jenetta said, scowling. To an ensign manning one of the tactical console stations, she said, "Ensign Danzig, you're with me; I might need help getting to Engineering."

It took several minutes to open the door to the corridor because they hadn't practiced using the modified manual release system in previous trials. Emergency lighting, like the type on the bridge, illuminated the corridor. The Marine stationed at the door to her quarters was still at his post, but he looked a bit bewildered. He hadn't been able to contact anyone in the security office.

Although it was unlikely that the lift was operating, Jenetta tried anyway. There was no way of knowing what power systems, if any, were still operating.

When the lift failed to arrive, Jenetta walked to the nearest access shaft that would permit travel to the Engineering Deck four levels below. After opening the shaft door, Jenetta peered into a semi-dark passage that extended from the lowest deck to the highest. The shaft was illuminated only by dim emergency lighting, but anyone in the shaft would have been clearly visible. Not seeing anyone above or below, she dove in head first.

The vertical shaft, like all of the engineering shafts and travel tubes in Space Command ships, were shielded from the artificial gravity inside the ship. Jenetta felt a momentary queasiness as she passed over the threshold of the door and gravity gave up its impermanent hold on her. Gravity deck plating was used inside lift cars and transit tube cars, so weightlessness was never a problem there. Ensign Danzig waited a couple of seconds for Jenetta to make some headway and then also dove into the shaft. The pneumatics on the hatch door slowly closed it behind him.

Using the hand grip depressions in the shaft walls, they pulled and pushed themselves along as they sailed almost effortlessly down to the lower decks.

Emerging from the shaft, Jenetta and Danzig found the corridor doors to the Engineering section already open. Commander Cameron was drawing a diagram on an electronic clipboard for two of his people while others peered into uncovered consoles with portable lights.

"Commander, what's the situation as you know it?" Jenetta asked.

"We've lost most power, Captain, but we haven't yet figured out why or how to restore it."

"Are we dead in space?"

"No, ma'am. We're still traveling FTL."

"How can you tell without instruments?"

"Put your hand flat against any bulkhead," he said, demonstrating. "You can feel the vibrations that occur as we're pulled from the old envelope into the new one. If we were stalled out, you wouldn't feel anything."

"Can you tell me our course?"

"Negative, Captain. Not until we get some power restored."

"Okay, Bill, keep at it. Send a runner to the bridge when you learn anything unless you can get the personal or shipboard com systems working."

"Will do, Captain."

Cameron turned immediately back to his two people. Jenetta and Danzig returned to the bridge using the access shaft.

"Commander Cameron is working on the problem," Jenetta announced to the bridge crew, "but we don't know the cause or how long it will take to restore power. Remain on the bridge, but you can move around and talk until we get power back. Ensign Danzig, why don't you be our town crier."

"Excuse me, Captain?" he said.

"Hundreds of years ago on Earth, a person would pass through the streets of a town shouting out the news. It was their only way of conveying important information because there were no telecommunications and many people couldn't read or write. I want you to visit the other decks and tell people that the reason for our power outage is unknown, but we're not being attacked. Tell them it's being worked on and they should remain calm."

"You want me to go to each deck?"

"Yes. Either yell out the information yourself, or conscript an NCO for the task and have them shout it out throughout the deck."

"Yes, ma'am," Danzig said before running from the bridge to complete his mission.

Jenetta waited for an hour according to her still-functioning chrono-patch, then went to the Engineering section again. Not much thicker than a tattoo, chrono-patches were powered by a harmless chemical reaction produced when it came into contact with human skin. It didn't have timekeeping functions and merely displayed the GST time being broadcast throughout the ship. But the broadcast signal equipment did require minimal power, so Jen decided it must be receiving its power from the emergency lighting circuits. The disposable waterproof patch could last several days before needing replacement.

Jenetta found Cameron working with several people at a wall console with all panel covers removed. Thick cables snaked along the floor and led into the open panels along the walls.

"Bill, can I interrupt you for a minute?"

"Just a minute, Captain. I'll be right with you."

Jenetta stood back and watched as Bill issued instructions to the other crewmen working with him. "Lower that light down a little, Tony. Good. Lock that connection down, Sam. Yeah, that's got it. Good, it's tight. Okay, everybody set? Get your arms out of the consoles and we'll see what we've got." The crewmen working with Bill stepped back out of the way. After verifying that everyone was out of the panels, he said, "Alright, Bonnie, give it a try."

A lieutenant(jg) standing at another panel flipped a switch and one wall of gauges and displays lit up. A cheer went up in the room.

Bill turned to Jenetta and smiled. "At last."

"Did you find the problem?"

"Not yet, Captain. My first priority was to get the life support systems operating again. In another hour it would have started to get noticeably cold in the ship, and in several more hours we'd have been breathing substantially elevated levels of carbon dioxide." Glancing at the displays, he said, "But we now appear to have life support systems functioning throughout the ship again."

"Good job, Bill. What next?"

"Ship's lighting. The emergency lights just don't give us enough illumination to work properly. Then we'll tackle the main problem. I did originally spend about half an hour trying to track down the problem, but I didn't find the cause and I had to stop to take care of the more immediate concerns."

"How long before we run out of power?"

"We won't. As you know, fully charged power cells are designed to support basic ship functions for several months. Since the engines are still functioning and the power cells are constantly being recharged, we don't have to worry about losing life support or the artificial gravity system."

"Good. I'll get out of your hair for a while. What do you estimate for time in getting the lighting restored?"

"About an hour. Maybe less. I'm going to use the same bypass arrangement I used with life support."

"Okay, Bill. I'll check back with you later."

Jenetta turned and left, satisfied with the progress and grateful that Cameron was aboard. Arriving on the bridge, she plopped down in the command chair. "Ensign Danzig?"

"Yes, Captain."

"Notify all decks that life support systems are back on line and we're working on getting our lighting restored."

"On my way, ma'am."

The overhead lighting popped on about forty minutes later. At the same time, the emergency lighting shut down and the doors between the bridge and the corridor slid silently closed. But for all the consoles remaining dark, things were taking on the appearance of being normal. It was warm, light, and the oxygen was plentiful. Now, if only they could see where they were headed at a hundred twenty-one million kilometers per second, assuming they had maintained their Light-412 speed. For all Jenetta knew, they could have dropped to Plus One, which was just one kilometer per second. If only they had communication with the *Prometheus*.

As if in response to her thoughts, several crewmen from the engineering staff arrived to work on the bridge systems. They spread out to examine the helm, navigation, and communication consoles.

Along with the ship's lighting had come other functions, such as lift power, transit car travel, and food synthesizers. When the latter was discovered, the first thing Jenetta did was prepare a large mug of Colombian, black and steaming. Then she personally visited each of the decks instead of sending Ensign Danzig. Some of the crewmen were eating now that food preparation devices and synthesizers were functioning again, and some were engaged in leisure activities, but everyone was calm and relaxed. Jenetta finished up at the Engineering section where everyone was as busy as on her previous visit. Looking around, she failed to see Bill Cameron. The normally tidy engineering section was in a complete state of disarray, with thick cables crisscrossing the floor and panel covers stacked up everywhere. A lieutenant, seeing Jenetta looking around, approached her.

"Are you looking for Commander Cameron, Captain?"

"Yes, I am."

"He's below this deck checking power couplings in one of the horizontal access tubes."

"I see. When he returns, tell him I've called a meeting of senior-level staff for 1600 hours. That gives him three more hours to learn what he can. The meeting will be in conference room 6-12-2-Quebec."

"Yes, ma'am. I'll tell him as soon as he returns."

The ship's senior staff, consisting of Lieutenant Commander Pulsen, the first officer, Lieutenant Commander Cameron, the chief engineer, Lieutenant Kerrey, senior helmsman, Lieutenant Matthews, senior navigator, Lieutenant Doran, the ship's medical doctor, and Marine Lieutenant Leese, the senior security officer, met with Jenetta at the appointed time for the briefing.

"Brief us on the situation, Commander," Jenetta said to Bill Cameron, who was still wearing the maintenance harness needed to work in an engineering tube. The leading edge of several thin straps that allowed engineering techs to tether themselves in the weightless environment as they worked hung from the harness in self-retracting coils.

"We have life support, lighting, and basic services restored. We've accomplished this by jury-rigging the power panels in Engineering. The ship is under power but we're still deaf, dumb, and blind. It may take days to get everything under control. We seem to have suffered a massive ship-wide power surge that fused half the electrical systems on board. Thankfully, life support, lighting, and basic services are on protected loops that weren't affected. We simply had to reroute power around the main distribution systems in Engineering."

"Excellent work getting the basic systems back up so quickly," Jenetta said. "It seems that our most important task right now is to get communications restored so we can relay our problem to the *Prometheus*. I'm sure they're trying everything possible to contact us."

"The bridge consoles are fried. The same is true of the Auxiliary Control and Communications Center; everything is fried. We'll have to completely rebuild each console, and I'm not even sure we have sufficient parts on board."

"If you concentrate on communications, how long to get something operating?"

"We might be able to get the bridge console functioning in four or five days, but the problem is not limited to that. We have to rebuild all the transmission and receiving equipment as well."

"Is the flight bay operational?"

"If not, we could make it operational, but we can't use the flight bay while traveling faster than light."

"Can't the temporal field generator be disengaged?"

"Not without doing permanent damage. Given time, I should be able to perform an orderly shutdown of the drive system. We can then repair the circuits when we dock with the *Prometheus*. But if we don't shut it down properly, a shipyard will require months to replace it. Maybe longer because of its experimental status."

"How much time?"

"I don't know. A week, maybe two."

"We can't run blind for two weeks."

"Our plotted course was clear, Captain," Lieutenant Matthews said. "There's little danger of encountering obstacles during that time."

"But we can't be sure we're still on course. For all we know, we could be traveling in one enormous circle or zigzagging through this sector of space. If only we could speak with the *Prometheus*. They could be our eyes."

"If we weren't traveling faster than light," Bill Cameron said, "I could easily make an old RF radio set for basic communication, but we need IDS to communicate with them while we're traveling at this speed."

"Okay, Bill. Get your people working on the com systems, and see if you can stop the drive system without destroying it. I've grown kind of fond of this little ship and I'd hate to see it docked with the *Prometheus* for years without any opportunity to use it."

"Aye, Captain."

"Anything else?"

"Are we certain this wasn't a deliberate attack by outside forces?" Lieutenant Leese asked.

"Nothing is certain yet," Commander Cameron replied, "but there's nothing to suggest that it was. Our outer skin is made of the new Dakinium, and it's many times more resistant to damage than tritanium. I know we're not breached anywhere, and the *Prometheus* was only a kilometer off our starboard stern quarter. Even if *we* had missed an enemy coming up from behind, they would surely have spotted them and warned us. So far, it looks like the attempt to go to full power overloaded the electrical system somehow."

"Anything else?" Jenetta asked. When no one replied, she said, "Very well. We'll meet here each day at 1600 hours until this situation is resolved. Dismissed."

The days passed slowly. There was little for Jenetta to do except keep morale up. She found herself spending more and more time working out in the gym or jogging around the flight bay with her cats. They had become the places for her to expend the excess energy that arose from her feelings of helplessness. As consoles were disassembled and slowly rebuilt, the bridge began to look as messy as Engineering. At the end of seven days they were still flying deaf, dumb, and blind.

"Let's start with a sitrep, Commander," Jenetta said at the start of the daily meeting with senior staff.

Commander Cameron was really looking haggard from the long days with little sleep. "We're still working primarily on restoring the communication system, but we're also working on the other systems as well. We're still days away from getting any of them operating. I wish I could give you a more optimistic estimate, but I can't."

"Thank you, Commander. We know you're doing your best under trying circumstances. Have you determined yet if the engines can be disengaged without doing irreparable damage?"

"I'm still working on it, Captain. I've tried a few things but I haven't been successful. I'm afraid of causing a problem in the antimatter containment since I don't understand all of the interface linkages on this new design. I don't have to tell you what would happen if the containment systems failed."

"No, we're all aware of what happens when antimatter comes into contact with matter, but we can't continue on like this much longer. I grow more fearful with each passing day that we're in danger of a collision. Let's set a time limit of one week. If you haven't figured out how to disengage the engines by the end of seven more days, we'll take whatever measures are necessary to stop the ship."

"Okay, Captain."

"Anything else that needs to be discussed?" After several seconds of silence, Jenetta said, "I realize these daily meetings have become shorter with each passing day since there's so little to discuss. Let's discontinue the daily meetings. We'll meet again in seven days or when our systems start to come online if that happens sooner. Dismissed."

After the meeting, Jenetta changed into her sweats and went to the gym. Hurtling through space without any control over speed or direction was also causing great distress among the rest of the crew, and the gym was crowded with crewmen working through their own feelings of frustration and helplessness. Jenetta took her cats to the flight bay instead. There were a few runners there but not enough that they'd be disturbed by her cats as she ran.

Five days later, the feel of the ship suddenly changed. Jenetta walked to the closest bulkhead and placed her hand flat against it. The vibration was gone. She hurried down to Engineering to find Bill Cameron. He was in earnest discussion with several of his top people when she arrived.

"Commander, the vibration has stopped. Have you disengaged the engines?"

"Not me, Captain, but something has. We're investigating."

"Do you think the *Prometheus* has found a way to halt us?"

"No, the change happened internally. My first impression is that the collision avoidance system dropped us out of Light Speed."

"Collision avoidance has been functioning?"

"Apparently, but without any of the consoles working, we couldn't know."

"I wish I had known. I would have been sleeping a lot better."

"As would I. We should know more in an hour, Captain. I'll let you know as soon as I do."

"Very good, Commander. I'll be on the bridge."

Jenetta wasn't the only non-engineer to notice the change in the ship. As she returned to the bridge she saw that everyone there was standing against the rear bulkhead with their hand on the wall.

"The ship's light speed drive has disengaged," Jenetta announced. "Our engineers are investigating and will let us know what they find very shortly. Now that we're stopped, the *Prometheus* can begin working on our problem also."

Commander Cameron arrived on the bridge a little over an hour later. He followed Jenetta into her briefing room where they both took seats around her desk.

"It appears that it *was* the collision avoidance system that was responsible for our drive shutdown. Even though our console connections to the DeTect sensor net are still offline, it appears the net was working fine and the ACS direct cutoff connection to the temporal generator was still intact. We hope to have the bridge tactical console back up today or tomorrow. We've been cannibalizing the helm, navigation, and tactical consoles in the Auxiliary Control & Communications Center to make usable consoles here on the bridge from each of the two."

"That's great. How about communications?"

"We're putting the transmission equipment back together now. We've had to cob the system together by using spare parts not originally intended for an IDS transmitter and receiver, but the system should function."

"Excellent, Bill. We'll need the com system to dock with the *Prometheus*. I wish we had a shuttle, tug, or fighter in our bay. It would have given us communications during this mess and would give us eyes now that we're stopped."

"We'll have to recommend that for future trips. Maybe we should open the flight bay so a ship from the *Prometheus* can dock."

"Good idea. They may already be outside just waiting for an invite." Jenetta reached for the com panel on her desk and then stopped. "You don't realize how much you take it for granted until it's gone."

Walking to the door, Jenetta called out, "Ensign Danzig, please go down to the flight bay and have the officer on duty open the bay door."

"Is someone coming in, Captain?"

"Perhaps. We just want to be ready in case the *Prometheus* sends over a shuttle."

"Yes, ma'am," the ensign said before turning and hurrying from the bridge.

Jenetta walked to the beverage synthesizer in her briefing room as the doors closed.

"Coffee or tea, Bill?"

"No thanks, I've already had three cups during the past hour. I've been living on the stuff for the past two weeks and I've got to cut down before I develop caffeine jitters."

Jenetta prepared a large mug of coffee and took her seat behind her desk.

"Were you able to extract any information from the sensor net? What caused the collision avoidance system to shut down the temporal field generator— an asteroid, planet, another ship?"

"We only know that it appeared to be a long-range contact, so it must be big."

"I wonder if it could have been the *Prometheus* cutting across our bow to trigger the system?"

"Not if we were running at, or faster than, Light-412. They would have had to be traveling faster than us, and we know they can't."

The door chime sounded and announced Ensign Danzig.

Come," Jenetta said.

Ensign Danzig ran into the briefing room as soon as the doors opened. Obviously agitated, he practically shouted, "Captain, we opened the flight bay door, but there's a problem. The stars are all wrong."

"Wrong? What do you mean *wrong*?"

"The configurations aren't what they should be."

"Have you allowed for twelve days of travel at Light-412?"

"Yes, ma'am, but the star groupings visible through the bay door are all wrong for what we should be seeing. It's not just me, Captain. Lieutenant Conover said the same thing. We couldn't get a real good look from the flight bay control room window, but nothing was recognizable."

Jenetta looked at Bill for a few seconds. "Could we have turned around and been headed back towards Vinnia?"

"Anything's possible, Captain. We should go take a look."

"Right. Let's go."

Twenty minutes later, Jenetta and Commander Cameron were suited up in extravehicular activities suits or, more simply, EVA suits. With the monitor systems down, they would have to physically go outside to get a good look at the space around the ship. They entered the flight bay through an airlock and walked towards the open door.

"They're right," Jenetta said. "What I can see from here is all wrong for what we should be seeing. I don't recognize any of the star configurations."

"We'll have a better view topside."

Once outside it only took a few minutes to maneuver up to the top of the ship using their suit jets. They stood on the highest point of the ship and scanned the area around them. The *Prometheus* was nowhere in sight.

"Any ideas, Bill?" Jenetta asked.

"Not really. Where do you suppose the *Prometheus* has gone? They shouldn't have left us while we were having a problem."

"I don't know. Maybe they didn't leave us. Maybe we left *them*. Maybe we achieved Light-487 and maintained that until the engines shut down. It may take a couple of days for them to catch up with us. That doesn't explain the stars though."

"Astronomy was never my strong suit," Lt. Commander Cameron said. "I rely on machines to tell me where we are."

"I was trained in astrophysics, and I first came into space as a science officer. I've spent thousands of hours studying star configurations, but I don't recognize the stars from here. We'll have to get the tactical console or the navigation console online so we can identify our position. It's as important now as the communications system."

"Aye, Captain. Let's get back inside so I can get to work."

"Just give me a few minutes to record some images."

Using the vid camera she had brought along, Jenetta performed a 360 degree horizontal and vertical pan to record the space around the ship before they headed back to the flight bay.

Once inside the ship, Jenetta gave the order to close the bay door. There didn't seem to be any likelihood that friendly visitors would be dropping by anytime soon.

While Bill headed for engineering, Jenetta went to the bridge. The consoles might be inoperable, but she had a portable computer that hadn't been connected to the power system when the problem occurred. She had only been using it to record her daily logs, but it also contained star charts for half the galaxy.

Downloading the video frames into the portable computer, Jenetta performed a search of the charts, looking for a match-up. When the computer completed the search, the results made her jaw drop in shock.

Chapter Seven

~ March 5th, 2273 ~

"Earlier today, Commander Cameron and I went topside for a look around," Jenetta said to the senior officers at the emergency meeting she had called. "Our walk was prompted by reports from Lieutenant Conover and Ensign Danzig. After the flight bay door was opened to provide entry for a shuttle that might arrive from the *Prometheus*, they observed that the visible star configurations were unfamiliar. Our initial observations bore this out, but we forgot about that temporarily when we discovered the *Prometheus* was nowhere in sight. After recovering from the shock of learning that we were alone, I shot vid images of the space around us.

"Upon returning to my briefing room, I downloaded the images into my portable computer and compared them to the star charts it contains. I've confirmed that we did travel in a straight line after our power problem occurred and that we're now roughly three hundred fifteen light-years inside the former Frontier Zone."

There was stunned silence around the conference table.

"That's impossible," Lieutenant Matthews, the senior navigator, said.

"Impossible or not, it's happened. We're here. We'll need the navigation or tactical station to get a precise fix, but my calculations should be accurate to within— a billion kilometers."

"To travel that far in twelve and a half days means that we would have had to be traveling at—" Lieutenant Matthews paused to punch the numbers into his tiny wrist calculator, "roughly one light-year per hour. That would make our speed greater than Light-9000, but there is no such speed."

"There *wasn't* such a speed *before*. Of course we don't know exactly how long it took us to get here. At least not relative to the rest of the universe."

"What do you mean, Captain?" Lieutenant Doran, the ship's medical doctor, asked.

"I mean according to Einstein's Theory of Special Relativity and his ideas about space and time distortions."

"But aren't we exempt from that?"

"Normally, yes," Commander Cameron said. "But no one's ever traveled this fast before, at least not to my knowledge."

"I don't understand. The mechanics of space travel has never been my strong suit, but it hasn't been a problem because I'm a good doctor and I understand medicine. How can we be exempt some of the time but not others?"

"Okay, doc," Commander Cameron said, "let me see if I can explain it in layman's terms. Every schoolchild knows that the engines on a starship aren't really engines in the old sense. They're nothing like the giant behemoths gobbling tons of liquid fuel every second as they did on the ships that first lifted mankind into the heavens. Early in the twentieth century and long before space travel was possible, Einstein postulated that the relationship between the four dimensions of space and time dictated that nothing could reach the speed of light because time slows down as the speed of light is approached. However, thinking changed when science first hypothesized about the existence of additional dimensions. By the end of the twentieth century, scientists had shown us that at least ten dimensions could be proven mathematically. It's difficult to think in such terms because we live in a three-dimensional world and our minds tend to accept only that which we can see and touch, but we must train ourselves to think differently.

"Faster-than-light speeds became a reality with the discovery of Dis-Associative Temporal Field Anomalies. Our antimatter engines generate the massive electrical power needed to expand a coalesced group of anomalies and create an invisible temporal envelope around the ship. When moving, the ship always remains inside the temporal envelope, so it's always isolated from the normal space around it. The envelope itself doesn't move so it doesn't exceed the speed of light. Rather, a new envelope is created slightly in front and the ship is pulled into that while the old envelope decays. During the process, the ship always remains disassociated from normal space. We steer by altering the shape of the new envelopes. The altered shape positions us in a new direction as the envelopes are created in a new direction."

"But aren't we traveling faster than light inside the envelope?"

"No, the temporal nature of the envelope generated by the antimatter-produced energy field separates us from normal space. It might be easier if you think of it as an envelope that constantly renews itself in a new position. We just go along for the ride, much as a rider on a surfboard, but we're completely isolated from the space outside the envelope. That's why we don't feel anything when we accelerate or decelerate. We're not actually moving within the temporal envelope; it's just shifted position to a new point in space. The *Colorado's* generator is the most advanced ever built, giving new meaning to the old expression of 'pushing the envelope.'"

After a few chuckles passed around the table, the doctor asked, "Then why aren't speeds faster than Light-487 possible?"

"Nobody ever said they were impossible; they just haven't been possible with our current technology. Our speeds are governed by our ability to regenerate the next temporal envelope at a new point in space. The *Prometheus* and the *Chiron* were the fastest ships in the fleet before this ship was built because of the massive power they can generate. Our oldest active-duty Space Command ships can only travel at Light-225 or maybe Light-262, while few freighters can exceed Light-187. Power innovations have resulted in faster and faster speeds, but I'm sure no one ever conceived that the *Colorado* would travel faster than Light-9000."

"I think I understand better now. You're saying that we've regenerated our envelope more than twenty times faster than anyone ever has before?" Lieutenant Doran asked.

"Well, yes— and no. Our theorists have always maintained that we could only achieve speeds as high as Light-862 with a single envelope dynamic and that only Light-500 was practicable in the foreseeable future. But while the Light-862 limitation has been accepted by almost everyone, there're two other theories that have been the subject of great discussion in recent years. The more pragmatic theorists believe you can generate an envelope within an envelope. The two-envelope theorists feel that the first envelope isolates the ship from the outside envelope, allowing the outside envelope to reestablish itself many times faster because it doesn't initiate any relationship to the vessel. It only 'sees' the inner envelope. It's true that at this point I'm guessing, and I really don't know what factors were responsible for creating a second envelope, if that's what happened."

"But wouldn't such envelopes merge, as when two ships get too close to one another and the two envelopes become one?"

"The theorists say no. They speculate that although the two envelopes are synched, they'll be slightly out of phase with one another. There's a lot to work out and better theoretical minds than mine will have to do that work. It might be the new hull, the new engines, the electrical problems, the equipment we used to replace failed equipment during the previous trials, or a combination of those and other factors. Did the electrical problems cause the generation of a second envelope, or did the generation of a second envelope cause the electrical problems?"

"And the second theory?" Lieutenant Doran asked.

"A few scientists believe that since we're already separating ourselves from time and space, it should be possible to have the replacement envelope appear at our destination, instead of just ahead of the old envelope. It would mean instant teleportation to any other place in the universe. Pretty wild, eh? If they ever get that one figured out, the universe will change overnight. I wouldn't hold my breath waiting though. They have no idea how to make an envelope appear at a distant location, much less one that retains a bond to the ship."

"Then that couldn't have happened to us? I mean, we couldn't have been instantly teleported across the galaxy and then simply continued on at Light-487 until the drive disengaged?"

"I don't know, Doc, but I don't think so. I'm more inclined to go with the double envelope theory. Now, if we had suddenly found ourselves in another galaxy, I'd have to support the second theory."

"As interesting as this discussion of theoretical physics is," Jenetta said, "right now we have to figure out where we go from here. Or rather, *do* we go anywhere from here? Are we going to be able to get the engines running again?"

"The power systems are running fine," Commander Cameron said, "and there should be nothing wrong with our sub-light engines. However, the drive circuitry to the temporal envelope generator is disengaged. I don't know yet if we'll be able to re-engage the drive. I'm fairly certain the entire generator won't have to be replaced, so a long period in a spacedock won't be necessary."

"Did you figure out what shut the drive down?"

"Not exactly. I have a theory, but I know you're not going to be comfortable with it. I know I'm not."

"I'm already uncomfortable," Jenetta said calmly. "Might as well lay it on us and we'll see if it makes us feel better or worse."

"Okay, here goes. At the speed I estimate we were traveling, there would have been less than one and one-half seconds from the time our DeTect system could have identified a stationary object in our path until we reached it. If the object was traveling on a reciprocal course, there might have been less than a second. But the ACS system takes two seconds to identify a danger that would result in a shutdown of the light drive. With normal speeds, that's more time than anyone ever thought would be needed. So— I think we flew *through* whatever caused the ACS to shut us down."

"You mean we destroyed a ship or small asteroid without even feeling it?" Lieutenant Doran asked.

"No. I'm not saying we impacted anything large enough to cause a problem. If we had, we'd certainly know it. In normal FTL, if an object is small enough to fit between our hull and the outside edge of our envelope, it's like encountering the object in normal space. Relatively speaking, we'd be at a standstill and the micro-meteorite would simply disintegrate as it impacted our hull or it would glance off and then disappear back out of the envelope. An object larger than fifteen-point-two-four centimeters wouldn't immediately fit inside our envelope and there wouldn't be time for the envelope to expand to encompass it before it came into contact with our hull. So the extent of the problems caused by a large object would be relative to the object's mass, direction of movement, and speed if it was moving at the time we made contact. It's likely that a tritanium-hulled ship encountering a chondrite asteroid would just smash its way through. That would be dependent upon the size and mass of the chondrules, of course. The specs for our hull indicate that such an encounter would be negligible, but we're not invincible."

"I agree with your earlier statement," Jenetta said, grimacing. "I'm not too comfortable with the theory that we flew *through* whatever caused the ACS to shut us down. You're talking about Transverse Phase Differential theory, aren't you?"

"Yes, ma'am."

"I don't understand," Lieutenant Doran said. "Did I miss something? What's Transverse Phase Differential theory?"

"As I mentioned when I explained the double-envelope theory, Doc," Commander Cameron said, "the inner envelope is expected to be out of phase with the outer envelope. If that's true, then the ship was also out of phase with time and space outside the outer envelope. I believe we might have passed directly through whatever the ACS saw."

"Passed through it? Without touching it?"

"We might have— *touched* it, metaphysically speaking. We just didn't impact it."

"But how is that possible?"

"Let me see if I can keep this simple," Commander Cameron said, running his hand through his hair. "Objects can only impact when they attempt to occupy the same three-dimensional point in space at the same time, right?"

"Uh, right."

"Time is considered a fourth dimension. Two people can occupy the same chair if they do it at different times, right?"

"Right."

"So with a fifth dimensional attribute, one requiring complete alignment with the others to cause a conflict in three-dimensional space, you're adding a new variable like time. If the new attribute, let's call it *phase boundary*, is different than that attribute for the other three-dimensional object, there's no conflict for the same space. So if we were outside the phase boundary of that other three-dimensional object, then we never attempted to occupy the same three-dimensional point in space at the same time as the object we passed through."

"I still don't grasp the intricacies. What is the phase boundary?"

"I'm talking about dimensional shift. A different plane of reality. The theory is that you'd occupy positions in two dimensions at the same time but not be sufficiently in either for the physical laws of matter in that dimension to apply to you."

"Could you become trapped between dimensions?"

"I honestly don't know. The theorists say no, and all we're really talking right now is theory. As far as we know, no one has ever accomplished it before. I'm not even sure if we've accomplished it now. I'm just guessing."

"Wow," was all Lieutenant Doran said, clearly out of his depth.

"Putting that aside for now," Jenetta said, "will we be able to use FTL speeds again?"

"I think we might be able to make repairs once we have access to the parts and equipment available aboard the *Prometheus*."

"Trouble is, the *Prometheus* is probably about ten months away. Are we dead in space until then?"

"We'll have the sub-light engines available once the helm console is repaired. Our hydrogen tanks are topped off and we can keep them that way by collecting as much as we need as long as we remain in normal space."

"Sub-light engines are designed for maneuvering the ship during battle or for approaching a station, but they're not going to get us home in our lifetimes."

"Sorry, Captain."

"It's not your fault, Commander. You and your people have faced a Herculean task and shown yourselves to be equal to the challenge. Thank you for everything you've accomplished." Jenetta paused and sighed. "It looks like we're going to be here for a while, so let's continue to concentrate on getting our communications up first. I'd like to let the *Prometheus* know we're alive and well. This ship was fully stocked before we left the *Prometheus*, so we have plenty of food aboard. Since we're not in any danger of starving for two years and life support functions are operational, we're fine. We'll just kick back and wait for the *Prometheus* to pick us up in ten months."

"I'll be back on the com system as soon as the meeting is over, Captain."

"Anyone have anything else to bring up?"

"Should we continue to fully man the bridge 24/7?" Lieutenant Commander Pulsen, the first officer, asked. "It hardly seems necessary with the ship being stationary and all the consoles unusable."

"We're still an official Space Command vessel and we'll follow regulations. Any other questions?"

When no one spoke up, Jenetta dismissed the group.

Commander Cameron's people had the communications console reassembled and apparently operating by 1830 hours. Jenetta sat at her desk in her briefing room to record the first message. She took a deep breath, let it out, stared into the vid lens, and then pressed the record button.

"To Captain Lawrence Gavin, commanding officer of the GSC battleship *Prometheus*, from Commander Jenetta Alicia Carver, commanding officer of the GSC scout ship *Colorado*. Begin message.

"Hello, Captain. As the result of a shipboard anomaly that we don't fully understand, the *Colorado* has traveled three hundred fifteen light-years into the former Frontier Zone. As the test of the *Colorado's* drive system began, we suffered a massive electrical discharge through all systems that rendered us deaf, dumb, and blind until now. Life support functions were restored soon after the problem occurred and we have adequate food stores. The crew is healthy and we suffered no injuries to personnel. We believe we have the communications systems functioning again and we're working on the other bridge functions. I'm estimating our position as being 8667-3212-7797.5691 ante-median 0101. I can't be more accurate until our navigation equipment is restored to working order. This position is based on my visual observation of the star configurations around us.

"Our engines are functioning, but the FTL drive can't be engaged so we're limited to sub-light travel only. We have no choice but to wait here until we're picked up. On all future trips of the *Colorado*, I recommend that a fighter, shuttle, or tug be part of the mandatory equipment on board. They would offer us additional options that would be very helpful in this situation.

"I estimate it will take four days for this message to reach the *Prometheus*, and I realize it will take time to decide upon a course of action, but I request an immediate simple acknowledgement that the message was received.

"Jenetta Carver, Commander, Captain of the GSC *Colorado*. End of Message."

The message was encrypted and sent immediately by the com operator. Jenetta fixed herself a cup of coffee and sat down to relax. Getting the message off had lifted a huge weight from her shoulders.

Over the next few days, the other bridge functions were restored. When the first images of the surrounding space appeared on the huge monitor screen at the front of the bridge, a cheer went up from everyone present. The ship couldn't move FTL, but the *Colorado* had eyes, ears, and a voice again.

Eight days after Jenetta sent the message to the *Prometheus*, a reply was received. The com operator buzzed her in her briefing room when it arrived and passed it through to her com. As she depressed the button to play the message, the face of a grinning Captain Gavin appeared on her screen.

"It was a relief to hear from you, Jen. We were deeply concerned when we weren't able to contact you. As the test began, you just disappeared from our sensors. We replayed the image logs over and over trying to resolve what happened. We finally determined that you had accelerated to a speed in excess of Light-7500. You departed so fast that we weren't able to determine your speed any more accurately than that. When we weren't able to contact you, we feared the speed might have been uncontrollable and the ship had impacted some object, or perhaps some other calamity had occurred. We've been traveling at top speed on our original course, scanning space for any sign of you.

"I've sent your message on to Space Command with my report of the incident, and until we hear differently we're proceeding on course to pick you up. I'm sure the significance of this event will not be lost on Space Command planners, so I don't expect we'll be diverted. Even so, it will take us more than nine months to reach your reported location.

"I'll send another message as soon as I've heard from Space Command. Rest assured that help is on the way. Captain Lawrence Gavin of the GSC *Prometheus*. Message complete."

Jenetta, her spirits buoyed by the message, immediately buzzed the com operator and instructed him to place her on ship-wide speakers. When the operator said "Go ahead, Captain," she began talking.

"Attention crew of the *Colorado*. This is the Captain speaking. I've just received a message from the *Prometheus*. They were happy to hear from us at last and are proceeding here at top speed. Still, it will be many months before they arrive. Beginning tonight we will transmit personal messages once each day. Don't give our location and don't mention anything about the incident that resulted in our being here. We've all been privileged to be a party to something momentous, and one day you'll be able to tell everyone that you were aboard the *Colorado* when it changed the history of travel in the galaxy, but for obvious reasons this information must remain classified as top-secret for now. The normal message limit of one minute is being extended for this date to three minutes. Forward your message to the com operator by 1800 hours. All messages received after that hour will be held until the next day's transmission. The burst transmission will be directed to Dixon Space Station, the nearest SC base, for forwarding. That's all."

* * *

Admiral Moore called the special meeting of the Admiralty Board to order as he took his seat at the center of the large horseshoe-shaped table. The gallery of the enormous meeting hall that the Admiralty Board used for both private and semi-private sessions at Space Command Supreme Headquarters on Earth was empty today, as it was for most meetings of the Board. "Good morning," he said as private conversations ended and everyone looked towards him expectantly. A couple of dozen aides and senior officers occupied chairs behind the admirals, but they would never dare return the greeting or even speak aloud while in this chamber unless specifically invited to do so. The four women and six men at the table were the most powerful officers in Space Command by virtue of their rank and their position on the Admiralty Board.

"Something completely unexpected has happened and it requires our immediate attention," Admiral Moore said. "While conducting a space trial of the new Dakinium sheathed Scout-Destroyer, Commander Jenetta Carver has discovered a capability we were unaware of."

"Oh, no," Admiral Hubera groaned loudly. "Not Carver again. We never should have let her leave Dixon. We had an entire year of peace and quiet with her posted inside that asteroid."

"If I might continue, Donald?" Admiral Moore said, glaring at Admiral Hubera.

"Of course. I'm sorry Richard. I just know what's coming."

"Oh? Then tell us, Donald."

"Uh, I didn't mean that I know exactly. I just know it's going to be something that will keep us awake nights until we bail her out again."

"I don't recall any incidents where we were required to bail her out. She's an exemplary young officer who has served Space Command with distinction."

Admiral Hubera simply scowled.

"And I don't expect this announcement to keep anyone awake at night, except of course every scientist, engineer, and ship designer entrusted with the details. It seems that Commander Carver has broken the speed record in space. In fact, she didn't just break it; she shattered it beyond what anyone could ever have imagined. According to the report she's filed, while in command of the *Prometheus'* new scout-destroyer she traversed most of the former Frontier Zone in just twelve days. The distance covered is estimated as being some three hundred fifteen light-years."

"What?!" Admiral Woo said, practically shouting as he jumped to his feet. "You can't be serious."

"I'm perfectly serious, Lon. If her reported position is accurate, our estimates of her speed are Light-9793.6. Captain Gavin confirms that she attained a minimum of Light-7500 before they lost all contact with the vessel. The instruments aboard the *Prometheus* couldn't be any more precise than that because they weren't prepared for the event when it occurred."

"This is incredible," Admiral Plimley said. "How did she do it? Has she prepared a report on her breakthrough?"

"Commander Carver is presently stranded near the new Frontier Zone border," Admiral Moore said. "Her ship has suffered a problem with its drive system and they don't have the necessary parts on board to make repairs. Captain Gavin is proceeding to her location with all haste, but at the top speed of the *Prometheus* he won't reach her location for nine months and twenty-one days."

"Stranded?" Admiral Bradlee echoed.

"Yes. She has sub-light power and thrusters, but no FTL capability. They have adequate food and life-support for two years, so the only danger seems to be from hostile forces."

"We must send everyone within a hundred light years towards her position immediately," Admiral Platt said. "We can't afford to have that ship and crew fall into Raider hands. If they learn the secret of such travel and we lose it, they'll be unstoppable."

"And while she's waiting for assistance, she must transmit everything she has on this breakthrough," Admiral Hillaire added, "so our people can begin working on ways to refine and improve on it."

"I don't know how much we can improve on Light-9793," Admiral Woo said as he dropped back into his seat, "but I agree with Arnold. We must have her report as soon as possible."

"At least we can look forward to almost ten months of peace and quiet with Carver stuck out there in the middle of nowhere and unable to get herself into trouble," Admiral Hubera said, chuckling to himself.

* * *

Two weeks later Jenetta received another message from the *Prometheus*. Captain Gavin's face appeared on her com screen as she pressed the play button.

"Hello, Jen. Space Command has approved our proceeding to your location with all due haste. As expected, they're anxious to learn everything possible about your extraordinary passage. I perceive from the tone of the message that the Research folks are in an absolute frenzy to receive *anything* you can relay to them about the anomaly. Please have Commander Cameron prepare a complete report that elucidates not only what occurred to the ship's systems but also what he suspects might be responsible for causing the anomaly. Encode it using the encryption algorithm November-One-Niner that can be found in your briefing room safe.

"Space Command has ordered a number of ships reported to be much closer than the *Prometheus* to head for your location with all possible speed. They'll stay with you until we arrive and they'll assist with your repairs.

"Good luck. See you when we arrive. Lawrence Gavin, Captain of the GSC *Prometheus*, message complete."

* * *

The routine aboard the *Colorado* settled into something almost normal after receiving the message from Captain Gavin. Lieutenant Commander Cameron finally got the rest he needed and he started looking like his old cheerful self again. His engineering team continued to work on the ship's systems, and the cables that had snaked around the Engineering deck slowly disappeared as equipment was repaired or replaced and the functions were moved back behind the panel covers. A report describing each of the steps necessary to restore life support and power in a similar situation was recorded onto a holo-tube and stored with the emergency information holo-tube manuals. Two months after first hearing from the *Prometheus*, the ship had the appearance of an ordinary GSC ship. They could just as easily have been hurtling through space at Light-412.

Just as the other watch officers were required to do, Jenetta spent much of her watch on the bridge and the remainder in her briefing room talking with her senior officers, reviewing reports, and preparing her own reports. She also spent at least two hours each day in the gym or running around the flight bay track with her cats.

Since the ship was stationary, Jenetta tried to make it blend into the background of space as much as possible. The naturally black color of the Dakinium hull helped immensely. All exterior lights remained extinguished, and sensors would only be used in passive mode so passing ships would not pick up an active signal. A dozen times each month, the *Colorado's* DeTect equipment had recorded the passage of a ship within four billion kilometers of their position, so before the communication messages were sent each day, the surrounding space was checked for the presence of any ships.

Jenetta was working out in the gym when she received an urgent message from Lieutenant Commander Pulsen. Her CT made it seem that her XO was whispering directly into her left ear as she heard, "Captain to the bridge. A vessel is approaching our position."

"Sound GQ," Jenetta said as she jumped up from the exercise machine and ran for the door, her cats just a step behind her. She reached the bridge in twenty seconds, sweat still dripping from her brow.

"What is it, Ken?" she shouted to Pulsen over the noise of the GQ message emanating from speakers in the corridor while the doors were still open.

"A ship has dropped out of Light Speed off our larboard stern. It's still too far away for viewing with the sensors in passive mode, but it's coming on at Plus Twenty directly towards us. Should we turn on our navigation lighting?"

"No, no lights. Let's prepare for unwelcome visitors."

"Unwelcome? It might be one of the Space Command ships sent to assist us."

"Space Command vessels will contact us as soon as they reach this sector so they can get a fix on our position. This contact appears to be a chance encounter. Until we know differently, they're to be considered unfriendly."

"Aye, Captain. We're already blacked out."

"The Dakinium should shield all life signs from their sensors. We know that the original material couldn't be penetrated. Even com signals were blocked. Let's just play dead and see who 'comes aknockin.'"

A ship glided cautiously into view during the next hour. The *Colorado's* crew was poised for action. All laser gunners were at their posts in the weapons centers, even though the hatch covers over the laser arrays remained closed. Torpedo guidance specialists were likewise manning their consoles, ready to override the programmed target lock and steer their charges towards the enemy hull if necessary, if it was an enemy. The torpedo hatches were still closed. All personnel not actively involved in offensive or defensive activities were in Secure rooms.

When the ship got close enough, Jenetta remarked, "It appears to be a light destroyer, but it isn't Space Command or Nordakian. It looks Uthlaro-made. It could be a private security company ship, or it might be a Raider ship."

"What should we do, Captain?" Commander Pulsen asked. "Should we hail them?"

"No. Let's wait and see what *they* do."

Several minutes later the com operator announced, "The vessel is hailing us, Captain."

"No response. Ignore their hails."

"Aye, Captain."

The ship stopped trying to hail them after ten minutes. As they watched the bridge viewscreen, several space tugs left the destroyer and approached the *Colorado*. Reaching the ship, they tried to cut their way into the flight bay, but their exterior-mounted plasma torches were totally ineffective against the Dakinium.

"They can't seem to cut their way in," Commander Pulsen remarked.

"No. The Dakinium can only be cut in a special chemical process used at the GSC spacedock where the ship was built. We carry special pre-cut and pre-shaped panels and vacuum epoxy to use for any hull repairs because even we can't work with the material. If they do manage to damage us, the real repairs will have to be made at the GSC spacedock at Mars."

"What will they do now?"

"I expect they'll either try to blast open the flight bay with explosives, or they'll use their laser arrays on the door."

"We should hail them before they do."

"No, they won't hurt us. At least not seriously. Let's wait before we reveal our presence."

Jenetta's prediction was correct. The space tugs moved out of the way and the ship fired a laser at the bay door. The coherent light hit the door dead center and remained on that spot for over a minute but was totally ineffective. Jenetta smiled as she imagined the surprise on the ship's bridge. After a few minutes, five arrays combined their pulses on the same point of the flight bay door. The laser pulses didn't even mar the surface.

"What next? A torpedo?" Commander Pulsen asked.

"If that happens, we'll try to destroy it before it reaches us, and we'll return fire immediately. Bomb-pumped laser and high-explosive warheads shouldn't hurt us, but a nuclear warhead could do some serious damage if it gets close enough. How well we'll hold up against a fission or fusion torpedo will depend on the strength of the warhead, but I don't intend to let them pound us with impunity. I'm betting they won't fire any torpedoes at us, though. They're going to want us intact."

"What exactly are we trying to accomplish, Captain? Are you testing the strength of the hull plating?"

"No, this is deadly serious. I'm hoping they decide to drag us home so they can get a better look at us without destroying the ship. This must appear to be quite a prize to the ship's captain."

"Drag us home? Where?"

"That's the question, Ken. Do you know what our biggest problem has always been in combating the Raiders?"

"Uh, finding them?" he said as the light suddenly clicked on behind his eyes.

"Exactly. Now, if we've convinced the ship's captain that we're a derelict, but one that can stand up to almost any pounding, that's a prize the Raiders, or anyone else, would want. Except for our unique sail required for docking with a mother-ship, we look a lot like a small GSC destroyer. But since we're the prototype, we won't match any configuration they're familiar with or have in their computers. Right now they're wondering if we're from this region of space or maybe from another part of the galaxy. They'll want our secrets and want them badly. After all, the GSC has kicked their butts all over space during the past six years. They have to be search-ing for an edge."

"You think they'll reveal the location of a hidden base?"

"It's a good bet. If it turns out they're legitimate salvagers, we'll thank them for towing us to a spaceport or planet and pay a towing fee according to scale. If they tow us to a Raider base, we can contact the ships on their way to find us and direct them to our new location."

"Brilliant, Captain."

"Let's wait to see how things turn out before we start tossing around superlatives like that, Ken. This could all be a big bust or a total disaster."

Less than thirty minutes later, three more tugs joined the three already outside the ship, and the destroyer moved off, resuming its original course. The six tugs placed themselves around the *Colorado* and began to move it. Placement was tricky because the tugs couldn't properly attach themselves to the ship, but in no time the ship was moving along at Light-

75. Tugs on either side were ready to guide the ship while three tugs positioned themselves at the stern for propulsion. The sixth tug, placed at the bow, initiated a temporal envelope in the same way a freighter creates an envelope that extends to the rearmost container section. That envelope merged with the envelope created by each of the other tugs so that all vessels would remain FTL if a gap between them momentarily exceeded the limitations of an envelope. Also, by combining their envelopes, the tugs reduced the power consumption of each to a fraction of what would have been required by one.

As the *Colorado* began to move, Jenetta sat down in the command chair on the bridge. For the first time since the red alert had sounded, she became consciously aware of the two cats that still flanked her sides. "I'm going to my quarters to shower and change, Ken. Call me if anything changes."

"Aye, Captain."

Knowing she would be notified in her CT immediately if anything significant occurred, Jenetta walked to her quarters with the cats. They had been extremely well behaved on the bridge, no doubt recognizing the smells of everyone there since most crewmembers worked out in the gym during the day. In fact, they had been so good that Jenetta decided to start bringing them to her briefing room each day. She would leave them there when she went out to the bridge, but she'd be able to spend a lot more time with them.

If Jenetta expected a short trip, she was mistaken. Six days later they were still being towed towards their unknown destination. Since the tug's sensors couldn't penetrate the *Colorado*, life continued on as before except that the bridge remained at a reduced alert status.

At the breakfast table in the Officers' mess, Lieutenant Kerrey asked, "Captain, how much longer do you think it will take to reach wherever it is we're being towed?"

"I don't know. I originally estimated about three days, but that was based solely on one fact. We'd had dozens of contacts in an area of space where I wouldn't have expected to have one contact in six months. That indicated there might be an unknown base operating around here."

"So you were developing your plan even before the destroyer showed up?"

"Not a plan, per se. I was trying to make sense of our observations. The plan didn't develop until our position was discovered and contact with a possible enemy vessel became unavoidable."

"When will we contact the fleet?"

"When the time is right. Every day we spend at Light-75 is another day the *Prometheus* draws closer at Light-412. Our course isn't taking us much farther away because we're running almost parallel to the new frontier border, so the *Prometheus* is closing on us quickly."

Eighteen more days passed before the tugs dropped out of Light speed. The sight that greeted the bridge crew surprised probably everyone except Jenetta. There in front of the ship was an enormous black asteroid with a huge, gaping maw. It appeared ready to swallow them up like a hungry, large-mouth bass about to swallow a fly after leaping from a Terran lake.

Chapter Eight
~ June 17th, 2273 ~

From a distance, one enormous hunk of rock floating in the depths of space looks pretty much like another. This one was in orbit around a Type F5 blue/white MMK class III giant with a large asteroid belt but no planets. But to Jenetta's trained eye, the hundred-twenty-kilometer-long asteroid looked similar to that of Dixon Space Command Base. Dixon had been a Raider base known as Raider-Three until Space Command attacked the Raider stronghold, defeated the garrison, and commandeered the base for their own use.

Using their sub-light engines and thrusters, the tugs slowly maneuvered the *Colorado* through the kilometers-long cavernous opening. The engineering effort required to create such a base never failed to impress Jenetta.

Like Dixon, the hollowed out interior of the enormous asteroid was about sixty kilometers long and thirty kilometers wide. And like the other Raider bases Jenetta had seen, it was a marvel of engineering. With walls that were probably thirty or more kilometers thick, it would be able to withstand an assault from almost any force. After being hollowed out, the interior surface had been covered with smooth, meters-thick, pre-stressed plasticrete. At Dixon, space between the inner 'shell' and the asteroid walls had been filled with a special plasticrete designed to harden in a vacuum. Jenetta had no reason to believe this base was constructed differently. To hide the base, giant doors several meters thick and cleverly camouflaged could be rolled closed.

A habitat building that appeared to be identical to the one at Dixon occupied an area along the wall on the larboard side of the ship as it was pushed to the work area where plundered ships were repaired either for service by the Raiders or for sale on the black market. If constructed to the same specs used at Dixon, the habitat would be three kilometers wide by one kilometer deep. Its eighteen levels would make it the size of a small city. Dozens of ships were moored at airlock piers that extended out from a pressurized docking platform that ran first along the length of the habitat and then continued into the cavern for some forty kilometers. Dixon could accommodate a hundred fifty ships at its docking piers. Jenetta counted sixteen large warships here, mixed in with dozens of smaller ships. She had no doubts that this was a Raider base, so the warships had to be Raider vessels.

After delivering the *Colorado* to the spacedocks, the tugs backed away and then zoomed off. Their two-man crews were no doubt anxious to get a decent meal after eating emergency rations for the twenty-four-day journey. Second on their priority list would no doubt be to get some sleep in a decent bed instead of restless sleep on a mattress pad laid out on the tug's flight deck.

Jenetta waited until the work parties began to approach the *Colorado* and then gave the order to Lieutenant Kerrey to execute the plan she had laid out as they entered the cavern.

Using its sub-light engines and deuterium maneuvering thrusters, the *Colorado* began to move quickly to a place along the wall opposite the habitat building. It took a few seconds for the work parties to get over the shock of seeing the ship suddenly come to life, but then the com channels came alive with screaming voices as emergency lights began to flash all over the cavern.

Taking up position almost twenty-five kilometers across from the habitat, the small ship could cover both the tunnel entrance and the entire habitat structure. Jenetta ordered the torpedo gunners to open fire on the sixteen warships that had stern torpedo tubes. Blinding flashes filled the dimly lit cavern as the *Colorado* emptied her ten bow tubes. Torpedoes streaked across the short distance to the airlock piers. With a torpedo reload time of just fifteen seconds, a second volley quickly followed the first. The sterns of all sixteen targeted warships were reduced to scrap in less than a minute. None got a torpedo off before their destruction was complete. It was a certain bet that many Raiders had died in those ships, but Jenetta hadn't had a choice. She couldn't allow the warships' gunnery crews to open fire on the *Colorado*. The ships without stern torpedo capability weren't targeted because they offered minimal threat with just their laser arrays. When the explosions ended, the cavern was strewn with hull pieces, Raider bodies, and assorted detritus.

"Com, I want to send a message to the habitat using RF communications in the three-to-thirty-megahertz range."

The com operator pushed a spot on his keyboard. "Go ahead, Captain. You're broadcasting on all frequencies on the High Frequency band."

"Attention, base commander. This is the captain of the GSC *Colorado*. I give you five minutes to surrender or suffer annihilation. If you commence an attack against us, we'll open fire on the habitat. If you try to send any IDS band messages to anyone, we'll open fire on the habitat. If you refuse to acknowledge this message, we'll open fire on the habitat. Respond on any RF frequency between three and thirty megahertz only."

The bridge was intensely quiet as they waited for a response to come. Almost the full five minutes had passed before a signal was received. When the com operator put the image up on the main viewscreen, Jenetta could see that the caller was red-faced with anger.

"Who are you?" the obviously frustrated man demanded.

"I've identified myself," Jenetta said, "I'm the one who's prepared to put several torpedoes into your habitat building. Now, who are *you*?"

"I'm Maximo Bacheer, the commandant of this base."

"And what do you call this base, Commandant? Raider what?"

"Raider-Eight."

Jenetta was shocked but didn't allow it to show on her face. She had expected it to be Four or Five. As far as she knew, the Raiders had only had six bases in Galactic Alliance Space when Raider-One was destroyed. The commandant could be trying to mislead her, though, by providing a fictitious number.

"Well, Commandant. Do you surrender, or do we open fire and finish what we've started?"

"Yes, dammit, I surrender."

"Very wise, Commandant. Here's what you will do. You will stand down and have your people go about their normal business *within* the habitat. You will not send any messages out, and you will not respond to any messages sent to you except for the ones that come from us on this frequency. No one will attempt to leave the base, and no one will attempt to fire at us. A violation of these rules will result in a spread of three fusion torpedoes being fired against the habitat. I destroyed Raider-One, and I won't hesitate to destroy this base also."

With both surprise and awe in his voice, Bacheer said, "You— you're Carver!"

"Yes, I'm Carver. I'm Commander Jenetta Carver, captain of the GSC *Colorado*. If you've spoken to the captain of the destroyer that happened across us in space, you're probably aware that this ship is practically indestructible. He fired his laser arrays at us point blank six times and didn't knick the surface. That was after his space tugs failed to cut their way in with plasma torches. We watched the efforts from our bridge. It was most amusing. But even though this ship is practically indestructible, I won't tolerate any resistance. Is that clear?"

"Yes."

"Very good. Now, recall your workers from your salvage area and other work areas, and summon all your people from the remaining ships. Then clear the docks and seal your airlocks so no one will be injured when we destroy the remaining vessels. You're all going to enjoy a nice long holiday until the rest of our task force gets here."

"You're not part of any task force. We'd know if one was operating in our territory."

"Just like you knew you were towing an occupied, armed, GSC warship into your base?"

Commandant Bacheer just scowled in reply.

"I'm serious about destroying the habitat, Commandant," Jenetta said calmly. "Don't make me prove it. You know who I am, and my reputation should speak for itself. After you've issued the orders to your people, get into a shuttle and come visit me. I'll have a lunch prepared. I'll expect you in thirty minutes. Oh, and bring two of your security runabouts with you. Carver, out."

The com operator alertly cut off the transmission upon receiving a signal from Jenetta, and the view from the bow returned to the main screen. Jenetta turned to the crewman at the tactical control station. "Keep an active torpedo target lock on the habitat so they know we're serious, but don't fire unless you're ordered to do so by the watch officer."

"Aye, Captain."

"Com, summon the senior officers to conference room 6-12-2-Quebec."

"Aye, Captain," the com officer replied, his fingers already keying the instruction that would broadcast the message to the CT's of all senior officers.

Jenetta walked directly to the conference room and was joined there in minutes by Lt. Cmdr. Pulsen, Lt. Cmdr. Cameron, Lt. Kerrey, Lt. Matthews, Lt. Doran, and Marine Lieutenant Leese.

"Okay," Jenetta said, grinning calmly, "we've neutralized a Raider base, but we've got a tiger by the tail and we don't dare let go lest it turn and rip us apart. I'm not sure how long it will be before our first help gets here, so we're going to have to stay alert. We know it will be months before the *Prometheus* arrives, but the timing wasn't our choice. If we had tipped our hand out in space, the Raiders might have stood off and used us for target practice as they zipped around us. Our problem now is how to play prison guard where the prisoners are all armed and dangerous and in control of the jail. We mustn't let the Raiders know we're not fully functional or how long it will take for support to arrive. Not knowing when our support ships are arriving will keep them off balance."

"Captain, they must have several thousand men and women in that habitat," Commander Pulsen said. "How can we possibly control them?"

"That count might actually be much higher, judging from the number of ships in port and their configurations. And based on the amount of activity in the reclamation area, I'd say it's early in their workday, so relatively few people were probably aboard ship. Our only effective means of control is the torpedoes we have aimed at them. They must believe without question that I won't hesitate to use them. We also have to keep them out of the ships remaining at the airlocks. At the first sign of movement by one of those ships, I want our laser gunners to target it and evacuate its atmosphere. We use torpedoes only as a last resort. Now, I want each of you to think like a Raider and tell me what action you'd take to break out or gain control so we can defend against it."

"I'd bail no matter what anyone said if I was a Raider," Lieutenant Leese offered. "I wouldn't care about the rest of the people in the habitat."

"Knowing that Space Command was guarding the only exit?"

"I'd create a diversion."

"What type?"

"I don't know. Anything to pull the guard off station."

"Okay. What could they do to pull us away from the entrance?"

"Blow something up so we'd have to investigate," Lieutenant Kerrey offered.

"Then we can't afford to be drawn away by explosions under any circumstances. What else?"

"I think they'll try to get a message out to whatever ships operate from this base," Lieutenant Commander Pulsen said.

"We're listening on all IDS frequencies, so we'll know if they try to send a message."

"Maybe we should jam all the frequencies instead," Lieutenant Doran offered.

"But then we'd be deaf and dumb as well. Jamming the band prevents us from receiving messages from Space Command or our approaching ships. We don't have a relay satellite on board. That's another thing I'm going to recommend that this ship have as part of its standard equipment."

Jenetta held up her hand to signal that she was receiving a message in her CT. She was notified that a shuttle and two smaller ships were headed towards the *Colorado*.

"I'm sorry to interrupt this meeting, but our visitors are approaching. Lieutenant Leese, I'll need you and your Marines to keep an eye on our visitors. Check them for weapons and hold everyone except the base commandant in or near the flight bay. The commandant should be brought to me in the Officers' mess, under guard. Assign a team to immediately examine the shuttle and security runabouts for explosive charges. Lieutenant Doran, would you come with me, please? Everyone else, keep working on our problem. We'll resume after our visitors depart."

Marine Lieutenant Leese headed for the flight bay, issuing orders through her CT as she walked, while Jenetta and the doctor talked in the corridor for a minute. The doctor then rushed off to the sick bay as Jenetta hurried to her briefing room before going to the Officers' mess.

The commandant of the Raider base was escorted to the Officers' mess after being thoroughly checked for weapons. Marine Lieutenant Leese and three Marines followed him in, then stood a meter away.

"Come in, Bacheer," Jenetta said from where she was sitting. "Have a seat. Lunch will be ready shortly."

"You don't take any chances," Bacheer said, nodding towards the Marines while his eyes remained locked on Jenetta's.

"There's nothing to be gained by giving you an opportunity to attack me, but I don't need the security detail if it bothers you." Looking at the Marine officer, she said, "You may wait in the corridor, Lieutenant." To the commandant, she said, "Sit down, Bacheer. We have a lot to discuss."

"You're as nervy as I heard," Bacheer said as he sat down. "Coming into this spaceport with just this one tiny ship shows you have more guts than sense. Now you send your guards out of the room."

"*Do* I have more guts than sense? I have an armed warship that's almost indestructible. Did you talk to the captain who tried to board us in open space?"

"I did. He confirmed what you said just before his own men killed him for bringing you in here."

"I'm surprised. I would have thought you'd exercise better control over your troops. Perhaps you're not the effective leader I was expecting."

"Who said they were out of control?"

"I see. So you ordered his death?"

"I allowed it. The fool shouldn't have brought you in here. If he couldn't crack this ship open, he should have left you alone."

"And would you have left such a prize as this floating in space? An apparently derelict ship that resisted all your weapons and attempts to board it? A ship that could redefine the defenses of the Raider organization? You'd have just flown off and left it there for someone else to find and use? Your hindsight is unusually blurry."

Bacheer scowled. Trying to change the subject, he said, "I suppose you expect me to play warden for you now?"

"No, I expect you to be a model administrator, and I expect you to keep your people in line. You see, we can't handle a mass revolt. You probably outnumber us, oh— thirty to one. Our only option is to destroy the habitat, killing everyone inside. We can't allow your people to escape, so we will exercise that option if you make it necessary."

"And what if I exercise my option to break your neck?" Bacheer growled, starting to rise from his seat.

Two large, black cats immediately stood up, bared glistening fangs, and snarled ominously. Bacheer's full attention had been directed at Jenetta and he hadn't noticed them sitting quietly against the wall just a dozen feet away. He froze halfway up as the cats prepared to spring.

"I'm quite capable of taking care of myself, Commandant, but in this case I don't have to. My pets would shred you into small, bloody, edible pieces before you could reach me, even though we're just a meter apart. I suggest you smile and sit down v-e-r-y slowly, and don't make any sudden moves again. Also, you'd better talk calmly from now on. You've already identified yourself to them as a threat."

Bacheer forced a smile and did indeed sit back down v-e-r-y slowly. The cats relaxed their posture when he was seated again but didn't lie back down.

The Officers' mess attendant further calmed the situation when he carried two plates of food over and set them down in front of Jenetta and Bacheer.

"Thank you, Ernest," Jenetta said. "Bring us a bottle of wine. Red, please."

"Would you care to trade plates with me, Captain?" Bacheer asked, keeping his voice very calm.

"The portions of food are identical, Bacheer, and you may have seconds if you wish."

"That's not what I was thinking."

Jenetta looked at him for a couple of seconds and smiled. "You think I poisoned your food?"

"Not poison, perhaps just a truth drug."

"You don't really think I'd do that, do you?"

"Why not? I would in your place."

Jenetta gestured towards the plates. "Feel free to take whichever plate you like."

Bacheer looked at her for a second. "No, you gave in too easily. You might have doctored your own plate, figuring that I'd demand a swap."

Jenetta smiled again and sighed. "I'm hungry, Bacheer. Pick whatever plate you like and I'll take the other. I have a runaway appetite and I'd like to have my lunch."

Bacheer swapped the plates, looking Jenetta in the eyes as he did. Jenetta waited a few seconds and then cut into the chicken breast cutlet. Bacheer waited a few more seconds and then started eating also.

"If I had wanted to drug you, Bacheer, I could have simply had you held down and had the drug administered."

"True, but then I'd know I'd been drugged."

"But you still would have told me everything I want to know. I don't want you drugged. I want you fully alert because your life and the lives of your people depend on it."

The mess attendant brought a bottle of wine and poured two glasses, placing them in front of Bacheer and Jenetta. The bottle was also placed on the table.

"You're welcome to swap glasses if you wish, Bacheer."

"Not necessary. I saw him pour both portions from the same bottle into clean, empty glasses." Bacheer took a sip of the wine. "You eat well, Captain. This is real wine from the Sebastian Colony. I didn't know Space Command provided alcohol on board its ships."

"Rank has its privileges. Most ships keep a small supply of spirits available for entertaining dignitaries. I'm sure you would offer me a glass of wine, were I visiting you."

"Definitely. Drop over any time."

Jenetta smiled. "Eventually. But not until our support ships arrive."

"When will that be?"

"Soon enough. I hope very soon for your sake."

"My sake?"

"Of course. You might be tempted to try something foolish with only one ship guarding the exit. Once the other ships arrive, you'll be more prudent."

"Exactly what is this ship made of?" Bacheer asked.

"A new composite material that's virtually indestructible."

"The stuff the door on Mawcett was made from?"

"Very similar. I expect the Tsgardi reported what they went through trying to enter the facility. They never succeeded, by the way."

"I know. If you hadn't killed them near Raider-Three, Mikel Arneu would have done it when he got his hands on them. When he learned that the Tsgardi had lost your clone, he raved and ranted for an hour."

"It wasn't their fault. Tsgardi are renowned for their ferocity, not their intelligence."

"Too true, but they do make effective minions for certain tasks. The chicken cutlet was excellent, Captain. Was it synthesized?"

"Yes. It's almost impossible to taste the difference with some foods, chicken being one of them. Have some more wine."

Bacheer filled his glass and then held the bottle to Jenetta's glass. "Would you care for more?"

"Just a half glass. I have a number of meetings today and I don't want to be falling asleep."

Bacheer grinned. "I know it won't affect you, Captain, and that you could drink me under the table without even getting a buzz. Mikel Arneu told me all about the recombinant DNA process he performed on you and himself. I've seen him drink an entire fifth of Scotch at one sitting and not be affected in the slightest by it. He might as well have been drinking water."

"You're unusually well informed."

"Arneu was the commandant here until just a few weeks ago. I was his deputy and we spent a lot of time talking. I must say I approve of the body he fashioned for you."

Jenetta ignored the remark. "Where's Arneu now?"

"He went to set up a new research facility on Raider-Ten. It's outside what you Spaccs call 'regulated space' and therefore beyond your reach. I don't know exactly where it's situated."

"Sure you do, but I'm sure you won't tell me."

Bacheer smiled.

"I'm going to need to hang on to your shuttle, Bacheer. And one of the security ships. I'm sorry it's going to be a bit tight going back, but it's only a few minutes away so you won't be inconvenienced for long."

Bacheer had stopped smiling. "Is that what this was all about? Getting your hands on one of our shuttles?"

"No, I wanted to meet you face to face. But I do need a shuttle since we don't have one on the ship. I guess I'm killing two birds, so to speak." Jenetta paused when the expression on Bacheer's face changed. "That was not a reference to the food. I didn't poison you." Bacheer's face relaxed. "Are you going to be able to control your people, Bacheer, or will we be forced to use the torpedoes?"

"I'll control them, Captain, for a while. The longer they remain cooped up in the station, the more desperate they'll become."

"Then I'll say goodbye now because the day after you lose control it'll be too late."

Bacheer stared at her intently. "With most other Spacc officers, I'd say they were bluffing. Space Command doesn't condone mass murder. With you though, I believe you're deadly serious."

"Good, because I am, and it's also good you understand that I won't hesitate to fire the torpedoes if you force my hand. And, just for the record, Space Command doesn't consider actions necessary for the suppression of an armed prisoner revolt to be mass murder. How many people do you have in the habitat, by the way? I'd like to know for my report in case I have to exercise our final option."

"Until you started firing, we had between seven and eight thousand. I don't know what the count is now, but it has to be closer to six than eight. We haven't had time to recover the bodies. May we have your permission to search the destroyed ships and also look for people trapped in airtight compartments?"

"Can you completely control your people? Because if just one of them decides to fire a laser at us or release a torpedo, or tries to send a message while aboard a damaged ship, we'll be forced to terminate the station."

"I'll control them."

"Very well. Use non-IDS frequencies to let us know which ship you'll be checking, and check just one ship at a time. Make sure you've evacuated all your searchers before you start on the next. Any sign of activity after you say you've vacated a ship will be considered an action against our authority. You have us vastly outnumbered and my gunners are very nervous. Don't give them an excuse to open fire."

Bacheer stood up slowly, eyeing the cats. "I won't, Captain. Thank you for a delicious lunch. Be sure to drop by so I can repay your kindness."

"You're welcome, Mr. Bacheer. I hope you survive the coming days."

Bacheer looked at her grimly and nodded, then turned. The mess hall door opened as he reached it, revealing an anxious-looking Marine guard. They escorted him back to the flight bay where he and the three pilots squeezed into one of the tiny patrol ships. The launch airlock was depressurized and the outer door opened, and the small craft moved out and headed towards the habitat.

Marine Lieutenant Leese returned to the conference room after the ship left. Jenetta had taken the cats back to her briefing room before also returning to the conference room.

"The shuttle and patrol craft that were left are free of explosives or listening devices, Captain. We disconnected the remote manipulation controls."

"Thank you."

"Were the two ships the reason for having him come over here, Captain?" Lieutenant Matthews asked.

"Partially. We needed a shuttle. I also wanted a chance to repeatedly impress upon him the fact that we would take action if any attempt to escape was made. I had one more objective, as well. Doctor Doran helped me with that one. The food and beverages we offered the pilots waiting near the flight bay and all the food and wine that was given to Bacheer were laced with a virile strain of the Kuwloon Flu. It takes a couple of days to fully incubate in a new host, but it then mutates into a highly contagious, non-lethal, airborne pathogen. In a few days to a week, with any luck, the entire station is going to be dreadfully sick. Or at least those who haven't built up the antibodies to fight it. It shouldn't kill anyone, but some will wish they could die. As you probably know, it takes a human as long as three months to fully recover from the effects of Kuwloon Flu, which is why Space Command requires that all military personnel receive an inoculation booster every five years. There hasn't been a reported outbreak in thirty years, so it's possible the station personnel are highly susceptible. Our own people are protected."

Lieutenant Commander Pulsen smiled and shook his head. "Oh, that was *nasty*, Captain."

Jenetta grinned. "It's better than firing torpedoes at the habitat to control the Raiders. We're lucky there are small samples of non-lethal infectious agents in the medical bay. This will buy us some more time for the cavalry to arrive. Let's get down to business. Did you come up with any ideas while we were gone?"

"Here's a list of the ideas put forth while you were gone, Captain," Lieutenant Commander Pulsen said as he handed her a holo-tube.

Jenetta looked at the list and said, "Very good. Let's discuss each one and define our responses."

Jenetta walked to her briefing room after the conference room meeting was over. Sitting down at her desk, she sat up straight and pushed the record button on her com unit.

"Message to Captain Lawrence Gavin of the GSC battleship *Prometheus*, from Jenetta Carver, Commander, Captain of the GSC *Colorado*. Begin recording.

"Hello Captain. While we were waiting for help to arrive, a Raider destroyer happened across our position. We had buttoned up the ship, trying to look like a hole in space, but we must have been directly in their path and they stopped to investigate. We didn't acknowledge their hails, and they were unable to board us, so they dispatched half a dozen tugs to tow us back to their base before they continued on. We could have destroyed the Raider ship or destroyed the tugs after the Raider ship left, but I decided it was best not to reveal our presence inside the ship and allow ourselves to be taken to their base.

"After being towed into their asteroid, the *Colorado* was moved to their reclamation area so it could be boarded. I waited until the workmen turned their attention to us, then made my move. Using our sub-light engines and thrusters, we maneuvered to a position across from the habitat, just inside the entrance of the base. We attacked and successfully destroyed all sixteen of the largest warships parked at the airlocks piers. We ignored the ones that didn't have rear torpedo capability. The base commander subsequently surrendered the station to us. Prisoner count is estimated as high as eight thousand, but as many as two thousand Raider personnel may have been killed when we destroyed the warships. We currently have a tenuous hold on this station and request that reinforcements proceed here with all possible haste. The commandant has identified the station as Raider-Eight; however, I can't independently verify the accuracy of that statement at this time.

"My navigator will append an exact position fix to this encrypted message. I realize the *Prometheus* is still about six months away, but it would be useful to know what other ships have been tasked to assist us. It would also be helpful if they were to contact us directly. Please respond as soon as possible.

"Commander Jenetta Carver, Captain of the GSC *Colorado*, message complete."

Jenetta calculated that the Commandant could control the Raider group for at least a month. He would first tell them he was preparing a battle plan to free the station. The intentional release of the flu used to infect the station might extend that by as much as another three months because no one would expect a plan to be implemented while everyone was deathly sick. But then he would start to encounter resistance. Eventually, the Raider personnel would revolt and probably take some reckless action rather than simply waiting for jailers to come take them into custody. Even a cornered rabbit would fight back, and these were anything but timid rabbits. Another possibility was that Bacheer would actually lead a revolt immediately, or just after the flu subsided.

In the hours following the visit to the *Colorado*, Raider personnel went through the wrecked ships and removed bodies and trapped comrades. The *Colorado's* laser gunners manned their guns and watched nervously, but no one started any trouble on that first day.

* * *

Admiral Moore took his seat at the center of the large table in the enormous meeting hall the Admiralty Board used for both private and semi-private sessions at Space Command Supreme Headquarters on Earth.

"Good morning," he said to the other nine admirals at the table and the room in general. He cleared his throat and said, "I've called this special meeting to discuss a situation that has just been reported from the new Frontier Zone border in sector 8667-3511-0131.5672. I have a copy of a message from Commander Jenetta Carver to Captain Lawrence Gavin of the *Prometheus* that I'll play now."

"Dear God," Admiral Hubera said, "not Carver again. What trouble has she gotten into *now*? I thought we would have some peace and quiet with her stranded in the Frontier Zone."

Admiral Moore simply nodded to his aide, who played back the message as everyone turned to look at the enormous monitor screen occupying an entire wall of the room.

When the message ended, Admiral Moore said, "In answer to your earlier question, Donald, it appears that Commander Carver has, with just a small, damaged scout ship, captured an entire Raider base, like the one she single-handedly destroyed in sector 8667-3855-1639.5273 *and* the one she helped capture and turn into Dixon Space Command Base. I wish we had a dozen more officers who consistently got into such *trouble*."

"This is a *fantastic* development!" Admiral Hillaire said. "If we can convert this base for our own use as we did with Dixon, it'll give us a ready-to-occupy base four hundred light-years beyond any other. We've been estimating eight to ten years before we'd have the first space station ready to occupy near the new Frontier Zone border."

"Yes," Admiral Platt said, "we must definitely support this operation with every resource available. Commander Carver and her crew must be commended for capturing this base intact without any loss of SC life."

"Commended?" Admiral Hubera said incredulously. "For what? Her incapacitated ship was dragged into a Raider base. All she's done is shoot holes in a bunch of unmanned ships parked at a space dock."

"Donald," Admiral Burke said, "it's obvious you don't appreciate the danger the *Colorado* and her crew are in. They're hundreds of light-years away from the nearest SC base in very hostile space. Other Raider ships can return to the base at any time and engage them in combat. Rather than destroying the tugs and then using her sub-light engines to lose themselves in the blackness of space until reinforcements arrived, Commander Carver *allowed* herself to be taken into this base. She had to have known what she was doing and voluntarily taken the risk, just as she did when she entered Raider-One. If that's not commendable, then I don't know what is."

The other admirals around the table voiced their support of Admiral Burke's statement while Admiral Hubera just muttered something unintelligible under his breath.

*   *   *

A week following the takeover, Jenetta contacted the base and asked to speak with Commandant Bacheer. It took some twenty minutes to get him on the com, and Jenetta understood why immediately. His face was red and puffy, his eyelids were drooping, and he kept blowing his nose. His slack-jawed look was absolutely pitiful.

"Hello, Commandant. I'm sorry to disturb you. I didn't realize you were ill."

"Didn't you? The whole station is down with the Kuwloon Flu. It had to be you who infected us."

"Me? I've never had the disease."

"Then it was somebody on your ship. The symptoms of the disease were first noticed in myself and the three pilots who accompanied me to your ship."

"And it was me who placed you together in that tiny little patrol ship so the infected person could spread it to the others. I am sorry, Commandant."

"I'm sure." The commandant suddenly stopped talking and his image dropped from the viewscreen. Jenetta heard the sounds of retching and then Bacheer reappeared, a long string of vomit or spittle dangling from his chin. "What do you want, Captain?"

"I just wanted to know how you're making out. My gunners are getting more nervous with each passing day. It's been so quiet that they think your people must be planning something."

"The only thing we're planning is to get some sleep and try to get healthy."

"Very well, Commandant. I wish you a speedy recovery. Contact me when you're well again."

The commandant scowled and his image disappeared from the viewscreen to be replaced with a Space Command logo. He never had a chance to see Jenetta's wry smile.

Jenetta waited several more days, allowing the flu to *really* get a grip on those infected, before commencing an action she'd been planning since they were first brought into the asteroid base. In the very early hours of the tenth day, the shuttle and security craft stealthily exited the *Colorado's* flight bay and approached the line of docked Raider ships. They maneuvered using only instrumentation and night-vision glasses that made use of the dim overhead lights in the cavern.

Starting with the largest of the ships that hadn't been destroyed by torpedo fire, the *Colorado's* Marines boarded through exterior airlocks and searched for any Raider personnel that might still be aboard. Once they'd certified the ships were clear, they were joined aboard ship by engineers who backed the vessels away from the airlocks and moved them to an area near the *Colorado*. They were then tethered to the asteroid's interior wall by waiting engineering staff in EVA suits. No alarms were raised and no resistance was offered. An additional group of shuttles were appropriated for the *Colorado's* use from the newly anchored ships.

It took the rest of the morning to search and move all the ships that had been docked at the airlocks in front of the habitat. In all, twenty-four intact ships were moved to the far wall. Either the illness or the fear of the *Colorado's* torpedoes, or both, kept the Raiders from interfering with their removal. The destroyed ships, or what remained of them, were removed and towed to the reclamation area at the far end of the cavern. When the task was completed, all of the airlock piers were vacated. The only way out of the habitat now was in EVA suits or in one of the small shuttles or patrol craft that were parked inside the habitat's flight bays. Neither type of craft could be used to mount an effective attack or escape.

Two days later, the com operator on duty picked up a message from the GSC destroyer *Geneva*. Jenetta was in her quarters but came to the bridge immediately, entering her briefing room to view the message in private. She pressed the play button on her com unit and the image of Captain Simon Pope appeared. She had first met him years earlier following the Battle for Higgins.

"Hello, Commander. I understand you've been busy taking the fight to the Raiders again. Congratulations on your latest Raider base acquisition. We're proceeding at top speed to your location, and we should arrive in forty-seven days to support you.

"See you soon. Captain Simon Pope aboard the GSC destroyer *Geneva*. End of message."

Jenetta pushed the com screen down and sat back in her chair. *Forty-seven days!*, she thought. They were going to be pretty haggard by the time support arrived, but it was far better than the six months until the *Prometheus* arrived.

Chapter Nine
~ July 8th, 2273 ~

It's amazing it didn't happen sooner, Jenetta thought as the enormous heavy cruiser entered the asteroid's cavernous opening.

It was the twenty-second day following the takeover, and a Raider warship had just arrived at the base. The *Colorado* had received plenty of warning, and they were ready. The ship had been transmitting a repeating message for over two hours.

The IDS bands were always filled with encrypted, unreadable traffic, but the repeating frequency of this one suggested the transmitting ship was not far away. Normally a message was sent and then hours, days or weeks might pass while the sender awaited a reply before sending the message again. The exceptions occurred when the ship was either very close or sending a distress signal. But distress signals were usually sent in the clear. The *Colorado's* computer had identified the repeating encryption pattern and alerted the com operator to the irregularity.

The computer couldn't decipher the message, but analysis of the signal strength showed that the source was getting closer. There was little doubt that the people in the habitat knew of the ship's imminent arrival, so an engineer was standing by on the *Colorado* ready to jam the band in case anyone attempted to warn the ship off. The garrison in the habitat must have been expecting a large, heavily armed and armored ship to easily overcome the much smaller *Colorado*, so no attempt at contact was made.

The warship entered slowly and cautiously, stopping while half the ship was still in the kilometers-long entrance tunnel. The small *Colorado* was off its starboard side, mixed in among the ships that had been pulled from the airlocks and anchored to the cavern wall opposite the habitat. To the eyes of the cruiser crew, the *Colorado* would look as innocuous as the other ships, although they must have found it strange that there were no ships docked at the airlock piers.

Working on the hypothesis that the eyes of the crew would most likely be looking forward once the cruiser started to move again, Jenetta waited until the cruiser was completely inside the asteroid's large cavern before giving the command to fire. Three torpedoes with high-explosive warheads flew from the *Colorado's* launching tubes, covering the distance to the Raider ship in seconds. Before its crew could even begin to react to the threat, the torpedoes slammed into the cruiser and plowed through inches of titanium armor before detonating. Explosions ripped great holes in the hull and filled the cavern entrance with flying debris. Jenetta would have preferred to take the ship peacefully, but she knew that was impossible. They'd fight before surrendering. By striking without warning, there was less danger to Jenetta's crew, and that was her first concern.

Pieces of the cruiser tumbled in every direction following the attack. Some of it struck the habitat, but didn't penetrate the heavily reinforced outer walls. A few pieces even struck the *Colorado*, but did no damage. With the excitement over, Jenetta ordered her engineers to clean up the mess. As several *Colorado* NCOs left to man the space tugs that would be used to tow the major hull sections to the reclamation area, two others left in the patrol ship to get one of the sweeper ships with a large scoop that was used to keep the cavern's interior clean of smaller items. In an enclosed space, and with the weightlessness of space, space junk was always floating around, and the port would normally be 'swept' several times a day.

When the mess was cleaned up, the *Colorado* was again ready to welcome new visitors. Search parties were assigned to search the broken hull of the cruiser to see if anyone was still alive. The ship's company in a Raider vessel of that size was normally around eight hundred to a thousand.

Amazingly, the search parties found two hundred thirty-one crewmen alive and trapped in airtight sections. It took hours to free them. Portable airlocks had to be set up at the air-tight doors and then the Raider crewmen had to be transported to the *Colorado* using the shuttles appropriated from the ships taken from the airlocks. A cargo hold was quickly converted to a holding facility, but guarding prisoners would add another layer of problems to the blanket of difficulties already covering Jenetta.

The day after the cruiser was destroyed, Jenetta was working in her office when a message was received from another GSC ship. The captain of the heavy cruiser *Song* announced that they were on their way to the *Colorado's* location and expected to arrive in two months. Jenetta had served as captain of that ship for more than a year and probably knew most of its current crew. She welcomed the news mainly because of the additional firepower it would add but also because it would give her an opportunity to renew old friendships.

Jenetta's spirits had been buoyed by the messages from the three ships coming to assist, and the situation continued to improve as three more ships notified her of their expected arrival date. The *Geneva* would still be the first, but the imaginary task force she had warned the commandant was coming was in fact really on its way.

The news naturally excited the crew. Some had acquaintances, friends, or even relatives on the ships, but most were just glad that reinforcements were coming as quickly as possible, and everyone began counting down the days until the *Geneva* arrived. The appearance of the first destroyer would make a world of difference. The crew of the *Colorado* would no longer feel so cut off and totally alone in this dangerous area of space.

After thirty days in the Raider asteroid, Jenetta wondered if Commandant Bacheer's influence over the Raider personnel was continuing to hold. Many of the Raiders would be some-what healthy again, although weak and dehydrated, the flu probably having run most of its course by now. But it was still twenty-nine days from the expected arrival of the *Geneva*, and over the following month Jenetta expected that many of the Raiders would return to full strength and begin hatching plans for escape. After the space-worthy ships had been removed from the airlocks, Jenetta had Lieutenant Commander Cameron's people sabotage their engines and weapons. The Raiders wouldn't know that even if they managed to get inside any of the ships they couldn't make use of them.

Jenetta was sitting on the floor in her quarters, wire-brushing the smooth, dense fur on Cayla's head while the big cat purred contentedly when the voice of Lieutenant Commander Pulsen began whispering in her left ear. Tayna, who had been busily licking her fur as she lay near Jenetta's feet, stopped and looked up. The two cats could always sense when Jenetta was receiving a message on her CT.

"Captain, there's something going on," she heard her first officer say.

Jenetta pressed the face of her Space Command ring with her thumb and said, "What is it, Ken?"

"The doors to the base are closing and Commandant Bacheer is demanding to speak with you immediately."

"I'm on my way. Carver, out." Jenetta jumped up and said to the two cats, "Stay here, girls."

As the cats settled comfortably back down, Jenetta hurried from her quarters and ran to the bridge, just down the corridor.

"General quarters!" Jenetta said as she entered the bridge. "Tactical, this might be a diversion. Watch for movement inside the cavern."

Lieutenant Commander Pulsen immediately announced on ship-wide speakers, "General quarters! General quarters! This is not a drill. Possible Raider action. Man your battle stations."

Jenetta walked to the com station and said, "Put Bacheer on."

The com chief touched a point on the console and said, "He's on, Captain."

"Commandant Bacheer, can you give me a good reason why I shouldn't let my torpedo gunner fire the three torpedoes we have armed and ready?"

"Captain, please don't fire! Three men have locked themselves in the control room, and they are the only ones responsible for this action!"

"What do they hope to gain?"

"They're drunk! They want an end to the waiting! They want you to fire the torpedoes!"

"You're asking me to believe that several men have decided to commit suicide and take everyone in the habitat with them?"

"That's about the size of it. As I said, they're drunk. I beg you to be a little patient. We're doing our best to get them under control, but they're heavily armed."

"Don't you have stun grenades and stun pistols?"

"Yes, but they're armed with lattice pistols and rifles."

"It appears your control has broken down. I warned you what would happen when it did."

"Captain, I have 6,246 men and women in here. They've been sick for weeks and they're frustrated with just sitting around. A few broke into the alcohol stores in a warehouse and drank far too much to listen to reason."

"Commandant, I'll give you one hour to get the base doors open. Do what you have to do to make that happen."

"They'll be open by the end of that hour, Captain, if I have to go out and crank them open by myself."

"Better not, Commandant. My gunners have orders to shoot anyone seen outside the habitat."

"I have to go now."

"One hour, Commandant."

The com officer terminated the connection, and Jenetta sat down to watch the front viewer. Motion detectors would sound alarms on the bridge if anything moved outside the ship.

After fifteen minutes, Jenetta went into her office to prepare a mug of coffee, then returned to her bridge chair to watch the forward viewscreen as she sipped the steaming black liquid.

Fifty-six minutes into the allotted time, the giant doors began to open up again. As the hour ended, the doors finished their travel and the cavern was open once again.

Jenetta stood up and said to Lieutenant Commander Pulsen, "Call me if we have any more problems. I don't believe the story about drunks wanting to die."

"What do you think they're up to?"

"I don't know. Maybe you'd better send a shuttle out to investigate. Have them look around outside the asteroid as well. Maybe there was something going on out there they didn't want us to investigate."

"Aye, Captain. I'll take care of it. I'll stay on duty until the shuttle returns so I can debrief the team personally."

"Thanks, Ken. Goodnight."

"Goodnight, Captain."

Jenetta was able to sleep through the night without interruption. In the morning, she checked her messages and saw that the team sent to check for any sign of activity outside the asteroid had reported nothing amiss. Changing into her sweats, she took the cats to the gym with her for her morning workout.

After she'd showered and had her breakfast, Jen relieved Lieutenant Kerrey on the bridge. As the rest of the first watch crew reported in and relieved their counterparts, Jenetta walked to the helmsman's station.

"Lieutenant, I'd like you to move the ship. Take us across the cavern and position us in the shadows just beyond the far end of the habitat with our bow facing the cavern entrance."

"Aye, Captain."

Using just thrusters, it took less than ten minutes to move to the new location and position the ship as Jenetta had ordered. Once in place, they were approximately forty-five kilometers from the site they had occupied since first arriving inside the asteroid. Satisfied with the new location, Jenetta walked to her briefing room to start her workday.

When Lieutenant Commander Pulsen arrived on the bridge just prior to 1600, he immediately noticed the position change as reflected in the front view on the large monitor. After receiving an update on the status of the ship, he asked, "Was there a problem with our location, Captain?"

Jenetta, who was sitting in the command chair on the bridge, said, "No, I just decided it might be a good idea to change our location. We've been at our former position for almost six weeks."

"But we had a better view of the habitat from there."

"We no longer have a need to closely watch the docking platform or piers, and we can still observe anything that might happen in the habitat. We have a better view of the entrance tunnel from here, and that might prove advantageous. We're in the shadows, and we're not showing any external lights."

"Are you expecting company?"

"I've got a feeling we might see more Raiders before our support ships arrive."

"But the *Geneva* should be here in less than two weeks."

"A lot can happen in twelve days. Let's make sure everyone stays on their toes, even more than usual."

"Aye, Captain. We'll be extra vigilant."

"Good. The bridge is yours, Commander."

"Goodnight, Captain."

Jenetta was having breakfast nine days later when the GQ alert sounded over the ship's speakers. She dropped the spoon into her cereal and raced for the bridge as the general quarters announcement was made.

"Sitrep, Don," she shouted to Lieutenant Kerrey, the third watch officer, as she burst onto the bridge.

"Warships, Captain. It looks like three of them from the sensor readings and communication signals we're getting."

"Where are they?"

"Since their arrival a few minutes ago, they appear to have taken up stationary positions outside the asteroid."

"Are the Raiders in the habitat communicating with them?"

"We haven't intercepted any com traffic yet. Engineering is standing by ready to jam the bands."

Lieutenant Commander Pulsen came running onto the bridge and ran to where Jenetta and Lieutenant Kerrey were standing. "What's going on, Captain?"

"Three warships have taken up positions outside the asteroid."

"Ours or theirs?"

"Must be theirs. We haven't received any com traffic, and the *Geneva* is still three days away."

"Think this is a rescue effort for the Raiders we're guarding?"

"It's probably an attempt to take back the station, although it won't be of much use to them now that Space Command knows where it is."

"We're being hailed, Captain," the com operator said.

"Who is it?"

"They're identifying themselves as the *Space Witch*. They want to speak to you."

"By name?"

"Yes, ma'am. They're asking for Commander Carver of the GSC *Colorado*."

"Tactical, turn off the alert lighting. Com, put an image of the individual hailing us up on the front monitor."

Jenetta sat down in her command chair as the alert lights stopped flashing. The Terran face of a Raider captain filled the front screen.

"I'm Captain Karlsaw of the *Space Witch*. Stand down and prepare to be boarded, Captain. You and your crew are prisoners of the Raider Corporation."

"That's a bit premature, Captain, don't you think? You haven't done anything to imprison us."

"The asteroid is surrounded, Captain. You can't escape."

"Escape? Who wants to escape? We hold this base and our task force should be here any time. Have you looked over your shoulder?"

"The *Prometheus* is still about four or five months away. You can't hold out until they arrive. Surrender now and you and your crew will be treated well."

"Treated well? As pleasure or hard-labor slaves? Captain, don't be absurd. Besides, we're holding two hundred thirty-one surviving crewmen of your cruiser, the *Space Titan*, in one of our holds. You'd be killing more of your own people than mine if you managed to destroy this ship."

"Casualties of war. Our six thousand people in the habitat more than make up for the few who will be killed aboard your small ship."

"And how many will be killed aboard *your* ship if you attack *us*?"

Captain Karlsaw scowled. He knew that demanding surrender from Commander Jenetta Carver was pointless. She had refused to surrender on Mawcett when faced by a vastly superior force. Captain Karlsaw knew he would have to defeat her, or kill her.

"Brave talk, Captain, but I expected nothing less. I hope you survive. The bounty that the Corporation has placed on your head will buy my entire crew a month's vacation at a resort planet."

"Trying to collect it will cost you dearly, Captain. I see little point in continuing this conversation. If you survive, I'll see that you get a comfortable cell of your very own when the task force arrives."

Jenetta looked over at the com operator and the connection was terminated. Everyone on the bridge waited tensely for something to happen but nothing did.

After an hour of waiting, Lt. Commander Pulsen said, "What do you think is holding them up, Captain?"

"They're trying to decide how to attack us without destroying the station. When we took Dixon, we didn't care if the station was destroyed, so we just threw everything we had at them. The Raiders panicked, climbed into their ships, and tried to escape. We were able to fight them outside where we could maneuver and had the tactical edge. But in this situation we're better off inside because we're limited to sub-light. We'll use the cover of the asteroid to our advantage. Like the Raiders at Dixon, we wouldn't stand a chance out-side. Eventually they'll have to come in after us, and they can't just send in fighters because their laser weapons and small rockets would be useless against our hull. They have a real dilemma."

Jenetta stood up and walked to her briefing room to get a cup of coffee. The Raiders might take hours to make their first move. Jenetta sat down at her desk and composed a message to the *Geneva*.

"Message to Captain Simon Pope of the GSC Destroyer *Geneva*, from Commander Jenetta Carver of the GSC Scout Destroyer *Colorado*.

"Captain, three Raider warships have arrived and taken up positions outside the asteroid. They've demanded our surren-der, and we've refused. We're expecting an attack at any time. I realize you're still days away, but I wanted to warn you now about the situation you'll be flying into in case we're not able to signal you later.

"I hope to see you soon. Commander Jenetta Carver, Captain of the *Colorado*. Message over."

Jenetta forwarded the message to the com operator with instructions to encrypt it and send it immediately and then took her mug of coffee out to the bridge. The *Geneva* should receive the message within an hour if they were within three day's travel time. Their top speed should only be about Light-262.

Jenetta climbed into her chair on the bridge and settled in for a long wait. She estimated that the first attack wouldn't come for hours, but they had to be ready because it would be fast and furious when it did come.

A reply came from the *Geneva* about two hours later. The response time meant they were definitely within three day's travel time. Feeling that it would be a morale booster for everyone to see that help was near, Jenetta had the operator play the message on the front screen.

"We've received your message and continue to proceed to your location at our top speed. I estimate we'll arrive at the base in seventy-six hours. Good luck, Captain. The crew of the *Geneva* salutes the crew of the *Colorado*. We know you'll show the Raiders what a Space Command ship can do, even against superior forces.

"Captain Simon Pope, GSC *Geneva*. Message complete."

The bridge was deathly quiet following the end of the message.

"Nothing's changed," Jenetta said. "We knew we were on our own. Stay alert and focused. If we can hold the Raiders off for three days, the *Geneva* will be here to give us a hand."

Four hours later the Raiders still hadn't made a move. Jenetta was on her fourth mug of coffee, and everyone was on edge.

"They should have attacked by now," Pulsen said. "They should have at least sent in a squadron of fighters to pinpoint our location."

"They believe they know where we are," Jenetta said, matter-of-factly.

"How could they?"

"The same way they knew we were here, knew the ship's name, and knew I was in command. The Raiders in the habitat told them."

"Impossible. We'd know if they were transmitting anything."

"You're forgetting the little ruse of closing the doors. I believe they used the diversion to launch a com rocket, probably from one of the conduit tunnels that connect to the laser arrays mounted on the asteroid's surface. It would have been programmed to send a prerecorded SOS message to any Raider ship within this sector after it reached a predetermined distance from the base."

"An act of desperation?"

"Essentially."

"So the ships outside the asteroid know everything the commandant knows," Pulsen said. "They haven't sent fighters in because they know that laser fire and limited-strength weapons can't damage us."

"Right. They'll only lose whoever they send without any chance of hurting us."

"Then the only answer seems to be a slugfest. They come in using thrusters and we fight it out with torpedoes."

"But that's not to their liking," Jenetta said. "If they use nuclear warheads inside the cavern, they'll destroy the habitat and risk destroying the entire asteroid and themselves. And they don't even know how effective their high-explosive warheads will be against our new hull. They know we'll score as many hits as they do, and they know the first ship in isn't likely to survive the assault. I'm sure they're trying to decide who faces almost certain death."

"Raiders aren't known for self-sacrifice. So we just sit here and wait until they screw up the courage to face our weapons?"

"We don't have much choice," Jenetta replied. After a few seconds of silence, she added, "Then again, maybe we do." Climbing down from the command chair, she said, "I have to prepare a message for the *Geneva*; you have the bridge, Ken."

"Aye, Captain."

Jenetta hurried to her briefing room and reappeared about five minutes later with a fresh mug of coffee. Retaking her seat, she said, "Be ready for action in about two hours."

"What did you send, Captain?"

"I just asked the *Geneva* to start sending us short messages of varying length every fourteen to eighteen minutes, varying the time slightly until I ask them to stop."

"What kind of messages?"

"It doesn't matter what they say. The Raiders will pick up the transmissions and believe the *Geneva* is very close. The Raiders won't be able to decrypt the messages because sending in the clear would have made it too obvious, but it will appear that they're responses to the messages *we'll* start sending every fifteen minutes beginning in an hour and thirty-five minutes. The Raiders should naturally assume that the message and reply travel time is about six to eight minutes, meaning that our support will be here in a few hours. They'll have two choices: Either face us immediately, losing at least one of their ships in the exchange and then turn to face at least one Space Command ship with a smaller force, or get away from here fast."

Pulsen looked at Jenetta with admiration in his eyes and grinned.

The *Colorado's* com chief had been sending random messages every fourteen to sixteen minutes for an hour, and seven or eight minutes after his transmission he'd receive one from the *Geneva's* com chief. The *Geneva's* operator was reading lines from a new book while the *Colorado's* operator was talking sports.

Suddenly, six torpedoes entered the cavern and exploded precisely where the *Colorado* had been until yesterday. They all had high-explosive warheads. Immediately, Captain Karlsaw of the *Space Witch* began hailing the *Colorado*.

"No response, chief," Jenetta said to the com operator. "Stop sending the messages to the *Geneva*.

"Aye, Captain."

After a tense five minutes of repeated hails, six more torpedoes entered the cavern and exploded in the same area.

"They want to make sure they finished the job before they expose themselves," Jenetta said.

"I'm sure glad you moved the ship yesterday," Pulsen said. "I know we're supposed to be impervious to high-explosive warheads, but I can't help wondering if we could have survived double salvos of six simultaneous torpedo hits. What if the habitat gives them our new location?"

"Commander Cameron's people are standing by ready to jam all frequencies at the first peep from the habitat."

"What will the Raiders do when no one responds?"

"They'll have to investigate. When they get only silence from the habitat, they'll become very uneasy. If they believe the *Geneva* will be here any time, they'll be doubly uneasy. They need to be sure there's no ship at their back when they turn to face Captain Pope. They might send in a sacrificial probe or single fighter instead of one of the ships, but I'm betting they believe they got us with that dozen-torpedo spread and that one of them will want to verify that fact and claim the kill. We'll just have to wait and see what they decide."

They had their answer about ten minutes later. A Raider destroyer of apparent Tsgardi manufacture appeared in the cavern entrance, stopping halfway into the cavern just as the *Space Titan* had done. But this time Jenetta didn't wait. She knew all eyes aboard the warship would be scanning the area where the torpedoes exploded. Three torpedoes from the *Colorado* were loosed as soon as the torpedo gunner had a lock. Thousands of glowing pieces of detritus flew in all directions as the hardened torpedo casings entered the destroyer's bow and plowed through numerous titanium bulkheads before exploding deep inside the ship.

The brilliance of the explosion lasted for only a second as flammable material inside the destroyer was ignited and burned until the oxygen was dispersed into open space. Fragments of the warship would continue to ricochet off the walls of the cavern for some time. When a cheer went up on the bridge, Jenetta let them release some of their tension before reminding them that there were still two more Raider ships out there.

The Raiders now knew the *Colorado* hadn't been destroyed by the twelve torpedoes and might suspect that the small ship was impervious to them, as well as being impervious to laser fire. With the arrival of the ship that was sending the signals, the odds would be even. The Raiders knew they hadn't fared very well against a Space Command vessel when they had a three-to-one superiority, so one-on-one wasn't palatable at all. And they had to believe that the ship at their back was virtually indestructible.

From his position manning the tactical console, Lieutenant Kerrey said, "Captain, sensors indicate that two ships are leaving the area, fast. They're traveling in different directions."

"Getting away as fast as their engines can take them," Lt. Commander Pulsen said, smiling.

"It looks like this battle is over," Jenetta said wearily. "I'd have to mark it down in the win column. Hmmm, it's after 1800," Jenetta said, glancing at her chrono patch. "I could use some dinner, but first I'd better send a message to the *Geneva* so they can stop sending messages."

Jenetta walked to her briefing room and sat down at her desk. Her energy seemed to leave her as the adrenaline that had been sustaining her drained off. She had managed to maintain an icy calm exterior while on the bridge even though her stomach was twisted in knots as the minutes and hours had ticked by. She took several minutes to relax before starting the message.

"Commander Jenetta Carver of the GSC *Colorado*, to Captain Simon Pope of the GSC *Geneva*.

"The *Colorado* has prevailed, thanks to your help, Captain. The Raiders attacked us and we torpedoed one destroyer. The pieces are still rebounding off the walls of the cavern. The other two ships have fled the area. I feel certain their attack failed because they weren't able to gather proper intelligence about our location within the asteroid. Using old information, they targeted our former position, hoping to finish us off quickly so they'd be prepared for your imminent arrival. Their haste was their undoing.

"You may stop sending the messages to us now, and we look forward to welcoming you in a few days. Thank you for your assistance, Captain.

"Commander Jenetta Carver, Captain of the GSC *Colorado*, message complete."

Jenetta sighed, stood up, and started thinking about what she'd like to have for dinner.

The *Colorado's* engineers began a cleanup of the cavern during first watch the following morning. Pieces of the destroyer were taken to the reclamation area after being searched for bodies and survivors. Surprisingly, seventy crewmen, including Captain Karlsaw, were found alive, although a few were critically wounded. The bridge section of the destroyer was partially crushed but otherwise intact. The dozen people there were almost out of oxygen when the engineers arrived.

Injured Raiders were taken to the sickbay under guard while the rest were taken to a hold after being searched by Marines and stripped of all possessions and clothing items that could be used as weapons. It was good that the *Geneva's* arrival was imminent. With more than three hundred prisoners in its holds, the *Colorado* was fast becoming overcrowded and its carbon dioxide scrubbers were working overtime. Supplies had been removed from the second hold and stacked in corridors so prisoners wouldn't have access to them. That hold had been packed wall to wall when the first hold was emptied for use as prisoner housing after the cruiser was destroyed.

By late afternoon, the mess was cleaned up and port sweepers were zipping around scooping up the floating debris, some of which were bodies or body parts. The grisly job of separating the collected matter would fall to bots that would place the body parts in empty shipping containers. They already had hundreds of bodies from the earlier action.

Jenetta was working in her briefing room when notified that the base commandant wished to speak with her.

"Put him through."

She lifted the com panel and was greeted by the face of Commandant Bacheer. His expression made him appear as if he had been sucking on lemons.

"Congratulations, Captain. You've survived another skirmish."

"Thank you, Commandant. I also managed to suppress my urge to torpedo the habitat. You're very lucky."

"Torpedo us? What for? We haven't resisted your authority."

"Of course you have, Commandant. You sent out a com rocket to transmit a message calling for help. Oh, did I mention that we have Captain Karlsaw and his entire bridge crew in one of our holds, as well as sixty other crewmen from the former *Space Witch*? They joined the surviving crew of the *Space Titan*. I knew you'd signaled them when they foolishly fired their torpedoes at our previous location. You see, after the incident with the doors, I moved the ship. I'm sure you knew about that, but you couldn't let the ships know without blatantly showing your resistance and earning a torpedo salvo for your efforts."

"I don't know what you're talking about, Captain. If Karlsaw says I sent a message, he's lying."

"It doesn't matter, Commandant. The situation is resolved. The first ships of the task force will arrive shortly. You've probably noticed an increase in com traffic during the past few days."

"We have, but I still don't believe there's any task force. You've been bluffing your way along since you arrived."

"Our torpedoes aren't a bluff, Commandant. You must at least realize *that* by now. You've had a front row seat to the destruction of two Raider warships. As I see it, you have two choices: Accept that you're a prisoner of the Galactic Alliance and stop resisting, or prepare your Last Will and Testament. I know you signaled the ships we just fought no matter how strenuously you deny it. I won't have you endangering my people any more. Further resistance will earn you a trio of torpedoes. The prisoners in my holds have been given essentially the same choice. Any revolt will result in my ordering the outer airlock doors opened in those holds. We're not prepared to defend ourselves in any way other than with brute force. Raiders who defy my authority will find themselves sucking vacuum in open space. This is my last warning, Commandant. I killed over eighteen thousand at Raider-One, five thousand at Raider-Three, and a yet-to-be-determined number at Raider-Eight. You fill in the number, Commandant. Carver out."

Jenetta terminated the call by pushing the com screen down. She knew the only thing Bacheer would understand was might and an iron will. She had to subjugate his will to her own. If she showed the slightest weakness, he would try to exploit it. The only solution was to keep hammering home how she had the power of life and death over him and the other Raiders. But the problem with making threats was that if they weren't enforced, they became hollow and meaning-less. The arrival of the *Geneva* would add an important card to her hand, but Jenetta feared that many more would die before the station was fully secured. She presumed the

Raiders had been rigging deadly traps inside the station since the first day.

When Space Command had taken Raider-Three, things happened very quickly. The Raiders hadn't had time to prepare defenses inside the habitat. Here, they'd already had two months and might have four more before the entire task force was assembled and ready to storm the habitat.

Chapter Ten

~ August 16th, 2273 ~

Three days later, the com operator notified Jenetta through her CT that they were receiving a transmission from the *Geneva*. She was showering at the time, following her morning workout. Turning off the water, she pressed the face of her Space Command ring and had the com operator route the call directly to her.

"Good morning, Captain Pope."

"Good morning, Captain Carver. I don't have an image on my com. I hope I haven't caught you at a bad time."

"I'm just washing up after my morning workout. I'm speaking via my CT."

"I see. I won't keep you, then. I just wanted to notify you that we expect to arrive at your location within an hour."

"That's wonderful news, Captain. I'll be on the bridge by the time you arrive. We haven't seen any sign of Raider ships since our last encounter, but you should keep a sharp lookout. They know we're expecting reinforcements. Contact us before entering the base."

"Will do, Captain. See you soon. *Geneva* out."

"*Colorado* out."

Jenetta was smiling and more relaxed as she finished her shower.

Jenetta arrived on the bridge just before 0800 hours and relieved Lieutenant Kerrey, who then left to have breakfast. Preparing a cup of coffee for herself, she sat down to relax and await the arrival of the *Geneva*.

At 0818 hours the *Geneva* requested permission to enter the asteroid. Jenetta nodded to the com operator and clearance was given. As the ship entered the cavern, it was the most beautiful and welcome sight Jenetta had seen since leaving the *Prometheus*.

"Com, open a line to the Captain of the *Geneva*."

"Aye, Captain." After a few seconds he said, "Go ahead, Captain."

A view of the *Geneva's* bridge appeared on the front view-screen.

"The crew of the *Colorado* welcomes the crew of the *Geneva*," Jenetta said.

"Thank you, Captain," Captain Pope said. "Let me extend my most sincere congratulations to the crew of the *Colorado* on the amazing feat of singlehandedly capturing a Raider base and then defending it against hostile forces for months."

"Thank you, Captain. I wouldn't recommend connecting to a docking pier as the habitat still contains over 6,200 Raiders, but you're more than welcome to dock with us. One of the bow airlocks should be used because of the large prisoner population in our holds near the stern."

"We'll dock with your larboard bow airlock and join you on your ship shortly."

"Fine. *Colorado* out."

"*Geneva* out."

Jenetta called the Officers' mess and asked them to set up the main conference room with coffee, tea, and breakfast deserts before turning over control of the bridge to the helms-man. Taking the lift down several decks, she walked to the forward airlock frame and stood near the lieuenant(jg) at the larboard airlock while the ships were linked. The connection was presurized, tested, and certified before the hatch was opened.

Captain Pope led the group that entered the *Colorado* and handled the introductions of his officers. Jenetta welcomed them and led the way to the conference room that had been set up by the Officers' mess attendant. Most of the *Colorado's* senior staff was waiting to greet the *Geneva's* senior staff.

Lieutenant Kerrey arrived a few minutes later, having just cleaned up after coming off duty and grabbing a little breakfast.

Both crews had eaten, but coffee, tea, and pastries were sampled as Jenetta related the events of the past months since arriving near the new Frontier Zone.

"How did you manage to get so far from your mother ship in this small— what did you call it? Scout-destroyer?" Captain Pope asked.

"I'm sorry, I can't tell you about our trip, sir. Supreme HQ has ordered me not to discuss it with anyone."

"I understand, but what prompted you to attack a Raider base with a tiny, damaged ship?" Captain Pope asked.

"Our options were limited. With our FTL drive system down, all we had were sub-light engines and thrusters. We were waiting for the *Prometheus* to pick us up when the Raiders came across us in open space. We knew they wouldn't easily be able to board us, so we pretended to be a derelict. We could have destroyed the ship that stopped to investigate, but that might have invited other attackers if our position had already been sent. I decided to let them tow us back to their base and thereby learn its location. If they *were* Raiders and were operating from an asteroid base, I knew that offensively we'd be on an equal footing once inside the port and defensively we'd be in a superior position.

"After arriving at the base, I waited until the ship was turned over to the reclamation people to 'crack us open.' When everyone's guard was down, we engaged our sub-light engines and quickly moved to a position across from the habitat. We destroyed all warships with stern torpedo capability, then issued our 'surrender or die' ultimatum. They wisely surrendered."

"Incredible. But what about the ships that came later?"

"The cruiser *Space Titan* flew in warily, not knowing the situation and unable to make contact with the base communications center. We were still in position against the asteroid wall across from the habitat. I used the ships we had removed from the airlocks as camouflage, and we blended in nicely. As soon as the cruiser was fully inside the cavern, we loosed our torpedoes. We rescued two hundred thirty-one prisoners from the broken hull after the engagement."

"And the last three Raider ships?"

"They were warned by the people in the habitat. I suspect that a small com rocket programmed to send a general alarm message after reaching a predetermined distance from the base was launched during a little diversion the habitat prisoners pulled. They could have used an access conduit to the surface for the launch. Suspecting that our former position might be compromised after their faked emergency with drunks in the station, I ordered the *Colorado* moved to a new position within the cavern. When the three ships made their move, they poured torpedoes into the spot we had vacated. We didn't answer their hails after that to make the captain of the *Space Witch* think we were dead, or at least severely damaged. They came in to check and finish us off, but it was us who did the mopping up. We rescued seventy from the hull. End of story."

"How about the habitat?"

"That's another whole story. We have 6,247 Raiders contained but not under control. As the senior officer here it's now your decision to make, but I'd recommend waiting until the other five ships arrive before we try to take them into custody. I've kept them under control by maintaining a three-torpedo lock on the habitat and threatening to destroy it if they tried to revolt."

"I agree we'll need more help. How are you making out with your three hundred prisoners?"

"It's put a severe strain on our limited resources. I'd appreciate it if you could take them off my hands. You have significantly more hold space than we do."

"I'll have one of our larger holds emptied and we can start transferring them."

"Thank you, Captain."

"How are you doing on food and supplies?"

"We're running low on a number of items. We only provisioned for my crew of a hundred eighty-five. Our hundreds of prisoners have eaten their way through half our fresh-food stores. I was planning on scavenging food supplies from the ships that we— liberated, but we hadn't reached that point yet."

"Anything you need, let me know. If we have it, it's yours."

"Thank you again, Captain. If you have sufficient crew, I'd suggest putting a small group in one of the Raider ships and posting it outside the asteroid. Our ship sensors are severely limited in here because of the thickness of the outer walls. Having a ship outside would substantially extend any advance warning of visitors and possible trouble. I wasn't able to do it because I couldn't split up my small force. The ship could come back inside quickly if any Raider ships were detected."

"Good idea, Captain. We can use a shuttle though."

"I thought one of the smaller Raider ships might be more comfortable for extended surveillance duty. The ship can then remain outside unless a problem occurs. The team of sentries would have a galley and real beds. All the ships have been disabled, but my chief engineer, Lieutenant Commander Cameron, can re-enable any of them easily enough. And the sensors would be a little more powerful."

"Okay, Captain, I'll designate a small crew for surveillance duty as soon as I return to my ship. Since you and your chief engineer are familiar with the vessels you've commandeered, you should select a vessel and re-enable it for use. Anything else?"

"No, sir. Except to say that I'll sleep a lot better now that you're here."

By dinnertime all prisoners had been moved to the *Geneva* in groups of five, and the *Colorado's* corridors had begun to clear as supplies were moved back into the holds. With the prisoners gone and responsibility for base security passed to Captain Pope as the ranking officer, Jenetta was free to relax.

After a leisurely dinner, she composed messages to her parents, sisters, and brothers, and then sent them to the com operator to be included with the next outgoing traffic. She spent the rest of the evening sitting on the carpeted deck in her quarters, grooming her cats. They purred contentedly and licked at her hands with their rough tongues as she combed and brushed their short, dense fur.

Over the next month, the GSC destroyers *Asuncion* and *Ottawa* arrived, each docking with the *Geneva* and *Colorado* so it was possible to pass through all four ships using air-locks. As required by regulations, a junior officer and Marine sentry was always standing by at each open airlock in each ship. In the event of a problem, the airlock could be closed and the connection severed in seconds.

Captain Crosby of the *Ottawa*, as the senior ranking officer, assumed command upon arrival at the base. Commandant Bacheer hadn't gotten any further with Captain Pope than he had with Jenetta, so he was happy to have a new contact among the Space Command forces. But he quickly learned he wouldn't be any better off dealing with Captain Crosby. After receiving complete reports from both Jenetta and Captain Pope, Captain Crosby repeated the threats that any attempt at revolt would result in torpedoes being launched at the habitat. Furthermore, he informed Bacheer that he would be held personally accountable for any trouble in the habitat and that he'd better keep a lid on things if he ever hoped to be a free man again.

While the ships were kept at elevated alert status because of the situation, off-duty personnel were allowed to socialize with friends and new acquaintances on the other ships. In a similar vein, the captains of the ships dined together almost every night. The loneliness of command wasn't quite so bad on those evenings.

The GSC heavy cruiser *Song* arrived at the asteroid base in the fifth month following the base seizure. The ship docked with the other GSC ships inside the asteroid, dwarfing the *Colorado*.

Jenetta was working in her briefing room when the computer announced that Lieutenant Ashraf of the cruiser *Song* was requesting to be admitted. "Come," she said, without even looking up from the report she was working on as the computer opened the sliding door to admit the caller.

The officer entered and walked to her desk, stopping at attention. Jenetta looked up and smiled at the officer who had previously served under her.

"At ease," Jenetta said as she came out from behind her desk and extended her hand. "How have you been, Lori?"

Lieutenant Ashraf relaxed, smiled, and shook the proffered hand lightly. "Fine, ma'am. We just docked. I thought I'd come over and say hello."

"I'm glad you did. Please, sit down. Tell me about yourself and the rest of the *Song* crew. What's it been, about three and a half years?"

"Just a little over four since you turned the ship over to Captain Yung. You don't look a day older."

"Courtesy of the Raider's illegal medical experiments. I've been told that I'll look like a recent Academy graduate until well after I retire from Space Command. Then, during my final few years, the entire aging process will happen very rapidly."

"The Fountain of Youth," Lieutenant Ashraf said whimsically, "everyone's dream for millennia. The formula would be worth hundreds of trillions of credits."

"The secret was probably lost when Raider-One blew up, although the Commandant of this base told me that Mikel Arneu has gone into the new Frontier Zone to establish another research base. He'll probably resume work on the process."

"I'm sure they'll have no trouble finding test subjects if they use you for an example of its effectiveness."

"The price is rather steep," Jenetta said. "You have to give up your freedom and become a pleasure slave in one of their brothels. They brainwash you to enjoy a life of complete servitude and self-sacrifice for the enjoyment of others and wipe your mind of all useless information, such as the ability to read and write. It's not worth it."

"Did they brainwash you?"

"They began the process, but I was able to escape before it had progressed very far. A doctor at Higgins was able to override the programming. Luckily, they hadn't gotten to the erasure step yet. But I still carry the 'slave' imprint on my chest. It can't be removed because they programmed it into my DNA. But enough about me, tell me about you."

"Well, I'm third officer now, so I have the bridge whenever the Captain leaves it during first watch. I have enough time in grade and I hope to make the next Lieutenant Commander Selection List. Captain Yung is a wonderful commanding officer. Lieutenant Commander Rodriguez is still our chief engineer, and he really took your advice to heart. He's worked hard at becoming less of a micro-manager and spends a lot more time training the officers under him to be self-sufficient. You'd be proud. We all benefited from your time as our captain. I'm happy to see that you have your own command again."

"This is only a scout-ship. A very large one to be sure, but still just a scout ship. As soon as the *Prometheus* arrives we'll re-dock with them, and I'll resume my duties as XO."

"I'm sure you'll have your own command soon. With the new territory opening up, we'll need a great many more ships, and there should be a lot of opportunity for advancement."

"No doubt, but it'll take years to build those ships. I wish *you* luck though. I'm sure a position will open up when you make the Selection List."

"Thank you, Captain. I hope you'll consider me for a posting to your command when you get your ship."

"I certainly will if you're still interested."

"I will be. If you'll excuse me, I have to be getting back now. The captain allowed me twenty minutes to come say hello in person and I think I spent ten minutes just climbing through airlocks."

"Of course. Goodbye, Lori. It was wonderful seeing you again."

"You too, Captain. Are you coming to the reception on the *Song* tomorrow night?"

"Yes, I am."

"Then I'll see you there." Looking at the cats lounging against the side walls, she said, "I must say that your pets are beautiful. Will you be bringing them?"

"No, they're uncomfortable in crowds, and they tend to be very protective. They'd make the attendees nervous."

"Too bad. They'd be the hit of the party."

After the lieutenant left, Jenetta finished her report and then called it a day. It was almost dinnertime and she was beginning to feel insatiably hungry, but first she had to take her cats to her quarters and feed them.

Captain Yung greeted Jenetta as she entered the reception party on the *Song*, which was limited to the senior staffs of the ships gathered at the base.

"Commander Carver, welcome," Captain Yung said. "It's wonderful to see you again."

"Thank you, Captain. It's wonderful to see you also and a pleasure to be back aboard the *Song*. It's a fine ship."

"Yes, it is. And it has a fine crew. When you turned the ship over to me at the Mars Ship Yard, I had no idea how very popular you were with my officers. They still talk about your fight with the assassin who managed to make it into your quarters just prior to the Battle for Higgins."

Jenetta smiled. "I prefer to think about the more pleasant aspects of our time together."

"Understandable. If you have time later, I'd love to hear how you captured an entire Raider base with just that small ship of yours."

"Of course, Captain. It's not much of a story, though."

"Really? I understood that you destroyed sixteen warships and captured two dozen others."

"We simply used the element of surprise to our best advantage, but I'll relate the details later if you wish."

Other officers were arriving so Jenetta let the captain return to his receiving line duties and walked into the conference room. She was surprised to see a civilian leaning against a wall, sipping on a drink. She walked over and introduced herself.

"Hello, I'm Commander Carver."

"Ah, so you're the one responsible for this assemblage of ships. I'm Trader Vyx."

Jenetta looked at his strong, rugged features. At five-foot-eleven, Vyx was the same height as Jenetta. His deeply tanned skin and dark brown hair and eyes gave him a look that one would describe as rugged. If anything, his features appeared even harsher than in the old picture she had seen while reviewing the arms investigation reports at Higgins. "I'm glad to see that you were able to get off the Gollasko Colony safely."

Vyx, who had appeared to be bored until then, was at once wary. Jenetta noticed the almost imperceptible tightening of his muscles.

"Gollasko?" Vyx said innocently. "I'm sure I don't know what you're talking about, Commander."

Jenetta smiled and said in a lowered voice, "I understand. Still, I'm glad that Shev Rivemwilth's bodyguards were over-matched. I won't mention it again. What are you doing aboard the *Song*?"

Vyx looked at her suspiciously. "Just hitching a ride. I had some merchandise I wished to offer Space Command and the captain was generous enough to give me a lift since I was headed this way. The *Song* is quite a bit faster than my own small ship, which fits nicely into a maintenance bay."

"Are you heading into the new frontier?"

"Yes. My immediate destination is the mining colony of Scruscotto. I think there are opportunities there for a savvy trader such as myself."

"How do you feel about the Galactic Alliance's decision to extend the borders by a hundred parsecs?"

"I think the Galactic Alliance has bitten off a hell of a lot more than it can chew and Space Command will be hard pressed to cover the new territory. I expect to see law enforcement efforts pushed back twenty years as an organization that is far too small for the space it's supposed to safeguard tries to cope."

"It might appear that way right now. The GAC has announced plans to expand the Academy system and double the current budget for new ship construction, but you're correct that it will take years to build our forces to where they'll be as effective as they were in the old, smaller territory. Space Command is going to need the unswerving dedication of *all* its people and resources."

Vyx stared at Jenetta for several seconds before responding. "No doubt. Excuse me, Commander," he said, before tossing down the remainder of his drink and holding up his empty glass, "I need a refill." Vyx stepped around her and moved towards the beverage bar.

Jenetta watched his walk, thinking that he moved with the same kind of relaxed, self-confident gait as her cats. Turning towards a group of senior officers from the *Geneva*, she joined their discussion about the reassignment of homeports now that the borders had changed.

Vyx, his glass refilled, moved to another solitary position against the far wall. Every time Jenetta glanced his way, she noticed that he was staring at her. He never looked away when she looked at him, but she didn't feel intimidated. She knew she had surprised him with her knowledge of his activities, and he was trying desperately to figure out how she knew what she knew.

After leaving the party, Jenetta took a few minutes to walk to the captain's quarters and say hello to the captain's steward, Woodrow Casell. He had been Jenetta's steward during the year she had served as the ship's captain. The Marine sentry immediately recognized her and, after hearing of her intention, allowed her to enter despite the fact that the captain wasn't in his quarters.

Jenetta was in her briefing room the following morning when she received a message that a civilian named Trader Vyx was at the larboard bow airlock requesting to see her. "Have him escorted to my briefing room," she said.

A short time later, the computer announced that Marine Corporal Pettle and an unidentified person were requesting admittance. Vyx was standing at the entrance with a Marine when Jenetta opened the door by saying, "Come."

Waving off the Marine guard, she said, "Come in, Trader. May I offer you a cup of coffee or tea?"

"Nothing, thank you," he said as he entered and the doors closed behind him.

"Please sit down. How may I help you?"

Vyx plopped into one of the floating "oh-gee" chairs facing Jenetta. "I came to apologize for last night. You surprised me by having knowledge I hadn't divulged to anyone aboard the *Song*. I was rude to have walked away."

"As I said last night, I understand completely. I didn't say anything that would compromise your position and I kept my voice low anyway."

Vyx's face scrunched up into a look of surprise and exasperation. "There you go again. What *exactly* do you think my position is?"

Jenetta smiled enigmatically. "You're Lt. Commander Victor Gregorian, a Space Command officer and undercover agent for SCI. You were at the Gollasko Colony to purchase stolen Space Command weapons from Shev Rivemwilth. Following a successful negotiation with Shev Rivemwilth, a convicted Tsgardi killer named Recozzi walked in and reached for his weapon. You killed him when you sliced off the top of his skull with your laser pistol, but as he dropped, wild rounds from his lattice pistol hit Rivemwilth and two of his bodyguards. The other bodyguards chased after you, believing you to be responsible, but you managed to evade them and reach your hotel. When Rivemwilth recovered, he called off the bodyguards. You sent a recording of the meeting, which included the serial number from a sample weapon. Space Command traced the weapon to the point where it disappeared from the supply channel. That point was the munitions depot at Delos-Anon."

Vyx had just stared at her, his mouth opening slightly as she talked. "I didn't know about Delos-Anon. Just *who* are you?"

"I'm Commander Jenetta Alicia Carver, first officer of the *Prometheus*, temporarily acting as captain of the Scout-Destroyer *Colorado*."

"I already knew that much. Hell, everybody between here and Earth knows that much. I mean the other. You know stuff no first officer, or even any ship's captain, would have access to. Stuff that no one in this part of space, except for myself, should know, or— *could* know."

"That's incorrect, but I'm not at liberty to discuss it for reasons of national security. I *could* tell you— but then I'd have to kill you."

Vyx just stared at her with a confused expression on his face. Jenetta held a serious expression for as long as she could and then chuckled.

"That was a joke, Trader. Okay, here it is. Twelve months ago, as you were fighting to stay alive on Gollasko, I was working in the Intelligence Section on Higgins. In fact, I was charged with reviewing all materials related to the stolen arms investigation and with making recommendations for subsequent actions. I was briefed on your situation by Captain Kanes."

"You were on Higgins twelve months ago?"

"Twelve months and two weeks."

Vyx stared at her for a few seconds. "That's impossible. Higgins is fifteen months from here in the fastest ship in the fleet. My information is that you captured this base almost five months ago. You couldn't have been on Higgins when you say you were."

"All joking aside, there are many things I'm not at liberty to discuss, but I can't hide the fact that I was on Higgins a year ago October. Too many people saw me. I also can't deny that I was in this base eight months later. Again, there are too many witnesses to my presence."

"You have two clones. You could be pulling some kind of 'twins' switch."

"Both of my sisters are in highly visible line officer positions aboard Space Command Battleships with thousands of crewmembers. Besides, how would I know about you if I wasn't working for Intelligence?"

"I don't know, and I admit that bothers me, a lot. But I know that no ship can travel faster than Light-375."

"No?"

"Isn't that the rated speed of the *Prometheus* class battleships?"

"That's the *official* rating."

"You're saying it can travel faster?"

"I'm not saying anything. Such information would be classified, if it was true, although I know you could be trusted to keep it confidential."

Vyx stared at Jenetta again for a few seconds. "Forgetting about Space Command for a minute and talking strictly about hypothetical situations, what's the fastest speed you believe we could achieve given our current level of technology?"

Jenetta grinned. "Speaking strictly hypothetically *and* in strictest confidence, I would have to say that Light-9375 is within the current realm of possibility."

"Light-9375?!" Vyx said with difficulty.

"I'm not saying such speed is feasible for normal travel yet, and I definitely wouldn't repeat the possibility of attaining such a speed outside this briefing room. There could be all sorts of problems associated with achieving such speed, and it may be years before it can be used with any real degree of control and reliability. For instance, the ship might suffer extensive damage to its FTL drive system during such a test that would prevent it from being re-engaged after the test was over."

"I understand," Vyx said with a glazed look in his eyes. "It will take time to work out all the problems and make such speeds practicable for normal use. Uh, I've heard this ship is damaged."

"Yes, our FTL drive system suffered extensive damage that prevents it from being re-engaged. We only have sublight engines and thrusters at present. We spent months drifting in space, waiting for our mother ship, the *Prometheus*, to arrive. A Raider ship happened across us and towed us here."

"You drifted for months before arriving here?"

"Yes."

Vyx wet his lips as he thought. "I'm surprised the Raiders didn't board you where they found you."

"They tried, but they couldn't get in. They went so far as to fire on us with their laser arrays, but they didn't even nick our hull while we just watched from the bridge. We could have fired our torpedoes and destroyed them, but I decided to let them tow us to their base while we played dead."

"This ship is impervious to laser fire?" Vyx asked, his eyes as wide as saucers.

"Yes. It's a new design, both hull and engines. I guess the hull is no longer a secret since the Raiders are aware of its existence, but you should treat the information as confidential. This ship was just completed at the Martian shipbuilding facility a year ago July."

"And you made it all the way from Mars to here in that time?"

"I guess you might say we caught a good tailwind."

Vyx smiled. "I guess. What are your plans now?"

"The *Prometheus* will be arriving next month. It has a special airtight docking collar for the *Colorado* on its keel, and our engineers can start making repairs to the drive system once we've docked. What are *your* plans?"

"My immediate destination is the mining colony of Scruscotto."

"So you said last night. Scruscotto is in the new Frontier Zone. I thought you might have changed your plans to a location within regulated Galactic Alliance space."

"Well, in my line of work, business is often more lucrative *outside* regulated GA space."

Jenetta nodded. "I just thought you might have some unfinished business to clean up within the old Frontier Zone before moving to the new one."

Vyx stared at Jenetta for a few seconds before making a decision to discuss his active investigation. "Rivemwilth is the key to solving this case. When the GAC announced the border expansion, he left Gollasko, as did practically every other felon on the planet. No one knew where he was heading, or if they did know, they weren't talking. All I can do is set up a new base of operations and wait until he surfaces again. When he does, I'll get there and resume the operation. In the meantime, it wouldn't do for me to be seen in the vicinity of Space Command operations too often or for too long. Not if I'm to continue in my present occupation."

"I understand, Commander. Naturally I wouldn't want to see your position compromised."

"Thank you, Captain," Vyx said, standing up. "And thank you for sharing your views with me."

"They were only hypothetical musings, you understand?"

"Of course, ma'am, just hypothetical musings."

"Good luck, Trader."

"You also, Captain."

After Vyx left, Jenetta thought about the conversation. She didn't regret sharing information that was still classified top secret. It was probably the most un-secret top secret in Space Command anyway. Her entire crew of a hundred eighty-five knew the whole story and she was pretty sure that the thousands of crewmembers on the *Prometheus* knew all the facts or had heard the rumors. Then there was the command structure at Headquarters and probably dozens of scientists and their assistants in Space Command and at the shipyard. Since the trial hadn't been part of a secret test, it would have been impossible to contain it for very long.

Chapter Eleven
~ December 27th, 2273 ~

The battleship *Thor* arrived forty-five days after the *Song*, and the *Prometheus* showed up two days after that. Captain Gavin, as the most senior captain among the officers, took immediate command of the forces inside the asteroid. Disconnecting from the other ships, the *Colorado* moved to its docking collar beneath the *Prometheus*, and after ten months of separation the two ships were joined once again.

After all Marines from the combined forces in the cavern were moved onto the *Prometheus*, Captain Gavin ordered all ships to disconnect and prepare for action. He then ordered all ships other than the *Thor* to vacate the asteroid. When just the two battleships remained, he contacted Commandant Bacheer. Jenetta sat next to him on the bridge of the *Prometheus*.

"Commandant, I'm Captain Gavin of the *Prometheus*. I'm sure you're familiar with my first officer, Commander Carver."

"I am."

"Commandant, we're now ready to relieve you of the burden of maintaining discipline within the habitat. I'll give you one hour to move all your people to the docking level and assemble them in the main cargo area. Marines will move in and take them into custody. If there's resistance, it will be dealt with severely. An organized revolt will result in our pulling out and exercising the final option. I've already moved all other ships but one out of the asteroid for safety reasons should that option be necessary. Are you ready to comply?"

"I'm ready, but I can't speak for everybody on the station. I've done my best to keep things under control, but there's a faction that's prepared to fight when you come in. You can't hold me responsible for the actions of a few fanatics."

"I'm sorry to hear that they prefer to die. How many are in this faction?"

"I would estimate about two hundred to three hundred. I can't be sure because they're operating clandestinely in defiance of my edicts. The other six thousand will go peacefully."

"That certainly complicates things, Commandant. It's unfortunate you're not able to control your people."

"You can't destroy the habitat, Captain. You'd be killing thousands who want to surrender peacefully."

"Stand by, Commandant, I'll get back to you shortly."

The com operator closed the connection.

Gavin looked at Jenetta. "In my briefing room, Commander."

Jenetta followed him in and took a seat as he paced around the room.

"I don't want to kill six thousand people who want to surrender peacefully," Gavin said, "but the rebels will probably attack if we try to set up a holding area in the main cargo section as we did at Dixon where we had fewer than a quarter of the prisoners we have here. They'll try to use the confusion to their advantage and hope more will join them. We could find ourselves greatly outnumbered."

"Let's reduce the odds, sir."

Gavin looked at her thoughtfully for a few seconds. "I'm listening. Tell me your thoughts."

"I've had quite a bit of time to think about this, sir, and determine how I'd handle it. Everything I've seen so far confirms that this habitat is constructed along the same lines as the one at Dixon. So, other than one enormous airlock capable of bringing full-sized shipping containers into the cargo area, there should be only narrow corridors running from the docking platform to the main habitat space. In the event of a pressure drop, say from a ship crashing into the protective wall outside the platform while docking, emergency airlock doors in each corridor will drop and seal to protect the main area. I'd move my Marines in and set up a fortified position around a docking pier entrance while the engineers close the emergency doors in all the corridors except the one closest to the Marine position. Then we have the personnel who wish to surrender come to the docking pier in groups of twenty through that single corridor. We'll let the Commandant handle that part. He won't send the next batch until the previous group has been processed. That way, if the rebels make a move, no more than twenty would be in our midst, and they wouldn't be able to charge our position as a group because they'd be constrained by a narrow, two-meter-wide corridor without cover. Between the *Prometheus*, *Thor*, and *Song*, we should be able to securely accommodate six thousand in the holds— not for a long term, but for a couple of days until the habitat can be fully secured. Once the non-combatants are removed, the rebels will be the ones who are greatly outnumbered. We can even resort to more severe means if you wish."

"Destroy the habitat?"

"I was thinking more along the lines of depressurizing it, sir. The rebels would either be incapacitated or be forced into identifiable, airtight sections where the Marines could more easily overpower them."

"What if the rebels have rigged explosive devices or a single massive device?" Gavin asked.

"The Marines have equipment for the detection of explosive devices, but if the rebels are thinking of destroying the entire station, we may not be able to prevent it. However, if that's their goal, why have they waited this long?"

"Perhaps they wanted to take as many of us with them as possible. That was in my mind when I ordered the other ships out."

"Then perhaps we should just remove the non-combatants and depressurize the station without warning. The rebels will be expecting an assault force and may not have time to activate a self-destruct device or even reach EVA suits. It will help protect our Marines from people who simply want to die fighting."

Gavin nodded. "I'd like to give the rebels a last chance to surrender, but prudence dictates that we simply act."

"They *will* have a final chance, sir. They can join the non-combatants in the evacuation. After that, their intentions to 'fight to the death' are clear."

Gavin raised the com panel on his desk. "Get me Captain Yung on the *Song*," he said to the com chief. A few seconds later, Captain Yung's image appeared on the desk top panel. "Captain, we've had a change of plans. We're going to temporarily evacuate all Raider personnel from the station. Clear as much space in your holds as possible, establish security around the areas, and move back into the asteroid. On my command you'll move to an airlock and begin loading prisoners. This is a temporary situation that won't last more than a few days, so pack them in like sardines. We have to evacuate six thousand while we secure the habitat. If you can take twelve to fifteen hundred, the *Thor* and *Prometheus* can take the rest."

"Aye, Captain, we'll be underway in minutes. Our holds will be ready."

"Thank you, Captain. *Prometheus*, out."

"*Song*, out."

To Jenetta, Gavin said, "Let's brief the Commandant."

They walked out and took their seats on the bridge. The com operator made the connection.

"Commandant, you have one hour to assemble your people in the main cargo area. When instructed, you'll begin sending your people to a designated docking pier in groups of twenty, but you won't send any groups until the previous group has been processed. I want you to send the prisoners from your detention center first. Is that clear?"

"It's clear, Captain. What about the rebels?"

"We'll take them on after the rest have been evacuated from the station."

"Very well, Captain. I'll begin assembling my people."

"Commandant, you'll stay behind until the last group of non-belligerent personnel is evacuated."

Bacheer nodded solemnly. "Yes, Captain."

"*Prometheus* out."

The line went dead as the com operator broke the connection.

"Helmsman, move us to airlock 1-Mike and commence docking procedures. Com, have the three senior Marine officers report to conference room 3-22-3-Quebec."

Both helm and com replied affirmatively. Gavin stayed on the bridge until the ship was docked and then said, "Commander, you have the bridge. Handle any problems that might arise. I'm going to brief the Marine officers."

"Aye, sir," Jenetta replied. She was prepared to order the ship undocked if a group tried to rush the ship. Once the ship's forward cargo bay hatch was opened, the Marines would be prepared to handle any armed resistance.

Gavin returned after twenty minutes.

"Any signs of trouble, Jen?"

"Not a bit, sir."

"Good. Com, notify the airlock officer that the hatch can be opened as soon as Major Visconti is ready to disembark."

"Aye, Captain."

As the forward cargo bay's enormous hatch was opened, the front screen on the bridge became a patchwork of images being fed from the video cameras carried by all Marine officers and senior NCOs. Every Marine was equipped with a helmet camera and their feeds were being recorded, but it wasn't possible or necessary to show hundreds of duplicate views. The bridge crew watched as the Marines moved out of the ship unopposed. In ten minutes they had secured the airlock area and established a perimeter that extended from docking pier 1-Mike to 1-Oscar. Engineers, operating under the protection of Marine squads, closed and sealed all corridors to the habitat except the one.

"Com, notify the *Song* to dock at pier 1-November."

"Aye, Captain."

After ten minutes the com operator said, "Captain, the *Song* reports that they're docked and the forward cargo bay hatch is open. They're ready to receive prisoners."

"Notify Major Visconti to commence the evacuation."

"Aye, Captain."

Within twenty minutes, the first evacuees were being processed. These were prisoners from the detention center, and they were still wearing their restraint bands. Like all who would follow, they were searched for weapons before being passed through in case the Raider insurgents tried to sneak someone through, but they were taken to a separate holding area after entering the *Song*. After that the flow never stopped. Major Visconti worked out how long it took to process a group and how long it took the next to arrive, so there was never a long gap between groups. All evacuees were asked their name, home planet, and job assignment at the base. A record was made for each individual. It contained their picture, retinal image, and handprints as they progressed towards the ship. Criminal identity nano-tags were injected into their bloodstream as they were processed. The tags would spread throughout their bodies and from then forward a scanning device could positively identify them. Once the chips were implanted, it was virtually impossible to remove them completely. Those who already had criminal identity tags in their bodies, indicating that they had previously served time in a penal institution, were excluded from receiving new nano-tags. Their tags were recorded and mated with the new arrest records before they were passed through. In two hours and twenty-eight minutes, the *Song* had taken on fifteen hundred prisoners. The hatch was closed and the *Song* backed away from the airlock, then moved out of the asteroid.

The *Thor* was next to load, and it was moving into position at airlock 1-Oscar even before the *Song* had cleared the entrance of the asteroid cavern. As soon as the cargo bay hatch was opened, prisoners were ready to step inside.

Over the next few hours, everything progressed peacefully. Then suddenly, alarms sounded. Sensors placed in the open corridor that led from the main cargo area had detected something. Ducking behind cover, the Marines ordered everyone to drop to the ground. One Raider stood his ground defiantly, refusing to drop. He put his arms out to the sides until shot by a Marine with a stun rifle. As he went limp, he dropped the live hand grenade he was holding. His falling body landed on top of it just before it exploded. Only one other person was injured by the blast, and the injury to that individual was not life-threatening. As the injured man was carried to the ship's infirmary, the remaining body parts of the rebel were scooped up and put into a body bag for later identification. There wasn't a lot left, but one reasonably intact hand was found so identification should be routine.

Upon reaching its quota of prisoners, the *Thor* was sealed, the airlock depressurized, and the ship backed away. Instead of leaving, it took up its former position inside the cavern so it could offer cover to the *Prometheus*.

The remaining prisoners were moved into the *Prometheus* over the next few hours. There were no more suicide bomber attempts, and the evacuation finished smoothly. The final count was six thousand eighty-eight, leaving just under two hundred unaccounted for.

As the evacuation progressed, several engineers were working at docking pier 1-November. Each docking pier that extended to a ship was equipped with five airtight doors. There was naturally one airtight door near the habitat at the beginning of the pier, and there was one at each of the three airlock ramps where, depending upon its configuration, a parked ship could access the pier. The size and shape of the ship, as well as the location of the ship's hatch to be used, determined which airlock ramp was used. There was also one emergency door just before the first airlock. That door would seal automatically if a drop in pressure was sensed while any of the three airlock ramps were open. The engineers overrode the automatic features so that all airlock doors on the 1-November pier could be controlled manually.

With the evacuation complete, engineers moved into the one open passageway that led to the main cargo area. While Marines provided cover, they jammed the emergency gate open. With the one passageway unable to seal, the entire habitat could now suffer depressurization.

Completing their work, the engineers withdrew into the *Prometheus* and the ship's forward cargo bay hatch was closed and sealed. The Marines still on the docking platform anchored themselves to secure posts and stanchions near airlocks 1-Mike and 1-Oscar. When all were secure, they donned oxygen masks.

Gavin and Jenetta watched the preparations from the bridge of the *Prometheus*. When everything was ready, Gavin gave the command to depressurize the habitat and Major Visconti operated the control mechanism left by the engineers. All three airlock ramps at airlock 1-November opened and the air flowed out like an invisible river gone wild.

As the habitat's life-sustaining atmosphere drained through the airlock, dust, dirt, and everything that wasn't tied or nailed down rushed out into the cavern. Paper, boxes, crates, garbage, small electric vehicles, and even a few bodies still grasping wildly at anything that offered a possible handhold, flowed into the airless void outside the habitat.

When the atmosphere had been reduced to forty percent of normal, the airlock ramp doors were closed. Forty percent of normal was equivalent to being at an elevation of twenty-three thousand feet on Earth. Anyone used to a full atmosphere, the normal condition in space stations, would only remain conscious for four to ten minutes, and then only in a progressively debilitated condition. Prolonged exposure would result in death, and even temporary exposure could have serious consequences. The habitat's life support systems were already trying to rebuild the pressure, and although it would take hours to return to normal, it should rise quickly enough to prevent any deaths in otherwise healthy individuals.

As soon as the airlock ramps were closed and the hurricane-like wind had subsided, the Marines unhooked themselves and moved into the main cargo area. Sensor equipment helped them locate rebels who had been lying in ambush. Securing the rebels, the Marines lifted their unconscious or semi-conscious bodies onto 'oh-gee' sleds for delivery to a central collection point. Most of the Raiders who had failed to report for evacuation were collected within the first half-hour, and those who regained consciousness as the pressure increased were still unable to function properly when they were taken prisoner.

It would have been great if every one of the rebels had still been incapacitated until the collection finished, but some had recovered by the time the Marines reached them. A few pitched battles took place in remote areas of the habitat, but the Marines slowly took the station, as everyone knew they would.

By 0800 hours the next morning the habitat was declared secure, and all rebels had been accounted for. The Marines had worked all night to clear the eighteen levels, using sensors that could pick up the heartbeat of a mouse at a hundred meters. Port sweepers had also worked steadily since the airlock ramps had been closed. Visibility outside had been restored by fifty percent. Half a dozen bodies picked up in the cavern cleaners were turned over to the station morgue, which had also received the bodies of the rebels who had continued to resist after recovering from the depressurization. The other rebels had been taken to the detention center and placed in cells after being fitted with Raider restraint bands.

The restraint bands, placed on a prisoner's wrists, ankles, waist, and neck, stretched like elastic until they were locked on by a signal from a small electronic controller. The neck band, capable of emitting a shock that would incapacitate a prisoner when a button on the controller was depressed, was the most despised. There were five levels of shock, but rarely was level two ever exceeded since level one was enough to cause the prisoner to fall to the ground writhing in pain. With the press of another button, the wrists were pulled to the waist. Raider captives had suffered broken bones while trying to stop that from occurring, and no one had ever succeeded. A different button pulled the prisoner's ankle restraints together. Space Command and Marine personnel were restricted from using the shock capability of the restraints, but they were permitted to use the constraint feature to help subdue prisoners.

Summoned to the bridge in the morning, Jenetta was directed to the captain's briefing room. She entered as soon as the doors opened.

"Did you wish to see me, Captain?"

"Have a seat, Jen," he said. He seemed ill at ease and Jenetta immediately felt a sense of intense foreboding. After a few seconds of uncomfortable silence, he said, "I don't know how to say this in any way that will please you, so I'll just blurt it out. Effective today, you're in command of this station."

"Oh, Captain," Jenetta groaned. "You wouldn't do that to me *again*, would you? Last time, it took me two years to get back to the *Prometheus*."

"I know, but it can't be helped. You're the most qualified individual we have among the officers in this task force. You took over Raider-Three in the first hour following our attack and in a matter of months converted it into a first class Space Command base. This base is even more crucial to our needs. We're only a dozen light-years from the new Frontier Zone. We need this base desperately to support our future operations in this territory."

"But there must be somebody else who would appreciate this *wonderful* opportunity," Jenetta said facetiously.

"This isn't my decision, Jen. You know the high regard I have for you. I don't wish to lose you as my XO any more than you wish to leave the ship. This comes directly from Space Command Supreme HQ on Earth."

"Earth? Then you knew about this before today?"

Captain Gavin sucked in his breath and exhaled. "I received the orders on our journey here. They were only to be given to you if we were successful in taking the habitat intact, but I can tell you that the Admiralty Board was ecstatic when they learned you had secured a base of operations for us so close to the new border."

Jenetta scowled. "Good thing I didn't know. I might have been tempted to fire my torpedoes into it before you arrived."

Captain Gavin smiled. He knew his first officer well enough to realize she wasn't serious. "I guess that's why they instructed me to tell you only *after* the seizure was complete."

"They knew I wouldn't be happy."

"They're all experienced officers. They know the service is made up both of individuals who wish to be posted to a ship and those who prefer being posted on Earth or to a planet-side base. I think you're looking at this all wrong; this isn't a punishment. You're being placed in command of *the* most important base in *all* of Galactic Alliance territory. It's our most forward base now, in fact the *only* base in the former Frontier Zone, and its proximity to the border means that it will become the focal point of operations for hundreds of light-years in every direction."

"Aye, sir."

"And being so far away from Earth, you'll have little contact with politicians and diplomats. That's usually an enormous plus for most line officers."

"After I completed my duty as base commander of Dixon, Admiral Holt confided in me that Supreme HQ had wanted me to remain there for a full five-year tour of duty. He said he had to fight to get me back aboard a ship. Sir, is this another attempt to turn me into a port administrator?"

"I honestly don't know if there are other motives involved here. I do know that you're the most qualified officer for the job, and based solely on that, I'm forced to endorse your appointment. You're the only experienced base commander this side of Dixon. You can whip that base into shape faster and better than anyone else within five hundred light-years, including me." Changing the tone of his voice from authoritative to friendly, he added, "Jen, I'd been advised that the *Prometheus* would have its home port assignment changed to this base if we were successful in taking it intact, so this time we'll be nearby when your service at the base is concluded."

"That's something, I guess," Jenetta sighed. "Very well, sir. When do I take command?"

"Immediately. Pack your things and leave when you're ready. Major Visconti has been informed that you've been named as permanent base commander. Your job should be easier here than at Raider-Three. Our ships are all intact, so we'll be able to supply you with all the manpower you need to get things straightened out. You'll have first access to all personnel not needed for security work or emergency repairs, and the entire task force will be standing by for at least two weeks. It will take that long for new orders to come through now that I've sent my report on the operation to Space Command."

"Aye, Captain. I just hope that 'permanent base commander' doesn't mean what it sounds like."

Jenetta walked to her quarters and packed her things. Stacking her cases by the door, she completed a second sweep of the four rooms to make sure she had packed everything. Once she located her new quarters, her bags would be brought over.

Jenetta turned to her pets and said, "Cayla, Tayna, we're moving into the station." The large cats sprang to position at her side as she left her quarters and walked to the airlock.

The passageway where the engineers had jammed the emergency bulkhead was a mess. It was filled with crates and objects that had gotten stuck as they were being sucked out, creating sort of a dam. Marines were busy trying to un-jam the debris and engineers were standing by ready to undo the measure they had performed to keep the bulkhead from dropping into position. The other passageways had been opened though, and Jenetta used one of them to reach the main cargo sorting area.

Depressurizing the habitat wasn't responsible for a tenth of the damage Jenetta discovered when she made it through the passageway. As a result of being cooped up as prisoners, the Raiders had apparently released pent-up aggressions by smashing walls, equipment, and furniture. Raider-Three had at least been neat and orderly when she had taken over. This station looked like the pictures of deserted buildings in the large Earth cities of the late twentieth century. She shook her head as she walked along.

"Pretty bad, isn't it, ma'am?" she heard from behind her. Turning, she saw Major Visconti walking towards her.

"Yes, but I guess it was to be expected."

"Prisoners are the same the galaxy over. They wreck the decent places where they're held and then condemn their jailors for forcing them to live in substandard conditions."

"How are the housing areas?"

"About the same for the general population. There are a few exceptions here and there. The officer's quarters are much better, and the base commandant's quarters are orderly. You can move in whenever you're ready, by the way. I've had Commandant Bacheer's personal effects boxed and removed from both his quarters and his offices."

"Thank you, Major. And congratulations on a successful operation. I'm sorry about the injuries your people suffered."

"Thank you, Commander. Only three were injured seriously, and all will recover and be back on active duty within a few months. It would have been much worse if you hadn't depressurized the habitat. They had stockpiles of weapons and explosives at the ready."

"Has the habitat been swept for mines and booby-traps?"

"Yes, ma'am. My people found a few crude devices, but I guess not knowing how long they were going to have to live here or whether their comrades would mount a successful counterattack against our forces stopped them from doing anything on a large scale. They didn't want to be blowing themselves up, or their own people."

"How soon can I borrow some of your Marines?"

"Most of them are sacked out right now. We worked all night searching the habitat. You can have them in eight hours."

"Good. Our first task is to clean out nine large warehouses and seal any alternate entrances/exits. You were at Raider-Three so you know what we did. We have more than double the number of prisoners here since we didn't have the ship-to-ship battle. I'll get the engineers ready to start constructing shower and toilet facilities in six of the warehouses. We'll have to house about a thousand people in each 'prison dormitory,' and we'll need at least two of them ready by tomorrow. The ships are bulging at the seams."

"Aye, Commander. We'll be on it as soon as my people are rested."

"Thank you, Major. You'd better get some rest also."

"Yes, ma'am. I wanted to wait until you assumed command."

"You're relieved, Major."

"Thank you, Commander. Goodnight."

"Good morning, Major."

Major Visconti turned and walked towards the passageway that would take him to the *Prometheus* as Jenetta walked along one of the fifteen-meter-wide roadways that ran for most of the length of the habitat on this level. Once beyond the large open area referred to as the main cargo area, enormous warehouses that extended from the deck to the twenty-five-meter-high ceiling filled both sides of the 'road' without interruption. The main cargo area was always kept as open as possible. Raider ships coming in had their entire cargo brought there so it could be inspected and sorted before being taken to the appropriate warehouses for storage. Cargo loads for outgoing ships were likewise assembled there before container loading commenced. Jenetta was able to confirm that the layout was almost identical to that found on Raider-Three, now Dixon Space Command Base.

After deciding which warehouses would be used to house the prisoners and which would be used as exercise compounds, Jenetta took an elevator to the third level up and walked to the Commandant's offices. They would now serve as her offices while she was the base commander.

Identical to her offices on Dixon, she had a full-wall, three-dimensional SimWindow where recorded vid images taken on Earth and other planets could be displayed, making it appear that she was really there. She could also view a real-time image of the cavern outside the base. Using special cameras and sensors, the computer would make it appear as though one were looking at the ships through a window. The computer enhanced the image of the cavern to make it appear like a large, well-illuminated warehouse instead of the dimly lit cavern that it actually was. Jenetta could imagine Commandant Bacheer sitting here, staring out at the *Colorado*, its torpedoes armed and locked onto the habitat. The smooth plasticrete walls where the *Colorado* had been parked had been blasted apart by the two volleys of torpedoes from the Raider attackers, exposing the rough surface of the asteroid. The ships on either side of the vacant area had likewise been severely damaged in the attack.

Taking a seat behind the desk, she touched the face of her ring to activate a carrier signal. "Commander Cameron," she said.

After a few seconds she heard, "Cameron here, Commander."

"Bill, I need your help. We'll need to set up showers and toilet facilities here like we did at Dixon."

"Aye, Commander. I've already got my people working on them. We'll be ready to start installing them as soon as you have some space emptied for us."

"Thanks, Bill. I'll also need a complete check performed on all airlocks and emergency bulkheads once the passageway near airlock pier November is cleared and repaired."

"Aye, Commander. I've already issued the orders."

Jenetta smiled to herself. "I don't suppose you've arranged for a hundred cooks for me?"

Lieutenant Cameron quipped, "Sorry, Jen. I can't even make toast without burning it."

"Okay, Bill. Thanks. Carver, out."

As her two cats explored and sniffed every inch of the large office, Jenetta started working on a list of the items and personnel she'd need to pull the base together. The place was a mess, but Captain Gavin had promised that the engineers of all the ships would be available for work in setting up the base if they weren't required for emergency work on their ship, at least for the next two weeks. She would have to press hard to get as much done as possible before ships started receiving orders to leave on patrol. She was also going to need a staff after the ships started to leave.

When her list was prepared, she placed a call to Captain Gavin.

"Sir, I've prepared a basic list of our needs."

"Transmit it to me, Jen."

Jenetta pressed a button on the portable pad and the list appeared on Captain Gavin's com panel. He nodded as he scanned it visually.

"This is quite a list. I'll get the personnel officer on each ship working on it. How do things look over there?"

"It's a disaster, sir. The Raiders had little to do over the past six months, so they apparently spent their free time trashing the habitat. I'm going to take a complete tour after I finish speaking with you, but I wanted to get this first list ready so people could start assembling the things we'll need. I'll probably have another list just as long after my tour."

"Very well, you have top priority for our resources."

"Sir, how can I build a staff from the few ships in the task force? It'll take one to two years for newly assigned administrative personnel to arrive here. And what will we do with the prisoners? We'll need dozens of prisoner transport ships, and there are fewer than a dozen in the entire Space Command fleet."

"Space Command has been working on those problems since you first notified us that you had captured this base last August. Ships and people are already on the way here and have been for months. Even if we hadn't been able to capture the habitat intact, we would have used the asteroid as a base. Personnel would have lived aboard ships until the habitat could be restored to usable condition."

"What about the prisoners, sir?"

"I don't think HQ realized we'd have so many, but we'll get by as best we can."

"We'll still have to wait for as long as six months for the first ships to arrive, even if they left immediately from Dixon after receiving my first report regarding our seizure of the asteroid."

"True, but other ships will be stopping here now. Personnel can be swapped and transferred temporarily until the permanent personnel arrive. I'm sure things will work out, Jen."

"Yes, sir. With Space Command resources being so stretched, will the standard procedure of never having fewer than five battle-ready warships docked at a forward base be continued?"

"I'm sure Space Command will do the best they can. As you say, we're stretched pretty tight right now, and we'll probably continue to experience limitations for quite a while. But I'm sure you'll always have several here at least."

"Aye, Captain. Well, I suppose I should be off on my tour. I'll contact you after I'm done to give you an updated report on the condition of the base."

"*Prometheus*, out."

"Uh, Carver out," Jenetta blurted out, suddenly realizing that there wasn't any official designation for the base yet. She couldn't very well use the Raider-Eight designation.

This base is eighteen levels of mess and destruction, Jenetta thought as she completed her tour. Commandant Bacheer obviously hadn't maintained very tight control over his people, but that was understandable. They no longer considered the base theirs, and in fact it had become their prison. Vital areas, such as life support and the power generation sections, hadn't been touched for obvious reasons. They hadn't been so crazed as to kill themselves. But non-essential areas had been trashed. The computer center wasn't damaged, but they had destroyed all backups and erased the files. As at Dixon, computer experts would be called upon to see if any important data could be recovered from the system before Space Command software was loaded. It would be difficult operating without a central computer, but they could use remote connections to a system aboard one of the battleships for now. The IT experts might have to content themselves with files they might recover from the ships damaged while they were parked at the docking piers.

It took most of the first watch period just to walk through the base and perform a cursory examination. Jenetta didn't even get to the housing section, but she knew what she'd find after Major Visconti's report. A call on her CT prompted her to wrap up her tour and return to the main level. The Marines had reported back for duty after eight hours off, and Major Visconti wanted to know which warehouses to empty.

Jenetta found hundreds of Marines sitting in the main cargo area eating breakfast. All six ships in the task force had docked at the habitat airlocks once the station had been cleared of holdouts. Food had been brought over from the

Prometheus and *Thor*. The delectable aroma of piping hot eggs, pancakes, sausages, toast, and other breakfast items reminded Jenetta that she hadn't eaten in half a day, so she fixed a heaping tray and joined the officers at the packing crates they were using for a table. There were no chairs, so they stood as they ate.

After draining the last of the coffee from her cup and popping the last piece of biscuit into her mouth, Jenetta handed a portable viewpad to the Major. "I've listed the nine warehouses to be cleared in order of priority. If any are found unsuitable for confinement, use the designated alternates. Since this facility appears to be fairly new, that shouldn't be necessary. I don't know what the warehouses contain, so I don't have any specific place for putting the contents. I'll leave that up to you. On this level, the three main roadways run the full length of the habitat. That gives us nine kilometers of road with warehouses on both sides, plus this cargo area. I'm sure you can find space."

"No problem, Commander. We should have your nine warehouses empty by the end of the second watch. The base's loader equipment appears to be in good shape, and we can borrow additional 'oh-gee' blocks and bot loaders from the taskforce ships."

"Very good, Major. The engineers are prefabricating shower and toilet facilities for us, and they'll move in to begin installation as soon as you've cleared some space. I'd like to start moving prisoners in by tomorrow. I'll need your people to function as guards until Space Command makes other arrangements to move them to a regular prison colony."

"Understood, ma'am."

Jenetta received a message through her CT that she was wanted in her office. "Thanks for breakfast, Major. I'll check back with you later. Call me if you run into any insurmountable obstacles."

Arriving at her office, Jenetta found the personnel officers from each of the ships waiting for her. Each was carrying a holo-tube that contained the complete files on all of their ship's personnel. Jenetta led the way to a conference room and invited everyone to sit down.

"We have a massive task ahead of us here. I've been led to understand that some ships may be leaving as soon as two weeks from now. Before I start losing available resources, we have to get this new base established and functioning. We have about six thousand, five hundred prisoners to feed and control. That means my task is doubly as difficult as it was on Dixon. I need both immediate temporary help and reassigned personnel who will remain until replacements can arrive from Space Command. To be fair, I'll take an almost equal percentage from each ship. The two battleships will provide most of the Marines needed for prison guards, and we can worry about the personnel reassignments after we get my immediate need for temporary help taken care of. Right now I need engineers, computer experts, cooks, clerks, laundry, and support personnel. This station is a mess and we need to get it in order, fast."

Over the next two hours, an entire personnel infrastructure was created. Temporary personnel would live on their ships and report ashore at the start of their shift each day. Reassigned personnel would be quartered on the base.

The engineers were beginning to install the shower and toilet facilities by the start of the third watch. The nine designated warehouses had been cleared, the boxes and crates stacked in eight-meter-wide piles that ran the length of the habitat on two of the roadways. A warehouse located between each two dormitory warehouses would function as an exercise 'yard.' They would be available to one dormitory warehouse at a time on an alternating basis.

Having learned a valuable lesson from the computer restoration effort at Dixon and not wishing to spend weeks waiting for the base's computer system to become operational, Jenetta had the computer experts swap the core with a replacement unit instead of trying to retrieve information now. The core would then be sent to Intelligence, and they could take their time trying to retrieve any data. The lead engineer estimated that the center would be operational within two days.

In the mess hall, bots were hard at work scrubbing floors, dining room tables and chairs, and cooking equipment, while cooks planned menus and familiarized themselves with the facilities. Mess attendants were busy itemizing and organizing food stores in the numerous freezers and food warehouses.

Laundry equipment was also being checked and prepared. The laundry would soon have to start cleaning clothes for eight thousand, along with bedding and towels. Being fully automated, it only required a small management staff. Bots would take care of pickup and delivery.

A small army of clerks were at work inventorying the contents of the kilometers of warehouses, and another army was at work renovating the living quarters. The latter force was mostly composed of robots. Skilled operators supervised the bots as they patched, cleaned, scrubbed, and painted. A good operator could keep three teams of robots busy at once. A pair of robots removed furniture so that another, larger team of robots could strip, patch, clean, and paint the four walls and ceiling of each bedroom and bath. A third group of bots followed behind, deep-cleaning the carpets before the first team returned to replace the removed furniture. A suite could be completed every hour by an effective operator with his or her team of bots, and there were twenty teams working. If the robots were kept busy during all three watches, they should be able to refinish all ten thousand suites within twenty-one days. Jenetta hoped she would have twenty-one days before the ships started to leave.

It was after 0300 when Jenetta stopped at her office just long enough to retrieve her pets and then went looking for her quarters. It was fortunate that she had left her cats in her office because her new quarters had been renovated sometime during the day. Although they had gotten used to the laundry and housekeeping bots on the ships, Jenetta wasn't sure how her cats would have reacted to having their quarters invaded by the teams of renovation bots.

Her new apartment was the most spacious she had ever seen on a base, and easily twice the size of her quarters on Dixon. She decided that one of the previous base commandants, perhaps Arneu, had consolidated the space intended for two top Raider officials. But the late hour diminished any desire to look around, so Jenetta just located a bedroom and fell onto the bed after removing her uniform.

Sleeping until 0900 hours, Jenetta hurried to shower and dress. She walked to the main mess hall to see if she could scrounge something for breakfast and was pleasantly surprised to find it in full operation. Freshly baked goods were available, and cooks were supervising the preparation of items such as eggs and pancakes by the automated machinery. People coming off third watch were eating dinner entrees. Jenetta grabbed a quick breakfast and headed for her office.

As she entered the outer office, she found three officers waiting. They immediately stood and came to attention.

"At ease," Jenetta said. Facing the most senior officer, a lieutenant commander, she said, "What can I do for you, Commander?"

"Lieutenant Commander Novotny from the *Thor*, ma'am. I've been ordered to report to you for temporary reassignment."

"Very well. Welcome Commander. I'll be with you shortly." Turning to the second officer, a lieutenant, she said, "Good morning, Lieutenant Ashraf."

"Good morning, Commander. I'm here for temporary reassignment also."

"Welcome, Lieutenant. Have a seat." Turning to the third officer, another lieutenant, she said, "Good morning, Lieutenant."

"Good morning, Commander. Lieutenant Graham from the *Ottawa* reporting for temporary reassignment."

"Welcome, Lieutenant. Please be seated." Turning to the lieutenant commander, she said, "Commander, come into my office."

Jenetta moved behind her desk and sat down after they were in her office. "Have a seat, Commander, and tell me about yourself."

After twenty minutes of discussing Commander Novotny's previous duties, Jenetta said, "I have a very important and difficult assignment for you Commander. I'd like you to be my warden."

"Warden, Commander?"

"Yes. We have sixty-five hundred prisoners to guard until they can be transported to proper facilities. They'll be housed in six large warehouses that are being converted for prison use. We expect to begin moving them in today, as soon as the warehouses are outfitted with the new shower and toilet facilities. The most difficult prisoners, those who decided to fight, are being housed in the detention center. The next most obstinate group will be fitted with Raider restraint bands that can disable them in a second if they get out of control, but we won't have enough for everyone. Marines will guard the prisoners twenty-four hours a day from catwalk positions in the warehouses. Stun rifles will be used on those prisoners not equipped with restraint bands. You'll have the unenviable task of keeping a potential powder keg from blowing. Are you up to it?"

"I believe so, Commander, although I don't have any prison management experience. I'm a line officer."

"As am I. We're all being called upon to do things that are new to us. The Marines will handle the prisoners. You just have to supervise and make sure the Marines get whatever they need to do their job effectively. You'll also supervise the detention center, but you shouldn't have any trouble there. The warehouses are the potential problem."

"Aye, Commander."

"Good. Why don't you track down Major Visconti and introduce yourself. Your office will be in suite 903, just down the hall. Welcome aboard, Commander."

"Thank you, Commander," he said as he stood up.

"Send Lieutenant Ashraf in please."

"Aye, Commander."

A few seconds after he left, Lieutenant Ashraf came in.

"Have a seat, Lori."

"Thank you, Commander," she said, taking her seat.

"I'm surprised to see you here. As third officer aboard the *Song* you should have been exempt from reassignment."

"I was, but I requested to be considered for a position on your staff."

Jenetta paused for a few seconds. "You realize that these reassignments will last from six months to two years?"

"Yes, ma'am. That was explained to me."

"Okay, Lieutenant. Lt. Commander Novotny is our new prison warden, leaving three main jobs open. I need a Port Officer, a Food Services Officer, and an Adjutant. Do any of those positions interest you?"

"I'll serve where ever I'm assigned, ma'am."

"Of course, but do you have a preference?"

"I suppose Adjutant would be my first choice."

"Good. You're now my Adjutant. You'll set my appointments, coordinate all functions for this office, and supervise the office staff. I'll go over the station floor plans with you later and show you how we assigned quarters on Dixon; then you can assign quarters to yourself and the other new officers. You're also the Housing Officer until it becomes a fulltime position and we have someone to fill it."

"Aye, Commander."

Jenetta smiled. "Let's get to work, Lieutenant. Send Lieutenant Graham in, please."

"Aye, Commander," Lieutenant Ashraf said as she stood and left the room. Having functioned as Jenetta's acting first officer on the *Song* following the Battle of Vauzlee, she knew Jenetta well and was delighted to occupy a post that would have them working closely again.

Lieutenant Graham entered Jenetta's office a few minutes later and came to attention.

"At ease, Lieutenant. Have a seat and tell me about yourself."

Fifteen minutes later, the new Port Officer/Warehouse Operations Officer left Jenetta's office in the form of Lieutenant Graham. His first job was to coordinate with the clerks doing the inventory work to get the computer database established.

Jenetta reviewed the work in the warehouses after lunch. Five of the six dormitory warehouses were equipped with showers and toilets, and four were already set up with gravity-shielding pads that would serve as beds. The pads, about the length and width of a bunk mattress, blocked gravity from the deck plating and caused the sleeper to float as much as a quarter of a meter above the deck, depending on their weight. Jenetta approved moving the male prisoners from the *Song* and *Geneva* into the new facilities.

The Raiders were brought off the ships in groups of twenty under heavy guard. Their IDs were checked and they were assigned to one of the available warehouses. There wasn't any opportunity for them to attempt an escape with two platoons of armed Marines watching their every move and they were, in fact, relieved to get off the ships. They hadn't showered since entering the ships, the toilet facilities consisted of plastic tubs, they hadn't been given clean clothes, and they were sleeping on hard decks with just a thin blanket. Wherever they were being put now had to be better than where they'd been.

By the time the prisoners from the *Song* and *Geneva* were transported and settled, the rest of the warehouses were set up and ready, so the Marines began to transport the prisoners from the *Prometheus* and *Thor*. It was almost midnight when the move was complete.

When she arrived at her quarters that evening, Jenetta received a warm and friendly welcome from her cats. They weren't used to being away from her so much during the day. She decided that from now on she would take them to the office with her as she had done on Dixon.

Chapter Twelve
~ January 6th, 2274 ~

Despite the condition of the habitat when Jenetta assumed command of the new base, she was able to turn it into the semblance of a real base within a week. It still needed a tremendous amount of work though. More than half of the living quarters still needed to be refinished, most of the common areas and offices hadn't been touched yet, and the main computer still wasn't able to link with Space Command, although it was fully functional for internal base use.

The lower half of the habitat, reserved by Jenetta for Space Command and Marine use only, was being equipped with security entrances requiring implanted CTs or IDs, handprint, retinal identification, and even voice recognition. While all officers had CTs implanted, NCOs and crewmen only had implanted ID chips. Lacking two-way communication capability, the ID chips were in all other respects like CTs in that they could receive com messages, could be used to locate an individual, and permitted identification and access for authorized areas and equipment.

The initial inventory work in all the warehouses had been completed, and work was progressing well on inventorying the contents of cargo containers in the cavern, albeit more slowly because of the zero atmosphere.

Captain Gavin waited a full seven days to come ashore for the tour required for his report to Space Command. They had already toured the warehouses used for the prisoners and were touring the main level using one of the small 'oh-gee' vehicles common around the base when he said, "Great job, Jen. You've done wonders in just seven days. I saw the early assessment vids and didn't think things would look this good for months."

"I've had to use the resources while they're available, Captain. You said that ships might begin leaving after two weeks so it was imperative that we get as much done as possible before then. I've pushed my people really hard, but by the end of the two-week schedule I've established, we should be in good shape. We'll be able to function moderately well after that while we continue the renovation work and slowly gear up to function as a normal base."

"I filed a lengthy report on the habitat takeover after you left the ship to take command of the base. It's a little over six days each way, so Supreme HQ should have the report by now. We should have updated orders and information in another week."

"I hope they have something in mind for our prisoners. We can't keep a population like this penned up in warehouses for an indefinite period. Eventually, even the threat of being stunned won't hold them back. They'll revolt and we might be forced to use deadly force to stop them, if we even can."

"Where did you put the Commandant?"

"I gave him private, deluxe accommodations."

"Private, deluxe accommodations?"

"Nothing like his former quarters, of course. He's got a private cell in the detention center."

Gavin nodded and chuckled.

"It really is a privilege when you consider that otherwise you're sharing a single bedroom with about seven hundred other prisoners. Also, it keeps him from fomenting rebellion. All the top habitat officials are down there, in addition to the Raiders who decided to fight to the death. The latter are being held three to a cell, so they're not nearly as comfortable, although they do have their own bathroom in each cell. All prisoners in the detention center have been fitted with Raider restraint bands, and we're doing the same with all prisoners who start trouble in the warehouses. Troublemakers are being segregated into one warehouse where we have triple the number of guards on duty at all times."

"Your latest report states that you aren't able to receive Space Command asynchronous computer updates."

"That's correct, sir. We're still getting our updates through the *Prometheus'* system while the computer people work on the problem. There's some sort of difficulty in the decryption process that's preventing us from disassembling the data stream. We'll find the problem soon. I'm sure it's not a major one."

The car had reached the elevator to the lower floors, and after passing retinal scans they descended into the Space Command section and continued the tour of the base's power systems and life support systems areas. Entire floors, each with three square kilometers of empty space, would support whatever functions and activities Space Command assigned to the base. At present, the only space being utilized was dedicated to the detention center, computer facility, power and life support functions, Station Control Center, and the base's new Combat Information Center.

Captain Gavin returned to the *Prometheus* after spending much of the day touring the facility and recording the information he needed to complete his report to Space Command. Jenetta returned to her office after he left and called up her messages. Knowing she'd be lucky to get to bed before 2400 hours again tonight, she took a short break to feed her pets and spend a little time grooming them before resuming work.

Jenetta was so busy handling a myriad of details that she hardly realized the passage of another week. The computer problems had finally all been resolved, and the new base was receiving daily data streams that kept the base computer up to date with everything happening in Galactic Alliance space. There were actually a number of channels dedicated to the same stream, which were broadcast at different time intervals. If something caused an interruption in the transmission, the computer would automatically seek to replace the corrupted packet with one from another channel until the data was complete and accurate. The IDS streams included broadcasts from hundreds of news and entertainment stations on a dozen worlds, and these entertainment programs were stored and rebroadcast on demand throughout the station.

The reassignment phase of staffing the station was going well. Almost seventy-five percent of the base's staff was now 'assigned until relieved by the arrival of a replacement.' Staffing the base was decimating the crews of the ships in the task force, but it couldn't be helped. Each ship would lose about twenty-eight percent of its complement. That wouldn't be enough to hinder operations in any way, but much of the crew would be working extra duty hours each week.

The renovation work in the housing quarters was progressing well, with almost sixty percent of the rooms now repainted and refurnished. Because of the damage caused by the Raiders, Jenetta estimated that she would have only about eight thousand rooms available for normal occupancy. The other two thousand would have partial furniture or no furniture until new could be procured or the old could be repaired. The top six floors of the habitat were devoted to living quarters, and walls had been erected in corridors to divide the floors into four distinct and separate vertical sections, each having its own bank of elevators. One section was designated for civilian use and another for bachelor officer quarters. The other sections were designated for crew quarters and family quarters.

The prisoners were growing restless, cooped up as they were in the warehouses, and fights were becoming more common, despite the certain knowledge that those involved would be stunned by Marine guards armed with stun rifles. Although the beam was quite narrow, there had been instances of innocent bystanders being stunned, so whenever a fight broke out, the nearby prisoners scattered quickly away. This sometimes led to new fights as people collided or got trampled. Most of the fighting was limited to Warehouse Three, the place where all recalcitrant prisoners were placed. Anyone responsible for starting a fight was immediately moved into W3, so the other warehouses were comparatively calm and trouble free. Still, Lieutenant Commander Novotny was kept busy responding to complaints and charges from the prisoners against their fellows. Novotny had placed large monitors in the corners of each warehouse and selected movies and entertainment specials were being rebroadcast. Sports were limited to non-contact sports because an early rebroadcast of a football game had resulted in a general melee among viewers, many of whom were fans of one side or the other. None of the participants in that incident had been moved to W3 because it would have immediately overcrowded that warehouse.

The base's exterior defenses had been checked, improved where possible, and greatly expanded. A dozen self-loading torpedo launchers had been added to supplement the laser arrays the Raiders had mounted on the asteroid's surface, and the number of laser arrays had been tripled by salvaging weapons from the ships destroyed in the initial action at the habitat. More, and better, sensors had been added as well. There was a lot to be said for having the best engineering talents from half a dozen ships available, even if it was only temporary, and Jenetta made the most of it.

When Jenetta received orders to report aboard the *Prometheus* for a meeting of ships' captains at 1000 hours, she presented herself at the designated conference room at the designated hour. Although she didn't hold the rank of captain, her position as base commander dictated inclusion in this select group. Several captains were already present, and she took her chair after preparing a cup of coffee.

Gavin arrived a couple of minutes before the appointed time and welcomed the attendees individually. At 1000 he took his seat at the head of the conference table and began the meeting.

"We've all received our new orders by now. You'll each have specifics not available to me, but basically the *Prometheus*, *Geneva*, *Ottawa*, and *Song* will be leaving here within a week. The *Asuncion* and *Thor* will remain at the base until other ships arrive in relief and they receive orders to embark on patrol.

"Space Command has now officially designated this base as Stewart Space Command Base. It's being named after Admiral Phillip S. Stewart, one of our earliest space pioneers. If we were closer to the center of Galactic Alliance territory, there would be a ribbon cutting, dozens of politicians giving long-winded speeches, and hundreds of news reporters providing coverage of the event. But since we're so far away and in hostile space, such activities are suspended. The news agencies have been apprised via press release that we've secured this base from the Raiders and been informed of the new name.

"If it was feasible, Space Command would leave five ships here to protect this important base, but we all know the situation. Commander Carver is in the unenviable position of trying to develop this base while guarding thousands of Raider prisoners with minimal staff levels. Before any ship can leave, it will be necessary to complete the formal reassignment of loaned personnel to Stewart. I'm sure your Space Command orders mentioned that new base personnel are already on their way in several ships and that you'll get your people back as soon as possible. We'll all have to make do for awhile.

"Commander Carver's staff has completed an inventory of everything in the warehouses. You can access the supply database and submit your supply requisitions through her office. The ships on their way here include quartermaster supply ships, and once they begin arriving Stewart should be able to supply anything not currently available.

"Should you receive a distress call from this base, I know you'll return with all due haste to assist in its defense. Before this base was captured by the *Colorado*, I had been notified that Dixon would be our new home port. Following the seizure, Space Command re-designated this base as the new homeport for both the *Prometheus* and *Thor*. I'm sure other reassignments will be made in the next few months. That's all I wanted to announce, so the meeting is open for discussion."

"Larry," Captain Yung of the *Song* began, "there's been quite a bit of scuttlebutt about the *Colorado*, but no official or verifiable information has been forthcoming. The main area of speculation centers on how a disabled scout ship could wind up being three hundred light-years away from its host ship. Are you free to clear up the mystery now?"

"I can say that the *Colorado* wasn't disabled until it reached this area. Prior to that it was under full power."

"But why was it so far from the *Prometheus*?"

"An unfortunate mechanical problem left the ship without communications or sensors while the drive system was locked. The chief engineer believed that disengaging the drive would destroy the drive circuitry, with repairs requiring substantial time in a yard. Commander Carver wanted the engineers to definitely determine that there was no other way to disengage the drive before giving orders that would incapacitate the ship."

"Shouldn't you have been trailing the ship during its tests?"

Gavin sighed slightly. "Okay, here's the story. It's still classified top secret and Supreme Headquarters has to be the one to officially declassify the information, but it's too significant and too widely known to really remain secret for long anyway. However, you should still treat it as such and not repeat what I'm going to say. I'm only telling you now because without the facts the Commander and I come off looking like incompetent fools.

"Commander Carver and the crew of the *Colorado* traveled the three hundred fifteen light-years in twelve and a half days. When the ship engaged its FTL drive, it disappeared from our sensors so quickly that we at first thought it had exploded. It was only after a close examination of the image logs that we discovered what had actually occurred."

The room was silent for a few seconds and most of the officers turned to stare at Jenetta while they computed the speed in their heads. Captain Crosby of the *Ottawa* was the first to speak.

"I heard the rumors that the *Colorado* had exceeded Light-7500, but I had dismissed them as fantasy. If it was anyone but you relating these facts, I would laugh."

"There's nothing laughable about Light-9750," Captain Yung of the *Song* said. "I never thought such speed would be achieved. The theorists have said that the most we could ever expect to achieve is Light-862."

"A couple of centuries ago, theorists said we'd never exceed the speed of light," Gavin said. "And before that, theorists said we'd never break the sound barrier. And before that, people believed the Earth was flat. The officially computed speed is Light-9793.48, but we've simplified that to just 9790. I concur with you, Charles. I never expected that such speed would be realized either, at least not in my lifetime. The *Colorado* was only rated at Light-450 Plus, and the top speed was to be officially listed as Light-225. The trip that brought her here was simply intended as a test of the ship at full power. Something unexplained happened that we may not be able to reproduce in the near future, but we now know it's possible. If it can be done once, it can be done again. My orders are to return the *Colorado* to the shipyards so the scientists and engineers there can try to figure out exactly what happened."

"Sir," Jenetta said, "that means you'll be gone for two years. Space Command can't seriously be considering removing such an important part of our protective shield for that long."

"Our orders are specific, Jen. We're to deliver the *Colorado* to Dixon with all possible haste. A special transport ship with destroyer escorts will meet us there to take the *Colorado* on to the shipyard. We'll return here upon completion of that mission. We should be back in twenty months."

"The drive wasn't severely damaged because the anti-collision system shut it down. Why not try sending the *Colorado* back the same way? The *Prometheus* can always shuttle the ship if it fails to achieve Light-9790."

"Space Command specifically ordered me *not* to try that. They don't want to intentionally risk having the ship travel that far without any control, and if the collision avoidance system should shut down the drive months from the nearest SC ship, the Raiders might have an opportunity to destroy the *Colorado* before the scientists get to examine it."

"Commander Carver is correct," Captain Payton of the *Thor* said. "Losing your ship for almost two years will place an additional hardship on this and the surrounding sectors— especially since the *Thor* is ordered to remain at the base."

"It can't be helped. Identifying what caused the speed anomaly could revolutionize space travel. Think of it. We could travel the length of the galaxy in less than eleven years instead of the two hundred seventy-five it would currently take in the *Prometheus* or *Chiron*. For the first time, travel to another galaxy within a lifetime seems possible with the use of stasis sleep. Travel to Andromeda would only take two hundred thirty years instead of the current five thousand, four hundred years."

The captains at the table nodded without remarking. No attempts to travel to another galaxy had ever been made, or even seriously contemplated before. The speed that the *Colorado* had achieved could open the universe to exploration if it could be duplicated and brought under control.

The meeting lasted for another half-hour, but Jenetta only listened half-heartedly. Until today she had thought she might be able to rejoin the *Prometheus* in as little as six months if Supreme HQ had selected and dispatched a base administrator for Stewart before the first troop transports and quartermaster ships left. But it now seemed clear that she would be stranded on the base for almost two years whether a new base commander arrived with the first group of personnel or not. Although disappointed, she resolved before the meeting was over to put her personal feelings aside and perform her assigned duties to the best of her abilities.

The *Ottawa* was the first ship to depart Stewart SCB. With its stores restocked from the base warehouses, it left to resume its patrol duties. The *Geneva* was the second to leave, also restocked and able to remain out for up to five years if necessary. Most ships tried to get into port at least once a year to replenish their fresh food supplies since one year was about the longest that most fresh foods could be preserved at peak freshness levels. After that, the mess had to rely either on frozen foods or synthesizers that could create acceptable imitations. But with Stewart being so far from the regular supply sources, it would be impossible to stock most fresh foods, and frozen foods would become the norm.

Jenetta was working in her office a few days after the *Geneva* had left on patrol when Lieutenant Ashraf messaged to inform her that Trader Vyx was in the outer office, requesting to see her.

"Send him in, Lori."

Trader Vyx strode into the office a few seconds later as the door opened to admit him. Instantly, both cats stood up. They sniffed the air and eyed the newcomer carefully. Vyx didn't miss the obvious movement of the cats and stopped in his tracks.

"Cayla, Tayna, Trader Vyx is a trusted Space Command operative," Jenetta said. "He doesn't present any threat."

Both large cats sank down again but never took their eyes off Vyx.

"Good morning, Commander."

"Good morning, Trader."

"Is it okay to move?"

"It is now. Come sit down."

Vyx sat down across from Jenetta. "Very effective security measures, Commander."

"They're just my pets, but they feel very protective towards me."

"I see that. I'll be sure not to make any sudden movements. Uh, do they understand Amer?"

"To be honest, I don't know if they understand my words, perceive my meaning from the tone of my voice, or if they have telepathic abilities. Most of Taurentlus-Thur is a bit primitive and little research has been done on its indigenous species. I always speak to them as I would to another person, and they always seem to understand."

"So it seems."

"How have you been getting on?" Jenetta asked, trying to change the subject.

"Quite well. I'm preparing to leave the base. I was inform-ed by the Port Officer that I needed permission from you to leave because there's no record in the computer of my having arrived. I'm told that if I try to leave without my ship, the *Scorpion*, first being registered in the computer, I'll be target-ed by automatic laser fire."

"Yes, you arrived in the *Song*, didn't you? I'll add a record to the logs so you'll be able to leave whenever you wish. You'll still need clearance from departure control before moving around the cavern. Still outbound for the colony on Scruscotto?"

"Yes, at least initially. Once I'm established there I might do a little traveling. We've made a little headway in the stolen arms case, but there's still a lot to do. Knowing where they disappeared from the supply line and who is acting as broker to sell them are only two parts to the puzzle. We still have to find out who actually stole them, how, where they are now, and who else is involved with the thefts and distribution."

"Are you traveling alone?"

"No. I have two associates from Gollasko who are travel-ing with me."

"Byers and Nelligen?"

Vyx nodded. "Kanes decided there wasn't any sense in them remaining undercover at Gollasko. It turned into a ghost colony practically overnight after the frontier boundary was moved. So they joined me as my business associates. Gollasko never had much to offer anyone, except the complete lack of governmental authority. And with Space

Command moving into the neighborhood, it suddenly became unhealthy for most of its inhabitants."

"Good luck, Trader. Let me know if there's anything I can do to help you out."

"There is one thing. I'd like to give you an envelope to hold for me. It contains a data ring and some vid wafers. I know I can trust you because you worked at Intelligence. If anything happens to me, it should be forwarded to Captain Kanes."

"I'll be happy to forward it for you."

"But only if I go missing for an extended period."

"Of course."

Vyx stood up and, after laying an envelope on her desk, extended his hand. "Thank you, Commander."

Jenetta stood up and shook the proffered hand. "You're welcome. Goodbye and good luck."

After he left, Jenetta picked up the envelope addressed to Commander Kanes and placed it in her safe.

The *Prometheus* and *Song* left within hours of one another. Jenetta had visited the *Prometheus* before it left to say goodbye to her friends and to take one last walk around the ship she wouldn't see again for almost two years.

Lieutenant Ashraf had similarly taken a couple of hours to say goodbye to her ship and friends, although the *Song* should be back in ten to twelve months.

Base personnel and crewmen from the *Thor* and *Asuncion* continued to assist in restoration of the base, and with things settling down, Jenetta started to work with design engineers to prepare plans for the new civilian concourse. She'd decided that it would occupy virtually all of the three-kilometer-wide level just above the docking level. Like the docking level, the second level had been designed for warehouse space, so, as on the docking level, the ceiling was twenty-five meters high. Jenetta used the knowledge and experience gained from her year as base commander at Dixon to prepare an even more grandiose vision for the new civilian area on Stewart. The concourse plan included construction of a centrally located stadium that could be used for athletic events, meetings, plays, or concerts. The area around the planned arena would be divided into four distinct shopping areas with specific design themes. Large and small shops with wide corridors for shoppers would consume most of the available space, but there would also be large common areas for gathering and relaxing.

With its close proximity to the new Frontier Zone, it was a sure bet that Stewart would eventually become a major freight hub. Some freight haulers wouldn't travel into the Frontier Zone, so this would be an ideal location for their hub. Short-haul freighters who were unafraid of traveling in the frontier, or were at least willing to do so for the substantially higher financial rewards, could pick up and deliver cargo to the hub, while the long-haul freighters would bring food and manufactured goods, and return with ore and special products not available closer to the center of Alliance territory.

Arriving at her quarters after the end of the workday, Jenetta was delighted to find that she had personal messages waiting. She sat down at her desk and selected the one from her mom first.

"Hello, dear. I just had to send you a message right away. All the news channels are talking about you again. Space Command just released a story about how with just a scout ship you captured an entire Raider base near the new frontier. They say you destroyed sixteen Raider warships and took almost seven thousand prisoners, then defended the base during two attempts to retake it by Raider cruisers and destroyers while waiting for reinforcements to arrive. The news announcer has said that GAC has designated the base as a Space Command Base and that you've been named as the Base Commander. I'm so proud of you, honey, but I'm worried about you. You always seem to be right in the middle of the most dangerous situations.

"I've sent notes to your brothers and sisters, but they probably know already. I guess I won't be seeing you again for a while with you being so far away, but I know you'll come home for a visit when you can.

"There's the timer. Take care of yourself, dear. I guess things will be much quieter for you now that you're posted on a base. I love you. Bye."

As expected, the message from her father was quite a bit different.

"Hi, honey. I'm so proud of you I could bust. I'm working on the base again while I wait for my ship to be refitted and re-commissioned, and you're the main topic of conversation everywhere I go. Everyone is talking about your coup and speculating on how you might have accomplished it. There's also some talk about your scout ship not being a scout ship at all but rather some new secret weapon, although I haven't been able to get any specifics. Some officers claim to have heard that you broke the theoretical speed barrier wide open, while others are saying that your ship is indestructible. I think some people just can't believe that one person could do the things you've been doing, and they're looking for some other explanation. It's about time Supreme Headquarters realized that if you can accomplish the things you do with old freighters and scout ships, they should give you a destroyer to command instead of a base. Our best line officers should be on the bridge of a ship, not negotiating contracts with merchants looking for shop space.

"My time is almost up so I have to close. Take care of yourself, honey, and keep pounding the Raiders at every opportunity. I love you."

The other messages were from Billy, Richie, Jimmy, Andy, Eliza, and Christa, all congratulating Jenetta on the victory and her new posting. They all talked about the news being on all the channels and how they wished they could be there to help defend the new base. Christa, aboard the *Chiron*, was the only one actually aboard a ship presently headed for Stewart.

Jenetta was having a meeting in her office a couple of weeks later with Lieutenant Jacoby, her engineering chief, when he raised the issue of the captured Raider ships.

"They're just sitting there anchored to the far wall, Commander."

"What are you proposing, Derrick?"

"That we bring them back to the airlocks for examination. Each should be thoroughly checked and certified. Space Command might want to use them, or sell them."

"Well, we do have forty kilometers of airlock piers with only two in use, so I don't have any objection to bringing them back over and putting them down at the far end. We don't want to put a lot of money and effort into repairing them though."

"We should pick one or two of the best and keep them for the station's use, Commander. You never know when we might need a ship for some special purpose, such as a rescue mission."

"I don't know if I'd trust any of them. Most have just two layers of titanium plating and no self-sealing membrane. One hit from a laser array and you're dead if you're in the damaged section without an EVA suit. And a couple of torpedo strikes can blow the ship to pieces, as evidenced by the fates of the *Space Witch* and *Space Titan*."

"Some of them are built better than others. You destroyed all the ships that had stern torpedoes, but most of these at least have bow torpedoes."

"I suppose it won't hurt to look them over and prepare a fitness report on each if you have time. You'll have to assign some people to pack up and store personal possessions of the former crews."

"Aye, Commander. Everything on the station is running fine, and it will give my people something to keep them busy until the Quartermaster Corps can deliver the building materials we requested for the shopping concourse. We'll start this week."

"Okay, Derrick. Thank you. Dismissed."

Chapter Thirteen

~ February 10th, 2274 ~

The *Scorpion* entered orbit around Scruscotto a few weeks after leaving Stewart. With no coordinated planetary approach or departure control on the planet, each ship was on its own until it started to descend to the surface. It wasn't uncommon to find planets without such control operations, but the traffic into and out of orbit at this one was considerably heavier than most uncontrolled planets. Even the final descent was dangerous since ground control exercised no real control. It simply tried to keep other ships informed about ships landing or taking off during an announced ascent or descent. It was early morning on the area of the planet where they were headed, so Trader Vyx moved the small ship into position to land and waited until a ground controller suggested that it might possibly be safe to begin entry into atmo. The controller wished them luck before signing off.

With Vyx flying left seat and Nelligen in the right, Byers was forced to use the one jump seat on the tiny bridge of the ship as it followed an approach lane down to Weislik Space Port. After safely landing the craft on its assigned pad, Vyx shut down the *Scorpion's* engines and sat back in his seat to take a deep breath and relax for a few minutes.

"I'm going to pay our landing fees and see what information I can pick up around the port office," Vyx said finally. "Someone has to restock our food supplies and someone has to get us checked into the hotel. You guys decide who does which."

"I'll take care of the hotel rooms," Byers said.

"Okay, I'll restock the food," Nelligen said, smiling. "That way I get to pick what I like."

"Just take it real easy on the hot and spicy," Byers said. "My delicate stomach can't take any more of those flame-thrower dishes you like."

"I'll pick up some senior citizen meal packs for you. You know, the ones with lots of bland oatmeal and custard."

"Some regular dinner packs will be sufficient, thank you. But speaking of custard, get some snack packs also."

"Why don't you *both* order up the supplies?" Vyx suggested as he stood up. "That way I won't have to listen to the same argument before every meal." He walked from the bridge and headed for the airlock, stopping to pull his oxygen support equipment out of a storage locker on the way. A half century of terra-forming effort had created a marginal planetary atmosphere on Scruscotto. It was thin and just barely qualified as breathable, so he slung the small unit over his shoulder. Contained in a soft bag about the size of newborn infant, the unit pulled oxygen from the atmosphere and supplemented what the body was able to draw on its own. A thin tube clipped onto the nose and released oxygen as the body needed it. The release was minimal unless the wearer had overexerted himself.

The planet's vast mineral resources justified the enormous expense of the terraforming operations that were slowly creating the atmosphere, but it would be many more decades before the oxygen levels compared favorably even to the grossly polluted atmosphere in Earth's major cities during the late twentieth and early twenty-first centuries. Each mine contributed a percentage of its gross income to support the operations because a breathable atmosphere made it easier to get good workers and keep them. An entire daily shift in full facemask breathing equipment wasn't fun, but an entire daily shift in a full EVA suit was nothing less than complete misery, not to mention being far less productive.

Vyx cycled through the ship's airlock and walked down the ramp, feeling the slightly lighter gravity of the planet as soon as he stepped over the hatch threshold. He found himself taking longer strides than normal as he moved to the terminal building despite the thinner air. The terminal was a sealed building, and after entering through an airlock, Vyx found normal Terran gravity and oxygen levels inside. He followed the signs to the port administration section.

As with most port-of-entry offices, there was a large waiting area filled with dozens of sleazy characters looking for an opportunity to turn a profit or just pick up some useful information. The attention of everyone in the room shifted to Vyx as he entered the office and stepped up to the counter. Every ear in the room was attuned to his voice as he explained who he was and paid his landing fee plus pad rent for a full week. After receiving his receipt, Vyx turned back towards the waiting room. The room's occupants immediately returned to whatever they had been doing before he entered, pretending they hadn't been straining to hear every word that passed between him and the clerk at the counter.

Vyx took time now to appraise each individual in the room as he walked through the seating area. About half the room's occupants were Terrans, but there were also Cheblooks, Nordakians, Wolkerrons, Alyysians, Tsgardis, Arrosians, and even a single Pledgian. It was unusual to see a Pledgian since they rarely left their home world. The short, furry creatures came from a society that wasn't technologically advanced and so were totally dependent on transportation from the advanced species. To Vyx, they appeared like a large, fur-covered ball. Their limbs only extended when they needed to move, so at rest they were completely round, with two eyestalks sticking up if they were awake. If Space Command suddenly began enforcing the ban on trading with planets having no space travel capability, sightings of Pledgians would quickly become even rarer than they were currently. This one must have paid a trader or freighter captain to bring him here, and Vyx wryly wondered where it stored its credits and documents since it wore no clothing and carried no bags.

Finding a vacant seat, he eased his almost six-foot frame into the chair, hanging his portable breathing bag on the side. He could tell fairly easily who the long-time residents were in the room because most scoffed at the use of portable units.

Their bodies had become accustomed to the thin atmosphere on this planet and they were quite comfortable without any supplemental oxygen. But miners, even long-time resident miners, often carried full rebreather backpacks because their level of exertion required much higher levels of oxygen than the breathing bags could possibly provide.

Picking up a newspaper lying on the seat next to his as he settled in, he saw that it was in Amer and only a week old, so he passed the next several hours watching the coming and goings as he read up on the news of the colony. Like the others in the room, he noted the arrival and departure of every ship by watching the monitors mounted around the room. He didn't really expect to find a lead to Rivemwilth here, but one never knew.

As the afternoon hours passed, Vyx's stomach reminded him that he hadn't eaten since breakfast, so he stood up, stretched, and strode out. Every pair of eyes in the room watched the departure of the dangerous-looking stranger who moved with the easy grace of a wild animal.

Returning to his ship, Vyx found Byers and Nelligen putting away the food stores in the galley.

"We stored the rest in the hold," Byers explained.

"Do we have rooms?" Vyx asked.

"Yes, three rooms at the Weislik Grand Hotel."

"What say we head over and get settled, then find a good place to eat? I'm tired of food packs and synthesized food."

"Sounds fine to me," Byers said, "Nels was planning on having some hot dish with cheese, onions, and peppers. My stomach was bothering me just thinking about it."

"I guess I can wait for another day to have that," Nelligen said, grinning. "Let's go."

An hour later, they were sitting in a restaurant that advertised itself as having the best steaks on the planet. Most of the steaks were cuts of Cheblookan Daitwa, a sort of horse-like creature, but with enough credits one could get real Terran beef. They had moved into their rooms in the hotel and cleaned up a bit before going in search of a restaurant, deciding upon this establishment after seeing the image of a Terran steer on the menu posted out front.

As the waitress cleared the dinner dishes and brought fresh tankards of the local ale, a tall Wolkerron stepped up to the table.

"Welcome to Scruscotto, gentlemen," the thin, Hominidae-like creature with a long yellow face and enormous, jet-black eyes said.

"Are you the planet's official welcoming committee, Wolkerron?" Vyx asked warily.

The Wolkerron offered what passed as his specie's equivalent of a grin, which looked menacing to the uninitiated. "I'm but a humble tradesman, sir."

"And what are you selling tonight?"

"Employment, gentlemen, employment. Might you be looking for jobs?"

"I'm Trader Vyx. I'm always looking for a deal or a trade but never a job."

"Perhaps I can put you together with a buyer or seller then. Filling mining jobs is not my only occupation. I also function as a trade broker. In fact, I'm the main broker in this city. Might I be invited to join you?"

Vyx looked at Byers and Nelligen, then nodded his head towards the bar. The two men understood the movement and stood up to move.

"Sit down, Wolkerron."

"Call me Ker. I'm Ker Blasperra."

"Very well, Ker."

"And what sort of deal or trade are you looking for, Trader?"

"With a few exceptions, almost anything that will yield a profit, Ker."

"If one is— flexible, there are always deals to be made. What sort of merchandise have you been handling lately?"

"My last deal involved purchasing arms from Shev Rivemwilth and selling them to a party that shall naturally remain nameless."

"Shev Rivemwilth? That's quite a recommendation. I trust that your deal with the Shev went well?"

"He was satisfied. He approached me again when he was moving his operation from Gollasko, but I wasn't in a position to take on anything at that time. I needed to move my own operation out of the territory."

"Yes, Space Command's expansion has proved most unsettling for a number of honest traders, but it has provided me with a small bonanza of opportunities. Have you ever considered working for the Raiders? If your references check out, I can place you with them almost immediately."

"I don't work for others."

"This would be strictly on a contractual basis. They've lost so many people to the Galactic Alliance in recent years that they're desperate for good, dependable people."

"What's the job?"

"Spotter. You take your ship where they tell you and observe ship movements. You spend five months on station and then get one month off before they assign you elsewhere."

"Sounds boring. It's not for me."

"It pays very well, very well indeed."

"Nope, not for me. The way Space Command is knocking off Raiders, I don't want any involvement that might make the Spaccs think I'm one of them. Is that all you have?"

"A wise and all too familiar sentiment lately," Ker Blasperra said as he reached into a pocket and brought out a notebook. As he flipped through several pages, he said, "A lot of these jobs are too big for your small ship."

"What do you know about my ship?"

"Trader, please, it's my business to know such things. I can tell you what pad the *Scorpion* is on, precisely what time you landed, and approximately how much cargo space you have available."

"And if I had a larger ship?"

"Well, I have a party looking to transport a cargo of slaves and another looking to send a shipment of Melwen powder to Crisce-Six."

"No slaves; you can't jettison your cargo if Space Command takes an interest in boarding you. How much Melwen powder?"

"Two thousand tons."

"Two thousand tons? Of a powder that explodes if the temperature varies too quickly? You can't even jettison it unless you've kept it frozen."

"That's why regular freighters won't transport it, but it pays very well. It might as well be two thousand tons as one ton."

"I don't mind risking my neck, but I'm not suicidal."

"Your ship is too small anyway."

"I can get a larger ship if I need it. But only for the right deal."

"How big a ship?"

"Oh, say about eight hundred fifty meters."

"Well, that's a different matter entirely! Why didn't you say so before? The ship you came down in is just your shuttle then?"

"No, it's my personal ship. But I could get the larger ship if I needed it."

"You mean steal one?"

"Yes, but none that will be missed. I might be persuaded to take the risk if the price were right."

"And where could you steal an eight-hundred-fifty-meter ship that won't be missed? Is it space worthy?"

"You've no doubt heard that Space Command seized a base from the Raiders recently?"

"Everyone knows that. It's only a few weeks from here, just over the border in regulated Alliance space."

"I stopped there on my way here to have a look around. They have a couple of dozen seized ships ripe for the plucking just sitting there in a storage area. Space Command won't use 'em because they don't have enough hull integrity for fighting, but the ships are fine for simple cargo duty."

"You're crazy if you think you could sneak an eight-hundred-fifty-meter ship out from under the noses of Space Command."

"Not so crazy. They're still all fouled up over there trying to organize the base. They're guarding almost seven thousand Raider prisoners, and they're severely short-handed until ships with more personnel arrive. Besides, their systems are designed to protect against outside attack. They'll never be expecting someone to sneak a ship out that they consider useless. I, uh, also have a contact on the inside who'll help me get the ship past the automatic port sensors."

"If you could get a ship that large, I have a dozen jobs I could offer you. I even have a listing from Shev Rivemwilth. He's looking to move his entire warehouse out of regulated Alliance space. He's desperate to transport everything into the Frontier Zone before Space Command locates his old base."

Vyx's attention had jumped up several notches at the mention of Rivemwilth's name, but he'd made no obvious outward signs. "I thought he kept everything on Gollasko."

"Not hardly. He only kept a small sample of his merchandise there. Even if you can get a ship as large as the one you say, it'll be difficult to fit everything in it from the way he described his warehouse to me."

"I can get it. What's the pay?"

"At Light-187, it'll take eight months to transport the cargo. The entire trip from here, loading, transport, unloading, and return should take about a year and a half, and you'll spend four months traveling in regulated GA space with a full cargo of illegal weapons. The pay is five hundred thousand credits."

"That's not a bad payday. Can you set it up?"

"I'll contact him right away if you feel positive that you can complete the contract. We should have an answer in a few days."

"I'll get the ship. Who pays you?"

"Shev Rivemwilth will deposit the contracted amount with me as the party listing the job as soon as I advise him that you've offered your services. That is, if he also accepts. When the contract is complete, I'll transfer the entire amount into whatever account you name. My commission comes from having the entire amount on deposit with my banker for a year and a half."

"I see. That's makes things nice and simple. You collect the interest on the money but can't be accused of accepting payment for any misdeeds should you ever be captured by Space Command because you turn over every penny of the arranged price."

"Yes, very simple and very clean." Ker Blasperra paused for a few seconds. "I feel that I should warn you, though. If you accept this contract and then fail to secure the ship, it would be best if you never show your face in this part of space again. Shev Rivemwilth has no patience with failure."

"I understand. Goodnight, Ker."

"Goodnight, Trader."

Byers and Nelligen returned to the table as soon as Blasperra was gone.

"What's up?" Byers asked.

"It looks like we're back in business already. Let's head back to the hotel and I'll tell you about it."

Vyx, Byers, and Nelligen spent the next several days infusing themselves into the rough fraternity of spaceport dwellers at Weislik. Occasionally they even ran into someone they knew from the Gollasko Colony. Each received a number of propositions for nefarious activities, most coming from two-bit hustlers looking to turn a credit in this new environment. If Ker Blasperra had the contacts he claimed, they needn't look for further offers, but their job was to collect information, so they listened carefully to every offer while not appearing to be listening very carefully or appearing too interested.

On the fourth day following their arrival, they stood at a bar drinking the house ale while trying very hard not to stare at the four Milora at the other end of the bar. A very ugly species by Terran standards, the home world of the warlike Milori race was roughly eight hundred light-years beyond the new outer border of GA space. Totally intolerant of Terrans in their own territory, it was highly unusual to see them outside their own borders. About the average height of Terrans, Milora were covered with a dense, brown, stringy hair that completely covered their body. They had what passed for two arms, ending not with hands but rather with what would more accurately be described as gripper claws, as might be found on a terran crab or lobster. Additionally, they had four tentacles. It was probably this fact that upset Terrans so much. The body hair completely concealed their tentacles when at rest, but it was said that they could dart out to coil around a person and then crush them to death, as would a boa constrictor on Earth. Four eyes offered Milora superior peripheral vision.

Vyx, Byers, and Nelligen were just about to leave when Ker Blasperra arrived and approached them.

"Gentlemen, it's a pleasure to meet you again."

"Hello, Ker," Vyx said.

Byers and Nelligen just nodded.

"If you gentlemen will excuse me, I'd like to speak with the Trader," Blasperra said.

"There're no secrets here, Ker," Vyx said. "They know everything. You can speak freely."

"Very well, Trader. I've been in contact with Shev Rivemwilth and he has accepted your offer." Reaching into his pocket, he took out a sealed envelope. "Here're the coordinates where you're to go, along with the route you're to follow precisely for the final month of travel. There's also a frequency and scramble code, and a code word to send when you're ten days from the final location. A ship will meet you there and lead you to where the arms are stored. Make sure you're not being followed or the other ship won't show. They'll have spotters watching you along the way. Give them a full day after you reach the destination. If no one shows, contact me. My frequency and encryption code are listed also."

"And the money?"

"It's been deposited with me. If you fail to show, I'll have to return it." Looking at Vyx ominously, he said, "I don't like returning payments, so don't let me down."

"We'll be there if we're not dead or in a Space Command brig."

"If you're dead, all will be forgiven."

"But not if we're simply jailed?"

"Shev Rivemwilth believes that people try harder if they know their lives are on the line. A Space Command brig won't spare you from his wrath. It will only delay the inevitable. Until the contract is fulfilled, he considers you his employees."

"It's nice to know where you stand," Byers said calmly. "Sort of comforting to know how much he cares," he added sardonically.

"Uh— yes," Ker Blasperra said uncertainly. Wolkerrons didn't understand the subtlety of Terran sarcasm. "Gentlemen, I bid you goodbye and good luck. If you're successful, I'll see you in about a year and a half."

"We'll see you again, Ker," Vyx said. "Just be sure you don't lose track of our payment."

Vyx and his two associates stayed around Weislik for another day before pre-flighting the *Scorpion* and preparing to leave the planet. When word spread they were departing, they were inundated with requests from people looking for a ride. They responded to all requests with the simple comment that all passengers would have to share their quarters with a dozen crates of Melwen powder. At the mere mention of the highly volatile substance, each requestor suddenly lost interest in hitching a ride. After filing their request for departure, they had to wait patiently for almost two hours before being given clearance by the spaceport control center to lift off.

The small craft achieved orbit without a problem and then was almost struck by an arriving freighter that had set up a similar orbit track. After a few heart-stopping minutes and some fancy maneuvering by Vyx at the controls of the *Scorpion*, both craft were established in their orbits with a mere hundred meters of separation. Given the three-kilometer size of the freighter, it might have appeared to an outside observer that they were linked.

Vyx performed the flight calculations using the Gollasko Colony as their destination, and the small ship moved out of orbit. The destination was designed to confuse anyone trying to track them, and they'd follow that course for a week before altering course to Stewart Space Command Base. The phony destination would only cost them about a day of extra travel.

* * *

Seven days out of Scruscotto, Vyx altered course for Stewart. The time alone on the bridge was calming, and he spent several hours there before returning to the lounge where Byers and Nelligen were playing cards. During the past week, the pair had spent most of their waking hours playing cards, watching recorded sporting events, or arguing about the food preparation. Vyx preferred to read, but the lounge was the only comfortable place to relax except for his bunk, and he didn't enjoy lying in bed all day. The anti-collision alarm would alert them in time to react if danger appeared ahead and even drop them out of FTL if they didn't react quickly enough.

At four billion kilometers from Stewart, Vyx dropped his envelope and engaged his sub-light engines to Sub-Light-100. FTL speeds were always prohibited by any inbound ship at a Space Command Base. It would be too dangerous to suddenly appear at the asteroid because, aside from the danger of impact with other ships arriving or departing, there was the danger of being fired upon by defensive weapons. Since the Battle for Higgins, any unannounced ship suddenly appearing within twenty-five thousand kilometers would be immediately targeted by every phased array laser on the station. Once identified, approach control would establish an approach vector for the vessel. There wouldn't be any danger of collision or defensive fire if the ship didn't deviate from their assigned approach path and speeds.

When Vyx contacted the base, they gave him approach instructions and told him to reduce his speed first to Sub-Light-10 at the outer pattern marker (fifty million km), then to Plus-100 at the inner marker (ten thousand km).

A shuttle with an inspection crew met them when they finally arrived at Stewart. A mandatory examination was required of every vessel before being allowed inside. The *Scorpion* was scanned for potentially explosive or bio-hazardous materials. It passed cleanly, in spite of Byers sarcastic comments about the volatility of Nelligen's food stores. Approach control then directed them to a vacant docking pier where they would be met by a port operations officer.

After completing the dock and lock, Vyx walked to the entry bay hatch and waited until the airlock tunnel was fully pressurized and certified. As he was opening the ship's door, a port worker was opening the door at the other end of the ramp tunnel. A light whooshing noise could be heard as the slight pressure variances equalized. Lieutenant Graham, the Port Officer, stood by as Vyx walked to the docking platform where he was required to hand over his identity papers for examination.

"Good day, Trader," Graham said, "what's the purpose of your visit to Stewart Space Command Base this time?"

"We just stopped by to see if your civilian operations were established yet."

"We have civilian housing accommodations available but little else. The civilian concourse is under construction, but at present there are only several temporary offices and one temporary restaurant open."

"Then we'd like to arrange for housing accommodations."

"Contact the base housing officer in the base commander's office. Do you have anything to declare in the way of restricted cargo?"

"Nope. We're empty. You're welcome to check."

"We will. I'll have someone escort you to the base commander's office."

"No need. I know the way to Commander Carver's office. She is still the base commander, isn't she?"

"Yes."

"Thank you. One of my associates will show you anything onboard that you wish to see."

Vyx walked to Jenetta's office and stopped at Lieutenant Ashraf's desk. "Good afternoon, Lieutenant."

"Good Afternoon. Trader Vyx, isn't it?"

"Yes, you have a good memory. Is the Commander in?"

"Yes. Let me see if she's available to see you." Lieutenant Ashraf pushed a button on her com unit and said, "Trader Vyx would like a few minutes of your time, ma'am."

"Send him in, Lori," appeared on Lieutenant Ashraf's screen in response to Jenetta's spoken words. The com panel was not visible to Vyx.

"You may go in, Trader," the lieutenant said.

Vyx walked to the door and stepped inside, stopping as the two large cats raised their heads, sniffed the air, and looked at him like he was part of the evening's dinner selections. They were always more alert to someone not wearing a Space Command uniform.

"Cayla, Tayna, you remember Trader Vyx," Jenetta said softly.

As the cats relaxed, Vyx walked over to the desk.

"Have a seat, Trader. I'm surprised to see you so soon. It's only been about two months, hasn't it?"

"Nine weeks. Eight weeks of travel and one week on Scruscotto."

"I assume things either went very well or very badly."

"Very well, I think. I was hired to move a large cache of illegal arms for a certain notorious arms dealer."

"Rivemwilth?"

Vyx grinned. "Exactly. Good guess."

"It wasn't so hard. He's one of the most notorious *and* the focus of your case."

"It's amazing how things happen. I was racking my brain trying to figure out how I was going to get that toad back into my sights when this deal fell into my lap."

"How large is the cache?"

"Rivemwilth is moving his *entire* operation into the new Frontier Zone. I got the job by promising I could provide an eight-hundred-fifty-meter transport."

"And you want me to provide the ship?"

"Yes," he said, smiling. "Can you help me out?"

"For an opportunity to confiscate his entire cache of weapons, I'm sure we can. How will you explain having the ship?"

"I told the broker that I'm going to steal it. I said things are so fouled up over here that I could sneak it out under your very nose. I told him I have a contact on the inside who will arrange for our departure clearance."

"Not a very flattering endorsement of myself or my staff," Jenetta said, smiling.

"I did explain how shorthanded you are and how you have almost seven thousand Raider prisoners to guard."

"What's your plan after you have the ship?"

"We'll go to the base and load up. On the leg of the trip that takes us towards the Frontier, I'll send you a message and you arrange for us to be stopped for inspection. I'll sabotage the ship so we can't make a run for it."

"That's a dangerous plan. You could get killed if Rivemwilth makes a fight of it. The big transports we got from the Raiders aren't well protected."

"As long as your people don't hit the bridge, my associates and I will be safe. Just make sure the corridor doors on the ship you select all close tightly in the event of a pressure drop."

"It would be better if you rigged the torpedoes so they can't explode. That way the Space Command ships wouldn't feel as compelled to return fire. Better yet, why don't we just move in and take the arms cache *before* it's loaded?"

"They haven't told me where it is yet. I only have directions for a rendezvous point, and they'll have spotters watching to make sure we're not followed. We have to give ten day's notice before arriving at the RP, so the cache could be ten days away, or even much more. It could even be at multiple locations."

"We'll put a tracking device in the ship so we can follow your movements."

"I can't risk them discovering a signal."

"They won't discover it. We'll set it to transmit just a single pulse every few hours on a rotating frequency. We can even have the time vary so a pattern can't be discovered. If they do happen to pick up one pulse, they'll think it was a reflection or an anomaly when it doesn't repeat. I'll make sure no one moves in closer than ten billion kilometers, but when you call they'll be there in about three minutes."

"Okay, I can live with that. But don't under any circumstances move in until I call."

"You've got it. Let's go look at the available ships."

"I can't be seen with you, Commander. There are civilians on this station who might pass on such information for a price. I came to your office under the pretext of getting rooms for myself and my associates."

"I see." Jenetta leaned forward and pressed a button on her com. "Lori, please arrange for three rooms in the civilian housing section in the name of Trader Vyx."

As the words appeared on Lieutenant Ashraf's com screen, she responded with, "Aye, Commander. He can pick up the card keys on the way out."

"Thank you," Jenetta said before punching a few keys on her computer terminal. Scanning the display as she leaned back in her chair, she said to Vyx, "Okay, Trader, you're all set with your housing. In my opinion, the ship at docking pier 4-Sierra, the *Maid of Mephad*, appears to suit your stated purpose best. It's the biggest we have and it has several enormous holds with easy access, but I'll leave the choice up to you. As soon as you decide which ship you want, I'll have my chief engineer, Lieutenant Jacoby, install the tracking device. He's checked the ships over and declared all of them spaceworthy, except for the one at docking pier 4-Tango, the *Baroness*. He says he wouldn't trust that ship for any duty other than as an unmanned marker buoy. He can help you if you have any questions or need any assistance. I'm sure you can think up some pretext for being seen with him. Tell people you were having a problem with your ship or something and needed his advice."

"Thank you, Commander."

"You're welcome. Good luck, Trader."

Vyx picked up the card keys on the way past Lieutenant Ashraf's desk. Upon entering the room for the first time, the room's occupant could record a thumbprint or a voiceprint to be used to open the door for the remainder of the stay. Vyx asked Lieutenant Ashraf to locate Lieutenant Jacoby and then arranged with him to come to Vyx's ship in an hour.

Arriving a few minutes early, Lieutenant Jacoby refused a beverage but accepted a seat in the ship's lounge.

"Lieutenant, I need your help," Vyx said.

"Commander Carver has briefed me that you need to borrow one of our Raider ships without anyone else knowing you borrowed it, sir. She says you have a very large cargo of special equipment to move."

"Good. That makes things easier. She recommended the ship at docking pier 4-Sierra."

"That would be my choice as well. Most of the *Maid* is devoted to large storage holds, but there're crew accommodations for up to twenty-five. The engines are in excellent shape, and you won't have any trouble maintaining Light-187. The ship can easily be handled by two crewmen. If the hull plating were better, it would make an excellent short-haul ship for the Quartermaster Corps."

"Excellent. How soon can it be ready to go?"

"It's ready now. The Commander wants me to install a special tracking device though."

"I have a couple of things I'd like installed as well. Let's go look at the ship."

Ten minutes later, Vyx and Jacoby were in a transport car zipping through the outbound tube that ran along the docking platform to the remotest part of the cavern. Stretching some forty kilometers, the tube passed the dozens of empty piers in Sections One, Two, and Three. The commandeered Raider ships were all arranged along the piers in Section Four.

It was just after 0300 hours two days later when the *Maid of Mephad* released its docking clamps and backed away from pier 4-Sierra. Except for the controller who issued clearance to leave the port, Vyx doubted that anyone else paid any attention to their departure.

Once clear of the base, Vyx built the temporal envelope, and the ship disappeared from visual sight of the station in seconds. The course had been entered into the computer, and there would be little to do over the next four months except relax and find ways to pass the time. The enormous ship gave Vyx numerous places where he could get away from Byers and Nelligen when he wanted a little peace and solitude to read. Having crew accommodations for twenty-five meant that there were no fewer than three social or gathering areas. And if that wasn't enough, there were always the cargo holds.

Jenetta had prepared and transmitted a message to Captain Kanes after her meeting with Vyx in which she gave a detailed report of their conversation and the action she had taken in turning over the ship. Vyx would be gone for days before she received a reply, but there were still things to be done. Ships would have to be diverted from patrol or other missions so they would be on station and ready when Vyx called for them. Jenetta knew the opportunity to capture Rivemwilth, or at least confiscate his entire inventory of weapons, would receive the highest priority at the Intelligence Section.

A reply from Captain Kanes arrived sixteen days after Vyx had left the base. Jenetta lifted her com screen and pressed the play button. A retinal scan was required to unscramble the message, and the face of Captain Kanes appeared after the computer was satisfied as to her identity.

"Hello, Jen. Your action was correct in providing the ship to Vyx. Space Command has dispatched two ships, the *Ottawa* and the *Geneva*, to points where they can monitor the *Maid's* approach to the rendezvous coordinates you sent. They'll lay off ten billion kilometers and monitor the movement of the ship using the electronic signal from the tracking device.

I've named you as director of this operation because you're familiar with the investigation and are best suited to coordinate the activity. Captains Pope and Crosby will make their reports to you, and then you'll report to me.

"Captain Kanes, SCI, Higgins SCB, message complete."

Chapter Fourteen
~ May 14th, 2274 ~

Managing the base consumed virtually all Jenetta's time and attention, so she didn't have time to dwell on Vyx's operation as the months passed. Her one diversion was the time she allocated to sending messages to her sisters, brothers, parents, new sisters-in-law, and friends. But because of the distances involved, she'd normally send two more messages before getting answers to questions raised in an earlier one. At the end of each day as she walked wearily into her quarters, she always checked immediately to see if there were any personal messages waiting. When there were, they never failed to lift her spirits.

Her mom was now home alone since her father was back on active duty in command of an older, retrofitted cruiser. The *Octavian*, named after the Roman emperor who ruled from 27 BC to 14 AD, was assigned patrol duties in deca-sector 8667-3179. Since that was hundreds of light-years on the other side of earth and it took weeks to receive answers to messages, they avoided asking trivial questions that would be forgotten before an answer could be received. Jenetta sent messages to her mom at least three times a week, hoping that the constant stream of news would help keep her from being so lonely with everyone else off in space. At least she had Richie's wife, Marisa, nearby. Jenetta also sent at least one message each week to her brothers, sisters, sisters-in-law, and father, and did her best to keep in touch with friends and former shipmates. Rarely did a day pass without a message arriving from someone, and frequently she would have several come in the same day.

More than four and a half months had passed since Jenetta had been appointed base commander of Stewart. By that time at Dixon, the base was already a thriving community of Space Command and civilian personnel, but not so at Stewart. The dangers of traveling in the former Frontier Zone had previously kept such travel to a minimum. Although safer now that another Raider Base had been neutralized and Space Command had started patrolling the territory, travel was still minimal this close to the new border. Jenetta knew that wouldn't last forever, so she kept pushing ahead with her plans for developing the station. The building supplies discovered in storage areas of the station and in containers in the port had allowed the engineers to make great progress. The concourse was far from complete, but the first block of stores was shaping up nicely and should be ready for partial occupancy by the time civilian entrepreneurs arrived to set up their businesses.

Several ships underway to Stewart for as long as eight months were getting closer with each new day. Carrying personnel and supplies for the new station, they were the ships so hastily equipped and dispatched soon after Space Command learned of the base's seizure by the tiny *Colorado*. One of the first to arrive would be the *Chiron*, which had happened to be in port at Dixon when the *Colorado* sent the seizure message. Jenetta was more excited about seeing her sister Christa than she was about the replacement personnel and supplies the ship was carrying. The *Chiron* was close enough now that replies to messages sent to Christa could come in hours.

* * *

As the *Maid of Mephad* reached the rendezvous point, Vyx brought the ship to a halt. Ten days earlier he had sent a message that would alert the people who would lead them to the arms cache location. There wasn't anyone waiting, so Vyx set the sensors to summon him if any ships were DeTect'd approaching. He then joined Byers and Nelligen, who were playing cards in the main lounge.

"No one here," Vyx said. "I guess we wait."

"They're probably watching to see if anyone tailed us," Byers said.

"You don't survive long in their business by being stupid," Nelligen quipped as he dealt the cards.

"Nor in ours," Vyx said as he sighed.

"Any changes in the plan?" Byers asked.

"No," Vyx responded, "no changes. We load the ship and get underway for the new base. After a few days I send the message to Space Command, and they move to block our path. Our anti-collision system will shut down the light engines and Space Command will take the ship. As I promised Commander Carver, I've removed all the detonation triggers so the torpedoes won't explode, and I've sabotaged the laser control system so it will overheat after only a few shots and then cycle down. The Space Command ships won't have to return fire."

"And Space Command won't move in until we summon them?" Nelligen asked.

"That's the plan. They wait until they hear from us. Until then they stay at least ten billion kilometers away."

"And they're out there now?" Byers asked.

"I assume so. I don't think either Commander Carver or Captain Kanes would leave us swinging in the breeze. But we won't know until we yell for help."

"But just for argument's sake, what if they don't show when we call?" Nelligen asked.

"We play it by ear. I'm sure Rivemwilth isn't going to trust us alone with his entire cache, so he'll want some of his people on board. For one thing, we don't know how many will be on the ship, and, for another, we don't know how closely they'll be watching us."

* * *

"Commander, you have a message from Captain Crosby of the *Ottawa*."

"Thank you, Lori. Pass it through."

Jenetta raised her com screen and pressed the play button. The face of Captain Crosby appeared.

"Good morning, Jen. Using triangulating information provided by the *Geneva* and Stewart, we've determined that the target has come to a stop at the coordinates you provided. We'll maintain the ten-billion-kilometer distance until they summon us or we receive new orders from you.

"Jeffrey Crosby, Captain of the GSC Destroyer *Ottawa*, message complete."

Jenetta hit the record button to send a reply. Captain Crosby should receive the message in about twenty hours.

"To Captain Crosby, GSC *Ottawa*, from Commander Carver, Stewart SCB. Begin message.

"Thank you for the update, Captain. Good luck.

"Jenetta Carver, Commander, Stewart GSC Base, message complete."

* * *

The *Maid of Mephad* sat at the RP for more than eighteen hours before a space tug arrived and approached without apparent hesitation, then docked to a starboard bow airlock. Byers and Nelligen watched the airlock door with weapons drawn as Vyx operated the controls and opened the door. A slovenly-looking Terran with several days of beard growth stepped into the *Maid* carrying a small backpack over his arm.

"I'm Wagner," he said causally, with seeming disregard for the weapons pointed at him. "Any of you Trader Vyx?"

"I'm Vyx." Pointing to each of the others as he introduced them, he said, "That's Nelligen and that's Byers."

"Hi, fellahs. I'm here to escort you to the base."

"Okay, we're ready whenever you are."

"I'd just like to get cleaned up a little before we go. Mind if I take a shower? I don't have one onboard the tug and I haven't felt clean for days. We have quite a trip ahead of us."

"Sure. What's in the bag?"

"Clean clothes," Wagner said, holding the pack out. "See for yourself if you want."

Vyx nodded towards Byers, who took the pack and looked inside.

"Just clothes and hygiene gear," he said, handing the pack back.

"Byers will show you to the crew quarters section where you can take a shower. We'll be ready to leave whenever you are."

"You fellahs sure seem to be in a hurry," Wagner said suspiciously.

"We've been underway for almost *five* months," Nelligen said. "We're just a little antsy to do something except sit around on our spreading backsides."

"Oh, I can understand that, and I only spent nine days in that freakin' little tug. I won't take too long, although I can tell you that I've been looking forward to this for several days."

"Take your time and enjoy your shower," Vyx said. "Another couple of hours isn't going to make any difference."

"Thanks, Trader. That's right neighborly of you."

* * *

Nine days later, the *Maid of Mephad* entered orbit around a small moon with no atmosphere and a greatly reduced gravity. As the tug piloted by Wagner prepared to land on the surface, Vyx and Nelligen climbed into a shuttle aboard the *Maid* to follow him down. Byers would stay aboard the ship and coordinate loading operations.

Vyx piloted the ship into an open flight bay that had been cut into the base of a rocky cliff. When the bay door was closed, or if it wasn't approached just right, it would never be spotted, so it was unlikely that anyone would just happen across it. They waited until the doors had closed and the bay was pressurized before climbing out of their seats and walking to the shuttle hatchway.

A man whom Vyx recognized as being one of Rivemwilth's personal bodyguards was there to meet them as

Vyx and Nelligen climbed down from the shuttle. The man nodded and Vyx returned the nod. Then the man tilted his head to the side, indicating that Vyx and Nelligen should follow. He turned and led the way through a series of brightly lit corridors, at last coming to a door that opened as they approached.

As they entered the ornately furnished room, they found Rivemwilth sitting in an enormous reclining chair surrounded by several of his bodyguards.

"Trader, come in. Welcome to my little castle."

"Hello, Shev. This is my associate, Mr. Nelligen. Nice place you have here."

"Greetings and welcome to you, Mr. Nelligen. Thank you, Trader. I expected this base to last me for the rest of my life, so I spared virtually no expense in its construction. It upsets me greatly to have to leave it. Who could have guessed that the Galactic Alliance would extend their borders by a hundred parsecs when they couldn't even control the space they had claimed before? My new base lacks so many of the creature comforts I've come to enjoy here. It doesn't even have a swimming pool. Ah, well, that's life. I was most surprised when Ker Blasperra contacted me and informed me that *you* were offering to move my merchandise. I had no idea you had the large transport I needed."

"I didn't until I learned of the available contract, but I knew where I could get one. I liberated it from Space Command, who had liberated it from the Raiders."

"And Space Command just let you take it?"

"No, I appropriated it from a storage area. They had no use for the ship so they probably haven't even missed it yet. We got away clean or they would have caught us months ago."

"Very resourceful of you, Trader."

"Just trying to turn a credit, Shev. So, where's the new base?"

"About sixty light-years inside the new Frontier Zone, but there's a lot of work to be done before then. When we've finished loading it, your ship will be full from bow to stern. This complex extends a kilometer into this mountain, and it's almost five hundred meters wide. It has a three-meter-thick reinforced roof, and beyond this living area it's divided into large warehouse chambers with two-meter-thick reinforced walls. In the event that an accident occurred, I wanted to minimize damage to other chambers. Most of the warehouse space is crammed with merchandise. I have almost as much inventory as some of Space Command's smaller supply armories."

"How many people do you have for loading?"

"I have eighteen. You?"

"Just myself and two associates."

"Just three of you?"

"I was asked to ferry the arms to the new base. Blasperra never said I had any responsibility for loading them. I only brought enough crew to handle the ship."

Shev Rivemwilth made a sound that Vyx assumed to be a sigh. "I should have been more explicit in my instructions to Blasperra. Well, that can't be helped now. We'll have to make do. It will just take us longer. Normally that's not a problem, but having a huge transport overhead is like having a sign announcing 'Secret Arms Base Located Here.' We'll just have to work around the clock until everything is loaded."

"We'll do our best, but we're Terrans. If my guys and I don't get at least eight hour's sleep each night, we won't be much good, and it sounds like this will take weeks."

"We'll stagger the schedules so everyone gets their sleep, and we can reduce the artificial gravity to one-sixth g. Each man will feel six times stronger than normal."

"How many tugs do you have, Shev?"

"Two tugs with ten quarter-size containers and one shuttle."

"That's our bottleneck then, since we only have two shuttles. Send six of your men up to my ship to help my guys and me. The rest can load containers or pilot the tugs up to the ship while we unload and pack it in."

"How soon do you want to start?"

"I'd like to have a tour of the warehouse first. I'll be able to direct the loading more efficiently if I have a feel for what's going up."

"Of course. Follow me."

The tour lasted several hours as chamber after chamber was visited. The amount of ordnance was phenomenal. For the first time Vyx began to wonder if the *Maid of Mephad* was going to be able to contain everything. He would have to make sure every cubic foot of hold space was used properly.

"Quite impressive, isn't it, Trader?" Rivemwilth asked at the completion of the tour.

"Staggering, Shev. It's going to be a chore getting it all into the ship though. I suggest you send up your more valuable merchandise first, leaving the least valuable until last just in case."

"You think we might have to leave some behind?"

"We'll pack it so tight that an Aluvian mamot couldn't squeeze into the hold, but it's possible we won't fit everything."

"Damn Blasperra! I told him to get me a ship large enough to carry everything in one load," Rivemwilth said angrily.

"My ship is eight hundred fifty meters in length and entirely constructed around cargo holds. Only the Space Command Quartermaster Corp has larger single-hull transports, and you don't have a chance of getting your hands on one of those. The next option is a freighter using link sections, but then you'd need five hundred empty, full-sized cargo containers as well. It's your call, Shev. Shall we start loading or should I leave?"

"I can't wait any longer. We'll have to take what we can. Make sure you pack your ship from bulkhead to bulkhead, Trader. When do you wish to start loading?"

"Now. We'll head back up as soon as you round up those six men to help on the ship. Send the first containers as soon as they're loaded. Make sure they're loaded with your largest pieces, such as the fighter ships, APCs, and underwater craft. We'll be ready."

*   *   *

All personnel arriving aboard the *Chiron* had been assigned quarters before the ship even docked. Several holds aboard ship had been converted into enormous makeshift dormitories to accommodate the personnel, and most of the replacements couldn't wait to move into their new quarters and get their first real privacy in more than a year. Two hundred replacement Marines would relieve many of those who had been guarding prisoners since Stewart was first taken, and three hundred eighty other SC personnel would relieve personnel on temporary reassignment, allowing them to return to their ships once the replacements had been trained in their new duties.

Jenetta was working at her desk when Lieutenant Ashraf notified her that Lieutenant Christa Carver was in the outer office.

"Send her in, Lori."

Jenetta jumped up from her desk and reached the door just as Christa entered. They hugged like close sisters who hadn't seen each other in a long time. The cats had followed Jenetta and sniffed at Christa, then stood watching the pair. After she and Jenetta finished hugging, Christa bent to pet the large cats.

"Hi Cayla, hi Tayna," Christa said, and the cats purred and mewled in response to the attention, brushing against her legs, pushing her backward a couple of steps until she braced herself against their affections. After a few seconds, she stopped petting them and stood up. The cats took that as a cue to stop rubbing against her and returned to their normal resting spots on each side of the room.

"Come sit down," Jenetta said. "Tell me everything that's been happening."

"You already know all the high points from our messages. The rest is just the normal day-to-day stuff, but I've been waiting almost a year to hear *your* special news. Specifically, how did you get here? One week I get a message from you and you haven't crossed the old border yet, and then two weeks later you're at the border with the new Frontier Zone. How did you travel a hundred parsecs in two weeks when it should have taken you ten months aboard the *Prometheus*?"

"It's classified," Jenetta said innocently and teasingly.

"Come on, this is me— it's almost like talking to yourself, after all. And it's hardly a secret. The rumors are that you were placed in charge of testing some kind of secret new ship."

"The rumors?"

"Sure. Everyone knows somebody who was aboard the *Prometheus* when you left, or knows somebody who knows somebody. You can't keep a thing like this secret when thousands of people know that something really spectacular happened. Everybody knows you did something that's never been done before. You crossed a hundred parsecs of space in two weeks. You *might* have been able to keep the travel quiet if you hadn't then attacked the Raiders and seized another base, intact, with just a crew of a hundred eighty-five. You should have seen the headlines back home. Good thing you're way out here or they'd still be throwing parades in your honor. So the travel isn't a secret. We just don't know how you did it."

"Neither do I, exactly. It wasn't anticipated at all. So far, all we have are theories. The *Colorado* has been sent back for testing so they can define the mechanics of what caused the anomalous speed."

"You're kidding."

"Nope, we were as surprised as anyone when we learned how fast we'd traveled."

"So exactly how fast did you travel?"

"What do the rumors say?"

"Light-9750."

"Close. Actually it was a touch over Light-9790, but we're calling it Light-9790."

"Why did you come so far? If you had only traveled a short distance, you could have kept it a secret."

"We were out of control— *literally* out of control. We lost communications, sensors, optics, everything. We didn't even know we were setting a new speed record until we finally stopped after twelve and a half days. We expected to find the *Prometheus* alongside us once we stopped."

"Light-9790! Wow! And you didn't even know?"

"Nope. We only knew we were moving because of the vibration of the ship. We thought that if we disconnected the drive, we'd do irreparable damage, but we were on the verge of doing just that when the anti-collision system shut it down properly. Even so, it needed repair before it could be reengaged, and we didn't have the proper replacement parts on board."

"It's a miracle you didn't hit something."

"My chief engineer believes we did. He believes we passed through at least one object harmlessly, according to the mechanics of Transverse Phase Differential."

"Double wow! TPD! You know, I understand now how our brothers must have felt when we were reaping all the attention a few years ago. And I'm not thinking about the glory but about the tremendous excitement. I've been sitting at the helm station of the *Chiron* punching in minor course adjustments during the third watch every day, while you've been setting galactic speed records and seizing bases."

"How exciting was it a couple of years ago while you were shackled to the wall of a Tsgardi cell in the *Boshdyte's* brig?"

Christa thought for a few seconds. "I guess you're right. It looks a lot more exciting to everyone else."

*   *   *

Vyx was really looking forward to completing the loading of the ship. Before beginning, he had lowered the artificial gravity to one-sixth normal, and they were using 'oh-gee' blocks, but he was still exhausted at the end of each day. After two weeks of sixteen-hour workdays, the ship was only half full. The holds were being packed bulkhead to bulkhead and deck to overhead. Normally, aisles were left in cargo areas so someone could get through the hold to check on problems, but aisles were considered an extravagant luxury on this trip. And considering the cargo, if a problem such as a fire occurred, the crew would be lucky to get to the lifepods before the ship disintegrated.

* * *

The *Chiron* was the first new ship to arrive since the base had been fully secured, and as had been her custom while serving as base commander at Dixon, Jenetta hosted a dinner for the senior staff on their first evening in port. Captain Powers wasn't at all surprised to see one of his junior officers among the attendees because he knew Commander Carver would want her sister there.

As on previous such occasions at Dixon, the visiting crew wanted to hear all about Jenetta's exploits and especially about the taking of the new base. Jenetta sidestepped questions about the trip in the *Colorado* by saying that Space Command had instructed her not to say anything, even though it was obvious from Christa's account of the rumors that there was no real secret to protect.

"It's a real story of David and Goliath," Captain Powers said, "taking this base and sixty-five hundred prisoners with just a crew of one hundred eighty-five. And then holding it, alone, for months through Raider attacks by cruisers and destroyers just makes it that much more amazing. You make it sound so matter-of-fact in your retelling, but it's a great accomplishment."

"Thank you. I had the support of a great crew. They always came through for me."

"Where's your ship now, Commander? I'd love to take a look at it. Our scout ship wasn't ready when we had to leave, so we won't be getting it for a while."

"The *Prometheus* was ordered to return it for repairs and testing. I doubt you would have been able to leave with yours once we reported our— problem, until they put it through a whole new series of tests and made some important modifications."

"A pity. We could really use such a weapon right now."

"Hopefully not immediately. My latest communication from Space Command states that you'll be remaining here for the present so the *Thor* can leave on patrol."

"That's correct. And two more ships should arrive over the next few weeks. We weren't the first to leave, but our greater speed allowed us to get here first. It was decided that the *Chiron* should arrive as soon as possible rather than traveling as a convoy with the other ships. The transport ships are sufficiently armed to travel in relative safety when there are two or more, and while traveling faster than light there's little danger anyway. Space Command will decide who will remain for the protection of the base and who will go out on patrol next."

"I imagine the destroyer *Asuncion* will be the next to be released. They've been here even longer than the *Thor*. I can empathize with their desire to be out on patrol again. At least my days pass quickly because of my workload."

"You didn't request this assignment?"

"No, I think of myself as a line officer, not a base administrator. I was posted here because I was the only experienced base commander among the officers of the task force. I'm anxiously awaiting the return of the *Prometheus*, but that might not be for another fourteen months or more. And I don't even know that I'll be relieved here once it does come back. It's up to Space Command HQ."

"For a base of this importance, they'll probably be sending someone quickly. It stated in my orders that this base was about to be designated as a StratCom-One base. No offense, Commander, nor is any slight of your abilities intended, but no StratCom-One base has ever been commanded by an officer below the rank of Rear Admiral, Lower, and the regs actually recommend that the base commander be a Rear Admiral, Upper. The next nearest StratCom-One base is Higgins at Vinnia where Rear Admiral Holt is base commander. As you're well aware, Holt's a two-star. The new base designation means you're not only responsible for the base, but for all of space as far as halfway to Higgins. Until you're relieved, you outrank everybody, including all ship's captains, within two hundred to three hundred light-years."

"Perhaps technically, following the strictest interpretation of the regs, but patrol routes around a StratCom-One base are supposed to be established by the base commander. Here, the captain of each ship receives his or her patrol routes directly from Space Command Supreme HQ. So I don't understand why they upgraded us from StratCom-Three."

"StratCom-Three is the lowest designation for a large military base also functioning as a home port for military vessels. The whole purpose of designating a base StratCom-One is to allow the base commander to override orders from Space Command because of distance or security issues. I was quite surprised when I learned that Stewart had been designated that way, considering the base commander wasn't a flag officer. It shows the confidence the Admiralty Board has in you. If a line officer does have to be posted off ship, I can't think of a better, more important, or more powerful position to be in. You're potentially right in the middle of the busiest place in Alliance territory. This sector faces the largest concentration of planets along our entire border, making it a gateway of sorts to Galactic Alliance regulated space, and you're far from Alliance politics and news reporters."

"It won't remain that way for long. From my experience with members of the press, I expect reporters are already aboard ships bound for this station. It provides a moderately safe place from which they can file their stories, and over the next year we'll be welcoming embassy staffs, freight hauler representatives, and private entrepreneurs looking for concourse space. We still have a lot of construction work to be done. With our construction supplies arriving soon, I hope

I can count on help from your engineering staff while you're here. "

"We'll assist in any way we can. Commander Elliot will contact your office tomorrow and arrange to meet with your chief engineer."

"Thank you, Captain."

* * *

After waiting in Jenetta's outer office for fifteen minutes, Lieutenant Commander Davis was permitted to go in when Jenetta's prior appointment left. He walked in and stopped at attention in front of her desk. "Lieutenant Commander Davis reporting to the base commander."

"Welcome, Commander. At ease. Have a seat."

"Thank you, ma'am."

"It's nice to see you again."

"It's nice to see you again, Commander. You've had a remarkable career since you were a young ensign assigned to my section at Higgins. And you don't look a day older than when we first met. Of course, everyone knows of your ordeal at the hands of the Raiders and the DNA experiments you were subjected to."

"It seems like a lifetime ago. How are you getting on? Have I assigned enough room for the new Science Section?"

"Very adequate, Commander. We have lots of room to grow as the section expands to meet the needs of Space Command."

"Excellent. What can I do for you today, Commander?"

"I wanted to discuss sending out a ship to begin making astronomical observations. There's not much that can be done from inside this asteroid."

"I don't have any ships that can be used for that purpose right now, Commander. The ships in the port are required to remain here for the protection of the base, and we need dozens more warships just to patrol the immediate sectors for which this base is responsible."

"I understand that, Commander, but I've learned that you seized a number of Raider ships when you took this base. We brought several optical and radio telescopes with us, but I'd hesitate to put them in orbit nearby with so much traffic expected here. We have no need of warships and special hulls. Any one of the ships you seized will provide us with the stable platform we need for our studies."

Jenetta thought for a few seconds. "I don't think that would be wise, Commander. This is still very hostile territory. We haven't had sufficient time here to secure an area of influence where you would be fundamentally safe."

"We won't go very far, Commander. I promise to remain within one hour's travel time of your slowest destroyer."

"In one hour you can be killed and your ship towed away without leaving a trace."

"Thirty minutes then. Commander, we can't do our job from inside this hunk of rock."

Jenetta leaned back in her chair. She didn't want to grant the request because of safety concerns, but as a former science officer and astrophysicist, she knew the science people had a job to perform also.

"Okay, Commander, I'll give you a ship. But since I can't give you a ship that can be depended on to provide adequate defense for your group, I'll only give you a very small ship that offers minimal value to the Raiders. It's unlikely that they'll venture within an hour of the base just to capture a small scout ship. We can equip it for basic research purposes, but it won't compare to a regular research vessel."

"I understand, Commander. How many people will it accommodate?"

Jenetta turned to her computer terminal and punched a few buttons, scanning the information for a few seconds.

"The ship I have in mind has quarters for eighteen. Since you won't be any further from this base than a hundred billion kilometers, any warship from this base will be able to reach you in no more than thirty minutes. And when I say a hundred billion kilometers, I *mean* a hundred billion kilometers, Commander."

"Yes, ma'am. One hundred billion kilometers from this base and not one meter more. I understand."

"Good. I'll speak to my chief engineer and have him start preparing the ship. The Raiders called her the *Poacher*, but we can rename her something more appropriate if you wish."

"How about *Star Gazer*?"

"That's fine with me. Computer, is there any ship in the Space Command Ship Registry presently using the name *Star Gazer*?"

"Negative," the computer replied. "There is presently no listing for any GSC ship named *Star Gazer*."

"Computer, file an application for that name with Space Command and request that an official identification be established. The ship currently named *Poacher* in base records will now be designated as *Star Gazer* unless our application isn't approved. Purpose is astronomical observation and investigation of celestial phenomena."

"Application completed and forwarded to Space Command HQ," the computer said.

"There you go, Commander. Good luck. I'll see that a crew of six is assigned to the *Star Gazer*, allowing you a dozen berths for your people. In the event of contact with hostile forces, the crew will have orders to return here immediately. We'll dispatch a ship to intercept and escort you back should that happen."

"Thank you, Commander. I know Lieutenant Kesliski will be very excited."

"Kesliski?"

"Yes. From our astrophysics section. She'll head up the team going out. I believe you worked with her at Higgins."

"Yes, I worked *for* her. I remember Lieutenant Kesliski very well. I'm just surprised to hear she's out here."

"I would have had trouble trying to keep her at Higgins once she learned there was an opportunity to work at this base. We've never had a research vessel out this far. As you know, Space Command regulations require that unarmed research vessels remain within regulated Galactic Alliance borders."

"Yes, and that reminds me. Although this is *considered* regulated Galactic Alliance space, make sure everyone traveling in the *Star Gazer* understands that this is still hostile territory. Every one of your people must be a volunteer."

"Very well, Commander, volunteers only. But I don't expect that to be a problem."

Jenetta's last appointment before lunch was with the senior officer of the new Weapons Research section, Commander Barbara DeWitt. She was waiting in the outer office when Jenetta finished her meeting with Lieutenant Reese, the new Housing Officer who was taking that responsibility off Lieutenant Ashraf's shoulders. It had become an increasingly time-consuming part of her daily activities.

When told to go in by Lieutenant Ashraf, Commander DeWitt entered the office and stopped in front of Jenetta's Desk. Coming to attention, she said, "Commander DeWitt reporting to the base commander."

"At ease, Commander," Jenetta said, smiling. Standing up, she offered her hand and Commander DeWitt took it. "It's good to see you again Barbara. Welcome to Stewart SCB."

"Thank you, Commander."

"It's still Jen, Barbara."

DeWitt smiled. "Of course, Jen. Thank you."

"Have a seat, Barbara. How are you getting on?"

"Fine. We've started organizing our space to fit our needs, although most of our equipment won't arrive for months. It's aboard one of the many slow quartermaster transports on their way here. But we have more than enough to keep us busy until then. How about you? You've come a long way since I first saw you during your court martial."

"A lot has happened, that's for sure."

"I don't think we've spoken in person since the day you were promoted to Lieutenant Commander, and here you are, practically a two-star admiral."

Jenetta laughed. "Please don't wish that on me. Admirals spend all their days sitting behind desks."

"Don't you?"

Jenetta grimaced slightly. "Right now, but I expect to get back into space after they send someone to relieve me. I'm only the base commander because I was handy. I can't possibly remain in command of a StratCom-One base when regs specify that the base commander should be a Rear Admiral, Upper."

"I admit it's unusual, but these are very unusual times. Space Command resources had already been stretched to the breaking point before you secured this new base for us. We just don't have any extra two-star admirals in need of a post, and you're the only Space Command officer to destroy one Raider base and capture another almost single-handedly."

"Now Barbara, it's never been *proven* that I destroyed Raider-One, only that I planted an explosive device that *could* have destroyed it."

"Oh, it was proven beyond any shadow of a doubt that you were responsible."

"It was?"

"I thought Space Command would have sent you a copy of the final report. Residue found on many of the collected samples of the asteroid and all of the samples from wrecked ships contained the marker tags the manufacturer had mixed into the shipment of Corplastizine the *Vordoth* was carrying. The explosion was definitely caused by the eighty-two metric tons you planted coming into contact with properly synthesized dithulene-35. The explosive force in the enclosed cavern was enough to destroy a base twice as large, which is why the destruction was so complete. I'm sure the official record has been amended to show that the base was definitely destroyed as a direct result of your actions."

"Hmm. I was never told, although I've always suspected that was the case. I guess Space Command just wanted to keep it quiet once the news of the event and the resulting court-martial died down. I'm glad they did."

"It's sort of an open secret anyway. Everyone credited you with the destruction long before we proved it, even while the court martial was still making headlines in every part of Galactic Alliance space. Oh, I want to thank you for sending that security ship to us after you became the base commander at Dixon. We learned quite a bit from it."

"I'm glad. Anything we're likely to see in new ships?"

"Not right away. The weapon they used to disable small craft by draining all power can really only be used inside the cavern where the ships are moving slowly. It won't function in open space where ships are traveling at FTL speeds because it can't move between temporal envelopes. It also has little effect on ships that are heavily shielded, such as Space Command Vessels, which is why we hadn't encountered it before."

"We haven't seen any sign of it in the large ships we've captured, but most of them were scrap when the engagements were over. The lightly armed ships we took here didn't have it either."

"I'm not surprised. I'm sure the Raiders are very aware of its severe limitations."

"How does it work?"

"Well, the security ship releases a collimated ball of highly charged electron plasma with magnetic properties that allow it to be directed by a theta-pinch device. It very much resembles ball lightening on Earth, which normally appears yellow or orange but in the vacuum of space would appear bluish. When the ball strikes a ship, the effect is like the explosive decay, and there would be a loud noise but for the vacuum. Any occupants of a craft would feel the effect, but that's not what causes the problem.

"A discontinuous magneto-plasmatic configuration of extremely high internal energy passes through the craft and acts like the Source Region Electro Magnetic Pulse that results from a thermonuclear device detonated at low altitude over a planetary surface. The extreme effect of the electromagnetic resonance in an unshielded ship either disorients or renders any crewmen unconscious. As you suggested on Higgins, a ship in outer space doesn't provide an easy migration path for the electrons at the outer part of the deposition region towards the burst point, and a large ship's artificial gravity system totally overwhelms the SREMP effect anyway. We're continuing to work on a solution."

"It would be great if your section could come up with something that would allow us to disable a ship traveling at FTL speeds. The envelope-merge procedure is so potentially hazardous that it could lead to a complete loss of life aboard both ships."

"We'd love to come up with something, but don't expect it soon. Everything that's been tried has been a complete failure. You know, there are days when you begin to think science has reached its zenith and there's nothing new left to discover, but then something happens, such as your twelve-day trip in a small scout ship, that makes you feel we've only scratched the surface. Several of our brightest minds at Higgins were sent to the dockyard at Mars to work on solving the mechanics question of your little ship. That must have been quite a ride you took."

"That's a good way of describing it, Barbara. Hey, it's lunchtime. If you'd like to join me for lunch in my dining room, I'll tell you about it. I know you have clearance to hear the facts about the biggest non-secret secret in Space Command."

"I'd love to, Jen."

*   *   *

The *Maid of Mephad* was at last fully loaded. Two workers had to hold packing crates to keep them from falling out of the last hold until the doors could be completely shut. For safety reasons, Vyx had refused to allow the corridors to be used for storing ordnance, but twelve crew staterooms had been filled. Only the bridge, engineering, and galley were totally free from boxes and crates.

With the completion of the loading, Vyx returned the ship's gravity to normal, then walked to his quarters and took a long, hot shower. As he was dressing afterwards, one of Rivemwilth's bodyguards came to find him.

"The Shev wishes to invite you to dinner on the surface."

"Thank him for me, but tell him I'm so exhausted that I wouldn't make good company. I'm going to turn in early and sleep all night."

"The Shev would prefer that you leave orbit and then catch up on your sleep while on route. He'll give you your course directions during the meal."

Vyx sighed. "Very well. Tell him I'll be there shortly."

Vyx headed towards the shuttle as soon as he finished dressing. He was anxious to get down to the surface, get the directions to Rivemwilth's new base, and get back to the ship and his comfortable bed. Arriving at the bay, he found Nelligen waiting for him in the craft.

"You get a personal dinner invite also?"

"Yeah, except it sounded more like an order."

"Mine too," Vyx said. "I wonder what he wants. I was hoping not to see that toad's face again for awhile."

"Maybe he intends to come along with us."

"That's a gruesome thought. I figured he wouldn't want to be anywhere near the shipment in case we get stopped."

"If this is everything he owns, he might not want to let it out of his sight."

"Where's Byers?"

"I saw him in the lounge about ten minutes ago."

"He wasn't invited?"

"I guess not."

"Good."

"Why good?"

"Because then I'd start to think Rivemwilth was looking for an excuse to get us all off the ship."

"Think he'll pull something?"

"I don't trust him if that's what you mean, but they have us outgunned six to one. I'm going to trust that his reputation will keep him honest. If he cheats us, then others won't trust him."

"But nobody knows we're here except for Space Command."

"We know that, but he doesn't."

"Gotcha."

"Buckle up and we'll go have dinner."

An escort was waiting at the flight bay when they landed, and he showed them to a dining room where Rivemwilth was waiting.

"Gentlemen, come in. Dinner is almost ready. Help yourselves to the appetizers. I especially recommend the pickled Keenie eggs and the fried Oulee. They're my cook's specialty."

Rivemwilth filled his plate with a little of everything on the appetizer buffet table and sat down to eat. Vyx took a few things and sat down while Nelligen filled his plate before taking his seat.

Speaking with his mouth half full and dripping food, Rivemwilth said, "I'm extremely pleased with your efforts thus far, gentlemen. We couldn't fit everything in the ship, but we got the best of it, and what's left is older ordnance of limited value. We'll seal up this base when we leave and trust that no one will find it until I can send someone to pick up the rest. I won't need a ship nearly as large as yours for the remaining stockpile."

Dinner was served before they had finished their appetizers, and Shev Rivemwilth continued to relate tales of arms deals in between mouthfuls of foods. Vyx was getting tired of the stories but was spared further tales when the door opened and Byers walked in. Vyx tensed visibly as a half-dozen, heavily armed bodyguards followed Byers in.

"Ah, the last member of our transport crew has chosen to join us."

"Chosen hell. I was brought down here at gun point after I refused to come earlier."

"What is this, Shev?" Vyx spat out.

"Just wrapping up our little deal, Trader. You see, we won't be needing your services any longer. But thank you for providing us with an excellent ship."

"If you kill us, I guarantee you'll never be trusted again. If I don't make it back to Scruscotto, I arranged for word to be spread that you murder your business associates and steal their ships. That'll put one hell of a dent in your arms deals. Your reputation isn't everything, but it's extremely important in a business where cheated customers can't complain to Space Command or justice courts."

"I'm not going to kill you, Trader. I'm going to leave you and these other gentlemen here alive, unless you give my people cause."

"And the punch line is?"

"The communications devices have been totally destroyed so you can't call for help. There's enough fresh food for a couple of weeks, and the synthesizers should keep you going for six months or more. Someone will be by to pick you up in a couple of months, but you'll never be able to tell anybody where my new base is located."

"This wasn't the deal, Shev."

"I'm altering the deal. If you make it back to Scruscotto, you can pick up the credits I've paid over to Blasperra."

"What about my ship?"

"I'll change the identification information and dispose of that for you. It wasn't really yours anyway; you stole it from Space Command. With the five hundred thousand credits, you can pick yourself up a nice little used ship."

"The *Maid* is worth fifty million credits."

"Yes," he said, smiling, "it seems I've done quite well on this deal."

"If you do this, Shev, it'll be the biggest mistake of your life. I warn you that you'll regret it very soon but not for long."

"Enough with the threats, or I'll forget my promise to leave you alive. Gentlemen, enjoy the rest of the food. I have a ship to catch."

Vyx just glared at Rivemwilth as the arms merchant and his bodyguards left the room. Byers hurried over to the door only to discover that it was locked. Nelligen tried the kitchen door and found that locked as well.

"I'm starting not to like that overgrown toad," Nelligen said.

Vyx sat down and calmly resumed eating his dinner.

"Are you just going to sit there and eat?" Byers asked excitedly.

"Might as well. It's getting cold. I'm not charging, unarmed, into a group of bodyguards with laser weapons. Try the champagne, it's excellent."

"But they're getting away."

"They're already away. After dinner we'll find a way out of here and then see what our situation is. Try the fish. It's like brook trout on Earth. The *late* Shev Rivemwilth set a good table."

Chapter Fifteen
~ June 26th, 2274 ~

Christa completed her duty shift aboard the *Chiron* at 0800 hours each morning, immediately changed her clothes, and hurried to the base gym to work out with her sister. Jenetta worked from 0600 to 0800, then took a two-hour break so they could have this time together each day before returning to her office and the staggering workload that always awaited her.

They began their morning routine each day with kick-boxing practice. Having had different practice partners over the past year, their techniques had altered slightly and they could no longer always predict the other's moves. After kickboxing, they ran on the track for an hour with Jenetta's cats and then showered. When Jenetta left for her office, Christa would go to her quarters to get some sleep. They would get together again at dinner each evening.

Christa was in Jenetta's quarters following their evening meal when Jenetta's com unit buzzed. Lifting the cover of the unit on her coffee table and depressing the 'play' button, the face of Captain Crosby of the GSC Destroyer *Ottawa* filled the screen.

"Good evening, Commander. I just wanted to let you know that the ship we have under surveillance is now moving towards the Frontier Zone after being stationary for the past month. We'll be trailing and standing by until we receive the call to move in.

"Jeffrey Crosby, Captain of the GSC Destroyer *Ottawa*, message complete."

Jenetta tapped the record button. "To Captain Crosby, GSC *Ottawa.*

"Thank you for keeping me informed, Captain. I would assume that our contact will be summoning you sometime in the next few weeks as an opportunity presents itself. Warheads on the ship's torpedoes have reportedly been neutralized, and all laser weapons will fail within seconds of first use. Please take care that no one is injured when you seize the ship.

"Jenetta Carver, Commander, Stewart Space Command Base, message complete." Jenetta tapped the transmit button and lowered the com screen.

* * *

Without proper tools it took over two hours to get the dining room doors open. Vyx, Byers, and Nelligen headed to the flight bay first. From the control room viewing window they could see that the outer doors were open and the bay was empty.

"Nothing," Byers said. "Not even an old tug we might try to get working."

"Let's check out the communications gear to see if there's anything I can do with it," Nelligen said.

After an hour of digging through the mess that used to be the communications room, Nelligen threw up his hands. "Not a chance. Everything is fried. I can't even rig up a simple RF transceiver with this junk. We'd be long dead by the time a message reached Stewart anyway."

* * *

Working in her office when a message came from the *Ottawa*, Jenetta lifted her com screen and pressed the 'play' button. An image of Captain Crosby filled the screen.

"Good morning, Commander. We've been paralleling the course of the *Maid* for about a month now. Two weeks ago they dropped their envelope. Should we continue to monitor them, or should we move in?

"Jeffrey Crosby, Captain of the GSC *Ottawa*, message complete."

Jenetta touched the record button. "To Captain Crosby, GSC *Ottawa*.

"Continue to monitor, Captain. I promised Vyx we wouldn't move in until he called. They might simply be trying to correct some engine trouble. It's better to keep our distance until we have some better indication to go by."

"Jenetta Carver, Commander, Stewart SC Base, message complete."

Jenetta tapped the transmit button, then pushed the screen panel down and leaned back in her chair. Why would Vyx stop the ship at this point? Had he tried to send the signal but experienced com trouble? Was dropping the envelope supposed to be a signal? They were still months away from the Frontier Zone so the reason couldn't be to stop the arms merchant from getting across the border, and Rivemwilth wouldn't order stopping a ship loaded with illegal arms. It must be a problem with the drive.

Another week passed before Captain Crosby contacted Jenetta again.

"Commander, the *Maid* is still not moving and we haven't heard from Vyx, so there must be a serious problem. Please advise.

"Jeffrey Crosby, Captain of the GSC *Ottawa*, message complete."

Jenetta sighed. She tapped the record button. "To Captain Crosby, GSC *Ottawa*.

"It would appear that something serious has occurred. Okay, Captain, coordinate with the *Geneva* and move in. Contact me after you've made contact with the *Maid*.

"Jenetta Carver, Commander, Stewart SC Base, message complete."

A new message arrived from Captain Crosby the following evening.

"We've moved in and are standing a thousand kilometers off. The *Maid* isn't responding to our hails. Her running lights are on, but there's no sign of life otherwise."

"Jeffrey Crosby, Captain of the GSC *Ottawa*, message complete."

Jenetta thought for a few seconds, then sent a message in response. "Board her and determine the condition of the ship, crew, and cargo. If they open fire, use your best judgment. Don't put your crew in danger, but try not to destroy the *Maid*. We have three of our people aboard. Contact me after securing the ship.

"Jenetta Carver, Commander, Stewart SC Base, message complete."

Jenetta sat sipping on a cup of coffee as she thought about this new situation.

The next message from Captain Crosby arrived a day and a half later.

"My people are inside the *Maid*, Commander, and they've found nineteen bodies. The hull is breached in a dozen places and the crew died when the atmosphere was lost. It appears that the damage came from within. The emergency doors never closed, so there were no protected areas. They all died in minutes. They're all Terrans, except for one Alyysian."

"Jeffrey Crosby, Captain of the GSC *Ottawa*, message complete."

Jenetta recorded her message and transmitted it.

"To Captain Crosby, GSC *Ottawa*.

"Okay, Captain. Send me their ID information when you have it, then bring the ship to Stewart under power if possible, otherwise, tow it with your tugs. You can release the *Geneva* so it can return to its regular patrol route. You won't be able to travel faster than Light-187 at best, so we'll see you in a couple of months. Thank you for your help with this operation.

"Jenetta Carver, Commander, Stewart SCB, message complete."

The images, retinal scans, and DNA of the dead aboard the *Maid*, along with the fingerprints of the Terrans, were forwarded to Stewart two days later. Several of the corpses contained criminal marker tags, making their identification easy, but it took several weeks to make positive identification of the remainder because the information had to be sent to Space Command to be checked against a central database. The desiccated corpses were grotesque-looking after weeks of being subjected to the cold vacuum of space. It turned out that none of the victims were Vyx, Byers, or Nelligen, but their bodies could have been sucked out of the ship when the hull was breached. Captain Crosby also forwarded images of each hull breach to Stewart. The damage had been patched, but they had recorded images before the work commenced. The *Maid* had been re-pressurized and was heading for Stewart SCB under its own power.

After receiving the images, Jenetta summoned Lieutenant Jacoby, her engineering chief, to her office.

"Look at these hull breaches, Derrick," Jenetta said as he sat down across from her. She tapped a button on her com console and they were projected onto a large wall monitor. "They appear to have been caused from within the ship."

Lieutenant Jacoby stood back up, walked to the monitor, and closely examined each high-definition image for a few seconds. He called on the computer to magnify certain parts before saying, "From these pictures, it's difficult to fully appreciate the size of the breaches, but they appear to have been caused by the small, shaped charges Vyx had me place against the hull. They were disguised as fire suppression devices and could be triggered from a remote detonator located in his stateroom."

"He asked you to place charges inside his ship?"

"Yes, ma'am. He said it was sort of a 'mission failsafe' device. He could set the trigger mechanism for up to thirty days. It looks like something happened that caused him to trigger it. That, or someone else found the remote and played around with it without realizing its purpose."

"You're absolutely sure your devices did this damage?"

"As sure as I can be from the images. I'd have to see the actual blast holes and take metal filing samples to be a hundred percent certain."

"Okay, Derrick. Thank you. That'll be all."

"Aye, Commander. Is Trader Vyx still alive?"

"That's the big question, Derrick."

* * *

The fresh food supplies were exhausted, so Vyx, Byers, and Nelligen were eating food exclusively from the food-synthesizer. After more than a month and a half in the deserted base, their nerves were on edge. Byers and Nelligen were bickering almost constantly, and Vyx was spending as much time as possible by himself. They always came together for meals though.

"I hope our rescuers get here soon," Byers said at dinner. "This waiting around without being able to contact anyone is getting on my nerves."

"Rescuers?" Vyx said. "You believe rescuers are coming?"

"Rivemwilth said he was sending someone to rescue us."

"Actually, he said that 'someone will be by to pick you up in a few months.' That's not the same thing. Why do you think I've spent so much time working with the explosives in the storerooms?"

"In case someone unexpected arrived."

"Not only that. I've been working to prepare for whomever the late Shev Rivemwilth has sent."

"Who are *you* expecting?" Nelligen asked.

"I doubt the late Shev Rivemwilth would have sent anyone unless he stood to profit. It could be relatives of Recozzi, the Tsgardi I killed. Rivemwilth might be hoping to collect the bounty the family is offering on my head. But I expect them to more likely be slavers. Or they could be both. They kill me, collect the bounty, then sell both of you as slaves. But, whoever's coming, I don't intend to simply let them kill me, or to live out my days mining ore."

"Slavers? You think that lousy toad has sold us? If that's true and I ever get my hands on him, I'll choke the life out of him."

"I expect you're too late. I believe the life has already been choked out of him."

"I've noticed you keep calling him the 'late Shev Rivemwilth.' I originally thought you meant that he was 'as good as dead.' Why do you think he's already dead?"

"I rigged the *Maid* with small explosive charges that would breach the hull in a number of places. When we came down to the surface, the detonator probably had about two weeks left of the preset thirty days. I suspect Rivemwilth died from asphyxiation about a month ago."

"Explosives? You never told us about any explosives."

"It was 'need to know' information. You didn't need to know, and it was one less chance for somebody to slip up and tell Rivemwilth. I told him he'd soon regret leaving us here but not for long."

"So, if he hadn't yet told anyone exactly where we are, we won't be seeing anyone. Not even slavers."

"I suspect those arrangements were made long before we arrived. Rivemwilth always planned well ahead."

"If he was so smart he would have taken us down as soon as we finished loading the ship and not given you a chance to set the detonator."

"It was set from the first minute we arrived at the rendez-vous point. I was resetting it every week to the maximum time, but we had been so busy with the loading that I hadn't reset it in a couple of weeks. I plan well ahead also."

"You mean we spent over a month working on that ammo-filled ship while the timer was running?" Byers asked.

"Yep. It was the only way I could assure that Rivemwilth didn't get away if anything should happen to us quite suddenly."

"Maybe he found the charges."

"It's possible but highly unlikely. They were well disguised, and the trigger is a remote detonator so there weren't any wires to spot. There's so much explosive aboard that they couldn't use sensors to find them, and it's totally unlikely that they could have found all the devices anyway. Since the emergency door controls are disabled if the detonator is activated, the entire ship could depressurize from just one breach. The Light Speed engines are likewise set to shut down, so we have plenty of time to recover the ship once we get out of here."

"You're awfully sure of yourself. Maybe you've blown the entire ship to pieces. It was loaded with ordnance, after all."

"The charges were tiny, all specially prepared just to evacuate the air in the ship and located with that in mind. The charges were shaped to blow outward only, and the crevice holes should only be about fifteen-centimeters across and thirty wide. The ship will still be around for us to find."

"You really think we're getting out of here, alive and free?"

"I'll believe that until the second I draw my last breath here."

* * *

As the door opened to admit her, Jenetta entered the bridge briefing room of Captain Payton. He welcomed her to the *Thor* and invited her to sit down.

"So what can I do to help the base commander today?"

"Captain, I'd like your assistance with a little problem that's developed. You're scheduled to depart the base tonight, and I don't know if you have a specific mission or if you're going on routine patrol, but if it's the latter I wanted to ask a favor."

Captain Payton smiled. "No specific mission this time out, Commander. What is it you need?"

"What I'm about to tell you is confidential, Captain. We've been conducting an Intelligence operation during the past six months, and at this moment the *Ottawa* is escorting a large transport loaded with seized illegal ordnance towards this base. We believe much of it was stolen from Space Command. As the senior officer on Stewart, Captain Kanes named me coordinator for the operation because the distance to Higgins prevented him from issuing more timely instructions in response to delicate situations. Following the seizure of the weapons, I released the *Geneva* and it resumed its normal patrol while the *Ottawa* has continued on as escort."

"I see, Commander, but what do you need from me? It would appear the operation is over."

"Three of our people, the three operatives responsible for recovery of the armaments, are missing. I wasn't sure until all the bodies aboard the seized ship were identified. It's possible they were lost when the ship's hull was breached, but it's more likely they weren't aboard the ship at all. I believe they might have been left behind at the arms merchant's former base. The transport was parked in orbit over a small moon for more than a month, during which time it was loaded with ordnance for its journey to the new Frontier Zone. I'd like to have someone visit that moon to see if our people are still there. I could order the *Geneva* back, but it would take her weeks longer to get there than it would you since the *Thor* can achieve Light-375. The *Ottawa* can't be freed up because it's needed for protection of the loaded transport."

"So you'd like us to check out the moon to see if we can locate a secret base, and then search that base for any sign of your operatives?"

"Yes."

"Where is it?"

"The Frassah system. It orbits the fourth planet."

"Computer," Captain Payton said, "display the deca-sector chart on the wall monitor showing our patrol route and highlighting the Frassah system." After looking at the chart, he said, "That's well outside our established patrol territory, Commander."

"These are extenuating circumstances, Captain. I know I can get approval for this deviation, but it will take almost two weeks for new orders to arrive. In that time you could be a quarter of the way there, or much further away if you deny my request."

Captain Payton was silent for a few seconds. "You're the base commander of a StratCom-One base, Commander. You can order me to do this."

"I didn't want to pull rank on a senior officer, but I'll make it official if it will make you more comfortable. Space Command doesn't desert its people, especially after they've served so valiantly. We have to learn their fate, even if we only ascertain their deaths and recover their bodies for proper burial."

Captain Payton nodded. "Very well, Commander. We'll check out the moon and see if we can find your missing people."

"Thank you, Captain. I'll send messages to Captain Kanes and Space Command Headquarters explaining that your patrol course deviation was on my explicit order."

*　*　*

Vyx was awakened sharply by Byers' voice coming from an overhead com speaker.

"Vyx, wake up, someone's here!"

"Wha? Who's here?"

"Two shuttles have just entered the bay."

Vyx came instantly awake and jumped off the bed. "Who is it?"

"I don't know."

"Where's Nels?"

"He's at the bay, watching the ships on the monitors."

"Good. Stay away from the control room window so they can't see who's in here. Get ready for action. I'll be there in a few minutes."

"Hurry."

After pulling on his pants and boots, Vyx strapped his laser pistol belt around his waist. It was an older model than the one he usually carried, which meant it was bulkier and not as efficient, but he had a dozen charged power packs on his belt. Byers and Nelligen were similarly armed. They had found a large cache of the older weapons in one of the storerooms.

Vyx finished dressing as he ran through the corridors to the flight bay. "What's happening?" he asked as he entered the control room, staying low to avoid being seen through the window. He raised up just high enough to see figures encapsulated in bulky EVA suits beginning to disembark from the shuttles and head for the airlock. "Tsgardi!" he said.

"I've blocked the controls so the outer doors can't be closed remotely," Nelligen said. "They had to suit up and must use the airlock to get in here. We should be able to pick off the first group before they know what hit them. Here they come."

"Let's get into the corridor outside the airlock," Vyx said, pulling out his pistol and checking the charge.

The three men tensed as the airlock finished cycling and the inner door began to open. Five Tsgardi warriors, the most that could fit into the small chamber at one time, stepped out of the airlock. They were all carrying laser rifles. As they started moving down the corridor, Vyx, Nelligen, and Byers stepped partway out from the doorways where they'd been hiding and opened fire. In an instant the corridor was filled with light pulses from laser pistols and rifles. The exchange of fire lasted less than ten seconds, and when it was over, the five Tsgardi were down for good while the three Terrans had suffered only minor injuries. Nelligen had been hit in the leg, but the shot had passed through the fleshy inner thigh without damaging the femoral artery. Vyx had suffered a hit to the shoulder, but the shot had only creased the flesh. Both wounds had been sealed as quickly as they had been inflicted. They were painful but not disabling.

"I'm glad they're using laser rifles instead of lattice rifles," Nelligen said, wincing as he placed his weight on the injured leg. "This wound could have killed me."

"Same here," Vyx said, rubbing his shoulder. "It's another indication that they're here to collect us as slaves rather than coming to kill us. Let's get moving. We can set up another ambush outside the galley."

"No, let's stay here and pick off the next group coming out of the airlock," Byers said.

Grabbing Byers by the front of his shirt, Vyx shouted in his face, "There won't be a next group coming out of the airlock! Now run!" Vyx released the shirt and took off down the corridor behind Nelligen.

Byers waited indecisively for a couple of seconds and then ran after the others. Stopping just past the second of two emergency doors, Vyx stabbed at the buttons as Byers passed. The doors slid quickly and noiselessly down the tracks, sealing off the flight bay area from the rest of the base an instant before a blast rocked the walls.

"What the hell was that?" Byers exclaimed.

"They've blasted their way through a wall from the flight bay to the corridor with an explosive charge so we couldn't ambush anyone coming through the airlock."

"Whoa!" Byers exclaimed. "We would have been killed from the decompression if not by the blast. How did you know?"

"It's what *I* would have done. The airlock is a death trap because it's too inflexible. There's only one exit point."

"What do you think they'll do next?"

"They'll move more cautiously now. If they blow these emergency doors, the entire base will depressurize. We'll be dead, and they'll lose their slaves, but more importantly, they'll lose the chance to torture us for mowing down their friends. If they close the outer flight bay doors, they can reestablish the pressure and come for us in force. Let's hope they exercise the latter option."

"How many will come?" Nelligen asked.

"As many as they can muster. They might even bring down more from their ship. They've already lost more than they hoped to claim, so we'll see how badly they want us."

"Should we just wait here?" Byers asked.

"No. Let's take up positions in the corridor by the galley. Then we can fall back towards the storerooms if they still want more. We'll see how they like the surprises I rigged for uninvited guests."

The three men jogged through the corridors until they reached the galley. Vyx retrieved the remote detonator he'd left there and turned on a monitor tied into the base security cameras. They watched an image of the flight bay as a third shuttle entered and the bay doors closed. Estimating that the internal systems would require fourteen to fifteen minutes before the bay and corridors were adequately pressurized, they sat down to wait and watch the monitor as Vyx switched to different cameras.

Once the pressure had risen to the base's normal level, several Tsgardi approached the first emergency door warily, their rifles at the ready. Vyx watched as one reached out tentatively and pushed the control that would raise the door.

"Now!" Byers shouted when the three Tsgardi came within a meter of the door.

"Not yet," Vyx said. "Be patient."

The door rose and the three Tsgardi moved towards the second door.

"It's too late," Byers said. "You blew your opportunity to get them. They're too far past it now."

"Yes," Vyx said almost absentmindedly as a group of twelve more moved into view of the camera.

Waiting until the first two Tsgardi in the second group had passed the wall panel where he'd secreted two old land mines, Vyx depressed the button on the transmitter. Instantly the corridor was filled with smoke and flame. The air purification system immediately began to filter the air as a fire suppression system smothered the flames with foam from a computer-directed nozzle in the ceiling. When the view was clear, Vyx saw that eight Tsgardi were down. Two of those were still moving, but barely. The downed Tsgardi, covered in dense, white foam, presented a surreal sight. It looked almost like a snow sculpture on Earth. The first three returned momentarily to view the bodies of their fallen comrades.

"That seems to have slowed them a bit," Vyx said.

"Not for long," Byers said as the remaining seven turned towards the base corridors again and began to move forward.

"They didn't even leave anyone behind to help the wounded," Nelligen said.

"They don't believe in helping a downed warrior until the enemy is neutralized or the battle is lost," Vyx said.

"Then let's help them understand that this battle is lost," Byers said. "What's next?"

"We greet them again in the corridor. Come with me."

Vyx placed the two men and told them not to leave their positions unless he was down no matter what happened. The Tsgardi worked their way slowly through the base, not finding any sign of their opponents as they searched every room and closet. It took almost an hour for them to reach the galley area. Vyx waited until five of them had entered the corridor before stepping out of the doorway and opening fire with his pistol. Byers and Nelligen joined in immediately. The Tsgardi tried to retreat around the corner of the corridor but not before four of them went down. The one that managed to reach safety stopped where Vyx had expected they would choose to regroup and was joined by the remaining two. As the three Tsgardi spoke hurriedly with their ship and formulated a new plan for attack, Vyx set off the other explosive charge he had planted inside the wall partition next to where the Tsgardi were standing. The two land mines took out the last of the Tsgardi that had so far entered the base.

Signaling to Byers and Nelligen to follow him, Vyx retreated into one of the storage rooms where he'd set up a tripod-mounted, rapid-fire lattice rifle. Byers and Nelligen took cover behind some packing crates as Vyx moved to the gunner's position of the rifle. Then they waited.

During the next few hours, the three Terrans waited for an attack that never materialized. Vyx cursed himself repeatedly for not rigging up a monitor in the storage room to use the base's security cameras. Only low rumbling noises and vibrations that shook the room repeatedly rewarded their patient vigil. After half an hour of such motion, they cautiously left their positions and walked to the door. The vibrations could be felt in the walls, doors, and floor.

"What *is* that?" Byers asked.

"I don't know," Vyx answered. "It feels like the Tsgardi are blasting the base apart. But it's not close, so it must be at the other end."

"Let's take a look," Nelligen said.

Vyx tapped the control to open the door and then slowly peered down the corridor. It was empty except for the bodies of the four dead Tsgardi. He led the way, silently and carefully skirting around the four Tsgardi warriors and climbing over the bloody mess that remained of the three taken out by the land mine in the wall. They reached the galley without encountering any resistance. Turning on the monitor, they saw that the flight bay was empty. The Tsgardi shuttles had left.

"There's what we heard," Vyx said pointing to the monitor as he changed to a view that showed the flight bay doors open and the entrance covered with rock. "They've collapsed the face of the cliff over the flight bay opening. Either they're burying their dead, or us."

"Or both," Byers said.

"That's the end then," Nelligen said.

"You giving up?" Vyx asked.

"What chance do we have? No communications and now the only entrance buried. We're dead."

"Not me," Vyx said. "I'm still alive. And hungry. I'm gonna make myself some dinner and then we can start cleaning this place up. I think it's a pretty safe bet to say the Tsgardi won't be coming back."

Only seven of the dead Tsgardi were inside the pressurized area of the base. The emergency doors had been closed again so the outer bay doors could be opened by the Tsgardi shuttle pilots. Vyx and Nelligen used an 'oh-gee' sled to take the seven Tsgardi bodies to a storeroom where they were sealed in empty, air-tight storage containers normally used for SAMs. Although not as cold as a proper morgue freezer would be, the remote storeroom was unheated and so barely above freezing. Without adequate refrigeration, the bodies would start to decompose soon, but the low temperature would slow the process dramatically and the storage containers would seal the odors in. Byers directed the base's maintenance bots to clean up the rubble from the mines placed in the corridor wall near the storeroom.

The work beyond the emergency doors would be more difficult to handle. Using the two emergency doors like an airlock, Vyx and Nelligen were able to tackle the problem of the damage created by the Tsgardi when they had depressurized that section with explosives. Since the wall sections were basically comprised of the same pre-fabricated construction throughout the base, except for the specially reinforced blast walls of the warehouse chambers, they used a section of wall from a utility storeroom to repair the damaged wall at the shuttle bay. After the area was pressurized and tested, the emergency doors were raised. The bodies of the Tsgardi found in that section had already been taken out and stacked in the flight bay. The extreme cold and vacuum in the depressurized area had already begun to mummify the remains.

"What now?" Nelligen asked over breakfast the next morning. "We've cleaned up the place and gotten the airlock working, but the outer doors are still blocked by hundreds, or maybe thousands, of tons of rock."

"We'll bury some of the anti-tank land mines in the rocks and blast our way through."

"What about the explosive blow-back?"

"We'll pile everything heavy that we can find behind the blast area. That'll deaden the effect of anything coming back. We have those three old armored personnel carriers in warehouse six. The engines don't run, but we'll reduce the gravity in here to the minimum and we should be able to position them where we want using 'oh-gee' blocks. After we restore the gravity in the base, they'll provide an excellent barrier."

It was late afternoon before the charges were placed and the APCs located to suppress the blast forces expanding back into the bay. Since the flight bay wasn't sealed, they'd had to work in EVA suits. The three Terrans retreated into the base and closed the emergency doors just in case. Vyx also increased the gravity in the base to 3 g's so any rock blown back into the bay would fall more quickly. The extra gravity also made the APCs three times more resistant to the effects of the explosion. Since the rock they were trying to remove was outside the area affected by the gravity plating inside the base, the increased gravity should have minimal effect on it.

"Any questions or answers before I detonate?" Vyx asked.

"Just blow it already," Byers responded. "I'm exhausted from just sitting in this gravity."

"Here goes," Vyx said as he depressed the button on the detonator.

As they watched the flight bay monitor, they saw the APCs shift slightly and then dust clouded the room for a few minutes. The gravity and lack of atmosphere caused it to settle quickly.

"It doesn't look like we even made a dent," Nelligen said.

"We won't know that for sure until we get in there. Let's suit up and take a look."

"Decrease the gravity first so I can stand up," Byers said.

It didn't take long to suit up since they had only removed their helmets when they had come back inside. The rocks had shifted a little, but there wasn't any indication that they had moved the pile covering the bay entrance.

"This pile must be more massive than I thought. With the moon's lower gravity I expected much more penetration. Well, let's try again. This time I'll use three anti-tank mines instead of two."

Two hours later they were ready to try again. As before, they closed the emergency doors just in case, and increased the gravity inside the base. Vyx detonated the mines, but they could tell after a few minutes that it hadn't done any good.

"It's just too massive," Vyx said. "The Tsgardi must have brought the entire cliff face down. The rock must be thirty meters thick or we would have seen some movement. They wanted to make sure we never tunneled out."

"It's understandable considering we killed twenty of their number," Byers said. "They were pissed and probably frustrated that they didn't get any of us."

"They got all of us," Nelligen said. "We'll just go a lot slower than their shipmates did."

"I estimate that the synthesizers can provide us with food for another four or five months," Vyx said, "unless one of you would prefer to check out earlier."

"What does that mean?" Nelligen said angrily.

"It means exactly what it sounds like. You're both talking like we're already dead. If one of you wants to end it, do it now. It'll extend the lives of the others." Vyx paused to sigh.

"But in the end we'll all die. Even if Space Command comes looking for us, there's no way they could find us. We're here until we die."

"I thought you never give up until you draw your last breath." Byers said.

"I never have, but then I've never been buried alive before. It tends to change one's perspective while limiting one's options."

Chapter Sixteen
~ August 11th, 2274 ~

The arrival of two large personnel transport ships, the *Hayworth* and the *O'Keefe*, at Stewart SCB increased the base's staff complement considerably and would allow virtually all of the reassigned personnel to return to their ships when it could be arranged. But none of the more than two thousand new personnel were there to relieve Jenetta. She wondered if she'd know in advance this time or find out when her replacement was standing in front of her, as when she had been relieved at Dixon.

Jenetta's workday filled all her waking hours for a couple of weeks as the new personnel were placed. Most of her days were consumed by meetings with the various senior officers in each section as the new staff members were worked in and space was adjusted to accommodate the changing workforce.

One officer among the new personnel was a Senior Food Service Administrator who would take over for the officer on loan from the *Asuncion*. The *Asuncion* was still in port, so he'd be able to rejoin his ship as soon as the new administrator was brought up to speed. Jenetta sent for them both to discuss the transition.

Lieutenants Charles Mergrove and Heather Gulvil reported to the base commander's office at the appointed time and were sent in after a short wait. They walked to Jenetta's desk and braced to attention.

"At ease. Sit down, please." To Lieutenant Gulvil, Jenetta said, "It's nice to see you again, Lieutenant."

"Thank you, ma'am. It's nice to see you again and an honor to serve in your command."

"I saw from your file that you've been the Senior Food Service Administrator at the Concordia base since leaving the Ethridge Space Station at Nivella-3?"

"Yes, ma'am."

"You'll have a lot more responsibility here. We'll be serving over ten thousand at each meal until we begin to ship the Raider prisoners to the justice courts for processing. As they leave, we'll probably have additional personnel arriving, so the number served will remain fairly constant for a while."

"Yes, ma'am. I've spent the past two days working with Lieutenant Mergrove. He's explained the current requirements and we've toured the five kitchens being used for food preparation, including your private dining facilities."

"Very good. How long do you feel it will take you to reach a point where Lieutenant Mergrove can be released back to his ship?"

"I feel confident that I can take over immediately."

"Very well. Lieutenant Mergrove, you may return to your ship for reassignment after this watch."

"Aye, Commander. It's been an honor serving in your command."

"Thank you for your excellent service. I've noted it in your file. You're dismissed. Lieutenant Gulvil, remain for a few minutes, please."

After Lieutenant Mergrove left, Jenetta said, "You're looking well, Heather."

"Thank you, ma'am. You haven't aged a day since we left the Academy, but you look very different. I used to be quite a bit taller than you, but now you have several inches on me."

"You can call me Jenetta when we're alone, Heather. My height and change of appearance is thanks to the Raiders. I'm sure you've heard all about that."

"Yes, I saw the entire court martial Space Command put you through."

Jenetta sighed. "I think everyone in Space Command saw that. I understand it's been declassified and released to the media now, so it will probably haunt me until I die."

"But you were cleared of all charges. Not only that, you've been promoted four grades since then. Obviously, Space Command isn't holding anything against you. In fact, it seems to have helped your career tremendously. You've come a long way since being assigned to the *Hokyuu*." Grinning, she added, "I still remember your happy dance in the Academy barracks on the day you got your notice to report to the ship."

"The happiest day of my life to that point," Jenetta said, smiling as she thought back to that afternoon in the barracks when she had received her orders. She had screamed so loudly with glee that everyone on the floor had come running to see if someone was being attacked.

"And now you're the base commander of a StratCom-One base, the closest thing there is to God within four hundred light-years. You've had so many firsts that I'm losing track. You were the first ensign to ever command a Space Command Battleship, the first Terran to be awarded the Nordakian Tawroole medal, the first Terran to be commissioned as an officer in the Nordakian Space Force, and a Captain at that, and now the first officer below the rank of Rear Admiral, Upper Half, to ever command a StratCom-One base."

"It's only a temporary assignment."

"Temporary or not, it's an official appointment. You've out-shone everyone from our class at the Academy, even Gary Bushnell. Heck, I think you've eclipsed everyone who ever attended the Academy. I never expected you to go so far, Jenetta, especially after you smoked the zero-grav lab at the Academy."

Smiling wryly, Jenetta said, "I've tried to forget that silly incident."

"Why? It's such a great story. Nobody else— and I mean nobody— would have had the temerity to pull such a prank in

Professor Hubera's class." Pointing to the two large cats that were half dozing and half watching from their usual places against opposite walls, Heather asked, "Are these the Jumakas I've heard so much about?"

"These are my pets. But don't approach them; they get nervous when strangers get too close. What do you mean 'that you've heard so much about?'"

"You're almost as famous for having them as anything you've done. It's like General Patton's pair of ivory-handled pistols, General MacArthur's unusual smoking pipes, or Admiral Winstead's iron-crystal walking stick made from a crystal formation he found on Costio during the first interstellar voyage."

"Jumakas are hardly unusual. They're quite common on Taurentlus-Thur where they've been domesticated for hundreds of years."

"But nobody else in Space Command has a pair, or even one— at least not that I've heard about. And they would have to keep them in their quarters if they did. Only the most senior officer, such as a captain or base commander, would have the privilege of keeping them with her during duty hours."

"I work such long hours that they're better off here than in my quarters, but I suppose I do claim that privilege of rank for myself. Do you have a pet?"

"Yes, I have a toy cocker spaniel. Your pets could probably swallow her in one gulp."

Jenetta smiled. "They wouldn't do that. They actually prefer their meat very well cooked. And they won't eat anything unless I put it in their food bowls, so your spaniel is safe."

"That's comforting. They look peaceful enough."

"They are, unless I'm threatened. When that happens, they look anything but peaceful. They're very protective."

"Considering your past adventures, I can see where they'd be very handy."

"I sleep a lot better at night knowing they're by my bed. The Raiders would revel at my death, but I know that no one can sneak into my rooms while my cats are there."

"You think an intruder could get into your quarters?"

"A Raider commander actually did sneak into my quarters while I was the captain of the GSC *Song*, so it's possible. The previous captain had ordered the Marine protection detail canceled and I didn't think to have it reestablished when I took command of the ship. I guess I'm like most SC officers in feeling perfectly safe while aboard our own ships. A detail was assigned to watch my door immediately after the incident, and since then I've always had security personnel stationed outside my quarters. On the *Prometheus* they weren't immediately outside my door since I wasn't the commanding officer, but my quarters were in the same corridor as the Captain's, so I benefited by his coverage."

"I wouldn't want to be an intruder in your quarters when you arrive with your pets."

"I hope potential assassins share that view. I'm sure any who have seen the images of the assassination attempt on Dixon will certainly think twice. Tayna and Cayla saved my life for sure that day. Tanya broke the arm holding the laser pistol, while Cayla ripped out his throat. He was dead almost immediately."

Lieutenant Gulvil put her hand to her throat and swallowed hard.

Jenetta grinned. "Don't worry. They've never attacked anyone else and wouldn't unless that person intended me harm or held ill will towards me and simply got too close. I don't know how they know, but they do. They seem to have some kind of sixth sense."

With the influx of new personnel and materials from Space Command, the available labor pool from the GSC ships docked in the port, and a small army of construction bots, Jenetta was able to make remarkable advances with the concourse construction. And along with the other career specialists arriving at Stewart were a dozen skilled intelligence analysts who would finally begin to interview the prisoners and begin processing them for transportation to judicial courts, and then to appropriate penal institutions. The interviewers started with the least violent of the Raiders and then moved them into the now empty personnel transports as they finished with them. The ships' holds were being fitted to function as brigs for the yearlong return voyage, but each transport could still only take about fifteen hundred per trip, which meant that more than half the prisoners would remain at Stewart until other ships became available.

As the new personnel were infused into the system, Jenetta was able to curtail her office hours to a normal workday. She was also able to start taking a daily walk through the new concourse, as had been her custom on Dixon. The walls of the warehouses in the twenty-five-meter-high area had been completely removed wherever possible. Only the few necessary supporting pillars remained, leaving a three-kilometer-square area that was almost completely open before the new construction work began.

The entire area now appeared to be ringed by two-and-three-story buildings, like those found on many planets. For retail shops, the upper floors could be used for storage, offices, or selling space. A number of buildings would have office space up and down. For restaurants, the upper area could be used for additional customer seating. About half of the planned restaurants would have open second floors with railings, giving the impression of outdoor dining. The concourse would be illuminated according to Galactic Standard Time. At 0500 hours, dawn would break from the back of the habitat. An enormous light, representing a sun, would intensify slowly and appear to move across a sky-blue ceiling over the course of several hours, reaching its zenith at 1200 hours. Sunset would occur at 2000 hours when the sun set at the front of the habitat. At that point, street lamps would provide illumination on the streets of the simulated city while tiny lamps mounted on the twenty-five-meter-high ceiling simulated stars.

Much of the rental space was now ready for occupancy by the merchants who were sure to be arriving soon. Jenetta had already received confirmation that almost a dozen commercial transports loaded with materials and supplies to set up shops and businesses were on their way to Stewart. Stewart was being touted as the newest 'golden opportunity' for entrepreneurs.

Christa began having dinner with Jenetta again most evenings, a practice that had been suspended when the transports arrived because Jenetta's work schedule didn't allow for a leisurely repast.

"Heather Gulvil is the new Senior Food Service Administrator," Jenetta said during dinner on their first evening back together.

"Heather? No kidding. I guess it's not surprising that someone from our class at the Academy is here. Now that I think about it, I suppose it's surprising there aren't more."

"There are so many ships and bases now that two officers from the same Academy class is probably about the average in any large command. Do you have any on the *Chiron*?"

"No, I'm the only one from our NHSA class who's part of the crew."

"We were asleep in stasis during the ten-year anniversary. I don't suppose we'll be able to attend the twentieth if we're still out in this sector."

"It's still several years away. Who knows where we'll be then? We should plan on attending though, if we can."

"Space Command won't give us two years off to return to Earth for a two-day party."

"I know, but if we're anywhere near there we should go."

"Okay, if we're anywhere near, we'll go."

"How does Heather look?" Christa asked.

"Fit, but older. It's funny to run into old classmates and see how they've aged. Especially since we haven't aged— externally."

"It's going to continue to get even stranger in the years ahead if Arneu was right about our longevity."

"Mikel Arneu," Jenetta said thoughtfully. "I've been so busy lately that I'd put him in the back of my mind."

"You can be sure he hasn't forgotten about us."

"I don't think I mentioned it to you, but he was the commandant of this Raider base until a few weeks before I seized it."

"No!?"

"What a prize that would have been!"

"Where is he now?" Christa asked.

"Bacheer said he had gone on to Raider-Ten in the new Frontier Zone to set up a new research facility. I can imagine what he's researching."

"Probably the same things he was into at Raider-One— DNA Manipulation and Life Prolongation. And I'm sure he still wants to reverse the effects of old age and live forever. If he's managed to convince the lower council of the Raider organization that it's possible, he'll probably have unlimited funding."

"He has only to point to us as proof of what's possible with DNA manipulation," Jenetta said with a grimace. "I'm just glad that part of the plan to turn us into pleasure slaves didn't involve diminishing our IQ."

"That would have been accomplished with the memory wipe they intended, but you're right. I never considered that. The scientists could have engineered our redevelopment with a reduction in thought capability."

"I don't want to upset you, but it's still possible that might happen. The full change will take eight to ten years, and we're only halfway through the process even though external changes have ceased. Heather commented about our height. She used to be four inches taller than us when we were five-foot-four. Now she's three inches shorter."

"We haven't grown any taller in more than a year," Christa said. "And I think that if our thought capability was going to diminish, it would have started already. We're probably worrying over nothing. The DNA recombinant process only takes eight to ten years because it takes that long for all bone cells to be replaced by new ones. All soft tissue and membranes have surely been rewritten by now."

"I hope you're right. I don't need anything new to worry about. Can you imagine living to be five thousand years old and not having a brain?"

"Let's just think about what we're going to do to Mikel Arneu when we catch up with him. What do you think? Boiled or fried?" Christa said, smiling.

"Both," Jenetta replied, grinning. "Boil him in oil."

The silliness relaxed the mood and both women laughed at the ridiculous thought of Arneu flopping around like a large fish in an oversized frying pan full of warming oil.

*   *   *

Things on the base had just begun to settle into a fairly sedate routine when the first convoy of civilian transport ships arrived. Jenetta marveled that business people could respond to new opportunities so quickly. They had to have loaded their ships and headed for Stewart after the first rumors that the base had been taken. That was months before the habitat was secured and before the complete story was released to the public. And the ships in the convoy were all newer types capable of sustained travel at Light-225. There must be dozens more slower ships on their way with additional eager merchants looking to cash in on the new opportunities.

Fearing that things were not as peaceful in the sector as they seemed, the convoy had pooled their resources and hired Peabody Protection Services to provide two destroyers for escort duty. On orders from Jenetta, all ships were required to stand off a thousand kilometers until they were cleared for entry into the station. Inspectors had to visit each ship looking for explosives, bio-toxins, or other hazardous material.

Normally, very large ships should only be delayed a day, but since twelve ships had arrived at once— fourteen counting the Peabody ships— the delay would be almost two weeks. Jenetta's office was immediately besieged by calls from irate merchants and business people who were anxious to land after more than a year in flight.

"Inform Lieutenant Graham that he doesn't have to treat the convoy as a single entity and hold all ships until the inspections are complete. He can release them as they're cleared. Have him inspect the passenger ships first so the least number of people will be inconvenienced. But there is to be no relaxation of inspection procedures regardless of who is on board or how important they believe themselves to be."

"Yes, ma'am," Lieutenant Ashraf said.

* * *

The following days were ten times worse than when the Space Command personnel transports had arrived. Jenetta's outer office was crammed with business people from morning to night. The volume of applications for concourse office and shop space overwhelmed the layers of Leasing Office personnel she had established to insulate her office from these negotiations. She had no choice but to become involved, taking on the more difficult cases. One of the cases forwarded to Jenetta involved a restaurateur who was unhappy with the locations being offered. He wanted one of two available locations that had previously been designated as 'retail goods' stores.

"Send in Mr. Harden," Jenetta said to her com unit when she had finished her previous task.

A minute later the computer announced that a visitor was at the door. Jenetta said "Come," and the door slid noiselessly open, allowing the din from the outer office to momentarily perforate the serenity of her inner office.

"Commander Carver," the short, dark-haired man said as he entered and the door closed behind him, "it's so nice to see you again. It's been far too long. Congratulations on your successful acquisition of this magnificent new base and on your appointment as base commander." He walked right up to the desk and took Jenetta's hand, clasping it between his own.

"Hello, Gregory. Welcome to Stewart SCB. I have to say I'm surprised to see you here. Your restaurant at Higgins has always been at the pinnacle of success. I'm surprised you'd leave it."

"Yes, it has been successful, but now I want to be at the pinnacle of success at Stewart, the new gateway to the galaxy."

Gently pulling her hand away and indicating that Gregory should sit down, she said, "But what of your restaurant at Higgins. Won't it suffer from your absence?"

"Perhaps a bit; I've left my brother-in-law in charge. My sister has been harping on me for several years that I never give him any responsibility, so now we'll see what he can do with it when he gets it. I haven't involved myself at all since I left, and the numbers are down ten percent already. But I intend to make up for that here if I can just get a decent location. You have to help me, Commander. The people in the rental office keep trying to put me in the center of a block, while I believe that I need a corner location. I'm not asking them to kick somebody out. The spaces are open, but they insist I can't put a restaurant in there. I have absolutely no problem with the higher rental charges for the more prominent location."

"The planners have worked very hard to lay out the concourse according to a set of rules designed to help all the merchants prosper. They've recommended that another restaurant not be located within a block's distance. If they put you on a corner, you would find as many as four other food establishments just half a block from you."

"I can stand the competition if they can. Please, Commander. We've been friends for a long time. I'm only asking to move five stores down from the center of the block."

Jenetta sat back in her chair. Gregory's request wasn't very far outside the established guidelines, but if she did this she'd be setting a precedent that could cause new headaches as other merchants requested similar re-evaluations of *their* locations.

"I'll see what I can do for you. Call the rental office tomorrow."

"Thank you, Commander. I really appreciate this. I hope you'll be a frequent visitor to my restaurant. I brought several of my best chefs with me."

"I will, Gregory. Call tomorrow."

Gregory stood up. "Of course, Commander. And thank you again."

Many of the problems she dealt with throughout the day were similar. Either merchants wanted a location different than the ones they were being offered, or they had a problem with restrictions that wouldn't allow them to sell certain merchandise. The station would always reserve the right to restrict the import and sales of certain items, even if they weren't illegal. One such item was Melwen powder, which was used in certain religious ceremonies in this sector. It was extremely unstable and would explode if the temperature varied too quickly. Like gunpowder, it was officially listed as a not-very-powerful explosive on the import lists. The inspection sensors were set to look for it in any vessels entering the station, although it wasn't illegal to own or transport outside of Space Command bases.

* * *

The change in the concourse was amazing after just a few weeks. Many new shops were already open for business, some as they continued to place fixtures and decorate the space they were leasing while other owners were driving their employees hard to get the shelves stocked so the doors could be opened to customers. Off-duty station personnel could usually be found wandering the concourse throughout the day, watching the activity and waiting for more businesses to open. The common areas were finished. Fountains with pools and small, colorful fish graced many intersections. Small trees and shrubs had been placed along the wide 'streets' in large decorative wooden planters. Purchased through a merchant hired to bring them from a nearby solar system, they were rotated once a week from a 'nursery' storeroom where special grow lights were used to reinvigorate the flora after its week on the concourse. Like the habitat's three swimming pools, most of the water in the fountains would automatically be evacuated to holding tanks if a decrease in gravity was detected. Since gravity deck plating consumed very little energy when operating at a reduced setting, the plates beneath the pools were connected to emergency sources. It was highly unlikely that uncontained water would ever become a concern.

At first, the newly arrived civilians ran for their lives when they saw Jenetta approaching with her large pets, but eventually they came to realize that the animals posed no danger if the Commander wasn't threatened. The un-tethered cats ensured that no one ever talked rudely to her, despite any feeling of frustration they might be experiencing at the time. On the one occasion when a merchant did yell, but only to get her attention after she had passed by his store, the cats both spun quickly, their fangs bared as they hissed and braced to spring. The merchant froze, calmly apologized for shouting, and slowly backed away. Jenetta had, of course, already calmed the cats, but the merchant felt it would be best for him to return to his quarters so he could change his shorts.

Jenetta began visiting the restaurants on the concourse for lunch as soon as they started operations. Gregory's was one of the first to open for fine dining, and Jenetta visited his establishment on his first day. There was a small line of patrons waiting, but Gregory, always alert, immediately spotted Jenetta and escorted her past the waiting diners while saying loudly, "Right this way, Commander. I have your reserved table all ready." Although pets were not permitted in the restaurant, he never mentioned the two cats that rarely left her side. As her protectors, they were as welcome in the restaurant as guide dogs had once been for the blind, but now that blindness was a correctable condition there was no more need for such animals.

As he held her chair, he said quietly, "Thank you so much for interceding with the rental office. I love this new corner location. I can already tell it's going to be worth every bit of the higher lease rate for the more prominent location."

"I'm glad Lieutenant Riley was able to find a spot that satisfied you. What's good today?"

"Everything we have," he said, smiling as he handed her a menu. "The menu is a bit limited right now because some of our equipment hasn't been installed yet. I refuse to permit installation work in the kitchen during business hours, unlike some of the other restaurant owners, but we have a good selection anyway. If you'd like a recommendation, the lasagna is most excellent today. It's made with a delicious meatless sauce, but we have a wonderful meat sauce to serve with it for those who desire it."

"That sounds delicious. I'll have the lasagna with the meatless sauce and coffee."

"I'll see that your waiter brings it immediately. Enjoy your meal, Commander."

"Thank you, Gregory."

Gregory stopped the waiter who was serving tables in the area where Jenetta was seated and spoke to him briefly before rushing off to greet another patron. The waiter immediately rushed off to the kitchen.

* * *

When the incessant buzzing of her bedside com unit awakened Jenetta from a deep sleep, she rolled over to lift the com unit's cover. The vid camera was always deactivated on this particular com unit unless intentionally switched on after a call was answered. The caller either received a simulated image of her sitting at her desk or a posed, still image when she was awakened.

"Carver," she said sleepily after stabbing at the answer button.

"Commander, this is Lt. Christopher in the Station Control Center. The *Star Gazer* has just declared an emergency. They report being surrounded by a large formation of unidentified warships. They say that the ships appeared to have been headed towards the base. They tried to make a run for it, but their temporal envelope generator was destroyed by laser fire. At the same time, we detected a fleet of ships on our DDG, so I can confirm the unannounced presence of the ships."

Jenetta was instantly awake. "How many ships?"

"We're seeing twenty-six large ships. There may be more though. The *Star Gazer* was operating at the very fringe of our network. The Distant DeTect Grid doesn't permit us to see much beyond a hundred billion kilometers."

Flinging back the covers, Jenetta leapt out of bed as she barked, "Sound General Quarters. Recall all personnel working outside the asteroid and close the outer doors. Notify the GSC ships at the docking piers of our alert status. Man all defenses and ready the Combat Information Center. I'll be in the CIC in ten minutes."

Pulling off her nightgown, she stepped into her trousers with both feet and then fell back on the bed to pull them up. She jammed her feet into her boots and pulled on her blouse and tunic as she ran towards the door. She paused just long enough at the door to say, "Cayla, Tayna, stay here," to the two cats that were already at her side. Her anxiety had them agitated, and they stared after her as she ran out. They paced nervously around the apartment for several minutes before lying back down.

Jenetta took the elevator down to sub-Deck Three. The lower eight decks of the station were reserved exclusively for Space Command use, and the elevators in the officers and crew quarters sections would drop to those decks if all occupants had an implanted CT or ID. Even so, all occupants of an elevator car still needed to prove their identity by voice analysis before the elevator would descend below the main docking level.

Jenetta arrived at the Combat Information Center in less than eight minutes from the time she was awakened. The small staff that usually occupied the room at this hour was swelling quickly as officers, NCOs, and crewmen swarmed in and activated work stations and equipment. The wall that separated the CIC from the Station Control Center had been rolled back to make one enormous room. The SCC encompassed the Port Operations Center.

"Where are the bogies?" Jenetta asked.

"About ten minutes away, ma'am," a chief at the com station said. "They still aren't answering hails, and we've lost all contact with the *Star Gazer*."

"Send out an emergency message recalling all GSC warships in this deca-sector while we still have IDS communications. Tell them we expect to be attacked very shortly by a force consisting of twenty-six warships of unidentified size and configuration."

The com Chief tapped several points in the com panel and spoke into his headset before turning to say, "Message sent, Commander."

"Open secure vid lines to all GSC ships in port."

A large wall monitor began to light up with images of the bridge on each ship. The captain of each ship was already on the bridge in response to the call for GQ. When all ships were represented, Jenetta turned to face the monitor. Her image and part of the CIC would be visible on each ship's bridge monitor. For the first time, she thought about her appearance— not out of vanity, but because she didn't want to give the appearance of complete disarray in the face of enemy opposition. But it was too late now, so she proceeded with her announcement calmly.

"Good morning. A large force of twenty-six unidentified warships is headed this way. They aren't acknowledging our hails, and we must assume that their intentions are hostile. I'm also assuming that they're Raider ships. I've ordered all personnel into the port and the station's outer doors closed. I've issued an emergency recall to all GSC warships in this deca-sector. The *Asuncion* and *Chiron* should disconnect from their pier as soon as their crews are aboard and back away from the habitat. Face the port entrance, arm all weapon systems, and maintain position. The *Hayworth* and *O'Keefe* should disconnect and move to the wall opposite the habitat, also keeping their forward weapons armed and aimed towards the port entrance.

"The port entrance is our only weak area. The walls of this asteroid are many kilometers thick, and to the best of our knowledge they can't be breached by any weapons the Raiders possess. The doors themselves are several meters thick and can't be damaged by most weapons the Raiders have, including torpedoes. Following our takeover of this base, I had the doors reinforced to make them less susceptible to the form of assault we used at Raider-Three. At the onset of an attack, we'll lower the habitat's emergency airlock gates to protect against a breach of the docking platform's outside wall. If the Raiders do manage to dislodge the large doors, they'll probably attack with fighters, but fighters won't be able to breach the habitat with the emergency gates lowered. Under no circumstances should any ship leave the protection of the base without specific orders because the Raider's superior numbers give them a decided advantage outside.

"This secure vid link will remain open for the duration of the attack, so you'll always have immediate information on the situation status. Any questions?"

"How many of our ships are nearby?" Captain Powers of the *Chiron* asked.

"We haven't received a reply to our message yet, but at last report the *Song* was five days out and the *Ottawa* was nine days away. Both the *Geneva* and the *Thor* are more than a month away. We're on our own for at least five days, but we're in an almost impregnable base here. The *Star Gazer* reported the first contact but it's not responding to our hails now. We can't send anyone to investigate so we'll have to assume it's lost."

"What are the outer defensives of this station?" Captain Wilmot of the *O'Keefe* asked.

"Mainly laser arrays, but I've beefed up defenses considerably since we took possession. It was one of my top priorities because of our proximity to the frontier and our distance from other bases. The Raiders had dotted the asteroid surface with phased laser arrays when they owned the station, and I tripled the number when we took over by salvaging arrays from the Raider ships we destroyed here, along with every usable array we found in the Raider's salvage area. The outside of the asteroid has more lasers per square meter than the *Chiron*. I've also installed a dozen torpedo-launching stations around the port entrance, again using salvaged equipment and munitions from Raider ships. Anyone trying to come in is going to get a pretty nasty surprise if they think the base's armament is the same as it was before our occupation."

When no further questions were raised, Jenetta said, "If that's it, let's prepare for action."

The four ships disengaged from the docking piers and took their assigned positions. No one questioned Jenetta's orders, although each ship's captain held higher GSC rank. They were in her port, and Space Command regs on positional authority for commanding officers put her in command here despite her lower rank and seniority. One of the captains could only assume command if she voluntarily relinquished it, else they risked facing charges of mutiny. And if they refused to follow her orders relative to the safety and security of the base, they could be court-martialed.

* * *

"I hear noises," Nelligen said upon entering the room where Vyx was relaxing in Rivemwilth's large recliner.

It was good that housekeeping bots cleaned the base regularly because the three men, fully expecting to die in a few months when the food ran out, had largely stopped caring about their personal hygiene or the cleanliness of the base.

"What kind of noises?"

"I don't know. They're coming from the flight bay. I picked them up on a monitor. At first I thought I was imagining it, but I wasn't, and they're getting louder."

Vyx moved the recliner to an upright position and then stood up. "Show me."

The two men walked to the communications center that Nelligen had taken over as his own. He hadn't been able to reestablish radio communications, but he had restored most of the security systems, and a wall of monitors showed every part of the base. He turned up the audio on one of the three monitors that offered different views of the flight bay. A distinctive noise could be heard.

"That's not a natural sound," Vyx said. "Could the video unit be causing it, like a feedback noise or something?"

"Nope. I checked that. It's external to the unit."

"It could be a boring machine. Perhaps we're about to have visitors."

"Think the Tsgardi are back?"

"I don't know. It doesn't make sense that they'd return, but nobody else could know we're buried here. Better call Byers."

Vyx continued to watch and listen to the monitor as Nelligen fetched Byers.

"Tsgardi?" Byers said as soon as he entered the room.

"Don't know."

"I know you don't intend to become a slave," Byers said, "but I've decided it's better than dying in here. I'll go with them this time. I'll have a better chance of escaping from that than from this tomb."

"Same here," Nelligen said. "A difficult life is better than no life, and there's always the chance of escape."

"Okay, if that's the way you want it." Vyx looked down at himself and sniffed. He hadn't showered in about a week. "I think I'll clean up since company is coming."

Chapter Seventeen

~ September 3rd, 2274 ~

"This is Captain Tolatsak of the Raider Battleship *Colossus*. I demand the immediate surrender of this base and all personnel inside." The face of a gruff and nasty-looking Terran filled the monitor.

"This is Commander Carver, base commander of Stewart Space Command Base," Jenetta replied. "This is a Space Command base in Galactic Alliance space, and I have no intention of surrendering this base to you or anyone else."

"This is Raider property, little girl. You seized our base illegally."

"If you have a complaint, you may file a lawsuit with the Galactic Alliance Council Court. If your claims are upheld, I'm sure the base will be returned to you."

"Very amusing, *Commander*, but we neither recognize your government nor its authority in this sector of space. That station is our property and we demand its immediate return. You won't be allowed to keep it. We'll destroy it, and you, rather than allow it to be occupied by Spacc forces."

"Whether or not you recognize the existence of the Galactic Alliance is immaterial, Captain. We certainly recognize your organization, and your days of piracy, slavery, murder, and theft are numbered in this part of space. You should find yourself a safer line of work because this one leads to a penal colony if you're fortunate enough to survive."

"Enough talk. My fleet of twenty-five warships surrounds the asteroid. We know you only have two warships in the port and no more than two more within a month's travel time. The *Song* and *Ottawa* will not arrive in time to make a tactical difference here. Do you surrender, or die?"

"We will defend this base against all enemies. Are *you* prepared to die for your pirate bosses?"

Captain Tolatsak scowled as the com line went dead.

Jenetta looked at the position table in the center of the room where the base's sensor net was creating a three-dimensional holographic image of the asteroid and the ships surrounding it. So far, the ships were holding position at twenty-five thousand kilometers from the asteroid, making Stewart's lasers largely ineffective. As Jenetta stared at their positions on the plot, several of the ships in the Raider force began moving towards the asteroid, firing torpedoes and laser cannons at the port's entrance doors as they came. They were smart enough not to waste torpedoes firing at the outer walls.

"Com," Jenetta said, "tell the Echo Group laser gunners to open fire on incoming torpedoes as soon as they get a lock on a target. Tell the other laser gunners and the torpedo gunners to hold their fire until the ships approach to within five thousand km."

As the torpedoes reached effective laser range, the designated Stewart gunners controlling laser arrays around the port entrance opened up, destroying either the torpedoes or their guidance systems. The light destroyers making the run didn't fare any better. As they reached a point five thousand kilometers from the port entrance, they experienced a rain of coherent light that no Raider captain familiar with the previous defenses would ever have expected. All three small warships were destroyed by the unexpectedly severe laser fire from the base before they could get back out of effective range. They continued to drift along their former courses, but it was doubtful that very many crewmen were left alive considering the abundance of holes in their hulls. One ship passed the asteroid and continued into space, but two impacted the surface. The base's seismic sensors registered the hits, but the kilometers of rock prevented any damage to the base. However, several laser arrays were damaged by the impacts.

"The titanium skin on those old Tsgardi-built vessels is like tissue paper," Jenetta said.

"That run doesn't make sense, Commander," Lieutenant Ashraf said to Jenetta. "He just sacrificed three ships. They could have fired their torpedoes from a safe range."

"They were three of his oldest and weakest ships. He was testing our defenses. If you look at their attack paths, you'll see they approached on routes that formerly wouldn't have drawn much fire because the array coverage there was very poor. He's obviously familiar with the station's former defenses and he now knows that we've substantially increased our laser strength."

"But he could have sent just one ship."

"If he had sent one, we wouldn't have responded with as much strength. Now he knows the position of every array and he knows they're manned by gunners who know what they're doing."

"What good does it do him?"

"All information about an enemy's defenses is useful when preparing for battle. It will help him formulate his next attack."

"What do you think he'll do?"

"Well, Captain Tolatsak is discovering the same thing we did at Raider-Three. It's difficult to get a turtle to stick its neck out so you can yank it out of its shell. Threats don't work, and he can't outflank us or launch an assault against our rear positions because there's only one way in or out. I don't think he really expected us to just surrender the base, but he had to try. Now he's being forced to admit that the only way to get to the turtle meat is to crack open the shell. He doesn't have the luxury of laying siege to wait us out. Aside from the fact that we could hold out for years, there's the matter of additional Space Command ships arriving. He believes he has a month to dig us out before a sufficient force can be assembled to threaten his blockade of the base. After that, he'll have a real battle on his hands."

"How come he hasn't blocked our communications?"

"Either through oversight, or he doesn't think it makes a difference. He would also be cutting off communication to his spotter ships and to whoever pulls his strings if he doesn't have an RF relay satellite available. He might even be aware that I've had several RF relay satellites placed beyond the range of jamming signals to preclude our being totally isolated. He knows he's got nine days before the *Song* and *Ottawa* could get here together. The *Song* is closer, but it can't take on twenty-two ships alone. Together they stand a better chance, but two against twenty-two is still too great for just a destroyer and a medium cruiser." Jenetta paused for a couple of seconds. "Com, notify the torpedo gunners to watch for a ship being launched directly towards the port's entrance doors. They have permission to fire at will on such a ship."

The seconds turned to minutes and the minutes to hours as the base defenders waited for a second attack that never came. Food was brought to the CIC so staff could eat without leaving. Gunners were relieved on a four-hour rotating schedule so they could eat or rest. After almost eighteen hours in the combat information center, Jenetta returned to her quarters so she could feed her cats, shower, and put on clean clothes. After she returned to the CIC, Lieutenant Ashraf left to shower and change clothes also.

A few hours later, Jenetta went to get some rest in a nearby room that had been setup with 'oh-gee' cots. She laid down fully dressed and was asleep in minutes.

Lieutenant Ashraf awakened Jenetta after a few hours of sleep. "The Raiders are up to something."

"What sort of something?"

"Our sensors indicate that tiny objects are moving towards the base. They're not under power."

"What do you think they are?"

"They look like individuals in EVA suits, or they could be bots."

"Tolatsak has got to be kidding. Does he really think they can get past our sensor net?"

"More tests?"

"Maybe. Okay, tell our laser gunners to open fire on all targets of opportunity. Then send out some bots afterward to look around. Wake me again if anything doesn't look right."

"Aye, Commander. Oh, one more thing. Another ship has joined the group outside, bringing their total to twenty-three."

"Another ship? What kind?"

"A destroyer."

"Hmmm. Either a little late to the party, or they were occupied elsewhere. The *Star Gazer* did report twenty-six originally."

* * *

Vyx, Nelligen, and Byers were watching the monitor when the tip of a boring tool suddenly popped through the pile of rock covering the flight bay entrance. It was withdrawn, and a video probe on a flexible cable replaced it. The probe revolved around the end of the cable briefly before also being withdrawn.

Over the next few hours, the sounds of heavy equipment could be heard on the monitor. The sounds grew consistently louder as the equipment got closer.

A little more than twenty-four hours after the first sounds were heard, the snout of an ore loader could be seen on the monitor. Because the rock blocking the entrance was all loose material, everything above the height of the shuttle door had to be removed before anyone could enter. As soon as the pile was low enough to allow entrance, the ore loader was retracted and several figures in EVA suits moved into the flight bay. They paused briefly to look at the mummified remains of the dead Tsgardi that had been piled in there, then proceeded to the airlock. As the outer door was closed and locked, the airlock pressurized. Completing its cycle, the inner door lock was released, and the visitors passed into the base. Standing there facing them were Vyx, Nelligen, and Byers with their laser weapons drawn.

To say that the three visitors were surprised would be a gross understatement. They stood facing the three Space Command operatives in what might otherwise have seemed to be an amusing situation. The mirrored faceplates of their suits masked their identities from the three SCI agents, so the guns pointed at them never wavered. After ten seconds or so, one of the visitors slowly reached up and removed his helmet, revealing himself to be a Terran.

"I'm John Denault of Bradley Mining Surveys, an independent exploration company," he said nervously. Pointing to his companions, he said, "This is Claire Dennis and Josef Sitz."

Vyx, Nelligen, and Byers just stared. This was a turn of events they hadn't anticipated. They lowered their weapons partway because the intruders seemed to be unarmed.

"We're sorry to burst in on you like this," Denault continued, "but we didn't know this place was inhabited. We were on the surface doing a survey when we saw a ship firing on the cliff wall to collapse it. We wondered what they were burying and decided to find out after they left orbit. Our sensors indicated that there was a hollow area behind the collapsed rock, so we thought it might be a cavern or mine. Uh, where's your other entrance?"

The other two visitors had removed their helmets by this time.

Vyx shook his head. "That's our only entrance. We owe you a debt of gratitude. We were attacked by the Tsgardi."

"Yes, we saw some in the flight bay."

"There's another large group down in one of the storerooms. I guess they figured that since they couldn't over-run us, they'd bury us."

"If you don't mind me asking, what are you doing here? Is this a mining operation?"

"Uh, no," Vyx answered, thinking quickly. "This is a Space Command remote outpost."

"Space Command?" Denault said with a confused expression on his face.

"Yes," Vyx said quickly. "There are a number like this sprinkled throughout the former Frontier Zone. We didn't operate any bases here, but we had small outposts for security and monitoring purposes."

"I see. Hold on, I'm receiving a message." Denault paused for a few seconds, cupping his hand over the ear that held a tiny receiver. "According to our com operator, a GSC battleship has just entered orbit. They've identified themselves as the GSC *Thor*."

"The *Thor*?" Vyx said, remembering that the *Thor* had been at Stewart when they left with the *Maid*. "Would you tell them they're most welcome and that we need their assistance cleaning up after an encounter with Tsgardi slavers?"

Denault relayed the message to his com operator, who relayed it to the *Thor*. After a minute of standing around, Denault again cupped his hand over his ear. "They'll be sending a party down shortly."

"Thank you. In the meantime, I offer you the hospitality of our little outpost. Would you care for some coffee?"

Denault looked at his companions, who nodded. "Thanks. I would like a chance to get out of this suit for a while and perhaps use a restroom. Now that we're in normal gravity, I'm really beginning to feel the urge."

"Of course," Vyx said, "follow me."

A shuttle from the *Thor* landed about an hour later. The entrance to the flight bay was still mostly blocked, so a half dozen crewmembers in EVA suits exited the shuttle outside the rock fall area and walked into the base as the mining people had done. Vyx was waiting just inside the airlock without the laser pistol this time.

"Lieutenant Commander Kinley," the leader of the group said after they had removed their helmets.

"Vyx," Trader Vyx said, identifying himself. "That's Nelligen and that's Byers," he said, pointing to his two companions. "Those folks over there are from Bradley Mining Surveys. They dug us out after the Tsgardi buried us."

"We've been trying to raise you on the com for two days."

"Our communications are out as well."

"We saw the Tsgardi bodies in the bay. It looks like you had quite a battle?"

"There are a lot more bodies in one of the storerooms. The fight was a bit one-sided even though we were outnumbered because we had the advantage of fighting on our own ground."

"I'm glad to hear you're all okay."

"We're glad you happened by."

"We didn't just happen by. Commander Carver ordered us here to search for you. This base is way outside our patrol area. I have to report in, and we need to talk. Is there a place where we can have a little privacy?"

"Sure. Let's use that room over there," Vyx said, pointing to a conference room.

Kinley spoke with the *Thor* and then turned to Vyx. "We've just received a message that Stewart is under attack by a large Raider force. If you're ready, we can return to the ship. The captain is anxious to leave orbit immediately."

"I'm definitely ready to leave this base, but there's still a large cache of weapons here. Its older ordnance, but some of it is pretty dangerous stuff."

"How long will it take to transport it?"

"Since we can't bring a shuttle into the bay, I estimate about a week. If we could get the flight bay entrance cleared, it could be transported in about two days."

Kinley whistled. "That complicates things. I'd better report this."

After relaying the information, he turned to Vyx again. "The captain is sending down a platoon of Marines. They'll garrison this base to protect the cache while we respond to the attack on Stewart. Get your things together. We'll be leaving shortly."

"There's no fresh food left and the synthesizer supplies are low."

"They're bringing sufficient food and supplies to support the detachment."

"I told the folks from the mining company that this was a Space Command outpost. It would have been better if I could have avoided connecting myself to Space Command, but at the time I thought we'd need their help contacting Stewart."

"I'll take care of it," Kinley said.

While Vyx left to get his few personal belongings, Kinley approached the people from Bradley Mining Surveys.

"Thank you for digging out our outpost," Kinley said. "If you'll submit an invoice we'll see that you're reimbursed for the effort you've expended. Would you be willing to clear the rest of the rubble away so we can use the flight bay properly?"

"We can do that," Denault said. "We've already moved the largest part anyway."

"Thank you. We appreciate it. One more thing," he said, pausing for effect. "If you ever again see any of the three people who were in here when you first arrived, you don't know them, their names, or their association with Space Command. That's for your safety as well as theirs. Do you understand?"

Denault nodded. "I understand, Commander."

The two additional shuttles from the ship arrived about thirty minutes later, and a tug dropped off a quarter-container loaded with supplies before returning to the ship. The container held sufficient food, clothing, and medical supplies to support a full platoon for up to twelve months. A complete communications equipment package was also standard issue when setting up a temporary base.

The original shuttle lifted off with the three Intelligence operatives aboard, and within an hour the *Thor* was leaving orbit at top speed. It would take about two months to return to Stewart, but a call for help from any Space Command ship or base meant that all warships in the deca-sector dropped whatever they were doing and headed there at their maximum speed.

*　*　*

It had been five days since the Raider captain had tried to sneak a few dozen people onto the asteroid with sacks of Corplastizine explosives. Their intent had obviously been to destroy the surface-mounted laser and torpedo platforms. Afterward, one of Stewart's bots had snagged a floating body, or rather half a body, and brought it inside for examination. About half of the bodies had been vaporized when laser pulses hit the small canisters of Dithulene-35, the catalytic agent for the Corplastizine, they carried. The plastic explosive immediately detonated as the two components came into contact with one another. Marker tags, mixed into the Corplastizine at the time of its manufacture, were found embedded in the recovered remains of the saboteur. The information would be sent on to SCI so they could attempt to track the source. Those not killed in explosions had met their maker when lasers perforated their space suits.

Jenetta was returning to the CIC after making a trip to her quarters to feed her pets, shower, and change her clothes when a chief petty officer intercepted her. He informed her that there were several merchants demanding to see her. They were waiting at the main entrance to the Space Command combat center.

"Tell them I'm not available, and that they should see the appropriate leasing office officer to handle whatever problem they have."

"They claim to be representatives of the Merchant's Association, Commander. They say they've received the run-around long enough, and if you won't see them they're going to close all the shops and picket the concourse."

"Just what I need now," Jenetta said, exhaling loudly. "Okay, I'll give them five minutes. Bring them to the conference room down the hall. I'll be there in a few minutes.

When Jenetta arrived at the conference room ten minutes later, she found six Marines guarding the door. 'War Active' status required that there be two armed guards in escort of each unauthorized civilian in a restricted area. The Marines braced to attention as she approached. As she entered the conference room, she recognized all three of the merchants.

"Well, Mr. Diggot," she said to the head of the local Merchants Association, "what do you find more important than our current crisis with the Raiders?"

"That's the issue we wish to discuss, Commander. We want to know what's going on. There has been no news released other than that the base is under siege by an overwhelming force of Raider warships."

"I'm handling the situation."

"What's Space Command doing about this?"

"I told you. I'm handling the situation."

"Not you. We mean your superiors."

"I have no superiors within four hundred light-years. We're too far away from any other base to expect support during this situation. I'm coping by using all the resources at my disposal."

"We should open a dialog with the Raiders. Perhaps we can offer them something to leave us alone."

"Buy them off? Not likely, Mr. Diggot."

"How do you know? Have you tried?"

"No, and I don't intend to. Space Command doesn't pay tribute to anyone. This is our base and we're going to defend it to the last man or woman."

"We're only suggesting that we might reach an amicable solution if we speak to the Raiders. They're business people."

"Business people?" Jenetta echoed. "They may call themselves a corporation, but they're not business people. They're pirates, slavers, murderers, and thieves. I've already spoken to them, and they've spoken to us with their attacks. There's only one way to deal with Raiders, and that's what I'm doing. Allow me to make myself perfectly clear, gentlemen. While I normally welcome suggestions and dialog from the merchants on the base, this is a military operation and I don't think any of you are particularly qualified to offer advice in that arena. I will handle this situation, and there will be no negotiations with the Raiders. Now, I suggest you return to your businesses and concentrate on *them*, while I concentrate on *my* business."

"I intend to file a protest with Space Command, Commander. You have no right to risk our lives like this."

"This is a military base in a very forward location. You knew that when you left your nice, safe former homes to come here. As the base commander, I am the first, last, and only authority in this part of space, but you're welcome to file all the protests you wish with Space Command HQ on Earth. You should have an answer in several weeks, but the situation will be over by that time. Now, if you'll excuse me, I have to get back to the CIC. The Marines will escort you out. Good day, gentlemen."

Jenetta turned on her heel and left the conference room while three very dissatisfied merchants remained behind. But she didn't have time to think about that since she had only been back in the CIC for a few minutes when one of the watch officers noticed that a ship was moving.

"What kind of ship and which way is it headed?"

"It's a light destroyer and it's headed directly away from the port's entrance."

"Com, notify all gunners to be alert."

"The ship is slowing, Commander."

Jenetta watched the holographic image in the center of the room. As the ship turned and began heading towards the station, she said, "Tactical, fire tubes four and nine as soon you get a lock. Hold fire on all other tubes."

The ship picked up speed quickly, heading for the base's entrance doors. Torpedoes armed with fusion warheads belched from launching tubes near the port entrance as the Raider ship's course was firmly established. The ship and torpedoes all reached the same point in space within micro-seconds of one another.

"Wow!" one of the junior officers manning a console shouted as the fusion warheads detonated and the ship suddenly erupted into a gigantic ball of plasma that burned as hot as a sun for several seconds. The blast winked out quickly and returned the area to relative darkness. In space, a nuclear explosion looked like a giant spotlight being turned on and instantly off. There was normally no fire, flame, or smoke. The effect they witnessed had to be the result of explosives inside the ship's bow, coupled with a hull full of oxygen and combustible material. Realizing he had screamed out loud, the young officer turned towards Jenetta with an anxious look on his face. As if he feared censure for his outburst, he said, "Sorry, Commander."

Jenetta smiled slightly and said, "Wow indeed, Lieutenant."

"That would have done some damage," Lieutenant Ashraf said. "It must have had ten tons of Corplastizine in it."

"That was the way we broke into Raider-Three," Jenetta said. "We filled the bow of a captured ship with explosives and flew it against the doors. They're using our tactics, but they didn't count on the torpedoes. Neither Dixon nor this base had exterior torpedo capability when we took it. That will probably change on other Raider bases now that they see the effectiveness in combating such an assault technique. At Dixon, we had the benefit of using a ship for which we had no other use, while they've used up a valuable asset. Even if it was their oldest ship, it was still a warship." Deep in thought, Jenetta said, "I wonder if the helmsman got out." She couldn't keep thoughts of Commander LaSalle's lifepod tumbling uncontrollably away from Dixon from flooding her mind.

"What now?" Lieutenant Ashraf asked. Her question refocused Jenetta's mind.

"We send out a ship while they're angry and upset that their attempt was unsuccessful."

"Who? The *Chiron*?"

"No, the *Baroness*."

"The *Baroness*? Isn't that one of the Raider transport ships you captured?"

"Yes, I had Lieutenant Jacoby rig the controls during the past few days so it can be piloted remotely at sub-light speeds." Turning to the chief engineering officer who was standing by at a combat station, Jenetta said, "Lieutenant Jacoby, are you ready?

"Aye, Commander."

"Com, have the Station Control Center open the doors according to the instructions I left. Lieutenant, as soon as the doors are open far enough, send out the *Baroness*. Com, notify all laser gunners that the Raiders may try to sneak some torpedoes in while the doors are partly open."

Everyone in the CIC not required to be monitoring other activities watched the movement of the *Baroness* on the monitors as it was maneuvered into position behind the giant doors at the entrance to the tunnel. Once it reached the outer end of the tunnel, it had to stop until the doors were open wide enough for it to squeeze through.

*   *   *

Captain Tolatsak sat in his chair on the bridge scowling and muttering invectives for his latest failure.

"Captain," the com operator said, "a laser gunner reports that there's something going on at the station entrance."

"Tactical, give us an extreme close-up of the entrance," Captain Tolatsak said.

Almost immediately a view of the station's giant doors appeared on the front monitor. They were definitely rolling back.

"What's that she-devil up to now?" Tolatsak muttered. "Com, alert all ships to be ready for anything. Torpedo gunners, fire a full spread at the opening as soon as the doors are open wide enough."

* * *

As expected, a number of torpedoes came at the base as soon as the doors rolled back, but the numerous laser weapons mounted on the exterior surface provided an excellent defense and the base's trained gunners made short work of the deadly missiles. The Raider ships, although outside effective laser weapon range at twenty-five thousand kilometers, nevertheless fired their laser arrays at the opening with abandon. Pulses harmlessly impacted the doors and surface of the asteroid due to the factors that made such weapons ineffective at such great distances. The *Baroness*, waiting in the tunnel just behind the doors, absorbed the few pulses that made it into the cavern entrance.

As soon as the opening was sufficiently wide enough to accommodate its body width, the *Baroness* surged ahead, immediately turning to larboard to head for an obvious gap in the coverage of Raider ships. As it pulled away from the base, two things happened: its sub-light speed increased dramatically, and every Raider ship opened fire on it with their laser arrays, regardless of the range. Four ships— a cruiser and three destroyers— immediately broke formation to pursue. The *Baroness'* engines died before it managed forty-thousand kilometers from the base, but it continued to fly on at the sub-light speed it had already achieved with the four Raider ships in close pursuit. As it reached a point fifty thousand kilometers from the base, one of its deuterium thrusters in the stern appeared to short-circuit because the ship began a 360-degree horizontal rotation to starboard. Stewart's port entrance doors were already closed.

* * *

Captain Tolatsak sat in his chair laughing almost manically as he watched the large ship spin. The bridge of his ship erupted in applause. "That'll show that she-devil," he said loudly. "Thought she could sneak a ship past us, did she?"

"Captain," the com operator said, "Captain Bradcock wants to know what your orders are regarding the captured ship, sir."

"Have him move in and board her. Anyone left alive is now a Raider slave. If the ship can be easily repaired, it will bolster our forces here."

* * *

The four Raider ships in pursuit had continued to accelerate for several seconds after the *Baroness'* engines died, closing the distance between the ships. The cruiser was closest and launched tugs that would attempt to stop the circular spin of the apparently luckless ship while the three destroyers looked on from a kilometer or two away.

The larboard and starboard engine nacelles of the *Baroness* were riddled with laser blast holes and the hull was scarred and breached in hundreds of locations, dozens of them in critical places, leaving the Raiders to assume the ship was completely incapacitated. Captain Bradcock, aboard the medium cruiser *Demon's Lair,* wondered if there was even anyone left alive aboard the ship to take as prisoners. Not a single laser pulse had come their way since the pursuit had begun.

* * *

"Standby, Lieutenant Jacoby," Jenetta said in the CIC.

Jenetta knew Captain Tolatsak would have the three destroyers move back into position around the asteroid now that the *Baroness* was about to be boarded. Waiting as long as she dared, she said, "Now, Lieutenant."

The *Baroness* had no stern torpedo tubes, but she did have eight in the bow. Jenetta had waited until the slowly rotating ship reached a point where the bow was almost turned towards the four nearby Raider ships before giving the order. Eight torpedoes suddenly erupted from the bow tubes and raced toward the Raider ships. The Raider laser gunners, busy celebrating their victory, never even had a chance to focus their laser weapons on the approaching missiles. Within seconds of leaving the *Baroness*, the fusion warheads were detonating against the hulls of the four Raider pursuit ships.

The eight torpedoes flickered like fireflies on a summer night, and the exposed skin of the four ships began to vaporize from the heat while the impulsive shock effect crushed anything along the leading edge of the blast. X ray radiation then coursed through any direct path no longer protected by shielding. Any enemy who managed to survive the heat of the blast, the crushing effect of the shock wave, and the loss of atmosphere would begin the slow, painful march towards death as their bodies were irradiated by lethal doses of unseen rays.

As the station's sensors readjusted after the final blinding explosion, everyone saw that there was little left of the Raider cruiser. Pieces of its broken and lifeless hull were tumbling slowly away from where two nuclear devices had detonated against its hull. The three destroyers had likewise each been crushed and broken by two torpedoes.

"Wow," the young lieutenant(jg) said again, but this time he said it quietly.

* * *

Captain Tolatsak jumped to his feet and screamed in anger and shock as his four ships died. "Target that ship," he screamed. "I want everyone still alive, dead!"

Torpedoes raced at the *Baroness* across the kilometers of space from the ships encircling the asteroid. No fewer than sixteen missiles found the ship and detonated either against the hull or inside the ship. When the explosions ended, there was nothing salvageable left, except perhaps seventy thousand tons of scrap metal in assorted sizes.

Captain Tolatsak flopped back into his chair, grinding his teeth and glaring at the image of the asteroid base on the front monitor.

* * *

Lieutenant Ashraf looked at Jenetta. "It was rigged to launch torpedoes after they caught it?"

"They didn't catch it. Lieutenant Jacoby shut the engines down before it had traveled forty thousand kilometers. The blast marks were on the hull and engines before the ship even left the port. I wanted the Raiders to think they had stopped it and killed everyone on board by breaching the hull. It was essentially just a *fire ship*."

"A fire ship, Captain?"

"A tactic notably used by the British, French, and Spanish back in the sixteenth and seventeenth centuries, but normally credited to the Byzantine Empire back in the seventh and eighth centuries on Earth. When the wind was right, they would set some of their own naval ships on fire and push them into the path of oncoming enemy ships or ships at anchor. The wooden ships of the enemy, without benefit of self-propulsion, were often unable to avoid the fire ships that sailed into their midst, so they would likewise catch fire and be destroyed. Our torpedoes were launched so close to the pursuit ships that they never had a chance to knock them down before they reached their objective and detonated. Eight guidance specialists in our weapons control center flew them into the cruiser and destroyers once they were fired from the *Baroness* by Lt. Jacoby. Essentially, I made the *Baroness* into a fire ship without the usual visible signs of danger— at least as much of a fire ship that's possible in the cold vacuum of space."

"But why did they even pursue it? It wasn't a warship and posed no threat."

"I speculated that they would lash out at anything in their anger and frustration. Tolatsak wanted a victory— needed a victory, no matter how small at this point."

"They came here with twenty-six ships and they're down to eighteen now," Lieutenant Ashraf said smiling. "They've lost more than a quarter of their force."

"Captain Tolatsak won't be sacrificing any more ships needlessly. He has all the information about our defenses now. He knows we're almost impregnable, so he won't send any more ships at us. He also won't be suckered by any more *escaping* ships."

"What will his next move be?"

"I can't see that he has any *new* options. He's tried threats, a tactical assault, sabotage, and brute force, and he's been suckered by a fire ship. I suspect he'll try brute force again, but he'll have to think about it for a while first. As you said, he's expended a quarter of his force and has nothing to show for it."

Stewart SCB received a daily report from each of the ships responding to the call for assistance. If Captain Tolatsak believed individual ships wouldn't attack an overwhelming force, then he didn't understand Space Command officers. Captain Yung of the GSC Cruiser *Song* had been ready to commit his ship to an attack of the Raider force as soon as he neared the base, but Jenetta had ordered him to wait and rendezvous with the *Ottawa*, who would arrive just a few days later.

It was obvious that Captain Tolatsak couldn't decide what action to take next because the days crept by without his initiating any attacks. He had tried everything he could think of, and he had only succeeded in losing a good part of his taskforce. This was a lot more difficult than seizing freighters or passenger ships, even when they were armed. He had risen to command through brutality and cunning, but he had no formal military training and he was ill-equipped for an operation like this.

* * *

"That's all of the facts as I know them," Admiral Moore said to the other nine admirals in the meeting hall. The special meeting had been called as soon as Admiral Moore received news from Commander Carver regarding the Raider attack on Stewart SCB. "I'm open to suggestions on how we should deal with this threat."

"Carver is too inexperienced to handle this problem," Admiral Hubera said. "Pulling the *Thor* off its assigned patrol route shows that."

"For once I'm in agreement with Donald regarding Commander Carver," Admiral Plimley said. "She showed poor judgment in reassigning the *Thor* to other duties with the base's protection force so limited. We should assign a more senior officer as Base Commander for the duration of the Raider threat."

After discussing the issue at length, the Admiralty Board made a decision to relieve Jenetta of command.

* * *

The *Ottawa* arrived at the rendezvous point just after midnight on the ninth day. The *Song* had been waiting there for several days just ten billion kilometers from the base and well outside the DeTect range of the Raider ships. Jenetta called for a private briefing between all ship captains and herself, establishing a conference linkup between her small office adjoining the CIC and the ships. There was no danger that the Raiders could eavesdrop as the signals between warships and the base were encrypted using the latest and finest equipment available.

"This plan," Jenetta began, "will require split-second timing in order to keep casualties to a minimum. If the *Song* and *Ottawa* approach the station at their highest FTL speeds, the Raider's DeTect equipment will see their approach almost a full minute before they arrive, giving the Raiders plenty of time to prepare a warm reception. But that's only the situation if they perceive a threat."

"How can they not perceive a threat?" Captain Powers of the *Chiron* asked. "They know the *Song* and the *Ottawa* are coming. They're going to fly into a barrage of torpedoes like the one let loose at the *Baroness*."

"There might just be a way to get them in close without alerting the Raiders to their presence until we're ready to strike," Jenetta said thoughtfully. "I've been toying with an idea since yesterday. It will take several days to set this up, but if it works the *Song* and *Ottawa* will be in the Raider's midst before they know they're coming. Then it will be up to all of us to follow through with the rest of the plan.

"Once it arrives, the *Song* will establish a wide, counterclockwise path just five thousand kilometers outside the ring of Raider ships, followed by the *Ottawa exactly* thirty seconds later. Just before the *Song* arrives, I'll open the outer doors of the base. This will put the Raiders on alert and they'll be focusing all their attention on us. They may try to sneak some torpedoes in again, but our gunners have so far proven themselves superbly adequate to the task of stopping them. As the doors begin to open, I'll fire six torpedoes from our surface-mounted tubes, holding the final six in reserve. The Raider laser gunners will then be occupied on defense, trying to shoot down our birds when the *Song* arrives.

"The *Song* will be attacking the sterns of the Raider warships, their most vulnerable quarter, so he should be able to target and launch torpedoes towards the Raider battleship, the only remaining cruiser, and perhaps a couple of destroyers before the Raiders can properly respond to the new threat.

"As soon as the Raiders become aware of the *Song's* arrival, they'll believe that opening the doors and firing the torpedoes was all a diversion. They'll probably turn all their attention, and their ships, towards the *Song*. They may even initially believe he's trying to run the blockade and enter the base. As they open fire, the *Chiron* will exit the base and turn to larboard, following a path five thousand kilometers inside the ring of Raider ships while opening fire immediately with all bow, starboard, and stern torpedo tubes, as well as all laser arrays that can be brought to bear on the enemy. Fifteen seconds later the *Ottawa* should arrive and begin *his* run. The *Asuncion* will depart the base fifteen seconds later, following the inside track path of the *Chiron*.

"If this goes as planned, we'll have the Raider ships caught in a crossfire with approximately a fifteen-second spacing between our four circling ships. The spacing should put our ships out of each other's range, but all GSC ships will be using the 'Alpha-twenty-eight' rotating frequency ship protection code, so the guns won't lock or fire on our own ships if they should happen to be too close. The *Hayworth* and the *O'Keefe* will move closer to the port entrance and help protect the base from any Raider ships that try to enter the port while the doors are open. Between their torpedoes and laser arrays and the defensive capability of the base, I doubt any Raiders will be able to enter the port.

"Any questions or suggestions?"

"Have you considered simply out-waiting the Raiders?" Captain Wilmot of the *O'Keefe* asked. "We're protected in here and they can't stand around forever. They have to know that other Space Command warships are on their way here with all possible speed."

"When I took this station, that was exactly my position. We were too vastly outnumbered to do anything else. We *could* wait now, parrying each thrust by the Raider fleet until we could assemble enough ships to take them on in equal strength, but given the number of ships in this deca-sector, that might take a year and a half. The *Star Gazer* crew, composed mostly of women, is being held either in one of those ships outside the base or in the *Star Gazer* vessel itself. I'm sure I don't have to draw you a picture of what is most likely being done to them. Then there's the matter of morale. We're little more than prisoners in here, just as the Raiders were when I took this base. If we do nothing, that has to have an effect on our people while emboldening the Raiders to be more aggressive in the future. Finally, there are eighteen Raider warships still out there. That's eighteen more chances for serious harm to come to innocent freight-haulers and passenger ships if we don't stop them here. I'm sure the Raiders have mustered as many warships as they could for this operation. That they could only put together twenty-six makes me more euphoric than you can imagine. They attacked Higgins with seventy-three. We've hit them hard during the past seven years and we're seeing the effect of those efforts. I don't want the Raiders to slink away into the darkness of space when a large task force approaches in a year and a half. I want to take them on while they're overconfident about their chances to win the day."

There was nothing but silence to Jenetta's rousing speech until Captain Novak of the *Asuncion* asked, "If this plan is successful, how do we deal with the Raider ships that try to break away?"

"Use your judgment. If the main threat from the Raiders has been neutralized, you're free to pursue. But don't travel further than thirty minutes. If you haven't caught them by then, return to the base."

"Do I assume correctly that the base's laser and torpedo gunners won't be participating in this action?" Captain Powers of the *Chiron* said.

"Yes, that's correct, Captain, other than the initial volley. Things will be wild enough out there without you having to worry about stray fire from the base even with the code protection system in operation. We'll only use our weapons to defend against penetration of the port by Raider ships. This is principally a ship-to-ship offensive operation."

"Commander," Captain Crosby said, "we had to leave the *Maid of Mephad* unprotected in order to come here. I have about a dozen of my people on her."

"I realize that, Captain, but there wasn't any choice and I believe there's little danger. The Raiders will have assembled *every* available warship for this assault. As soon as this battle is over you may return and intercept her. Should your ship be incapacitated in the engagement, I'll send someone else."

"Thank you, Commander."

"Anything else? If not, we'll kick off at 0312 hours three days from now. The *Song* should arrive at exactly 0320 hours, and the *Chiron* will exit the base fifteen seconds later. Your CIC vid link will continue to remain open until the end of the operation, so you'll all have up-to-the-second information."

Chapter Eighteen
~ September 13th, 2274 ~

The DeTect equipment at the tactical station aboard the Raider battleship *Colossus* identified a potential threat at 2052 Galactic Standard Time. The Captain wasn't on the bridge at the time.

"Commander," Lt. Bannock said, "I'm picking up something on the DeTect grid."

Instantly alert, Lt. Commander Villas said, "The *Song*?"

"It doesn't look like it, sir. There are multiple targets, and they're coming in real slow."

"How slow?"

"So slow I didn't even realize they were moving until now. The computer puts their speed at just under 80 kps. They won't reach us for more than six and a half hours."

"How many targets, Lieutenant?"

"It looks like two large targets and about thirty to forty smaller ones of varying sizes. It's difficult to tell because the small targets are so small that they keep winking in and out."

Lt. Commander Villas, who had been on the verge of ordering a call to general quarters, climbed down from the command chair and walked calmly to the tactical screen. He looked at it for a couple of minutes.

"I don't see any indication of power signatures."

"No, sir. They aren't under power."

"What would you say they are?"

"It looks like a small asteroid that's broken up, sir, but it's not in the navigation hazard database. A collision with another asteroid could have altered its original course. It'll pass about five thousand kilometers off our stern."

Lt. Commander Villas scrunched up his face as he wondered if he should alert the Captain. Tolatsak had gone ballistic when the *Baroness* destroyed those four ships, and he hadn't calmed down yet. He was in such a foul mood that he turned on anybody bringing him insignificant news.

"I think you're right. An asteroid must have collided with another and broken apart while changing its direction of travel. In addition to the forty pieces we can see, there are probably dozens, maybe hundreds, of smaller pieces that aren't even showing because of their size. Log it into the navigation hazard database and ignore them."

"Aye, Commander," the tactical officer said as he set the computer to ignore the contact. He also sent a message to the other tac officers alerting them to the approach of the tiny asteroid cluster and telling them to have their computers ignore it's approach and log it into their navigation hazard database.

* * *

At 0312 hours the giant doors that covered the opening to the port began to roll back. Jenetta could picture in her mind the activity aboard the Raider ships. They would be running about trying to get to their battle stations and gunners would be directing their sights on the opening. Everyone who had access to a viewing screen would be watching the base. Up until now, the siege had gone according to the Raider time-table, so it was to be expected that they would be confused by this sudden movement at the base.

At 0315 the doors stopped moving. They were only a little more than halfway open. The opening was actually twice the space needed by the *Chiron*, one of the two largest warships in Space Command, to pass through, but the narrower open-ing reduced the margin of error and would usually dictate that they move very, very slowly, using thrusters to keep the ship properly aligned in the middle.

"Com," Jenetta said quickly, "tell Station Control that I want the doors fully open!"

"They're reporting that the doors are jammed, Commander!"

"Tell them to un-jam them, now!"

"They report that that the doors won't move either way. They're checking the control panel wiring."

Jenetta looked over at the wall monitor that contained the image of the *Chiron's* bridge. The captain had been listening to the talk in the CIC. "Your call, Captain. Should I cancel the operation?" Jenetta asked Captain Powers.

"Negative, Commander. My helmsman won't have any problem. Right, Lieutenant Carver?"

"Right, sir," Christa replied.

Jenetta smiled and nodded. "We're still 'go' then, everyone. Fire torpedoes."

* * *

Just about the time the doors on the station jammed, alert horns and klaxons began sounding on every Raider ship. Third watch tac officers searched their screens for danger. They spotted the approaching blips on the DeTect screen, but their navigation computer told them it was a logged asteroid cluster contact so they ignored it. If they had known it had been logged by the tac officer who had just gone off duty at midnight, they might have been a little more suspicious.

Half-asleep gunners throughout the ship raced for their stations in various states of undress. Pulses of coherent light reached out for the six approaching torpedoes and all six were shot down. All eyes watched the station to see what their next move would be.

* * *

The *Song* was just five thousand kilometers from the *Colossus* when Captain Yung ordered the helmsman to wake up their sub-light engines and commence a circular course around the Raider task force. The dozens of fighters, marine-armored transports, tugs, and shuttles peeled off and headed away from the station. This was no place for lightly armed and unarmed small craft. They had performed their task of acting as a screen for the two warships and would sit back and watch the action from a safe distance.

Imminent threat alarms began sounding on every Raider ship as the *Song's* tactical officer fired a full spread of torpedoes the instant the sub-light engines kicked in. Since the ship was already moving at 80 kps, it would take just seven seconds for the torpedoes to begin reaching the Raider ships. Guidance specialists took control as the torpedoes left the ship and flew them into their targets.

Captain Yung had already given his orders to his helmsman, laser gunners, and torpedo specialists, so he sat rigidly in his bridge chair and watched the large monitor at the front of the bridge. The ship began to turn on its planned circular course around the station five thousand kilometers from the Raider ships while the helmsman slowed the ship to Sub-Light-5.

*   *   *

Captain Tolatsak awoke to the sounds of the alert klaxon. He slipped into his trousers and headed for the door of his quarters without grabbing further clothing. He reached the bridge of his ship at about the same time the *Song's* fusion torpedoes reached the *Colossus*. For just an instant his world was on fire and then all was black. The *Colossus* was no more.

*   *   *

In the four seconds following the appearance of the *Song* on the holographic display in the center of the CIC, twelve missiles of death flew from its bow torpedo tubes. While those tubes were being reloaded, the Raider battleship *Colossus* and the Raider cruiser, targeted with four torpedoes each, were wiped from existence.

As the Raiders became aware of the threat at their rear and attempted to direct fire at the *Song*, the two Raider destroyers initially targeted by the *Song* were also destroyed by fusion torpedoes. The Raider force now stood at just fifteen, and, more importantly, the command structure had been interrupted with the loss of Captain Tolatsak and the cruiser captain who was probably second in command. Still, one lone Space Command cruiser trying to run the blockade wasn't going to frighten them away because they had a fifteen-to-one superiority outside the base, or so they thought.

As the Raider gunners shifted their attention away from the base and helmsmen began to turn their ships to bring a greater percentage of the ship's lasers to bear on a target behind them, the *Chiron* made its move. Accelerating to ten kilometers per second— a speed that when used in port under normal circumstances would cause a captain to be court-martialed for reckless endangerment— the ship slid evenly through the entrance and turned sharply to larboard. As it began its arc inside the ring of Raider ships, its tactical officers and gunners began to release their deadly volleys of laser fire and torpedoes.

Raider gunners quickly began to shift their emphasis back away from the *Song* and towards the *Chiron*, but that act alone exhausted precious seconds of fire control time. Raider captains began screaming at their helmsmen to stop turning the ship. By that time some had shifted completely around, trying to line up on the threat on their stern, a warship's weakest quarter. As Raider ships turned again towards the station, the *Chiron* was beyond target range for most as it continued its flight around the diminishing circle of blockading warships. The *Ottawa* suddenly appeared and reminded the gunners that there were other ships besides the magnificent *Chiron*. The ring of Raider ships was already beginning to fall silent by the time the *Asuncion* rocketed out of the port at Plus Ten. It quickly gained speed as it turned to larboard to join the deadly trio of Space Command ships that were decimating the Raider ranks.

When the *Song* completed its first pass around the circle, half the Raider fleet of eighteen was just a memory, and the rest had suffered crippling injuries. With each strike, less fire came at the four Space Command vessels, but the Raider hits had done little to reduce the fire coming from the *Chiron*, *Song*, *Ottawa*, and *Asuncion*.

At 0332 hours, the first Raider ship applied power to its sub-light engines and left the area while building its temporal envelope. There were only five ships still firing back at that time, so the *Asuncion* left its position and pursued. Months of inactivity sitting in port had made Captain Novak yearn for even a quick trip at faster-than-light speeds.

The old Raider destroyer *Urodella* was no real match for the same-sized but much faster *Asuncion*. Captain Novak hailed the ship twice, demanding its surrender, but the Raider ship didn't acknowledge. Once a ship in space had achieved FTL speed, there were only two known ways of stopping it. If the pursuing ship was fast enough, it could pass its quarry and cut across its bow. This action would cause the Anti-Collision System aboard the fleeing ship to abort its envelope. The pursuer would then have two minutes to sufficiently damage the fleeing ship so that it couldn't rebuild a temporal envelope and resume its retreat. However, most ships attempting to flee would have already disengaged their ACS system to prevent this from happening.

The other procedure was one of the most dangerous maneuvers a space ship could attempt. The pursuing ship must approach the fleeing vessel and attempt to merge its temporal envelope with that of the quarry so only one envelope covered both ships. If this could be accomplished, laser weapons or torpedoes could be used to disable the fleeing ship. The danger of bringing two enormous ships traveling faster than the speed of light to within five-point-two-four centimeters of one another should be readily apparent. The tiniest miscalculation could result in the loss of both ships.

Captain Novak, determined to see that the Raider ship didn't escape, ordered his helmsman to pass across the bow of the fleeing Raider ship. In his haste to escape, the captain of the *Urodella* had neglected to disengage his ACS, so the system on the Raider ship immediately cancelled its temporal envelope when it perceived a possible collision.

The *Asuncion* turned to face the *Urodella*, which was trying to rebuild its envelope, this time with the ACS disengaged. Captain Novak was prepared to finish the Raider ship with torpedoes, but the Raider ship's captain signaled his surrender and the coalescing envelope evaporated as the generator retracted into its storage container. Captain Novak ordered the Raider captain to begin sending his crew over, unarmed, in the ship's shuttles. He left the threat unsaid that any resistance would be met with deadly force.

It took an hour to transport all of the *Urodella's* crew to the *Asuncion*, check them for weapons, and place them in a secure hold for the ten-minute trip back to the base. Captain Novak had maintained the open com line to the CIC, so he knew the *Asuncion's* presence hadn't been missed. The *Chiron*, *Song*, and *Ottawa* had finished mopping up the Raiders within a few minutes after the *Asuncion* had left. No other Raider ships had managed to escape the carnage.

Once all Raider prisoners were secured in the hold, Marine patrols searched the Raider ship for anyone who might be in hiding. Finding no one, Captain Novak assigned a small crew to man the Raider ship and return it to Stewart with the *Asuncion*.

Approaching the asteroid from open space gave the *Asuncion* bridge crew a unique perspective of the battle scene. The space outside the asteroid base was littered with broken and twisted ships. The *Chiron*, *Song*, and *Ottawa* had already docked inside the base and begun making emergency repairs to their ships when the *Asuncion* and *Urodella* moved into the port and proceeded to docking piers assigned by the port operations center. The *Hayworth* and *O'Keefe* were now outside the asteroid assisting in the cleanup as teams checked the broken ships for any signs of life. Raider crews lucky enough to be trapped in airtight and radiation-shielded compartments were being brought to either one or the other of the two transport ships. Twenty-five of the twenty-six ships that had come to reclaim the asteroid for the Raiders had been destroyed, and only the ship that the *Asuncion* had chased could ever be fit for use again. The rest were essentially broken and twisted hulls drifting in space. As the *Asuncion* completed its docking, the station's sweeper ships were moving outside to assist with the cleanup.

Jenetta addressed the bridge crews of the ships just before the com lines were closed. "Well done, everyone. Very well done. Thank you for your heroic actions here this day and during the previous days. Please extend my compliments and praise to your crews. Every ship's company performed its assigned duty with skill and bravery. I'm deeply saddened by the loss of crewmen in this engagement and I hope our losses were minor. We have dealt another horrible blow to the Raider organization during this operation, and I'm sure they'll hesitate before ever trying anything like this again. God bless you all. The status condition of the CIC is now lowered from 'War Active' to 'War Ready' on my order."

The com lines to the bridge of each ship were closed and Jenetta relaxed. The CIC would continue to operate in a more relaxed mode now. It would collect information from each ship and coordinate assignments of whatever additional manpower and equipment was needed for ship repair operations. Jenetta watched the monitors as damage assessments came in. The *Song*, the first ship into the battle, had lost eight crewmen when the hull was breached by a torpedo on the larboard side. Several dozen other crewmen had suffered injuries during the battle, but none were life-threatening. The *Ottawa* had lost three crewmen from a hull breach in a larboard torpedo room and had over a dozen crewmen injured. The *Chiron* and *Asuncion* hadn't lost any crew but suffered dozens of minor injuries. The *Chiron* had been hit more often than any of the other ships, but its three layers of reinforced tritanium hull plating with self-sealing membranes had prevented the loss of atmosphere. Hits to the *Asuncion* had likewise immediately self-sealed.

While the loss of eleven crewmen was depressing, it paled in comparison to the losses suffered by the Raiders during a battle that lasted just twenty-one minutes, if one only considered the final action. One of the officers in the CIC prepared an estimate of crew sizes aboard the Raider ships based on type, size, and knowledge of normal staffing levels aboard Raider ships. He calculated that the total crew complement of the original force of twenty-six Raider warships could have been as high as nine thousand, three hundred. They didn't yet know how many would be found alive and rescued, but it would surely only be a fraction of the original number.

Jenetta remained in the CIC for the next several hours as the cleanup and repairs continued. She had an urge to go check on Christa, even though she knew the bridge of the *Chiron* hadn't suffered any damage, but suppressed the urge and finally just left and returned to her quarters to get some needed rest.

*   *   *

Jenetta spent the entire next day preparing her report of the operation. It was forwarded to Space Command, along with a complete video record from the CIC and all sensor information while it was in 'War Active' status. The captain of each ship involved also forwarded his report and the video log from his bridge, along with all sensor information. From the supplied data, Space Command would reconstruct a simulation of the entire eleven-day period and the actions of all ships. The Intelligence Section and War College analysts always studied such records in great detail.

Jenetta dispatched the *Asuncion* to intercept the *Maid of Mephad* and escort it back to the base while the *Ottawa* continued its repairs. The *Maid* had continued to travel at Light-187 since the *Ottawa* had left it to race to Stewart, so the intercept distance was greatly reduced. They reported that they hadn't encountered any difficulty following the *Ottawa's* departure.

The next day, a funeral service was held in the as yet unfinished stadium/convention center on the concourse. Except for those personnel on duty in essential positions, virtually the entire military complement of the base and the ships in port attended. Jenetta, as base commander, officiated, along with the captains of the deceased crewmen and their ship's chaplains. After the ceremony, the bodies would be cryogenically frozen for return to Earth.

Following the funeral service, Jenetta went to the base hospital to visit the crewmen injured during the battle. The entire crew of the *Star Gazer* had been found alive in the brig of the damaged destroyer that had arrived at the station later than all the others. The crew had been brutally treated but all would survive. They had been told by the Raiders that they would be sold as slaves after the station was retaken. The officers had been anxious to enjoy their opportunity before they had to turn them over to a station commandant, so the nine women had been raped repeatedly during the eleven days they were aboard the ship. The small research ship had been badly damaged during the attack but was recovered and towed back to the base.

About halfway through the visits, Jenetta came to Lieutenant Kesliski's room. Jenetta had been assigned to work for the lieutenant following her court martial on Higgins while she was still an ensign. The lieutenant hadn't made any secret of the fact that she disapproved of Jenetta's attitude towards the Raiders. Jenetta had once spent almost a month in captivity, during which time she had been subjected to torture, humiliation, and an experimental DNA process that would alter her forever in preparation for her being made a pleasure slave at a kinky resort in the Uthlaro Dominion.

Pushing open the door, Jenetta walked into the hospital room. Lieutenant Kesliski, her face a puffy mask of multi-colored bruises, at first appeared to be sleeping. But her eyes opened as much as they could as Jenetta turned to leave.

"I'm awake, Commander," Kesliski mumbled through her swollen mouth.

Jenetta turned back. "Hello, Lieutenant. How are you feeling?"

"Better now, ma'am. I've been assured there's no lasting damage, and most of the swelling should go down in a few days."

"That's wonderful news. I'm glad you and the other crewmembers of the *Star Gazer* have all survived your ordeal."

"Thank you, ma'am."

"I'm sorry we couldn't rescue you sooner, but we were vastly outnumbered and couldn't take on the Raiders until the *Song* and the *Ottawa* arrived back here."

"I understand, Commander. I've heard all about the siege and the battle. If it wasn't for you, we'd all be headed for a life of slavery and degradation. I couldn't have stood much more of what I experienced. I would have killed myself if I had had to face that for the rest of my life."

"The Raiders brainwash you into believing that you love it. Then they wipe all your old memories so you don't remember your former life. They end up with a compliant and obedient slave."

"Is— is that what they did to you?"

"Just the first part. I escaped before they wiped my mind. The doctors at Higgins removed the programming the Raiders had performed, or at least covered it up. It hasn't been a problem."

"I want to apologize for my behavior at Higgins, Commander. I didn't really appreciate what you'd been subjected to." Lieutenant Kesliski's voice had become very hard and, although starting quietly, grew louder and more vehement with each word as she remembered the things that had been done to her. "If I could have done what you did after becoming a prisoner of the Raiders, I wouldn't have hesitated for a second. I won't ever hesitate again if given the chance. I'll kill every one of them before letting them take me again." The last words were almost spat out.

Jenetta nodded and calmly said, "The Raiders are a malevolent group, opposed to the organization and rule of law that the Galactic Alliance brings with it because it threatens to end the slavery, piracy, murder, and theft that's their life's blood. We have to end the stranglehold they've had on this part of the galaxy and destroy them at all costs. I'm glad you've come to see that. I'm only sorry you had to experience their brutality firsthand."

"I was only interested in my work and I allowed myself to be blinded to everything else. I'm sorry. I support your efforts a hundred percent now."

"Thank you." Trying to calm the lieutenant and lighten the mood in the room, Jenetta added, "Speaking of work, you should concentrate on getting better now. There's enough work waiting to keep your section busy for decades to come."

"We don't have a ship. The engines of the *Star Gazer* were destroyed according to the captain."

"There are other ships available. We can have one outfitted and ready in a couple of months. In the meantime, we've recovered the *Star Gazer*, and its computer still contains all the data you've collected already. There's plenty to do, Lieutenant."

"Yes, ma'am."

"You come visit me after you're released here and we'll get to work on preparing another ship for your work."

Lieutenant Kesliski actually smiled slightly until her face reminded her of the swelling.

"Get well, Lieutenant. I'll see you soon."

"Goodbye, Commander. Thank you."

Jenetta nodded and turned. She stopped just outside the door to think about the short conversation. Lieutenant Kesliski had undergone an amazing change of attitude, but the experience of being beaten and raped repeatedly would do that to anyone. It was fortunate that not everyone had to be subjected to such pain and cruelty to see the truth.

Most of the other women were in better physical shape than Kesliski. They hadn't resisted the inevitable quite as fiercely. All would begin counseling immediately to help them overcome the trauma of the captivity and their treatment at the hands of the Raiders.

Continuing her visits until she had seen everyone captured by the raiders or injured in the battle, Jenetta returned to her office in a melancholy mood. Although gratified that Space

Command had so many dedicated crewmen, she was sad that so many had been injured as a result of orders she had given.

Jenetta had forwarded a report to Space Command immediately after the Raider ships arrived, but she didn't receive an answer until three days after the battle was over. In the message, Space Command instructed her to immediately turn command of the base over to Captain Powers of the *Chiron* for the duration of the Raider threat.

Jenetta listened to the week-old message, leaned back in her chair, smiled widely, and said, "Oops."

*   *   *

The meeting hall where the Admiralty Board conducted its sessions was unusually quiet after the composite vid record of the battle at Stewart had been viewed. The video report, prepared by the Intelligence Section from days of CIC log videos, lasted several hours and included all pertinent actions and communications that had occurred from the moment the CIC was activated with 'War Active' status. The gallery was empty, but all ten of the admirals were present, along with the usual complement of aides and clerks who sat dutifully behind their admirals around the perimeter of the horseshoe-shaped table. The earlier conviviality over the victory had dampened and the Board was now assessing the tactics of the battle plan.

"Would anyone care to view the record again?" Admiral Moore asked of the other board members. As he looked at each, they just shook their heads slightly. "It would seem that our order to Captain Powers placing him in command of the base during the recent crisis didn't arrive until three days after the battle was over owing to the distance to Stewart. Commander Carver did a magnificent job responding to the surprise attack, defending the station, and defeating the Raiders. I'm deeply ashamed. The order to replace her during a difficult period, arriving on the heels of her outstanding victory, had to have come like a slap to her face."

Silence descended over the room again until it was broken by Admiral Hubera. "Let's not forget she recklessly ordered the *Thor* to leave its assigned patrol route to run off on a crazy search for three people, thereby endangering the base and thousands of Space Command personnel in the first place."

"Even *with* the *Thor*, she would have been outnumbered twenty-six to five," Admiral Hillaire said. "She can hardly be accused of endangering the base in the first place because the presence of one more warship in the port would not have dissuaded the Raiders from attacking. One of the basic tenets of our military service is that we never leave a man behind. The three individuals Commander Carver was trying to recover could very well have perished if not rescued. She couldn't know that a mining survey crew would happen across them. I believe Commander Carver did a splendid job under impossible conditions and turned what might have easily been a major blow into an incredible victory."

"I *also* believe that we acted very rashly when we voted to replace Commander Carver during the emergency," Admiral Platt said. "If we had such little faith in her abilities, we should never have named her as base commander to begin with. We must show her that we have confidence in her ability to command by rewarding her in some way."

"Rewarding her?" Admiral Hubera exclaimed. "We've already placed her in a position that's never before been held by an officer below the rank of Rear Admiral, Upper Half."

"You equate heaping a ton of responsibility onto a young officer's shoulders with receiving a commendation for a job well done?" Admiral Bradlee asked.

All eyes turned towards Admiral Hubera and he scowled, then looked down at the table while muttering something under his breath.

"Evelyn is right," Admiral Moore said. "We must do something to erase the embarrassment of being ordered to surrender command to a more senior officer, and Commander

Carver must understand that we appreciate her efforts and continue to have confidence in her judgment."

*   *   *

Jenetta was glad news reporters hadn't gotten to Stewart yet. But even without their onsite presence, the news broadcasts received in the daily data stream were overwhelming for a couple of weeks. Headlines such as 'Carver Repels Raiders, Carver Annihilates Fleet,' and similar sensational headlines were commonplace. Space Command had released a number of press statements and the press had filled in between the lines, digging back into Jenetta's military history and even replaying segments of the video record from the court martial where she testified about the raids she had led to retake the battleships and the final destruction of Raider-One.

After the news of the battle was released, Jenetta received hundreds of messages from former classmates and people she had met during her military career. Even a few friends from high school— mostly people from her inner circle of 'computer geek' friends— sent notes. She responded to every one personally, even though her responses all started to sound the same after a few dozen.

Her family was naturally relieved that she was safe and her brothers were envious that Jenetta was once again in the thick of things. Jimmy seemed to be particularly envious, vociferously stating that he thought Space Command should rotate officers from behind the lines with officers who had seen a lot of action. His ship was on routine patrol in an area that rarely ever saw any real trouble.

*   *   *

It took weeks to complete the repairs to the four warships that had participated in the battle. There wasn't any great urgency since the ships were all fully space worthy after a few days, so the engineers took the time to do the repairs right. It might be years before they got back to a shipyard and this was the only protected base within almost four hundred light-years.

The *Maid of Mephad* had arrived with the *Asuncion*, and the cargo of weapons and munitions was unloaded and brought to an armory below the docking level where each piece could be examined and their serial numbers recorded.

The *Thor* returned to port with Vyx, Byers, and Nelligen aboard. Each man had prepared a report during the return trip and transmitted it to Captain Kanes at Higgins Space Command Base. Jenetta arranged for a clandestine meeting in her office with the three men to thank them for their participation in the weapons retrieval operation. Vyx had explained to Byers and Nelligen while in Rivemwilth's base that Jenetta knew every detail of the operation from having worked at Intelligence and they talked openly. They told her about loading the ship and then being brought to the planet's surface so Rivemwilth could strand them on the base.

"I'm glad he didn't just shoot you and have your bodies tossed out an airlock," Jenetta said.

"Well, it's true that he couldn't just let us go after stealing our ship," Vyx said, "but Shev Rivemwilth was also never one to pass up an easy credit. If word had gotten out that he had broken a contract and then stolen the assets of the other party, his business would have suffered greatly. There's always someone desperate enough to buy from anybody, but the price would have to be very low to attract the less desperate customers— those wary of a bad reputation. Rivemwilth had to make sure we disappeared permanently, so we couldn't tell anyone what he did. He could have just killed us and buried our bodies on the moon, but there's no profit in that. By selling us into slavery, he turned a profit and buried us at the same time. I'm sure the Tsgardi were there to take us away as slaves to a far-off mining colony. He must have had himself a real good laugh as the *Maid* left the moon's orbit."

"I'm sure he wasn't laughing when those explosive charges fired," Nelligen said, grinning, "and the atmosphere evacuated."

"No," Vyx said, "that would have wiped the smile off his ugly face. I'm sure the end came too quickly though. I wonder if there was even time for him to realize that I had done him in."

"If all the charges fired," Byers said, "and the emergency doors didn't close, they probably had less than a minute before the atmosphere was so depleted that they were struggling to get their breath. That wouldn't allow much time for reflection.

"They probably used their last seconds trying to get the emergency rebreathers to work," Vyx said without remorse. "I removed the control chips from all rebreather masks just before we reached the RP. By the time they realized that was a lost cause, it would be too late to get to lifepods. Rivemwilth was responsible for his own demise. If we hadn't been stranded on the base, it would have turned out much differently. But it's doubtful he ever would have enjoyed freedom again. Who knows, perhaps he would have preferred it this way. A jail cell wouldn't come close to providing the comforts of the base he had built on that moon. If you had to be stranded in a deserted base, you couldn't ask for a better place. If we'd had communications and ample food, we could have just kicked back and relaxed until someone could stop for us."

"From the way it's been described to me," Jenetta said, "the base is extremely well constructed. Pending confirmation from Space Command Supreme Headquarters, I've decided to designate it as an official outpost. At sixty light-years from Stewart, it offers a good location to function as a resupply point so ships don't have to travel the extra two or three months to Stewart when they're short on food or supplies. A small staff can be rotated in and out every six months. If it's approved as an official outpost, Quartermaster supply ships will make it one of their regular stops in this sector."

"I have something else for Captain Kanes, Commander. One of the Tsgardi who died in the attack on us is the spitting image of Recozzi. I'd like to have him identified before the body is disposed of."

"Certainly. Where's the body?"

"In the morgue aboard the *Thor*."

"I'll have the Intelligence Section here examine it as soon as possible. Is it in good condition?"

"He took a hit to the heart that killed him instantly. He didn't smell too good when we took him out of the storage container, but then he didn't smell too good when we first put him in. Come to think of it, Tsgardi never smell very good anyway."

Jenetta grinned. "As long as they can get elbow prints and DNA, they should be able to identify him and his origins."

"I'll be interested in learning those myself."

"Our Intelligence people here found Rivemwilth's records aboard the *Maid*," Jenetta said. "They positively identify Rivemwilth as the arms dealer behind the thefts and name his accomplices. His demise and the recovery of the ordnance will probably close the active investigation. Rivemwilth's records will put the others away for a long time."

"I guess we have some downtime coming," Vyx said.

"You deserve it," Jenetta said. "On behalf of Space Command, I want to commend you on a job well done. The recovery of those weapons will go a long way in helping us keep peace in this part of the galaxy. Thank you."

Before the three operatives left, Vyx requested the return of the envelope he had left with her for safekeeping.

"Also, what about my ship?" Vyx asked.

"The *Maid*?"

"Noooo, *my* ship, the *Scorpion*. The small transport I use to travel around."

"It's still where you left it in the port. Thinking about leaving us right away?"

"As soon as I get new orders. I also have a little side trip to Scruscotto in mind. Someone there owes us," he said enigmatically.

* * *

A DNA check performed on the body of the Tsgardi who looked like Recozzi proved that he wasn't a clone, although the family ties were very close. He had to be either a brother or cousin. Knowing that the Tsgardi blood feud code required all family members to know the face of the enemy, it wasn't surprising that another brother or cousin on Gollasko would have recognized Vyx immediately. Each Tsgardi carries the images of family enemies with them on playing cards and are required to study the faces nightly. The personal belongings of the Tsgardi killed at Rivemwilth's base must have been aboard his ship because they weren't on his person.

In any event, Vyx would have to be on the lookout and be careful around all Tsgardi because he couldn't count on there being such a striking family resemblance in the future. Very few people survived a Tsgardi blood feud unless they returned to Earth or at least remained at the inner core of the Galactic Alliance system. The Tsgardi rarely ventured there.

* * *

A week after the *Maid of Mephad* docked, Jenetta received a message from Space Command. It turned out to be a copy of a transmission sent to Mr. Diggot, the chairman of the Stewart Merchant's Association. The face of Rear Admiral, Lower Half, Wright appeared as Jenetta tapped the play button.

"Greetings, Mr. Diggot. Space Command Supreme Headquarters has received your complaint and investigated the matter thoroughly. Essentially, your grievance seems to stem from a lack of confidence in the ability of Commander Carver to function as base commander. Let me assure you that the Admiralty Board does not share that opinion. Space Command has full confidence in all our base commanders or they would not occupy such strategic positions of authority and responsibility, and Commander Carver has repeatedly proven herself to be one of our most able base commanders. Her response of ignoring your request to negotiate with the Raiders was one hundred percent correct. We find that you were very much out of line for even suggesting such an action. It's not the place of merchants to criticize the military decisions of Space Command officers during battle situations.

"Forgetting for a second that the Raiders have shown repeatedly that they can't be trusted to honor agreements, Space Command does not endorse appeasement of criminals. Your complaint calling for Commander Carver's immediate removal states that you and your organization will neither accept Commander Carver's authority nor obey her directives. Since this is in direct violation of the lease agreement you signed for space on the Stewart concourse, you force us to demand that you vacate the premises within 30 days from the receipt of this message. We will not hold any other members of your organization responsible for your words, but they will be likewise evicted should they be found to be in violation of the terms of their leases. Space on the concourse is a privilege, not a right. You're located on a military base, and a base commander is the final authority outside of Supreme Headquarters. In Commander Carver's case, she is the final authority in all Space Command matters over hundreds of light-years in every direction of Galactic Alliance space. She will be directed to return all unused rents and deposits once you have vacated your leased space.

"Admiral Wright, Space Command Supreme Headquarters, message complete."

Later that day, Lieutenant Ashraf informed Jenetta that Mr. Diggot was requesting to see her.

"Send him in, Lori."

Diggot wasn't even through the doorway before he began apologizing for the letter he sent to Supreme Headquarters.

"I was scared, Commander," Diggot said. "I didn't know what I was doing. I see now that I should have trusted your judgment. Please forgive me."

"I forgive you, Mr. Diggot," Jenetta said nonchalantly.

Diggot brightened. "Then I don't have to leave?"

"I didn't say *that*. I said I forgive you."

"Please, Commander," he whined, wringing his hands roughly. "Don't kick me out. I'll lose everything. I hocked my soul to get here." He started to walk closer but stopped short three meters from Jenetta's desk as the two cats stood up and snarled.

"Space Command Supreme Headquarters made the decision, Mr. Diggot, not me. They're the ones who ordered you to vacate the space you've leased. You wanted a Headquarters intervention and you've received it."

"Commander, please, I made a mistake. I'll never do it again. Please let me stay. Space Command has said you're the final authority in this part of space. Since this is a StratCom-One base, as the base commander you're empowered to override their directives. Please," he pleaded.

Jenetta sighed. She didn't like the man, but she didn't like to see people grovel either. She knew she could insist and that it would ruin him, but she didn't really hold any malice towards him.

"Mr. Diggot, I'll allow you stay on two conditions. One, that you submit your resignation as president of the Stewart Merchant's Association effective today and that you never again run for either of the top two leadership positions."

"Of course, Commander. Anything you say. I'll resign immediately."

"And two, that you send a letter to Space Command apologizing for wasting their time and requesting that they endorse my decision to lift the eviction order. If they do, you may stay."

"Of course, Commander. I'll send the letter today. Thank you so much. Thank you. Thank you."

"Very well, Mr. Diggot. The matter of the eviction is suspended pending the response from Admiral Wright and subject to the provision that you send the request today."

"I will, Commander. Thank you. Thank you."

Jenetta had to walk Diggot out the door to get him to stop thanking her.

Two weeks later Jenetta received a message from Admiral Wright approving her action concerning Mr. Diggot and expressing his satisfaction that she settled the matter amicably. He also congratulated her on her handling of the base and the battle for the station.

Chapter Nineteen
~ December 15th, 2274 ~

Three months following the battle, the station was back to normal. The *Hayworth* and the *O'Keefe* were filled with Raider prisoners and ready to depart for the penal colonies where the Raiders would be tried, sentenced, and incarcerated. The *Thor, Ottawa,* and *Asuncion* had received new orders to leave on regular patrol, while the *Chiron, Song,* and *Geneva* would remain behind to provide base security. Other warships were on their way and would arrive in the coming months, freeing up the three for patrol activities.

Captain Powers requested that Jenetta and the senior officers of each ship involved in the battle have a dinner together before any left the port. Jenetta also invited the senior officers at the station who had worked in the CIC. The *Geneva* and *Thor* had missed the action, but their senior staffs were invited as well so they wouldn't feel slighted. Jenetta's private dining room was far too small to accommodate everyone, so the Officers' mess, located very near Jenetta's private dining room, would close for the evening at 1700 to be used for the special dinner. Officers who didn't have dinner before that time would either have to eat in the NCO mess or try to get an invitation to dine at an Officers' mess aboard one of the ships in port for this one evening.

Lieutenant Gulvil took personal responsibility for the meal and everything was excellent, from the appetizers to the dessert. Since no dinner party such as this could ever be held without a few speeches being given, Captain Powers stood up to speak after the mess attendants had removed the dishes and begun serving coffee and desserts.

"My friends, I'm delighted to be here tonight and equally delighted that you're all here to enjoy this delicious meal.

There was some question a few months ago of whether we'd still be around to celebrate after the battle. The Raiders definitely had us out-numbered and outgunned. It's interesting that a few days after the battle was over, I received orders from Space Command Supreme Headquarters instructing me to take control of the station for the duration of the Raider threat. But by then the Raider threat was ended. I assume Space Command wanted a more senior officer in charge during such a dangerous and critical time.

"Well— following receipt of that order, I sent a reply to the Admiralty Board thanking them for their confidence in me. I also included a statement praising the tactical brilliance of Commander Jenetta Carver. It's true that I would have handled it differently. I'm sure every officer in this room would have had some variation for responding to the Raider threat, but I'm equally sure that not one of us could have had greater success. We destroyed twenty-six Raider ships while losing none, and we lost only eleven people while the Raiders lost many thousands. I firmly believe that the tactics used here since the day Commander Carver first seized this station with a tiny, incapacitated ship and a crew of just a hundred eighty-five will be documented, taught, and studied at the Academies for many years to come."

Captain Powers sat down to applause and Captain Yung, as the second ranking officer at the engagement, stood up immediately to speak.

"I'm very happy to be here tonight also. I was honored to captain the first warship to engage the Raiders during this battle, although I must say that flying into the fight in the *highly* unusual and daring manner ordered by Commander Carver was a bit unnerving. We entered the engagement area at just 80 kps and didn't employ our sub-light engines until we were just five thousand kilometers from the ring of Raider ships. The base had, of course, provided complete information on every target and its position. Still, it's a bit unnerving to expose yourself as the sole target to eighteen enemy warships." Smiling, he said, "Having the port entrance doors at the base jam halfway open didn't make me feel any better at the start of the operation. I'm glad Captain Powers has such an excellent helmsman that the smaller opening didn't delay his arrival. His timely exit from the port took much of the gunnery attention away from my ship. Every battle is fluid and unexpected events will always occur at the worst possible moment, but the jammed doors didn't affect the outcome of the battle and I add my praise to that of Captain Powers in congratulating Commander Carver for her excellent battle plan."

The speechmaking continued around the room, ending with Captain Payton of the *Thor*.

"The *Thor* was, unfortunately, too far away to assist in this engagement. If we had been on our scheduled patrol route, we would probably have been able to get here in nine days, but we were on a special mission for Commander Carver that took us well away from our patrol area. I'm indeed happy that things turned out as well as they did. I've studied the battle plan and examined the sensor data, and, as Captain Powers has stated, I too would have done things differently. But I don't think I would have had the tremendous success and miniscule losses against such an overwhelming force. I salute Commander Carver's brilliant tactical direction during this battle."

Jenetta stood to talk as Captain Payton sat back down, but Captain Powers stopped her with, "There's one more person to speak yet, Commander."

Jenetta sat back down, scanning the assembled officers for the next speaker. The huge monitor on the wall behind Jenetta suddenly came to life and a six-foot-high, head-and-shoulders image of Admiral Holt appeared and began speaking.

"I'm sorry I'm not there tonight to join this elite group of Space Command's finest. If the after-dinner activities have gone as planned, I'm the last to speak in praise of Commander Carver. We've examined all the reports, videos, and sensor data submitted to Space Command and performed re-creations of the siege. No disrespect to Captain Powers— nor is any slight to his abilities intended; he knows the high regard we hold for him— but the Admiralty Board now realizes it was a— miscalculation to order him to assume command of Stewart. The base was in excellent hands all along. For those of us who study tactics, and few military officers don't, the battle plan was slightly reminiscent of the plan used at the Battle of Vauzlee. I'm sure all of you know that engagement was commanded by Captain Gavin of the *Prometheus*, but some may be unaware that the tactics used in the other sensational victory were developed by then acting First Officer, Lieutenant Commander Jenetta Carver. Captain Gavin decided to use her plan in the final hours before the battle instead of one proposed by the planners at the War College. In a report to Space Command, he credited her plan with being mainly responsible for the huge success of that engagement. Commander Carver also devised the brilliant battle plans we used at the Battle of Higgins. We were out-numbered seventy-three to seven and managed to cut those odds almost in half within the first minutes of battle thanks to the inspired tactics of Commander Carver. It seems that the Admiralty Board forgot those little details when issuing the order that Captain Powers assume command of Stewart.

"I don't have to tell this group of officers how important it is to a line officer to be in space. Line officers are a very special breed and are just not happy being moored on planets or even space stations. Commander Carver is such a line officer, but she serves where sent without complaint and serves spectacularly. Despite my objections, the Admiralty Board has decided that Commander Carver will remain on Stewart as Base Commander for a full five-year tour of duty. I'm sorry, Commander. You've done your job so well that they can't find anyone better qualified or perhaps even *as* qualified."

Jenetta could feel her heart beginning to sink.

"But all is not bad news. The room will come to attention."

The officers in the room were confused as to whether or not they should take orders from a pre-recorded video message, but they followed Captain Powers' lead and stood up, then came to attention.

There were a few seconds of uneasiness because the admiral had wanted to give ample time for everyone to comply. He actually allowed too much time, but Captain Powers never flinched so everyone remained at attention.

The image of Admiral Holt finally began to speak again. "Commander Jenetta Alicia Carver, by special order from the Space Command Admiralty Board and with unanimous approval by the Galactic Alliance Council, you are immediately advanced to the rank of Captain. Congratulations, Captain. Would you do the honors please, Captain Powers?"

Jenetta turned to face Captain Powers, who produced the proper insignia from his pocket and replaced the three-bar commander insignia on Jenetta's shoulders with the four-bar insignia of a captain. He then saluted her, and after receiving her return salute, said, "The room shall be at rest. As you were." He extended his hand to Jenetta and pumped hers warmly. "I can't think of anyone who deserves it more. Congratulations, Captain Carver."

"Thank you, sir," Jenetta said, out of habit.

"Call me Steve."

"Of course, Steve. Thank you for all this. I assume you arranged it all."

"Admiral Holt actually set the format. I just went along with his wishes. But it's been my great privilege to pin on your new rank insignia. I'm sorry that you're dry-docked for a while."

"Thank you. I'm sure the tour will go quickly and I'll get back aboard a ship again."

"You will if they're smart. It's where you belong."

The rest of the officers began to crowd around and congratulate Jenetta while waiters emerged from the kitchen area with glasses of white wine so everyone could drink a toast. After that, a waiter pushed a portable bar into the room for those who wanted something a little stronger. The party lasted until after midnight.

Before going to bed, Jenetta called the bridge of the *Chiron* and the watch officer allowed Christa to take the personal call from the base commander. Christa immediately noticed the new insignia on Jenetta's shoulders.

"Oh my God! Is it official?"

"Yes. Admiral Holt, in a recorded vid message, made the presentation at the end of the meal. Captain Powers actually pinned on the bars. I'm sorry you couldn't come, but they wanted only senior officers there and felt that your presence might tip me off that something special was in the works."

"It doesn't matter. I'm so happy for you, sis."

"Thanks. That's the good news."

"There's 'not so good' news also?"

"Yes. I have to remain on as base commander for a full tour."

"That's not so bad. Just one tour?"

"So far. Admiral Holt said it's because I've done such a good job. They reward good work by assigning you to do a job you don't want."

"The time will pass before you know it. Have you sent a message to mom and dad giving them the good news?"

"Not yet. I'll do it in the morning. I'm exhausted right now and I want to appear fresh and alert. If dad was right, Billy may feel some slight embarrassment about my making Captain first. I want to think about that message and choose my words carefully."

"Okay. I won't say anything to them until I know you've broken the news."

"Okay. You'd better get back to work. See you at the gym in the morning."

"See ya."

The screen went blank and Jenetta pushed it down. She changed into her nightclothes, crawled under the sheets, and immediately fell into a deep sleep.

The grapevine had already spread the word of Jenetta's promotion so no one was surprised to see the four bars on her shoulders the next morning, but everyone took the opportunity to congratulate her as she walked to breakfast and then to her office.

Lieutenant Ashraf stood up and saluted, welcoming Jenetta with a "Captain on the bridge" announcement as she entered the empty office.

Jenetta smiled and returned the salute.

"Congratulations, Captain."

"Thank you, Lori."

"Does this mean you'll be getting your own ship now?"

"Not yet," Jenetta said sadly. "Admiral Holt broke the news that Supreme Headquarters wants me to complete a full tour here. Even if they count the tour as starting when I first seized the base, I'll still have three and a half more years. But they probably won't consider the tour as starting until I was officially named as base commander by Captain Gavin."

"I'm sorry, Captain. I guess I thought they'd be sending a two-star to take over now."

"So did I," Jenetta sighed. "I suppose it's a great honor— as everyone's been telling me. There's no reason to keep you stuck here though. I'll approve your transfer back to the *Song* whenever you're ready."

"If you're not unhappy with my performance, I'd prefer to stay here with you, Captain. I still have a lot more to learn from you, and I'd like to make my transfer to your staff permanent. I know you'll get a ship eventually and I'd like to go with you when you do."

Jenetta was touched by Lieutenant Ashraf's statement in the face of news that she was stuck here for probably four more years. For a line officer to be willing to ground herself to remain with a commanding officer showed great loyalty and great sacrifice.

"I've been extremely satisfied with your performance, Lori. You've done a wonderful job here, as I knew you would.

I certainly won't try to talk you into leaving; I appreciate having you here too much. But I don't want to keep you stuck on a station when you could be in space."

"We'll get back into space again, Captain. Maybe we'll get one of the next group of new battleships— one incorporating the new engine design of the *Colorado*."

"Perhaps, Lori, perhaps. You know, as base commander I'm entitled to a more senior officer as my adjutant."

"Yes, ma'am. I'll be happy to serve in whatever other capacity you wish."

"That's not what I meant. I noticed that you made the new Promotion Selection List for Lieutenant Commander. I'm going to contact Space Command Headquarters to see about having your position here upgraded so we have a slot to move you into."

"Thank you, Captain," Lieutenant Ashraf said, smiling. "That would be wonderful."

"You're welcome, Lori. Well— I guess we'd better get to work. When's my first appointment?"

"Lieutenant Commander Napole at 1100 hours. He wants to discuss the planned computer system upgrades."

"Okay, call me when he arrives. I have a few messages to send before the meeting."

"Aye, Captain."

Jenetta went into her office and sat down at her desk. Raising the com panel, she pressed the record button.

"To Annette Carver, Officer Housing, Potomac SC base, Earth, from Captain Jenetta Carver, Stewart SC base. Begin message.

"Hi, Mom. I just wanted to drop you a quick note to tell you I've received a promotion. I'm now the second Captain Carver from the family on active duty. In a few years' time, the service is going to be populated with Captain Carvers as Billy, Richie, Andy, Jimmy, Christa, and Eliza join dad and me. By then dad will probably be Admiral Carver though.

"Supreme Headquarters has decided that I should complete a full five-year tour at Stewart, so I guess I won't be home for a while. I'll come back just as soon as I can though. Since Christa and Eliza are still on ships, they'll have a much better chance of getting back home before I can.

"Everything is going well now and the Raider threat seems to have diminished even more following our recent battle for the station. Stewart has taken on the appearance of a small city and looks more like Dixon every day. I guess I could think of lots worse places to spend five years.

"I'll be sending messages to everyone else, so you don't have to forward this note. I love you and I'll come home for a visit as soon as I can.

"Jenetta Carver, Captain, Base Commander, Stewart SC Base, message complete."

"New message. To Captain Quinton Carver, GSC Cruiser Octavian, from Captain Jenetta Carver, Stewart SC Base. Begin message.

"Hi, Dad. By now you already know the news if you've read the 'from' address on the note. I received my promotion last night by video recorded message from Admiral Holt. Steve Powers pinned on my new bars following a dinner party of senior officers who participated in the recent battle here. I wish you could have been here for the party. I'll send you a copy of the vid as soon as it's edited. Right now it's just raw footage from several cameras placed at locations around the room. My PR people will be preparing a final version for distribution to the media.

"Admiral Holt has informed me that the Admiralty Board has decided I'm to remain here as base commander for a full tour, so I won't be seeing you for a while unless you get re-assigned to one of my sectors. I guess our messages will have to suffice. Perhaps once you become an Admiral you can get me posted someplace closer to home aboard a ship.

"I'm going to send a note to Billy next. I want him to hear it from me instead of on the news. Take care of yourself, Dad. I love you.

"Jenetta Carver, Captain, Base Commander, Stewart SC base, message complete."

"New message. To Commander William Carver, GSC destroyer St. Petersburg, from Captain Carver, Stewart SC Base. Begin message.

"Hi, Billy. I've received your latest message about visiting Eulosi to deliver the Ambassador from the Galactic Alliance Council. I think it's a shame that Eulosi has been requesting entrance into the Alliance for so many years but was always refused because they were located just inside the old Frontier Zone. I feel that any planet in the zone should be allowed into the Alliance if they request it, but that's just my opinion. The zone is technically Alliance space after all, even if it isn't Galactic Alliance regulated space.

It's been great having Christa around so much, and I wish you and the other guys could stop by for a visit. I've just been informed that Space Command intends for me to remain here for a full tour, so if you guys don't come to visit me, we can't get together. I guess I won't be seeing dad, mom, or Jimmy for a while since they're so far away. Maybe after my tour is up I can go back to Earth for a visit. Christa and I were hoping to make it back for our NHSA twentieth anniversary, but that's not possible now.

"I'm still amazed that Supreme Headquarters wants me to remain in charge here instead of sending a two-star, but they're really short-handed since the expansion. As you know, the recommended rank for a StratCom-One base commander is Rear Admiral, Upper Half. At a dinner party last night, Captain Powers pinned on my four bars while a presentation video made by Admiral Holt played in the background. I guess they decided to promote me in order to reduce the disparity between the recommended rank and mine.

"There's the timer. I love you and I miss you. Take care of yourself, Billy.

"Jenetta Carver, Captain, Base Commander, Stewart SC base, message complete."

Jenetta had rehearsed what she would say since waking up this morning. She tried to mention the promotion without showing any emotion that would anger her brother or bruise his ego. He had been in Space Command seven years longer, but she had just surpassed him in rank.

Jenetta continued recording messages, sending them to her other brothers, Eliza, her two sisters-in-law, and a dozen friends. She had finished by the time Lieutenant Ashraf paged her with the news that Lieutenant Commander Napole had arrived and that she had a message waiting. She told Lori to have the Lieutenant Commander wait for a few minutes and she played a message bearing the address of Admiral Holt at Higgins. Jenetta tapped the play button and the image of Holt appeared.

"Good morning, Captain. I hope I've timed this right. If I have, then this is the morning after you received your four bars. I'm sorry that I couldn't attend the ceremony in person, but I'm sure you understand.

"I did my best to talk Supreme Headquarters out of making you stay on at Stewart for a full tour, but I couldn't break you free. The expansion has drained our senior officer ranks as we've spread out to regulate a territory twice the size of the old one. As one of our most experienced base commanders who wasn't already assigned to a base, the Admiralty Board decided that you should remain on Stewart despite your rank. I *was* able to convince them to advance you to Captain *now*, although you would definitely have received it before your tour was up anyway.

"I won my bet with Admiral Hubera by the way. I'm sure you remember him. He was your instructor at the academy when you pulled that stunt of switching the power cables so the zero-grav lab would fill with smoke when he flipped the switch to power up the O'Connell Power-Cell Regeneration Unit. He bet me that you'd never be the first of your class to make Captain, if you even made it at all."

Admiral Holt chuckled. "The man has no sense of humor.

"I know you really want to be aboard a ship, but it's just not possible right now. We desperately need you there. I can't over-emphasize the importance of your position, and you already know how dangerous the situation is.

"In addition to your promotion, Space Command has decided to award you the Space Command Cross for your seizure of the base and its defense against repeated attacks until additional ships could arrive. The rest of the crew of the *Colorado* will each receive the Space Command Star for their service. The crews of the *Song*, *Asuncion*, *Chiron*, and *Ottawa* will be receiving various medals and commendations for their participation in the defense of the base, and the wounded will naturally all receive the Purple Heart.

"That's the end of the official stuff, Jen. Now I'd like to speak to you like a trusted uncle." Admiral Holt shifted in his seat and leaned closer to the monitor. "I can't think of anyone— not anyone— whom I would trust more to handle that base and supervise the surrounding sectors. You have the full support of the Admiralty Board also. After reviewing the reenactment created from the CIC videos, ship's bridge videos, and sensor information, they were *more* than a little embarrassed about sending that message to Captain Powers. The main reason for their attempt to shift command to Steve was because of your countermanding the orders of the *Thor*. Its patrol route was carefully planned so that it would never be more than fifteen days from the station. Your countermand sent it sixty days away and eliminated its effectiveness as protection for the base. They considered that a case of poor judgment on your part.

"Captain Kanes has defended your actions and explained that the missing operatives were responsible for recovering an entire transport ship full of stolen Space Command weapons. After further review, they decided your action was not out of line given the mitigating circumstances. I think I can assure you that they won't underestimate your abilities or rush to judgment again. Your unique position allows you to countermand Space Command orders to ships in your part of space, but I know you won't abuse the privilege. Your proximity to the Frontier means that you're susceptible to more attacks from the Raiders, so stay ever vigilant. Even though they've got to be plenty shorthanded these days because of the way you've consistently decimated their numbers, they're still a very serious threat to your base. And I'm sure they'd like nothing better than to bring you down. Be very careful. Message me if you need anything. Good luck, Captain.

"Brian Holt, Rear Admiral, Upper Half, Base Commander, Higgins Space Command Base, message complete."

Jenetta sat back to think about what Admiral Holt had just said, but her rumination was interrupted by Lieutenant Ashraf announcing that she had another message from Admiral Holt. Thinking that he must have forgotten something, she tapped the button to listen to his additional words. But instead of Admiral Holt's image, she was greeted by the visage of Mikel Arneu.

"Hello, Angel. Forgive the phony address, but I knew you'd take a message from Admiral Holt right away. I just wanted to congratulate you on your promotion. I've always known you had it in you to reach the big chair." He shook his head slightly and sighed. "What a team we would have made.

"It's too bad we missed one another last year. I wonder— would you have been able to take and hold the base if I was still the commandant there? I guess we'll never know, will we? I told the Lower Council they wouldn't be able to take the base back with just twenty-six ships, but the Upper Council was pressuring them to do something while there were only two warships in port. They thought that if they recovered it, they could push it across the border into the Frontier Zone before Space Command could recover enough to stop them. They put that fool Tolatsak in charge because he had a good record in seizing unarmed freighters and passengers ships. But he was no match for Jenetta Carver.

"I'm continuing to hold your place open at the resort. Some of the Lower Council members wanted to change the bounty back to 'dead or alive' after this latest encounter with you, but I convinced them that you'd be so much more valuable alive. And with you being stuck inside that hunk of rock for the next four years, you pose little threat to us now. So they decided just to increase the bounty on you again.

"So long for now, Angel. I have a new lab all set up to handle your reeducation when you're brought to me. Be seeing you."

Jenetta scowled as she pushed the com screen down and then started thinking. Unless Arneu had advance information about her promotion, which she doubted, word couldn't have been sent to him more than fourteen hours ago. Allowing time for the signals to travel both ways meant that he had to be within twenty-one light-years of Stewart. The border to the new Frontier Zone was only eleven light-years away, so Arneu must be within ten light-years inside the frontier. It was unfortunate that he was probably inside the Frontier Zone, but that fact might make him overconfident. It might make him think he was safe. Jenetta leaned way back in her chair and appeared to be studying the ceiling.

~ finis ~

Jenetta's exciting adventures continue in:
Milor!

Appendix

This chart is offered to assist readers who may be unfamiliar with military rank and the reporting structure. Newly commissioned officers begin at either ensign or second lieutenant rank.

Space Command	Space Marine Corps
Admiral of the Fleet	
Admiral	General
Vice-Admiral	Lieutenant General
Rear Admiral - Upper	Major General
Rear Admiral - Lower	Brigadier General
Captain	Colonel
Commander	Lieutenant Colonel
Lieutenant Commander	Major
Lieutenant	Captain
Lieutenant(jg) "Junior Grade"	First Lieutenant
Ensign	Second Lieutenant

The commanding officer on a ship is always referred to as Captain, regardless of his or her official military rank. Even an Ensign could be a Captain of the Ship, although that would only occur as the result of an unusual situation or emergency where no senior officers survived.

On Space Command ships and bases, time is measured according to a twenty-four-hour clock, normally referred to as military time. For example, 8:42 PM would be referred to as 2042 hours. Chronometers are always set to agree with the date and time at Space Command Supreme Headquarters on Earth. This is known as GST, or Galactic System Time.

Admiralty Board:

Moore, Richard E.	Admiral of the Fleet
Platt, Evelyn S.	Admiral - Director of Fleet Operations
Bradlee, Roger T.	Admiral - Director of Intelligence (SCI)
Ressler, Shana E.	Admiral - Director of Budget & Accounting
Hillaire, Arnold H.	Admiral - Director of Academies
Burke, Raymond A.	Vice-Admiral - Director of GSC Base Management
Ahmed, Raihana L.	Vice-Admiral - Dir. of Quartermaster Supply
Woo, Lon C.	Vice-Admiral - Dir. of Scientific & Expeditionary Forces
Plimley, Loretta J.	Rear-Admiral, (U) - Dir. of Weapons R&D
Hubera, Donald M.	Rear-Admiral, (U) - Dir. of Academy Curricula

Ship Speed Terminology — *Speed*

Plus-1	1 kps
Sub-Light-1	1,000 kps
Light-1 (*c*) *(speed of light in a vacuum)*	299,792.458 kps
Light-150 or **150 c**	150 times the speed of light

Hyper-Space Factors

IDS Communications Band	.0513 light years each minute (8.09 billion kps)
DeTect Range	4 billion kilometers

Strat Com Desig	Mission Description for Strategic Command Bases
1	Base - Location establishes it as a critical component of Space Command Operations - Serves as homeport to multiple warships that also serve in base's defense. All sections of Space Command maintain an active office at the base. Base Commander establishes all patrol routes and is authorized to override SHQ orders to ships within the sector(s) designated part of the base's operating territory. Recommended rank of Commanding Officer: **Rear Admiral (U)**
2	Base - Location establishes it as a crucial component of Space Command Operations - Serves as homeport to multiple warships that also serve in base's defense. All sections of Space Command maintain an active office at the base. Patrol routes established by SHQ. Recommended rank of Commanding Officer: **Rear Admiral (L)**
3	Base - Location establishes it as an important component of Space Command Operations - Serves as homeport to multiple warships that also serve in base's defense. Patrol routes established by SHQ. Recommended rank of Commanding Officer: **Captain**
4	Station - Location establishes it as an important terminal for Space Command personnel engaged in travel to/from postings, and for re-supply of vessels and outposts. Recommended rank of Commanding Officer: **Commander**
5	Outpost - Location makes it important for observation purposes and collection of information. Recommended rank of Commanding Officer: **Lt. Commander**

c

Sample Distances

Earth to Mars (Mean)	78 million kilometers
Nearest star to our Sun	4 light-years (Proxima Centauri)
Milky Way Galaxy diameter	100,000 light-years
Thickness of M'Way at Sun	2,000 light-years
Stars in Milky Way	200 billion (est.)
Nearest galaxy (Andromeda)	2 million light-years from M'Way
A light-year (in a vacuum)	9,460,730,472,580.8 kilometers
A light-second (in vacuum)	299,792.458 km
Grid Unit	1,000 Light Yrs² (1,000,000 Sq. LY)
Deca-Sector	100 Light Years² (10,000 Sq. LY)
Sector	10 Light Years² (100 Sq. LY)
Section	94,607,304,725 km²
Sub-section	946,073,047 km²

d

The following two-dimensional representations are offered to provide the reader with a feel for the spatial relationships between bases, systems, and celestial events referenced in the novels of this series. The mean distance from Earth to Higgins Space Command Base has been calculated as 90.1538 light-years. The tens of thousands of stars, planets, and moons in this small part of the galaxy would only confuse, and therefore have been omitted from the image.

Should the maps be unreadable, or should you desire additional imagery, .jpg and .pdf versions of all maps are available for free downloading at:

www.deprima.com/ancillary/agu.html

The first map shows Galactic Alliance space after the second expansion. The white space at the center is the space originally included when the GA charter was signed. The first outer circle shows the space claimed at the first expansion in 2203. The second circle shows the second expansion in 2273. The 'square' delineates the deca-sectors around Stewart SCB, and shows most of the planets referenced in Books 4 through 6 of this series. The second image is an enlargement of that area.

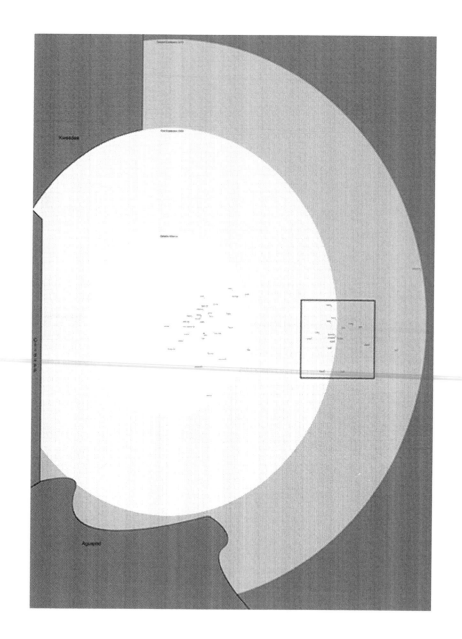

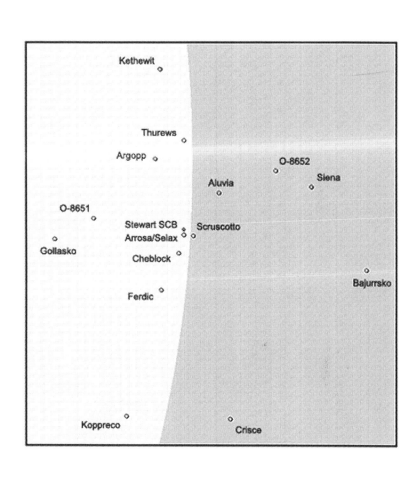